CW00631861

Ramble Through Nossex

Steve Saxton

Four Points Ramble Association

Published by the Four Points Ramble Association, 18, Bullfinch Walk, Manchester M21 7RG. www.fourpointsramble.org.uk

ISBN: 978-0-9555297-9-5

Printed and bound by: DeanPrint Ltd, Cheadle Heath Works, Stockport Road, Stockport SK3 0PR

The drawings on pages 1, 8, 84, 105, 120, 136, 153, and the cover are by Becky Knight. The drawings on pages 31 and 115 are by Peter Field. The maps and the drawing on page 66 are by the author.

Nossex Se'nstep, Buffaloes Brawl, Thatcher's Se'nstep, Ursula, The Capering Abbot and *Megs' Approval* are by the author. *Barefoot Bethany* is by Ishbel Saxton. All other songs & tunes are traditional or in the public domain. Some chords and arrangements are supplied by Ishbel Saxton and the author; others are traditional or in the public domain.

On the Facebook page:
www.facebook.com/pages/Four-Points-Ramble-Association
many colour photographs relating to other books in the series can be seen.

Also available from the same author and publisher:

Four Points Ramble Book One: Ramble Through West Yorkshire.
Four Points Ramble Book Two: Ramble Past Manchester.
Four Points Ramble Book Three: East Cheshire & North Staffs Ramble.
Four Points Ramble Book Four: Ramble through the Heart of England.
Four Points Ramble Book Five: Northants & Oxfordshire Ramble
Four Points Ramble Book Six: Upper Thames & Wiltshire Ramble
Four Points Ramble Book Seven: Ramble through Somerset.
Four Points Ramble Book Twenty-Three: Cumberland & Westmorland Ramble
Four Points Ramble Book Twenty-Four: Ramble through North Lancashire.

See the website www.fourpointsramble.org.uk (or the Facebook page) for details of the beneficiary charities, which are different from this book. Details are given on the website, and on the Facebook page, of how the books may be purchased online.

Contents

3

Introduction

This book is, and yet is not quite, part of a series describing a *potentially* continuous walk of rather more than two thousand miles, taking in the four extremities of England: the northernmost, southernmost, westernmost, and easternmost tips of the mainland. This is the tenth book to be published, and represents a pause in onward progress on the journey south, and a turning aside to explore the curious and little-known county of Nossex.

This is in no way a prescription or recommendation of a route to follow, nor a guide book or gazetteer, but a slow travel book, a description of a leisurely ramble of around 60 miles through Nossex from west to east and back again. It makes no claim to be a comprehensive survey, nor a representative sample of everyday Nossex life. I was only in the county for just under a fortnight, and for much of the information about the present, and all of the stories from the past, I was dependent on the accuracy and truthfulness of the Nossexfolk.

The gradual discovery and exploration of the peculiar culture of this most secret of counties gave plentiful opportunities to sidetrack into some, if not quite all, of the interests that are pursued in other volumes in the Four Points Ramble series: wildlife, history, literature, music, biography, genealogy, church history, topography and story-telling.

The exact location of Nossex has been left rather vague, and even possibly a little misleading, in deference to the wish of the Nossexfolk to remain hidden from most, though not necessarily all, of the rest of England.

In addition some, though not necessarily all, of the personal names may have been changed in order to respect people's privacy.

Possible route of the entire project, showing sections already completed (Nossex is not marked).

One: Yew Tree Stair to Pinrose *(9 miles)*

Monday 22nd September 2014

I had started the day by train from Manchester, made one change in a busy big city station by the skin of my teeth, and travelled on a few stops on a more rural service, until I came to a station amid green fields, just beyond the edge of the small town it served. A footpath ran alongside a small brook, on the far side of the station from the town, and I followed it eastwards. Thus far I was on the map, but my vague and rather hare-brained plan was to follow the footpath until it fell off the edge of the map, and as far as possible to continue in the same direction and see where that took me. I wanted a change from meticulous planning, knowing in advance where I would be and what I would find when I got there. I wanted freedom from booked destinations, buses to catch, and deadlines to meet. I wanted to get creatively lost.

My wife Ishbel had given me two weeks' leave from househusbandry and retirement tasks; she had even refrained from attempting to force me to buy a mobile phone, and the only stipulation was that I should make some sort of contact over the coming weekend. That was some way off; it was still Monday morning, and I intended to get a couple of hours' walking in before pausing for a packed lunch.

It was mild, even warm, as the sun struggled through a thin haze. A fresh breeze from a vaguely northerly direction helped the brisk walker to avoid overheating. The path seemed little used, but remained just traceable alongside the brook, which was lined with alder trees: the tiny cones crunched under my feet. A pair of speckled wood butterflies spiralled upwards through the alder branches: not a breeding pair, but two males battling for territory.

At this time of year there were fewer flowers than in the spring, my favourite season for walking, but colour and interest still caught the eye as I walked: yellow sow thistles, hawkbit, ragwort and charlock; pink campion and hedgerow cranesbill; and white yarrow and bindweed. Glossy blackberries were well worth picking singly, without breaking stride, just to moisten the tongue with a little sweetness. The hawthorn bushes were especially heavily laden with dark red berries, and the brighter red of bryony, rose hips, and rowan berries was also visible everywhere.

Here and there I came across dark elderberries, and took a few selected sprays from each tree as I went, in the first mile filling a small bag which I stuffed in a spare compartment of the rucksack. It seemed a waste just to leave them on the tree, and I hoped I might find myself that night at the kind of B&B where the landlady might appreciate the gift of some fresh elderberries.

The path appeared to bend away to the right, southwards. I was by now perhaps half a mile off the map, and had no idea where it might be going. Straight ahead, a mile or more away, the land rose in a fairly high hill, and I had a notion to climb that hill and see what lay beyond it. First, however, I had to find some means of getting there, which would involve crossing the brook. Smallish as it was, it ran in a deep ditch and did not look easily fordable.

5

Casting around, I saw or imagined the faintest of paths towards a particularly dense barrier beside the brook. This possible path twisted aside through shoulder-high nettles (I put my hands on my head to save my forearms) and dry brown stems of hogweed taller than I was, until between two trees a sturdy wooden beam crossed the brook. There was no handrail, and it was clearly not an official footbridge. Health and Safety would have closed it in a twinkling, and yet it was more substantial and better-engineered than you would expect a casual and unofficial bridge to be. I crossed it very cautiously, and paused to look ahead. A robin sang sweetly from the top of a thorn bush, and a wood-pigeon set off with a sudden clap of its wings. At the far end of a long meadow, a roe deer flashed a white rump as it bounded away.

The hint of a path continued towards a strip of woodland at the base of the hill. I saw now that the lower part of the hill was actually a rough rock cliff, scalable perhaps by proper climbers, but it did not look very manageable for a rather mature walker. This cliff ran right and left as far as I could see; above it were pleasant grassy slopes, though these were also quite steep. Altogether it seemed a much more formidable hill than it had looked from a distance.

The sensible thing would be to alter course and go round the hill, but somehow I now wanted more than ever to climb it, or at least to see what those high slopes were like. Accordingly I continued to follow the faint path – if it was a path. Continuing in a fairly straight line, it entered the wood and ran right up to a broad and ancient yew tree, growing close in front of the rock face of the cliff. The girth of the tree alone marked it as ancient; it had once clearly been very much taller: the main stem stopped abruptly some thirty feet up, while great boughs grew out sideways, one curving right down to the ground under its own weight.

I wondered if the tree might be hollow, and walking round it, found that indeed a gap, almost man-high, appeared towards the cliff face. I ducked through this and stood in the open space inside the hollow trunk, sky visible through branches above, to be confronted by a rough ladder. It was of a lighter coloured wood than the natural yew surrounding it, built within a strong frame that rather supported the ancient tree than depended on it.

I began to feel as if I might be living in a nursery rhyme or fairy story. Would I find myself among giants if I climbed the ladder? All the same, it hardly seemed possible just to look at the ladder and then go away again, so of course I climbed it.

It didn't take more than a moment. Perhaps twelve or fifteen feet up, the ladder reached a platform, opposite another narrow gap in the hollow trunk. The platform ran through the gap, across to a crack in the cliff face: not a cave, but an opening that led to a turn left and a natural stairway, which climbed diagonally sideways up the cliff. I was reminded a little of the Fairy Steps near Arnside, or Jack's Rake in the Lake District. These steps were longer and higher than the former, but shorter, less steep, and less exposed than the latter; and less natural than either, for here carefully chosen rocks had been added and others worked, to give a more even stairway, though natural matching stone had been used, and the work had been done a good while ago.

Delicate fronds of spleenwort and parsley fern grew in cracks and crevices, and the edges of each step were well worn. There was nothing as crude and modern as a handrail; but on the outer side was a rough low natural parapet that gave a sense of security and the chance to enjoy the widening view without vertigo. Within a few minutes I had come to the top of the cliff, and put my head back to look up the steep and grassy slope towards the hilltop that was out of sight.

Near the skyline was a rocky outcrop, and on a natural rock chair, almost a throne, sat a slim figure that seemed to be gazing in my direction. I felt the familiar uneasy sensation of being watched, and wondered if the path I was on was a right of way. At the same time I felt the warmth of the familiar, though in this setting bizarrely unexpected, sensation of being prayed for.

Putting what was presumably just a daft flight of fancy out of my mind, I set off upwards on a path that was clearer now, with indentations in the slope giving the feet a clear grip. The steepness encouraged pauses at intervals, when I would turn and look back at the growing panorama behind, with the encouraging sense of height gained each time. The hill was not of Pennine or Lakes proportions, but it was certainly bigger than it had seemed from a distance, and I had ascended some hundreds of feet when I decided to take a longer pause and have lunch.

The figure on the rock was closer now; it had not moved, and seemed lost in contemplation rather than watching me. I found a comfortable tussock of soft grass, grateful that the weather had been dry for several days at least, and faced westwards as I ate and drank, enjoying the view of the broad undulating patchwork of fields and woodland below.

An orange butterfly perched on brambles close by, its jagged-edged wings identifying it as a Comma. Other spots of colour on the hillside were pale blue harebells and scabious, yellow specks of tormentil, and in a little gully, drooping purple water avens, and upright orange spikes of bog asphodel. The sun was obscured by hazy cloud, but the scene was still very beautiful, quiet and peaceful.

A simple lunch was soon eaten, and after refilling the sandwich box with blackberries from the bramble patch, I headed onwards and upwards, finding that the path would lead right past the outcrop on which the motionless figure still sat. It was a tall and lean woman with cropped grey hair, I saw as I approached, dressed all in leather, but not a biker's leathers, nor anything shiny, tight, or fashionable, but rather rustic, brown, simple and well-worn, with the patina of old harness.

I said 'Morning,' and made to pass by, but she stood to face me, almost to block my route, and asked 'Do you know where you're going?'

I wondered if I was on a private estate. The woman did not seem quite like a typical rich landowner. Her lean and tanned face was dominated by a hooked nose and strong eyebrows above beautiful deep brown, almost black eyes, eyes that were warm and yet somehow sad.

'I was just wondering what was on the other side of this hill,' I said.

She smiled, and any hint of sadness vanished in merriment. 'The other side of the hill is Nossex,' she answered, and paused as if expecting a reaction.

'Nossex?' I said blankly.

'Yes. Did you want to visit Nossex?'

'Well, I don't know; I don't think I've ever been in Nossex, or even heard of Nossex. Would you recommend it?'

At this she laughed. 'I certainly would. I'm going that way shortly; I can take you in the right direction, if you don't mind walking with me.'

I hesitated, momentarily unsure how to reply, or even what I would prefer.

Over the brow of the hill, a little way above us, came a shortish, bearded, broad-shouldered young man in white (or, rather, off-white, almost buff) robes. My first impression was of a monk, though I wasn't sure why I thought that. He had brown curly hair, cut short but not shaven in any tonsure, and in fact he was wearing a plain rough shirt and trousers, rather loose, almost like judo kit.

In a few moments he joined us.

'All well?' he asked.

'All well,' she answered. 'This is…' and she looked at me.

'Steve,' I said.

'Alan,' he said, offering a bulky calloused hand with a firm yet gentle grip.

'Cennis,' said the tall woman in response to my glance in her direction. 'Steve was just deciding,' she added, 'whether he wants to visit Nossex.'

'Not to be missed,' said Alan.

'I'll go for it,' I said.

'Good,' she said. 'Let's go, then.' I noticed that both of them had an accent I couldn't quite place, with something of a Welsh lilt yet rather powerfully nasalised.

'Good watching, sister,' said Alan, and a flicker of his eyes suggested that he was referring to me, as if I were a fish she had caught.

'Good watching, brother,' she answered, and this sounded more like a handing over of responsibility. It seemed as if they were sharing in some kind of patrol or guard duty, though I wondered whether in his case it was more in the nature of a spiritual vigil. Might a monk (if he was a monk) go up in the hills to pray, as Jesus did?

We set off in the direction Alan had appeared from, and just before going over the top of the hill I turned to take a last look at the view westwards, and noticed his broad white-clad figure settled in the same rocky chair Cennis had occupied.

She had turned, too, to gaze at the view, and I thought I saw the sadness again.

'Beautiful view,' I said.

'Yes,' she answered. 'So much beauty… and so much empty selfishness.'

I thought about this, as we turned again and followed the path, now very clear and well-trodden, diagonally over a summit ridge that might well, I thought, be quite boggy in wetter weather. In places where the peat might have been exposed, stone slabs had been strategically placed.

9

Views began to open out eastwards down a long valley; I would have paused, but Cennis did not slacken pace.

'There's a better view further on,' she said over her shoulder, and I followed her long stride another quarter of a mile to a slope that commanded two valleys at once. It was indeed a better view, and we gazed for some moments in silence. A muscle moved in her throat, and I had a feeling she was praying.

'From here,' she said, 'you can see most of West Nossex, and a bit of East Nossex as well. That,' – she pointed left – 'is the valley of the North Brook. Let your eye run along the long hill beyond it…' – I did, and saw a cluster of buildings – 'and you can see Chittock. Now this way,' – she waved her long arm ahead and to the right – 'is the Middlebrook valley.'

She pointed out Pinrose, half-hidden, tucked under the slope below us, and then the village of Icclescombe, some way off on the far side of the valley on a low hill, and beyond that, what appeared to be terraced houses stacked up on a steep hillside.

'That's Quarrytown, one of the wonders of Nossex. Quite spectacular, once you get a closer look. And between Icclescombe and Quarrytown is the valley of the South Brook. These three valleys, and the hills that frame them, are all there is of West Nossex. Look a little to the left of Quarrytown, and beyond it, and that low wooded hill is East Nossex, but we can't see much of that from here.'

'How long have you got?' she added abruptly.

'Up to two weeks, perhaps.'

'Then you could stay in Pinrose tonight, Icclescombe tomorrow night, and Quarrytown on Wednesday night, and take it from there. Three rather different communities, but what they have in common is the Nossex spirit.'

'Sounds good. Is there a guest house in Pinrose?'

She laughed. 'Pinrose *is* a guest house – in a manner of speaking. At any rate you can stay there, and eat there, for nothing, if you're just passing through.'

'Can't I make a contribution?'

'You'll be able to contribute, don't worry. But not money. Pinrose doesn't bother with money.'

We set off again, skirting a low knoll on the edge of the ridge, to find a truly lovely hilltop tarn, fringed by low slopes on three sides, and with an apparently man-made dam on the fourth, though any earthworks must have been done ages ago, for the vegetation matched the surroundings. Through a notch in the dam a small leat flowed away on a near-level course along the hillside; and our path joined the leat, becoming a flagged bank alongside.

A little way ahead, a middle-aged man and a young woman were repairing the edge of the leat.

'Need a hand?' asked Cennis, and without waiting for an answer, she shrugged off her leather jacket to reveal sinewy brown arms left bare by a sleeveless linen tunic. The two workers straightened their backs and stood back, the man murmuring 'Thanks, sister.'

The girl, who had been standing barefoot in the water, stepped up out of the leat and sat on the ground.

'When in Rome…' I thought, and slipped off my rucksack. Cennis' arm was already plunged into the void in the bank, feeling around for gaps that needed filling. She seemed to know what was needed, and the repairers trusted her not to wreck what they had done so far, so I concentrated on passing boulders or lumps of clay, as Cennis' gestures indicated.

After a few minutes, the barefoot girl stood up and stretched, swivelling her shoulders right and left, looking keen to get back to work; and the man, who could well have been her father, as far as age and looks went, also rose. Both were short and strongly built, brown-haired and brown-eyed; her complexion glowed a light olive, while his, above the beard, was tanned and weatherbeaten.

Cennis put one more boulder in the void. 'You'll have that job done today,' she said, as we rinsed our hands in the leat and shook them dry.

'Yes,' said the stocky man, already back into the swing of work, 'it's been a dry month, we've knocked off a good few of these little jobs.'

'See you at Compline, Sister,' said the girl with a smile.

'Is Pinrose a monastic community, then?' I asked Cennis as we left.

'Yes,' she said. 'Would that put you off?'

'Not at all,' I said, and was about to follow up with questions of my own, but somehow I was forestalled, and although Cennis' questions, as we walked, were few and brief, they were probing, and I found myself recounting many episodes of my Christian life so far, considerable detail about my home church in Manchester, and certain things about myself that I'd hardly thought of before, at least not in the light I now saw them.

As we followed the slight gradient on the artificial stream, that twice took a hairpin turn over a little weir, we zigzagged down the slope to where I had seen the edges of the roofs of Pinrose. By now I was very curious about my companion, about where I was going, and indeed where I was. She, meanwhile, I felt already knew me rather well, and perhaps a little better than I was quite comfortable with.

As we dropped lower, we came into woodland, and passed another couple of workers busily coppicing. Once more Cennis paused: 'Can I help?' she asked, but picked up a short saw without waiting for an answer, and began trimming long poles into four-foot lengths as the two men greeted us laconically. Seeing a second saw, I swung the rucksack off again, and followed suit; Cennis passed me a pole as a template.

'That long,' she said, and for a quarter of an hour we worked away amid the sweet smell of freshly cut wood, my muscles eventually beginning to protest at the unaccustomed exercise, until she bundled up some gathered offcuts and handed them to me, taking charge herself of a couple of dozen poles.

'Work with God, brothers,' she said.

'Go with God, sister,' answered one.

Just out of the wood we came to Pinrose, long buildings of brown stone stretching round three sides of a broad courtyard open to the south-east. A continuous colonnade ran all around the three sides; we entered at the left-hand end and walked past several doors, some ajar.

Out of the half-open doors came smells of leather, grease, and varnish, and gentle sounds of steady tapping or rubbing, before we came to a door that Cennis pushed open. Through some of the doors we had passed I had seen evidence of a leatherworker, a cobbler, and a dressmaker. A quick glance around this workshop, as we dumped our bundles of poles and offcuts, showed that it belonged to a woodworker, who produced both simple items like rakes and brooms, and fine work in the shape of fiddles and harps. There was a marvellous aroma of new-cut wood.

A skinny girl of perhaps thirteen rushed in.

'Hello, Sister Cennis,' she said, 'can I help?'

'You could take brother Steve up to the guest room – the one in the corner is free.'

So although I would have liked a closer look at the musical instruments in various stages of crafting and assembly, I found myself scurrying along the colonnade in the wake of this teenage dynamo, named Cilla, I found, short for Priscilla. A spiral staircase in the angle of two wings led up to the second floor, where the guest room was small, clean and bare, with a window facing the hillside behind.

Breathing a little heavily, I dumped my rucksack by the solitary upright wooden chair. As I did so, I noticed how beautifully made the chair was, with a tall elegant back of spokes and a central carved panel, and I wondered if it was Cennis' work – then suddenly remembered the elderberries and blackberries.

'Where's the kitchen?' I asked, guessing, correctly, that Pinrose had a communal kitchen.

'I'll take you,' said Cilla, and was about to dash out again; I managed to prevail on her to wait while I dug out the berries, and then we hurried back down the staircase and out onto the courtyard, crossing it diagonally to a separate building just beyond the end of the far wing. Inside, this building was a single large chamber with ranges at both ends and tables in the centre, at which a middle-aged man and woman were working separately.

'Brother Steve has some berries for you – I'm helping Sister Cennis,' said Cilla, and shot back out of the door.

'Who's in charge?' I asked uncertainly, looking from one to other of the two busy workers.

'He is / she is,' they said simultaneously, each pointing to the other with perfect timing, then chuckled and chortled respectively; so I placed the berries halfway between the two, at which the man reacted first.

'Elderberries – the Lord bless you!' he cried. 'You're an answer to prayer – we had some, but not quite enough.' He dropped the carrot he was peeling, and began stripping the berries off their stems.

'Can I help?' I asked. It seemed the right thing to say in Nossex, and I soon found plenty of employment in peeling carrots, then apples, then onions. The piles of vegetables were dauntingly high; clearly we were preparing to feed a considerable number. Still, as I worked away steadily, the piles were eventually finished. Three more children of various ages had come in, wanting to help, and one was deputed to show me where to take the peelings. I followed the lad round the outside of the kitchen to an extensive kitchen garden, where he showed me a trench alongside a row of onions.

I tipped the peelings in, and looked around the rows of herbs and vegetables. There seemed to be a considerable variety of different produce, all carefully tended and kept very neat and organised. Nearby, a little old lady was bent over, steadily weeding a row of brassicas.

'Can I give you a hand?' I said, already into the groove of culturally appropriate Nossex behaviour.

She straightened up, gazing at me with a serious, deeply-lined and strong-featured face, framed by short white hair.

'Yes, if you like. You're Steve, is that right? You came in with Sister Cennis this afternoon. I'm Sister Christina. You could work along the next row, and I could tell you a little about Pinrose – I daresay you have questions.'

'Thank you.' I began pulling out little tufts of grass and tiny willow-herb seedlings, among other weeds. 'This is a monastery – is that right?'

'Yes, that's right. They call us the White Friars. It's a double monastery, which was fashionable when it was founded in the seventh century – in the year 666, which is nice and easy to remember.' I noticed that her accent was even stronger than Cennis or Alan's had been, the thickly nasalised pronunciation making it a little difficult to catch every word.

'So this place is over thirteen centuries old,' I ventured.

'No, older than that. It was actually built as a Roman villa in the early fourth century – soon after Christianity became the official religion of the empire. A man called Gaius retired here from a distinguished career of imperial service; he had already been a Christian before it was respectable, and his children and grandchildren were brought up in the faith. He brought a large extended family here, and some Christian friends, and servants who were Christian and soon became more or less part of the family. Gaius had been a rich man, and as a Christian he'd never been quite comfortable with this. When he founded Pinrose he sank his money in constructing the buildings, and then tried to put Acts 4 into practice – *no-one claimed that any of his possessions was his own, but they shared everything they had.*'

'Where did the name Pinrose come from?' I asked. 'It doesn't sound Roman.'

'No, it isn't; it's Nemsh, which is a British dialect related to Welsh, Cornish, and Breton. There was a tiny village here already, who were Christian, and they just became absorbed into the community.'

'And how big is the community now?'

13

'We are a hundred and eighty-three at the moment, not counting those who are on their Years Out, a couple of whom are actually here on holiday now. Most of the number are lay brothers and sisters; the monastic community are just twenty-five, which was the original foundation: twelve brothers and twelve sisters, and an abbess who is nominally in charge.'

'Nominally?'

'In any Christian community, the person truly in charge is Jesus Christ. The Holy Spirit works in all believers, so we seek God's will collectively. In practice, the daily routine rolls on, the daily tasks have to be done, and there is seldom any need for a difficult decision. When that happens, the community as a whole comes to a consensus, and only if we were hopelessly divided would I have to exercise authority. It hasn't actually happened yet in my time, and I hope it doesn't. If I start ordering the community according to *my* will, then I am not performing my role as I should.'

'So you're the abbess,' I said, suddenly catching up.

'Yes, indeed. Somebody has to be, unfortunately.'

And you said it's a double monastery. Are you – nominally – in charge of both monks and nuns?'

'Yes, that's how the earliest double monasteries were usually set up, often by noble, even royal, women who wanted their own religious community, and needed some men to fulfil functions that women weren't then allowed to. And Cennis, who founded Pinrose, was of noble blood.'

'Cennis?'

'The Cennis you met was named after our original founder; it's a common name in Pinrose. I'll tell you the tale; it's time for a break. Guy!' she called to a passing ginger-headed lad.

'Yes, sister?'

'Fetch us a jug of tea and two cups, if you don't mind.'

We settled on a wooden seat, and once the tea had swiftly arrived, proving to be delicately-flavoured rose-hip, I was able to hear my first of the Twelve Tales of Nossex.

Two: The Tale of Cennis and the Yellow Plague

'More are the children of a desolate woman than of her who has a husband,'
says the Lord. Is 54:1

Cennis was born into a noble family in Northumberland, a few years before King Edwin accepted the faith. She had four brothers, two older, Cedd and Cynibil; and two younger, Caelin and Chad. As a child, everything her brothers did, Cennis would do too: she ran with them, wrestled with them, climbed trees with them, swam with them, went fishing with them, rode with them, and hawked with them. In nothing would she be left behind, and, indeed, they never wished to leave her behind; she was the perfect companion, and they loved her dearly.

As they grew older, they left behind the more childish pursuits, and became more studious, and here too Cennis would not be left out. She studied everything that her brothers did, learning from the older and helping the younger brothers keep up. One by one they fell under the spell of the deep teaching and the humble dedicated lifestyle of Aidan, who was based on nearby Lindisfarne, and one by one the boys became priests – in fact two of her brothers, Cedd and Chad, later became bishops. However, Cennis could not become a priest, because she was a woman.

At first she found this very hard. She could have become a nun, of course, but her active spirit rebelled against this choice. And then Cedd was commissioned to take the gospel first to Mercia, at the request of Peada son of Penda, and then to Essex, at the request of King Sigbert.

Cennis persuaded her brother to take her along as assistant on both missions, and while he preached largely to the men, she found a role explaining the faith to women, and especially children. She knew how to keep children involved and interested with a blend of teaching, singing, and lively games; and after growing up with four brothers she knew how to deal with boisterous lads.

Later, she travelled a lot with Chad, developing a diverse ministry not only with women and children, but also in tending the sick, sometimes taking one or two other godly young women along and sharing the fruit of her growing experience. Her brothers had great success in spreading the faith, and some of this was due to Cennis' work, for if a whole family is convinced and believes, their faith is the more secure.

It is said that Cennis was flaxen-haired and beautiful, and many men desired her; but she said she would only give herself to one who was the equal of her brothers in every way, and such was their reputation that this deflated most of her suitors, until in the passage of time she was no longer of marriageable age, as folk judged things then.

She came to Nossex – or Nemet as it was then called – by chance when astray in a storm with Chad and two other companions. They ministered to the people, and Cennis and the woman with her worked chiefly in the infirmary, for it was the year of the Yellow Plague, and there were many sick and dying.

Chad preached strengthening and consoling words, and then was keen to press on, because he wanted to attend the great Synod that was to be held that year, 664, at Whitby. Cennis, however, elected to remain, because there was such need of her services, and also because she had no particular interest in the Synod. She tended the sick, and buried the dead. Some say she even dug graves, when the gravedigger had died and a replacement was not yet found.

She had great respect for Howel the Infirmarer; they worked in harmony as a team, and soon it became clear that love had grown between them, while death ruled all around. As the summer went on, the disease retreated, and fewer died each week. Howel and Cennis began to talk of marriage, but then he too sickened, and died in two days, exhausted as he was from the work they had been doing.

On the very evening that Howel died, Chad returned, with the news that the plague had also taken their brother Cedd. Cennis went out, and walked up the hill, returning, grey and gaunt, in the twilight of the following evening.

'It was prophesied long ago,' she said to Chad, 'that I should lose two men in one day, and yet gain many children. I have always thought that these would not be children of my body, and now I know it. So where are my children, those that I should gain?'

'They are everywhere,' said Chad. 'There are orphans in every village. How many shall I bring you?'

'How many can you carry?' she answered.

In the weeks and months that followed, Chad returned several times, each time with a cluster of children and a few adults, young mothers with infants, and one or two ailing older folk: all houseless wanderers whose families had been wiped out by the plague. Nemet had lost fully a quarter of its people in the plague, so there was ample space for the newcomers in most of the nine settlements.

Life was hard for them at first, for as soon as they had built up a little strength with better nourishment, they had to pitch in and work, completing tasks that had been neglected during the plague, and swiftly learning the rudiments of trades whose practitioners had died. Only the very youngest of the children could enjoy the luxury of play; the older ones had to grow up before their time.

But after two or three seasons of hard toil and good harvests, it was possible to take thought for the education of the newcomers, and after consulting Owen, Bishop of Noaster, with the support of her brother Chad, Cennis founded a double monastery within the community at Pinrose, modelled on Hild's establishment at Whitby. There were places for twelve monks and twelve nuns, with herself as Abbess, and it was not long before it was fully occupied. In the early years they served mainly as teachers, and Cennis was able to enjoy the shouts and laughter of children at play. The records hint that she joined in rather more than was strictly fitting, bearing in mind her age and her position.

The language of instruction was Saxon, as none of the newcomers had learned much Nemsh. Cennis found herself in demand as a translator of schoolbooks, as well as the Scriptures; she had known Strathclyde Welsh in her earlier days, and Nemsh was not dissimilar.

Indeed, at that time language became an issue for the whole of Nemet. For nearly three centuries before the plague, there had been a steady trickle of settlers of Saxon origin, but they were still a minority, and Nemsh was the first language of most of the communities, though some used both Nemsh and Saxon. Now death, and the influx, had changed the balance somewhat, and also it was clear that the Saxons were much slower to learn Nemsh than the natives were to learn Saxon.

So there was a Gathering in Noaster to decide on this issue alone, and it was agreed that the language of Nemet as a whole, and of most of the settlements, would thenceforth be Saxon, while Chittock and Caermorgan chose to retain Nemsh.

'Nemet has become Nossex,' said someone as a rather sad joke; but the name stuck, and gradually it was rumoured in England that there was a territory of the North Saxons, though few knew where Nossex lay, and many thought it a myth.

17

Three: Overnight in Pinrose; walk to Icclescombe *(5 miles)*

'A beautiful story,' I said, when Sister Christina had finished. 'So the monastery has survived unchanged from that day to this?'

'By no means unchanged. As they found so often Outside, monastic life very easily loses its focus – most often it gets soft and lazy, but sometimes it gets stupidly fanatical in extreme asceticism. Pinrose has been challenged many times to reform, but because we were never part of the Roman church, we have had no reform imposed from Outside or above, only from within. And we return often to the last Rule of St Albert: *See that the bounds of common sense are not exceeded, for common sense is the guide of the virtues.*'

'Very wise.'

'It could have been written for Nossex, the home of common sense. At least, we think so.' She smiled.

A small bell rang somewhere, a soft high note.

'Vespers in a quarter of an hour,' she said. 'you'll join us? It's only short – dinner afterwards at seven o'clock, then there's a break till Compline at half past eight. I should say that we observe another of St Albert's Rules: we *keep silence from after Compline until after Prime the next day* – that is, in our case, until half-way through breakfast. Guy! – Show Steve where the men's washroom is.'

I followed the willing Guy, a wiry lad with red hair, across to the very far side of the complex. There was just time, thereafter, to return to the tallest part of the main building, and enter a hall that was long and high, but not particularly wide, very plain and simple in construction, and with very little decoration, the walls plain and whitewashed.

A good number of people were filing in, so that it appeared that most of the 183 community members were present. All remained standing, facing the east window, as the monks and nuns entered. I recognised Cennis and Christina, looking rather different in plain off-white clothing, rather simpler, lighter and more practical than nun's habits I'd seen before, and Alan, returned from his vigil on the hill. They took up positions facing each other, like a conventional church choir, and their numbers were augmented by a few lay singers, Cilla the teenager among them.

Vespers began with a prayer and a psalm recited antiphonally with the congregation, who seemed to know it by heart, which was more than I did, though it was familiar. After a set prayer and a reading from a Gospel, another psalm was sung, to a fine melody I didn't recognise, then the women in the choir sang a Latin text to a soaring melody that I was sure must be by Hildegard of Bingen (as I later checked it was). The sound, seeming to float above perfect stillness, gave me gooseflesh from head to foot. Finally there was an extempore prayer for members of the community with particular needs.

The congregation quickly withdrew from the centre of the hall, while a well-practised team, mostly youngsters, brought tables and benches into place from where they had been stacked in the side aisles. In no time the hall had been transformed from a church into a dining-hall, and as Sister Christina was giving thanks to God for the food we were about to receive, and to the children for helping, more helpers were bringing bread and water to the tables, and then serving large bowls of mushroom and vegetable stew.

I found myself sitting next to the man who had been repairing the leat: Mark, his name was, and the girl who had been working with him was indeed his daughter Carys. As the stew was served, I learned that she was only temporarily in residence, on a brief holiday back home during her Years Out, due to leave the next day.

'I could show you the way to Icclescombe in the morning,' she said, 'if you don't mind a slightly roundabout route.'

'Not at all, the more I see of Nossex the better.'

The stew was magnificent, with generous chunks of root vegetables and broad slices of nutty mushrooms that I guessed were of a greater variety than I was used to, all in a thick broth and accompanied by dark wholemeal rolls and yellow butter.

Conversation died away somewhat as people got stuck into their food; then the small bell rang again, and there was silence as a woman stood at a lectern to read. Once again I noticed the distinctiveness of the thickly nasalised, yet softly lilting Nossex accent, which came across more strongly in the measured public reading. The text seemed to be advice for the monastic life, and was well worth listening to. I was struck, and encouraged, by an observation amid the exhortation:

> *God does not require from those still under obedience prayer completely free of distractions. Do not despond when your thoughts are filched, but remain calm, and unceasingly recall your mind. Unbroken recollection is proper only to an angel.*

And again, a little later in the reading, came a section that I found very wise and helpful:

> *The devil suggests to those living in obedience the desire for impossible virtues. Similarly, to those living in solitude he proposes unsuitable ideas. Scan the mind of inexperienced novices and there you will find distracted thought: a desire for quiet, for the strictest fast, for uninterrupted prayer, for absolute freedom from vanity, for unbroken remembrance of death, for continual compunction, for perfect freedom from anger, for deep silence, for surpassing purity. And if by divine providence they are without these to start with, they rush in vain to another life and are deceived. For the enemy urges them to seek these perfections prematurely, so that they may not persevere and attain them in due course. But to those living in solitude the deceiver extols hospitality, service, brotherly love, community life, visiting the sick. The devil's aim is to make the latter as impatient as the former.*

Of course I'm not now able to quote that passage from memory. When the stew had been cleared away, and a confection of berries and cream cheese was served, the reading ended, conversation began again, and I asked Mark what we had been listening to.

'*The Ladder of Divine Ascent,*' he said. 'It's a very old book, by a Greek monk who lived at the end of the sixth and beginning of the seventh century. So it was written before this monastery was founded, and yet it's still absolutely relevant. It's timeless.'

'People don't change much,' I suggested.

'And God doesn't change at all,' he answered.

Coffee was served, which smelt like, and when tasted turned out to be, some variety of coffee substitute. A real coffee-lover wouldn't have accepted it for a moment, but I felt it was interesting, with a kind of woody tang that one might actually come to like as much as the real thing. Like the *Malzkaffee* I remembered from the DDR before *Die Wende*, it was pleasant if you didn't think of it as coffee.

Before long the youngsters were taking the lead in clearing the tables and benches away again. I found myself carrying a pile of dirty plates, and since I knew the way to the kitchen, I took them there, and found a job for myself washing up. This is one of my specialities; I once even earned a wage doing it for a couple of weeks, and so I quickly felt at home, despite the lack of detergent. There were two sinks, so that rinsing was possible, and then the clean wet things went into extensive wooden racks along the wall, which reminded me powerfully of a particular Christian house party I had attended almost fifty years before, where 'orderly duty' had been enlivened once by spontaneous hymn-singing; the scullery acoustic had been rather fine.

Unconsciously I began humming 'Trust and obey', and suddenly the worker alongside me, a man of about my own age, burst into song. We managed a couple of verses and choruses, then found it easier to remember the words of short choruses: The Gospel of Thy Grace; We Have an Anchor; Break Thou the Bread of Life; Wide, Wide as the Ocean; and many more. The ginger-headed Guy brought in the last pile of plates, and made a third in the chain, taking the rinsed plates and placing them in the racks, joining in the singing with a fine treble voice, then he led off Dona Nobis Pacem, to my great delight. I learned this ancient three-part canon many years ago in the old DDR, and there have been too few opportunities to sing it since.

Our voices blended rather well; the man on my right had a deeper, richer voice than mine, and Guy's treble floated beautifully over the top. My neighbour then set off various very simple chants that I guessed stemmed from Taizé: even though I didn't recognise them, they were easy to pick up almost instantly. All too soon the last knife, spoon and bowl were done, the water let out and all surfaces cleaned.

'Do you play chess?' said Guy. 'There's half an hour before Compline.'

'I do,' I answered, adding like a true Englishman, 'though not very well.'

'Me neither,' he said. 'Good job you don't have to play well to enjoy it.'

He led the way to a small lounge, with a few rather more comfortable chairs than I had seen so far, mostly occupied by older folk. We took two upright chairs by a small table, all handsomely if plainly made, the wood showing the warm patina and rounded edges of age and continuous use, and Guy fetched a chess set that was also rather fine, the white pieces in what looked like yew, and the black perhaps in walnut: the design based on Staunton, but with individual interpretation of the detail.

'Nice, aren't they?' said Guy. 'Peter made them, Sister Cennis' husband. He died four years ago.'

'You remember him well?'

'Of course. He taught me to play. I never beat him – but I might now, if he was still alive.'

'Well, see if you can beat me,' I said, which he did, though it might have taken him a little longer if I'd focused exclusively on the game, rather than soaking up the atmosphere of Pinrose. The room was full of the buzz of conversation; yet several people, including a couple of youngish kids, were totally absorbed in reading, their books presumably taken from the shelves that filled two walls from floor to ceiling. It made for a pleasantly old-fashioned sight: most of the books were hardback (quite a few looked freshly bound, and I wondered whether bookbinding was one of the crafts practised in the workshops), and there was a set of wooden library steps with a seat at the top, all in solid dark wood rubbed light and shiny where generations of hands had gripped.

The titles on the nearest shelves, close enough for me to read off the spines of the books, seemed an eclectic mix of devotional books from different Christian traditions: Julian of Norwich, Thomas à Kempis, Jean-Pierre de Caussade, the anonymous *Cloud of Unknowing*, but also Spurgeon, McCheyne, and CS Lewis. There were other less familiar names, and I wondered if *Unintelligent Silence*, by Christina Powell, newly tooled in gleaming gold letters on the spine, was actually by the Abbess.

'Mate,' said Guy. 'You should concentrate more.'

'Sorry,' I said, 'this is all so interesting.'

The distant bell chimed its soft note again.

'Are you coming to Compline?' asked Guy.

'Gladly. How many services are there in a day?'

'Services? Offices,' he corrected me. 'Four. But you don't have to go to all of them. I suppose really you don't *have* to go to any of them. I often don't make it to Matins. But I like to go to the others; I like singing.'

Compline was a very simple service in the candlelit hall; a couple of prayers and a couple of psalms, and a verse from Psalm 133 in the original Hebrew: Hine Matov Uma Naim, to a melody I recognised:

As a conclusion, Cennis read out the following, with a moment's pause at every comma, and I thought I caught a special emphasis on the last word, at which the silence came down like a soft blanket.

Intelligent silence is the mother of prayer, a recall from captivity, preservation of fire, an overseer of thoughts, a watch against enemies, a prison of mourning, a friend of tears, effective remembrance of death, a depicter of punishment, a delver into judgment, a minister of sorrow.

It was barely nine o'clock, but felt later in the dim colonnade, as I found my way to the washroom, which reminded me of my boarding school fifty years before. After a quick cold wash, I wondered whether there might be enough light in the lounge to sample a book from the shelves; but I had made a very early start, and it had been quite a tiring day, so I went up to the guest room, groping for the rope handrail on the spiral staircase, and turned in. As I arranged the sheet sleeping bag I had brought on the trip (in case I stayed at any youth hostels), together with the blankets provided, I wondered if this was my earliest bedtime since childhood.

I woke once in the darkest part of the night, to hear a young child crying; not a baby or an infant, but a little older by the sound; then the murmur of an adult voice speaking reassuringly. It was comforting to know that the rule of Silence was breakable if need be – though not surprising, for I already had the impression that the community used rules as convenient guidelines rather than a straightjacket.

Tuesday 23rd September 2014

As always on my first night away from home, I woke ridiculously early, then needed to relieve myself, wondered about the chamber pot under the bed – after all, that was what it was there for – but felt sufficiently awake to prefer to go down to the latrines. It was surprisingly cold, perhaps the coldest morning since early spring. From there I went across the silent starlit courtyard (there was no moon) to the kitchen, where I guessed I would find someone already at work, as proved to be the case. Remembering just in time that Silence was still in place, I simply raised my eyebrows, and this was taken as a 'can I help?' – a smile and a gesture from the elderly woman preparing cereals giving me the task of cracking hazelnuts.

At this early hour there were no eager children wanting to help, and the pile of nuts was big enough to keep me busy for quite a while. Eventually there was the familiar sound of the small bell, and my co-worker downed tools, took off her apron, and suggested to me with a small inclination of the head that we should make our way to the hall, where people were gathering for Matins.

The short service, or 'office', as Guy had called it, was similar to Compline in its simplicity, though including more extempore prayer as well as composed prayers that I didn't recognise.

Breakfast included a mixture of nuts and grains not unlike muesli, plain yoghurt, apple juice, rose-hip tea or coffee substitute (which I chose, and found I was already acquiring a taste for), plentiful bread and butter and poached eggs. The silence was broken first by a monk reading from another improving book, that I discovered soon after was the *Serious Call to a Devout & Holy Life*, written by William Law in the early eighteenth century, Mark told me later, not to convert unbelievers, but to challenge lukewarm believers to full commitment.

> *For our souls may receive an infinite hurt, and be rendered incapable of all virtue, merely by the use of innocent and lawful things.*
> *What is more innocent than rest and retirement? And yet what more danger-ous than sloth and idleness? What is more lawful than eating and drinking? And yet what more destructive of all virtue, what more fruitful of all vice, than sensuality and indulgence? How lawful and praiseworthy is the care of a family! And yet how certainly are many people rendered incapable of all virtue, by a worldly and solicitous temper!*
> *Now it is for want of religious exactness in the use of these innocent and lawful things, that religion cannot get possession of our hearts. And it is in the right and prudent management of ourselves, as to these things, that all the art of holy living chiefly consists.*
> *Gross sins are plainly seen and easily avoided by persons that profess religion. But the indiscreet and dangerous use of innocent and lawful things, as it does not shock and offend our consciences, so it is difficult to make people at all sensible of the danger of it.*

Once the reading was over, a buzz of conversation broke out, and Mark, sitting near me, asked if I had slept well. I said I had, truthfully enough, for though I had woken early, I'd also turned in very early, so I'd had my ration. After finishing, I was ready to head for the scullery again, but young Guy persuaded me to let someone else have a turn at washing up; he wanted another game of chess, and since there seemed to be no shortage of willing helpers, I agreed, checking first with Carys what time she was setting off, and claiming a few minutes to clean my teeth.

'Are you going far?' Guy asked, as we went through the opening moves.

'Just to Icclescombe,' I said.

'And after that? Will you be at the Gathering in Noaster on Sunday?'

'Maybe,' I said. 'What's a Gathering?'

'Everybody in Nossex – well, most people, everyone who can – meets in the Cathedral, three times a year, and there's all kinds of announcements and debates and ceremonies and a concert and things. I'll be singing in a choir.'

'Well, I guess I'll be there if I can, then,' I said.

'And before that, I'm moving to Caeriago, I'm starting work in the Nossex Purse.'

I sat back in astonishment. 'Do people normally start work at your age? What will you be doing?'

'It's fairly normal; it depends a bit on how you're getting on with the school work. And it's not full-time. I'll do two days at the Purse – which is like a bank for all of Nossex, so I'll be doing finance work – and three at the Blackfriars School. Some people do one and four, or three and two, or four and one. It's flexible. If I work hard on the three school days I could go down to two.'

'That's an incentive,' I agreed, 'assuming the banking is more interesting than the school work.'

'If it isn't,' said Guy, taking my queen with a rook, 'I'll do something else.'

All at once, there was Carys with her merry smile, and Guy and I finished the game at blitz tempo, which was why I lost again.

'Mate,' he said. 'Sorry.'

'No, you're not,' I said. 'I am, though, I'll have to pretend it's best of five now. I'll beat you sooner or later. See you in Noaster, perhaps.'

I hastily grabbed my rucksack and settled it on my shoulders, following Carys as she led the way out of the courtyard and then headed nimbly up a steep path into the woods, making light of her old brown rucksack of leather and canvas. I did my best to keep up, and just as I was beginning to breathe heavily, Carys paused and darted aside with a cry of glee, taking a knife from her hip and cutting several large slices of a bracket fungus from the trunk of a tree.

'Oysters,' she said; and before long she had added Horn of Plenty and Ceps to a cloth bag. A second bag came out of the rucksack to take some elderberries; then we came across hazelnuts, then more mushrooms.

'You know the ones to avoid, I suppose,' I said, stating the obvious.

'Of course,' she answered. 'They teach us useful things in school here. Not just what will kill you, but where you might find it. Just over there I saw a Death Cap once. But most of what you'll find is edible, and some of it is delicious. If we take what God provides, we don't need to import food from Outside, much less from halfway round the world.'

All the time she was gathering food (and I was helping here and there) we were moving on through the woodland, and I was aware of the variety of herbs, ferns, flowers, and birdsong, from the sweet trill of a wren to the rough squawk of a jay. The rich pink of campion was abundant, with both white and red dead-nettle, purple vetch and knapweed, and yellow birdsfoot trefoil; and there were many other flowers I couldn't immediately identify. The bright red berries of bryony, rowan, and rose-hip were all around. Carys saw how my eyes were drawn time and again to the wildlife, and especially to the butterflies: Whites, a Red Admiral, Brimstones, and countless Speckled Woods.

'I've got a treat for you,' she said. 'I thought you would like it, but now I'm sure you will.'

We crossed a clearing, and on the far side were abundant brambles, blessed with a heavy crop of blackberries and also a number of butterflies: orange Commas and Small Tortoiseshells, but also some of a brown and gold variety that I didn't recognise.

'Aren't they gorgeous?' said Carys, focusing, I saw, on one of the unfamiliar examples.

'Yes,' I agreed, 'what are they?'

'Brown Hairstreaks. They're not very common, and becoming rarer. We're very glad to have some in Nossex, so we make sure we preserve the habitat.'

I admired the contrasts of brown and golden-orange amid green and black, as the butterflies basked amongst the brambles, hardly stirring as we began to collect berries, filling my sandwich box and a box of Carys's before moving on.

'So how did you like Pinrose Whitefriars?' she asked.

'Wonderful,' I said. 'The singing, the silence, the sense of peace and harmony, the simplicity, the setting – of course everywhere looks nice in good weather, but it's still an impressive place anyway. But all those things might be expected in a monastic community, and the happy younger children are perhaps not unusual. What I was most struck by, I think, was the teenagers: their enthusiasm, their willingness, their maturity – not bored, not rude, not negative or unhappy, not nervous or awkward.'

'Perhaps you saw them all on a good day,' she laughed. 'Everyone has their off moments. But yes, they're totally different to teenagers Outside. I started my Years Out at a sixth form college, and I found it really difficult, even though they're beginning to grow up and are better than the younger teens. So much posing, so much gossiping, so much hanging around doing nothing to speak of, so much insincerity, so many so-called friends yet so much loneliness, so little hope or enjoyment. So much consumption, so little production. They all have their digital devices and their huge collections of music to listen to, yet hardly one in a hundred can play an instrument to any decent standard, and not one in a thousand can sing in tune – except for those in the churches.'

'You exaggerate,' I suggested.

'About the singing, maybe. Not the other things.'

'So you're not enjoying your Years Out?'

'Oh, yes, now I am. Wider horizons, different ideas. And once you know your way around a bit you can join clubs, volunteer for things, and as a volunteer you meet people who are much nearer the Nossex spirit. Once I found the right church, too, and I was among Bible-believing Christians – Evangelicals, they call themselves Outside – it felt much more like home.'

We paused to listen to a wren singing, somewhere close by, and to watch a tree-creeper, working its way up the bole of a tall ash. Carys drew a deep breath, as if to memorise the smell of the woodland. This automatically made me aware of the scents of leafmould and ivy, garlic and all manner of unidentifiable woodiness.

'What did you volunteer for?' I asked. 'Apart from church, that is?'

'I started with St John Ambulance,' she said, 'and that was fun at first, and the training was useful. It's the kind of handy knowledge and experience we're supposed to pick up on our Years Out. But when we were actually on duty there was a lot of just standing about, which is not my favourite activity, and I didn't care for the uniform.

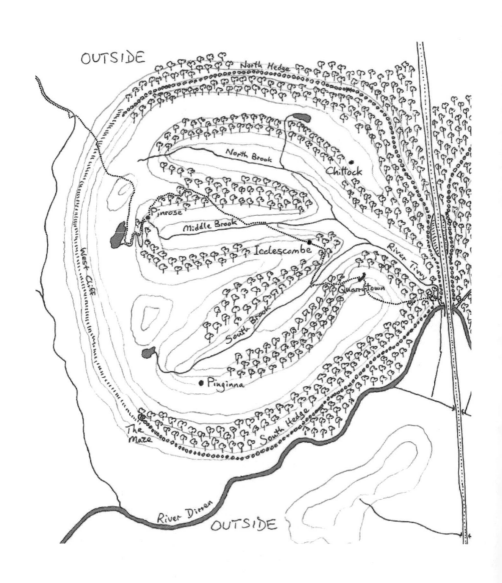

Map of West Nossex with outward route

I don't quite have the figure to look good in it, and I don't really do 'smart' anyway. After that I discovered the Waterway Recovery Group. Splendid stuff – restoring derelict canals. Proper hard labour, out in the country, gets your hands dirty and stops your palms softening. And then Fix The Fells, repairing paths in the Lake District. Now those people worked like Nossexfolk, and the jobs they were doing, the objectives, were worthwhile. I'm a real Nossex girl – I like repairing, restoring, fixing things so they keep going. Outside there's so much dereliction and neglect, so much abandonment or demolition or throwing away, mountains of junk and garbage, so much waste.'

'It's a society of waste, isn't it?' I agreed.

'Totally. Even committed Christians – I lodged with a church family at first – and they have Nossex connections, too, that's why I was there – and now I share a house with Christians my own age, and you would not *believe* the amount they throw away.'

'Didn't they recycle?'

'I suppose they did,' she admitted. 'And I suppose the amount of stuff that arrived in the house wasn't all their fault – the junk mail and all the packaging they couldn't help. But coming from Nossex, it still seems wasteful. We prefer reusing to recycling.'

In the course of the conversation we had descended a long leafy slope beneath tall trees, oak ash, beech, and Spanish chestnuts laden with green globes, before emerging from the woodland near the bottom of the valley. We joined a track running down the valley, through meadows full of wildflowers, alongside the winding Middle Brook. A heron flew upstream, towards Pinrose, with slow and stately wingbeats.

After a mile or so, the flower-filled meadows gave way to arable fields of vegetables or barley, and one of sunflowers, now bereft of their yellow petals, the broad seedheads dry and drooping, ready for harvest. In fact a small group were doing just that, and Carys called out: 'Can we help?' slipping off her rucksack at the same time. I followed suit, knowing by now that the answer wasn't going to be 'No', and that we were sure to be involved.

The group was of mixed ages, and a couple of the oldest workers took the chance of a break and passed their secateurs to us, an old woman showing me where to cut the stem, some six inches down from the flowerhead. A girl of nine or ten held a sack for us to drop the flowerheads into, and we clipped away for perhaps fifteen minutes before heading on our way. The fields either side of the track, which became broader and well-trodden, included long aromatic rows of lavender, and walled orchards of a great variety of apples and pears, green, yellow, russet and streaky red. Against the south-facing walls stood tall greenhouses.

Icclescombe was now close at hand, near the top of the south side of the valley, and we took the path that branched upwards towards the village. Unlike Pinrose, here there was a cluster of small thatched cottages around a separate hall of modest proportions.

We made our way into the hall and through a door at one end into the kitchen, a generous space designed for mass catering, not unlike Pinrose's kitchen once one was inside. Our contributions of mushrooms, fruit, and nuts were gratefully received, but would not find their way into lunch, which was almost ready; so we went back into the hall, dumped the rucksacks in a corner, and helped with table laying.

Lunch was simple in essence – soup, bread, water, cheese, tomatoes, onions and apples – but that bald list understates the depth of flavour of the carrot and fennel soup, crusty wholemeal bread, hard tangy cheese rather like mature Lancashire, tomatoes bursting with sweetness, and apples that looked like Pearmains and tasted magnificent with the cheese.

Carys and I found a place at a long table, but before she had started on the soup she spotted a friend on the far side of the room and went over to join her, so I turned to greet my neighbour on the other side, a young woman with blonde hair and a dazzling smile, who introduced herself as Megs. She was smaller and slighter than most of the stocky or burly folk I had met so far. She taught music, she said, apart from pitching in with the communal tasks as everyone did in Nossex.

I said I was retired, but had taught English to overseas students, and Megs was delighted.

'I'm doing a little bit of that,' she said. 'We have some new members who are refugees, from different countries, and I run a conversation class at the end of the afternoon, but I haven't done very much language teaching before – could you sit in and tell me what you think?'

'I'd love to,' I said. 'Where will I find you?'

'I'll find you, don't worry.' She turned away to speak to someone else.

Across the table were a mature couple, perhaps in their sixties or early seventies, both white-haired and in his case, white-bearded. Glancing around, I saw that here as in Pinrose, most adult men seemed to be bearded, though generally the beards were well-trimmed. The couple introduced themselves as John and Ruth and asked where I had come from. Pinrose this morning, I told them, adding that my home base was Manchester.

'So you're visiting? What do you think of Nossex?'

'Very unusual,' I said. 'And with an interesting history.'

'Have you heard any of the Tales of Nossex?' asked John.

'Just the Tale of Cennis and the Yellow Plague,' I said. 'How many Tales are there?'

'Traditionally, twelve – but of course there are many more than that really. I'll tell you the Tale of Alain FisBos, it's one of my favourites.'

'No,' said his wife, 'I'll tell it. You'll go off at tangents, and then I'll be tempted to interrupt.'

Her husband laughed, and gestured for her to begin.

Four: The Tale of Alain FisBos, First Earl of Nossex

Ask, and it will be given to you; seek, and you will find. Lk 11:9

Alain FisBos came over to England with William the Conqueror, though Alain always referred to his liege-lord as William the Bastard, and there was no love lost between them. It was never recorded why Alain followed William, instead of remaining quietly in his native Brittany. His heart did not seem to be in the invasion, for it is said he struck no blow at Hastings, nor took any prisoner, though he saved the lives of several, and was in the thick of much of the action. Afterwards his shield was beyond repair, from the countless dints and gashes.

Few dared criticise Alain, whose surname, or originally nickname, 'FitzBos', the son of the ox, hinted at his formidable bulk. He was an intimidating figure, short but immensely broad in the shoulder, black-bearded and heavy of brow, though his eyes were mild if you looked closely enough, and those who knew him intimately had no fear of him.

King William despised Alain as soft-hearted, and never missed an opportunity for mockery, so when the time came for parcelling out this rich land of England to his supporters, and someone whispered the tale of the mythical shire of the North Saxons in the king's ear, he saw the potential for a splendid joke. He told Alain that if he could subdue the North Saxons and win their allegiance in a year and a day, he could be created Earl of Nossex. Those that were in on the joke smiled at Alain; some congratulated him. He knew that there was some catch, but assumed innocently that Nossex would simply be hard to find.

In some ways Alain FisBos was a very straightforward man. He trusted God; he needed to find Nossex; so he went into Westminster Abbey and prayed that he would be able to find Nossex. As for subduing it, he was not yet sure whether it ought to be subdued, so he left that out of his prayer.

He did not like the idea of hunting around at random with a large retinue, and in any case he had little money to pay retainers for an indefinite period of time, so in the end he rode north with no more than a dozen men, besides his wife Judith, who would not be left behind, and Alice his little daughter, who his wife would not leave behind, and a couple of maids.

As chance, if it was chance, would have it, several of his men fell sick within the first two days, but Alain felt impelled to press on, leaving them to recover as best they might; and his wife was sure that they would find Nossex soon.

'You prayed,' she said. 'Does God not answer prayer?'

'Yes, Judy, of course He does. But will we like the answer?'

They had few specific clues to where to search for Nossex, other than the name, which suggested that it lay northwards from Middlesex, the fact that it was hidden, and therefore did not lie on any major route, and the rumour that it was far from the sea, which suggested somewhere in the broad midlands. They lodged at abbeys, and each time they asked the way and were directed vaguely onwards.

Some of the men were grumbling about the futility of their search, and the weather, which was grey and gloomy, and their lodgings, where the food was scanty, and especially the roads, which were awful. Judith in her turn became irritated with the despondency of the men, and so Alain took to asking three men to ride well ahead, ostensibly to guard against ambush, and three men to ride well behind.

They came to a place where trees grew close on either side of the rough track they were following, a prime place for ambush indeed, and yet the men riding ahead and the men behind were all out of sight. Alice chose just that moment to insist on a stop for a call of nature. Once set down on the ground, however, minx that she was, she ran off giggling into the undergrowth. Running away, in order to be chased and caught, was her favourite game; and in the right setting at the right time, Alain enjoyed it too, growling and pretending to be a great fearsome bear.

Here, though, there might be a real bear, for all he knew, and he crashed through the bushes after his daughter, cursing and praying by turns. Some way behind him, Judith and the maids followed, abandoning the horses rather than be separated from the only man they trusted to protect them.

There was a low opening where a great willow bough had grown down to the ground: little Alice trotted through without even needing to duck, but her father had to grovel on his knees to follow, while the three women scrambled through close behind. Beyond was a little clearing, in the middle of which Alain caught up his daughter, and was about to begin scolding her when he realised that the five of them were surrounded by olive-clad archers. The bows, he noted, were light hunting bows, made to kill wildfowl rather than men, but even a light arrow can kill a man if it strikes in a vital place; and they could certainly hurt his daughter. He plucked out his sword and hurled it away from him in one move, and folded his long arms around Alice, while the three women in their turn clung to him.

It so happened that the archers were from Chittock, and among themselves they spoke Nemsh.

'A man of peace,' said one.

'A brave man, nonetheless,' said another.

'And he surrounds himself with women,' said a third.

'I surround myself with good women,' retorted Alain in Breton, 'and a man could do much worse.'

Judith squeezed him a little tighter, but the men surrounding them reacted as if they had all been kicked simultaneously. Some lowered their bows, others pointed them upwards, and one loosed off an arrow high into the treetops, then dropped his bow altogether in surprise. There was a silence, broken only by the sound of the stray arrow falling through leaves to earth.

What are you doing here?' asked one of the archers.

'Looking for the land of the North Saxons,' answered Alain, 'though from the language you speak, I must be astray. Is this Wales?'

'Why do you seek the North Saxons?'

'King William said that if I could subdue the North Saxons, I could be Earl of Nossex. I thought I would try and find the North Saxons at least, though as for subduing them, it seems I cannot even subdue a three-year-old girl.'

'It's a skilled man that can do that – and she seems well enough subdued now.' The speaker unstrung his bow and approached, gazing at Alice, who looked up at this stranger and suddenly smiled, unleashing all the charm of her big brown eyes, black curls, and dimpled cheeks. He smiled back, the goofy smile of a man who had a little girl of his own.

'What would the Earl of Nossex do for the North Saxons?' he said to Alain, still smiling at Alice.

'Keep William the Bastard out of their hair,' said Alain.

'We should go and talk to the Bishop,' said the other. 'He might like the sound of that.'

Less because of Alain's powers of persuasion, than because Bishop Leofrith and the Nossexfolk liked him, and liked his wife and her women, and most especially loved his daughter Alice, it was agreed at an Extraordinary Gathering that Nossex should for the first time have an Earl, if King William kept his promise at the end of a year and a day. The FisBos family settled in Chittock, where they and the community enjoyed converting a redundant barn into a dwelling that was at first jokingly dubbed the Tower of FisBos. Later it became known as Portervert Castle, from its ever-open door.

Meanwhile Alain's six remaining men, finding no trace of their master or his womenfolk, but only four riderless horses, concluded that they had been abducted and slain by outlaw Saxons. So they returned in haste to London, where they took service with other masters. King William lost no sleep over FisBos' disappearance, though he was a little disappointed that his joke seemed somehow incomplete.

A year and a day after the royal pledge had been made, Alain FisBos, who had been discreetly waiting for the right moment, presented himself to King William at a banquet and announced that he had found and subdued the North Saxons.

'How many men-at-arms can they provide for my army?' asked the king.

'None at all,' admitted Alain. 'They are most unfitted for war. However, they are excellent craftsmen.' Two men with him unrolled and held up a finely-embroidered altarcloth, that caused eyes to widen all around the king, though he scowled.

'Craftswomen, you mean,' he objected.

'Men and women, my lord. I had a hand in some of the plainer and simpler parts myself.' There was a general intake of breath at this, and the king laughed.

'Very well,' he said. 'You and your heirs may hold Nossex, on payment to the crown of one fine altarcloth, on this day each year.'

Alain FisBos did not venture into the king's presence again, but sent the altarcloth every year, and William presented them to whichever abbey, minster, or cathedral he wanted to ingratiate himself with at the time.

The many descendants of Alain FisBos are found all over Nossex to this day.

Five: Overnight in Icclescombe; walk to Quarrytown *(4 miles)*

'What about Domesday Book?' I asked. 'Would the Conqueror not have expected a detailed survey of Nossex to appear there?'

'We don't know for sure what King William thought,' said John. 'Certainly Nossex isn't in Domesday, so the commissioners never found it. Probably he assumed that Nossex was mythical after all, and that Alain FisBos had simply bought himself a meaningless title at the cost of an altarcloth per year.'

'And is an annual altarcloth still paid to the crown?

'Oh no, the tribute was discontinued when the Nossex borders were completely closed during the civil war between Stephen and Matilda, and the payment never resumed. So roughly sixty-five or seventy must have been made, but as far as I know none survive.'

'I like the image of him entering Nossex on his knees,' I said.

'Yes,' said Ruth, 'and he spent time on his knees before he set off to find it. He was a man of prayer, and everything you hear about him points to his amazing humility, in an age when most big strong men were arrogant bullies. He'd been brought up in a landed noble family whose members hardly needed to work, and would certainly have scorned to work with their hands; but when he settled in Chittock as Earl of Nossex he worked as a quarryman and stonemason. They said that whenever Earl Alain was in the quarry, the laughter rang louder than the hammers.'

'Humility,' said John, 'was why he was an object of scorn in William's court, and why he fitted in so easily in Nossex.'

The meal was over. John and Ruth got up to go; Megs had already slipped away after eating very frugally, which helped explain her slim figure. Carys had been chatting to her friend at another table, but as I was carrying a pile of soup bowls to the scullery, she looked up and hurried over to catch me.

'It was a nice walk,' she said. 'Thanks for keeping me company. I'm off to Quarrytown this afternoon, but I'll probably see you at the Gathering in Noaster.'

'Thank *you*,' I said, 'for the guided tour, and especially for the butterflies. Go with God,' I added.

'Stay with God,' she smiled. 'You're sounding like a Nossexman already.'

I felt I was beginning to adjust to the life in this singular county, as I formed part of a team washing up again, before finding my way outside to the kitchen garden, where there was weeding to do, then potatoes to lift, and after that I was invited to join a small group gathering windfall apples and pears. Each task took a while to complete, and I was fully ready to sit down and rest my back, when a couple of children brought refreshments for the workers.

Megs was with the children; I guessed she had been teaching them.

'I said I'd find you,' she said with a warm smile, and sat next to me. The tall brownstone walls that enclosed the orchard also kept out some of the breeze, so that it felt as pleasant as high summer. I was enjoying Nossex life.

The tea was sage this time. 'It reminds me of Turkey,' I said, remembering Çanakkale and the Dardanelles.

'I'd love to go there,' she said, 'that's partly why I wanted to try English teaching; I think it might take me further than music.'

'Very easily,' I answered, 'if you're prepared to go to the less popular places at first.'

Within a few minutes, once the tea was finished, I was in one of the cottages, listening to Megs' adult English students, two men and two women aged between twenty-five and fifty, telling their life stories with different degrees of fluency and a great deal of grammatical inaccuracy. They had come from various backgrounds of conflict, persecution, or deprivation, and had arrived in England hoping for peace and security. Their optimism had been dented by the difficulty of arguing their case to the British immigration authorities, and each of them had somehow found their way into Nossex. Luckily they had no common language other than their imperfect English, and so plenty of meaningful communication was happening.

I was impressed that Megs did very little overt teaching or correction, and her brief interventions served mainly to stimulate more exchanges; she sounded genuinely interested in what they had to say, and nothing as boring as grammar was mentioned for the whole hour.

A bell rang somewhere outside, a deeper and stronger sound than the soft high Pinrose bell, but I guessed with the same meaning: a communal event would soon take place. The students stood up, taking the lesson as finished.

'You go to prayer meeting, Miss Megs?' asked a tall African, Titus by name; and when she shook her head, he turned to me: 'Mister Steve?'

'Yes, I'll come,' I said, wondering what, if anything, lay behind Megs' refusal. Titus led the way back through the clustered cottages to the hall. A good number of adults, and a few older children were gathering. Each person took a wooden chair and stood behind it; I followed suit and waited while Ruth introduced the meeting with news of a medical missionary couple in Uganda. Once the update was complete, everybody knelt on the hard wooden floor behind their chair, resting their arms on the back of the chair, and everyone at once began praying fervently aloud: the hubbub was considerable. I hastened to kneel, registering the hardness of the floor at once; it reminded me powerfully of a prayer meeting I'd attended in Romania in the eighties, before the fall of Ceaucescu.

Because there was no turn-taking, it was not long before a new topic could be introduced; this time Titus spoke briefly and effectively about the persecuted Christians in his homeland, the Central African Republic, and the difficulty of restraining those who wanted to retaliate. There was another burst of simultaneous heartfelt prayer, then another topic, closer to home, sick or bereaved individuals whose names meant nothing to me. The forthcoming Gathering was also an item for prayer, with particular focus on several baptisms to be held in the morning beforehand; and before long (though it seemed long enough to my unaccustomed knees) the meeting was over.

The noise and energy of this time of prayer contrasted powerfully with the sense of calm and quiet security with the White Friars at Pinrose; two Christian communities only a few miles apart, within sight of each other, and yet how different they are, I thought. All the same, I reminded myself, a similar contrast might be found between two churches in neighbouring streets in any English city Outside. And at some deeper level, I could feel a common culture between Pinrose and Icclescombe, a sense of deep-rootedness and communal solidarity.

'You certainly have lively prayer meetings here,' I said to John as we helped rearrange the long tables for the evening meal. The smell of some kind of stew was floating through from the kitchen and making my stomach rumble.

'It's all down to Titus,' he answered as we set out cutlery. 'We were getting rather stale, and very laid-back and relaxed, and when he arrived he gave us such drive and energy. He has a special need to pray for his own country, his family and his friends, of course, and that's infectious, it makes us all more aware of the need for prayer, and the seriousness of it.'

'Good things come to Nossex from Outside,' said Ruth. 'People find their way in for a reason: God has something He wants them to contribute.'

'Cennis said I would be able to contribute,' I remembered, 'but I guessed that would just mean working my way, pulling my weight, not freeloading.'

'Of course, that goes without saying, but there will be something before you go that only you can do, something that you were brought here for.'

I pondered this, as the meal was served: monster rabbit and mushroom pies, one for each long table, plus potatoes, carrots and cabbage. The mushrooms considerably outnumbered the rabbits, if my portion was typical, but the modest quantity of meat was made up for by the glorious gravy, dark and rich and full of flavours that were almost unfamiliar, and yet not quite: it tasted of the smells of woodland, and I guessed that all manner of herbs whose virtues had been forgotten Outside were contributing to this noble pie. Presumably much of what Carys and I had gathered in the morning was somewhere within, along with the gatherings of other wanderers.

There was a lull in the conversation while people were fully engaged with the pie. I glanced around the hall as I held a bread roll and waited for Ruth to pass the butter. There were well over a hundred present including children, I estimated, but clearly the community was a little smaller than Pinrose. The hall was relatively plain, but the cruck beams supporting the roof were impressive; I guessed they must be several hundred years old. Megs was sitting over on the far side; she flashed a smile in my direction, and I nodded back.

'How old is the hall?' I asked John.

'If you mean the roof beams you were looking at, five or six hundred years, perhaps; but the hall? It's hard to say. It's like the broom that's had three new heads and two new handles. There's been a hall of some sort here for well over a thousand years, but how much of it is original is more than I can tell you.'

As people were piling plates, I made to pick up a stack, but John forestalled me.

35

'Let someone else do that,' he said. 'Do you have any instruments with you? We'll be playing together for a while.'

'A couple of whistles,' I admitted, and fetched them from the rucksack, while chairs were being moved from alongside the tables to round the fire, making a double or in places triple semi-circle. John took a seat, shrugging into the shoulder-straps of a melodeon, and pointed me to a chair beside him; on the other side of him Ruth was tuning a fiddle. Across the semi-circle, I saw that Megs was strapping on a hurdy-gurdy. She caught my eye and smiled, and a moment later began a rhythm on the wheel that led into *Sellinger's Round*, an ancient melody that everybody seemed to know, for they all joined in. Happily I knew it and could join in too.

There must have been twenty-five or thirty musicians, blending into an impressive sound, as together as any session I remembered back in Manchester. There were mandolins and citterns, small pipes and concertinas and recorders, and a double bass keeping the pulse, while Titus added all kinds of rhythm on a djembe. The tempos were reasonable; none of these players were competing to show how fast they could play, and almost every tune was led off by a different player, though I could discern no pattern in the turn-taking. I knew perhaps half of the tunes, and was able to busk along with some of those that were new to me.

After a little while, someone appeared with a large stoneware jug and a tray of mugs, and served what turned out to be really excellent cider, dry and sharp and full of character. I said as much to John.

'Icclescombe makes the best cider in Nossex,' he said, 'and 2014 promises to be a good year, even by our high standards.'

'I don't remember anything like this being on offer in Pinrose.'

'No, Pinrose doesn't touch alcohol – that is, the White Friars don't, and the lay brothers and sisters abstain while they're at home, so that the place is dry. But some of the layfolk would be happy enough to try our cider if they were here; a few of them sometimes come down and join our sessions.'

Someone struck up a melody that I didn't recognise, but clearly I was alone in this; everyone joined in with a readiness typical of total familiarity. I had a go at joining in: the melody seemed rather plain and simple, but I kept finding myself on the wrong beat, so stopped and began to count.

'It's in seven,' said John with a smile.

Meanwhile, some teenagers and a couple of younger ones began to dance, behind the rows of musicians. There were lines of girls and lines of boys, arms around each others' shoulders, sliding left, sliding right, pausing and splitting into individuals that briefly swung an opposite-sex partner, then back into the same-sex lines, drifting sideways and back again. I watched absent-mindedly, trying to get a grip on the tune. On the third time through, I was just beginning to pick up parts of it, when the musicians shifted seamlessly into a rather spikier and more challenging tune with the same underlying beat: the dancers kept going, but a couple of the players took a pause and a pull at their cider. I didn't venture to join in, simply enjoying the swaying rhythm and the tune, which was followed by a third tune before the dancers stopped.

'What was that?' I asked.

'The original *Nossex Se'nstep*,' answered Ruth. 'Esther Breeze's most famous dance and best-known tune, followed by...' she hesitated.

'*Rowan Berries* and *Andrew's Delight*,' said John promptly, and perhaps just a little smugly. Another tune began before I could ask any more about who Esther Breeze was, and before long I had forgotten the name. All too soon, as I felt, the musicians were packing up, the cider was finished, and although my watch said it was still relatively early, there was a sense that the day was over.

I wondered if there would be any equivalent to the White Friars' Compline, but it seemed not. Megs came over, the leather hurdy-gurdy case slung on her shoulder. I picked up my whistles and stood up, looking round for my rucksack.

'So where are you staying tonight?' asked John.

'I don't know,' I admitted. 'A day and a half in Nossex, and I'm already assuming that'll take care of itself.'

'We've a spare bed,' said Megs.

'And so have we,' said John. 'Would you be able to take Steve to Quarrytown in the morning?'

'All right,' she smiled.

'So we'll share our guest around. We'll do the bed and breakfast, you do the guiding – you're teaching at Quarrytown in the afternoon, aren't you?'

It was all very hospitable and perfectly friendly; seemingly casual, and yet I wondered whether John was just a slightly controlling character, or perhaps my progress through Nossex was being carefully planned and monitored. I recalled that within a short while of my arrival in Pinrose, every adult I met there had already seemed to know about me; and the border had apparently been guarded. Perhaps Nossex was totalitarian enough to make sure visitors only saw positive things.

The bedroom I was given to sleep in, like the rest of John and Ruth's small cottage, was much less bare and spartan than the accommodation at Pinrose; but still there was a clear difference in style to the average modern dwelling Outside. I decided that this was due to the absence of clutter: what was there was comfortable and attractive, but there was nothing superfluous, very little in the way of ornamentation, bits and pieces, knick-knacks or the stuff that often gets dumped in bedrooms.

I slept much later on my second night in Nossex, and was woken by Ruth with a cup of fruit tea. It was already full daylight, and I drank the tea quickly, hoping I hadn't missed breakfast.

It turned out that I had, more or less, but something had been left for me: oatmeal and nuts, a frugal muesli-equivalent, together with yoghurt, and a couple of oaty pancakes with berries and a little honey. There was also coffee, no more real than in Pinrose, but quite different in taste, darker, and with a powerful roasted bitterness.

Ruth was ready to go. 'I'll leave you to finish the washing-up,' she said. 'You can work out where things go – there aren't too many possibilities.'

It was indeed a fairly simple kitchen, with relatively few cupboards, by standards Outside.

'How shall I lock up?' I asked.

'Lock up?' she said in mock horror, as she went out. 'This is Nossex – we don't lock doors.'

I finished the breakfast quickly, and cleared away, washed up, and used the bathroom all in a few minutes, before heading outside with my rucksack and looking around for Megs. There was no need to look far; she was sitting on a bench beside the door, enjoying the morning sunshine. Since she didn't immediately get up, I sat down next to her.

'Good morning,' she said.

'It is, too. Sorry to keep you waiting.'

'It's a nice day for waiting.' She paused. 'Can I ask you – I didn't have a chance before – what did you think of the English lesson?'

'How did *you* feel it went?' I asked.

'I didn't do anything of what I'd planned, and I hadn't really planned very much anyway. I sometimes wonder if I'm an English teacher or a therapist. They enjoy talking, and they seem to think the time is worthwhile, but I wonder whether their English is improving.'

'It will be,' I assured her. 'Maybe not fewer mistakes, but more familiarity with the language, more ease of use. Presumably they don't need to pass any exams, just to be able to function as full members of the community. You're a very encouraging and non-threatening presence, and you enable them to relax – that has to help learning.'

'Could I do the job somewhere else, though?'

'Of course,' I said firmly. 'You instinctively do the right thing, which is not to interfere with their learning. That's the best approach in any context.'

'Well, thank you for that,' she said, 'Shall we head off? Quarrytown isn't very far; I usually make the journey a little longer by taking the scenic route. You don't mind seeing a bit more of Nossex?'

'That's what I'm doing here,' I answered. 'Sightseeing. Which way will we go?'

'Up the South Brook to Deborah's Stones, and back down on the far side.'

'Sounds good.' I swung the rucksack onto my back, and Megs settled a hemp bag on her shoulder, and we set off over the slight rise behind the village. As we came over the brow I caught my breath. Across a fairly narrow valley, the curved terraces of Quarrytown faced us, row above row of warm brown stone houses stacked on top of each other, the top terrace almost reaching the level of the hilltop opposite, which was some way higher than our vantage point.

'Cennis said it was spectacular,' I said. 'She wasn't exaggerating.'

'Yes, it is impressive, isn't it?' Megs had the unmistakable air of someone who has seen a view a thousand times before: not that she didn't seem to appreciate it, just that she had no need to gaze at it for more than a moment or two. With no camera, I could only try to memorise the sight. Meanwhile my companion moved on at a brisk pace. Clearly she was fit and a regular walker, but then everyone in Nossex probably was, for I had seen hardly any riders or cyclists and no sign of anything like a road, so Shanks' pony was obviously the normal mode of transport.

One path ran on ahead, directly downhill towards Quarrytown, but Megs took a right turn along a path that slanted more gradually downwards, heading towards the upper end of the valley, which disappeared from sight as we came down into the woodland that lined the slopes on both sides of the valley.

Sunlight filtered through the high green canopy, and there was birdsong in all directions, as well as the sudden clap of wings as a wood pigeon set off, the raucous squawk of a jay, and the cackle of a green woodpecker not far away. My eyes were drawn in all directions: here a nuthatch, there a great tit, over there a wren flitting through the undergrowth; ancient oaks with moss-grown limbs festooned in polypody ferns; tall grey-skinned beeches towering over holly bushes; sprays of ash leaves underfoot on the path; Speckled Wood butterflies everywhere.

Megs seemed less fascinated by the fine detail, and apparently had none of the instinct for gathering food that Carys had shown the day before; but she obviously enjoyed her surroundings, and paused once or twice to show me particular vistas where the woods were more open. Her preferences suggested an artist's eye rather than a naturalist's.

'You're here about three weeks too early for the best autumn colours,' she said, and I could imagine how extra beautiful the scenes might yet become. But it would have been ungrateful to grumble; the woods were still wonderful, and I said so.

Down on the level floor of the valley, we emerged from woodland into flowery meadows, green tinged with the brown of dock and sorrel flower spikes, and the yellow of buttercups. The path gradually approached the South Brook, a lively stream a little wider than the Middle Brook had been. Ahead of us, the path continued as a line of a dozen large stepping stones that crossed the brook diagonally in a place where it was broad and shallow.

As a gentleman, I was ready to offer assistance with the stepping stones, but I needn't have concerned myself; the small blonde figure flitted across ahead of me with the light and confident steps of a gymnast, which perhaps she was.

She was certainly a multi-talented young woman. I followed more cautiously, though the twelve stones were good and solid, flat-topped, and just a very manageable stride apart. Ahead, the path ran onwards, climbing gradually through woodland on the south side of the brook. Far off, above and beyond the trees, I could see the small houses of another village, high on the hillside at the head of the valley.

However, that was not our destination. Quarrytown now lay downstream to our left, and as I expected, Megs turned sharp left on the far bank, and headed downstream. But almost immediately, she stopped at a spot where smooth turf ran down close to the water's edge.

'A good place for a pause,' she said, slipping off her sandals, seating herself on the bank and dangling her bare feet and calves in the water; her light knee-length skirt no encumbrance to this arrangement. 'Have a seat,' she added with a smile.

I sat down alongside, but decided against paddling. 'It is a beautiful spot,' I agreed. The brook bubbled and rippled past; the sun behind us peeped out from a passing cloud and turned the meadows and trees a brighter green; birds sang in the woods above, and yellowy-grey wagtails bobbed on rocks in the water. A big Brown Hawker dragonfly zipped past on bronze wings.

'I used to run down here as a little girl, playing truant from school,' Megs admitted, 'or escaping from helping out with chores. It still feels deliciously naughty, just doing nothing in the middle of the day, when everybody else is working.'

'What should you be doing just now?'

'Oh, there's no *should* – I've done some work in the garden already, I didn't have any teaching this morning, I'm teaching in Quarrytown this afternoon. I'll see my parents at lunch, but if I'd gone straight there I suppose I could have worked alongside them for an hour or so. It's quite acceptable to be taking a break by the riverside – after all, what's the point of Nossex if you can't take the time to appreciate it? Besides, I'm showing a visitor round.'

'And this place is well worth showing someone,' I agreed. The valley was deserted and quiet, with only the sound of the water and the birds, and very little wind. There were sheep in a meadow, some way off upstream, but we were the only humans in sight. Yet for a moment, just as at my first approach to Nossex two days before, I had the oddest sense of being watched and prayed for. Clearly not by Megs, however, whose eyes were closed and her head tilted back, enjoying the autumn sunshine. With her pale skin, she probably had to keep out of the sun in high summer.

I felt a reluctance to move from this very pleasant spot, and thought of a way to prolong the moment.

'Tell me another of the Twelve Tales of Nossex,' I commanded.

'Alright,' she said, opening her eyes, 'Ruth told you the Tale of Alain FisBos, so I'll follow that with the Tale of Judith FisBos – though it's not just about her.'

Megs took a deep breath, paused, and went into dramatic story-telling mode, adopting a different voice for each character and carefully timing every phrase.

40

Six: The Tale of Judith FisBos' conditional forgiveness

Who can say, 'I have kept my heart pure; I am clean and without sin?' Pr 20:9

Judith FisBos, Countess of Nossex, was a short and rather dumpy woman with unruly auburn hair and a more or less permanent cheerful smile. She enjoyed her new life in Nossex immensely, and the only thing that might have made her even happier would have been a second child, a baby brother for her growing daughter Alice.

One day, when life in Portervert Castle was going on as normal, and the Countess was singing sweetly as she kneaded dough for bread rolls, she was startled to see Tilflæd, the Abbess of Pinrose, enter the kitchen, in a state of great agitatation.

'Judy,' she said, 'Oh, Judy, I'm so sorry, but I must talk to you. Now. But not here.'

The Countess knocked the dough and flour off her hands, delegated the unfinished task to a lad nearby, and came outside, just as she was; the day was sunny and mild, with the first light green leaves of Spring unfurling on the birch trees. They walked up to the crown of the ridge, Tilflæd appearing a little calmer, Judith turning over in her mind what all this might be about. Why would the Abbess seek her out? She had other advisors or confessors to call on. It had to be something to do with Alain: he might have caused offence in some way, and it would be her job to deal with him and perhaps also with the injured party. Or perhaps he had met with an accident? But then the Abbess would not be the obvious person to break the news…

Her thoughts trailed off as they came to an open space, above the woods, and Tilflæd, glancing round to see that none was in earshot, burst out:

'Judy, I have wronged you…!'

'…with Alain,' Judith finished the exclamation for her, quietly, sensing the blow a moment before it landed. She held the taller, but far slighter figure of the Abbess as she wept. For some time neither woman moved or spoke.

'Did he force you?'

'No! Did I tempt him? Not intentionally. It just happened. We met on the path. In a narrow place. We greeted one another, quite normally. He stood aside to let me walk by. I stumbled and fell; he caught me up in his arms. So natural! So dangerous! The strength of him! The spicy … smell of him! I was never so close to a man before. I had no idea… My body answered, my will disappeared. I seemed to take no decision – and I think it was the same for him.'

'He had less excuse,' said Judith. She looked at her friend, now perhaps her rival, with sympathy, understanding, and jealous rage. Most women, outside Nossex, had to put up with their husbands picking any tempting fruit they saw along the way, but Alain had never been like that, even before they came to Nossex. She realised now why he was late returning from his two-day trip to Noaster: he was afraid to face her. With good reason, she thought grimly.

'Can you forgive me?' asked Tilflæd.

41

'I hope so,' said Judith; then, to her own surprise, she heard herself adding: 'If there is a child, and you give me that child, I will forgive you.' How could she ask that? She did not normally make such conditions.

What the Countess said to the errant Earl of Nossex was never recorded. Alain said once that when she had finished with him 'I felt smaller than a shrivelled hazelnut.' What the sisters and brothers of Pinrose said to their errant Abbess was not recorded either, though it appears that they were most reluctant to let her step down, as she fervently wished. Finally the Bishop overruled them, and an Extraordinary Gathering was held in Noaster Cathedral on October 1st, 1071.

In a breathless silence, Bishop Leofrith began with words from Old and New Testaments: '*Both the adulterer and the adulteress must be put to death*'– then, after a pause – '*The wages of sin is death, but the gift of God is eternal life in Christ Jesus our Lord*'.

Then Alain and Tilflæd entered from doors on opposite sides of the cathedral, he barefoot and in sackcloth, she barefoot and in a long white shift that showed the swelling of her growing child. They recited Psalm 51 antiphonally, half a verse each. Then the Bishop spoke again.

'*Offer yourselves to God, as those who have been brought from death to life.*[1] People of Nossex, you see before you a good man and a good woman, as other men and women would judge it. If such as these can fall, who can stand? Do not doubt the power of sin. Yet Christ is far stronger, and no sin is too great for Christ to redeem.'

He developed this theme, using many texts, while the two penitents stood with bowed heads on either side of the nave. Finally he concluded with a prayer, then made an announcement.

'Sister Mary of Pinrose is appointed Abbess of Pinrose. Tilflæd, former Abbess of Pinrose, is called from celibacy into matrimony. Brother Godwin of Pinrose is also called from celibacy into matrimony. Tilflæd and Godwin are to be married in Pinrose on November 1st.' Nothing was said of Tilflæd's child.

The silence was broken by a sigh and a stirring; none spoke, but many reacted, for this was news to all but the people of Pinrose.

A son was born to Tilflæd just after Christmas, and named Leofrith, since the Bishop stood godfather. Judith, often together with Alice, frequently visited Godwin and Tilflæd, helped with bathing and changing baby Leofrith, sang to him and played with him as he grew bigger. Finally, when Leofrith was a little over a year old, fully weaned, and his half-sister Judith had just been born, he was formally adopted into the Fisbos family and went to live in Portervert Castle.

[1] Lev 20:10; Ro 6:23; Ro 6:13

42

Seven: Overnight in Quarrytown; walk to Caermorgan *(5 miles)*

I felt rather unsettled as the brief Tale concluded, realising that I had just listened to a story of an unexpected illicit sexual encounter in the countryside, while out in the countryside, alone in idyllic surroundings with an extremely attractive young woman. It was an odd coincidence, and yet the story followed naturally on from the one I had heard the previous day, so there was no reason to ask Megs why she had chosen precisely that Tale.

'A dramatic Tale, and well told,' I said, 'but not as positive a story as the one I heard yesterday.'

'I often wonder about Tilflæd,' she answered. 'Was she happy? Did she miss the celibate life? The Tale doesn't say.'

'How do you imagine it?'

'I imagine – at least, I really hope – that she was far more fulfilled as a wife and mother than she could have been as Abbess. So Alain's loss of self-control did her a favour. But that's just my imagination. She wasn't only a character in a Tale, she was a real historical person, and she may have felt very differently.'

'The Tale says she was keen to step down as Abbess,' I said. 'That could mean she was deeply disappointed in herself, which suggests she had had a sincere vocation to the celibate life.'

'It could also mean she had discovered she rather liked men,' said Megs, standing up. 'We'd better move on, if we don't want to miss lunch.'

The path to Quarrytown slanted upwards, away from the brook, under immense pines, both Scots pines and other, heavier varieties. They were well spaced, allowing some underbrush of ferns and garlic, and a few holly and birch trees in between the tall straight trunks. Jackdaws chattered above, and I saw a spotted woodpecker tapping at one of the pines. Alongside the path, flowers added colour to the woodland scene: pink herb Robert and campion; purple knapweed; yellow hawkbit and white dead-nettle and yarrow.

The path levelled out, and ran on through the woodland, pines gradually giving way to oakwood, before we suddenly emerged and were confronted with a much closer view of Quarrytown, its nearside towering up over us. I was stopped in my tracks, staring upwards, while Megs at first went on without slackening stride, until she realised I'd halted.

'Sorry,' she said, returning. 'I'd forgotten how impressive it is, when you stand here for the first time. I was born here, so it doesn't strike me the same way.'

'But you live in Icclescombe now,' I answered, probing a little, as I took in the view of the curving terraces, eight floors high, set into what had presumably once been two quarries, divided by a tall narrow near-vertical crag that still split the terraces now. Each two floors were set back by a couple of feet, leaving space for a narrow balcony with an iron railing.

'I felt the need to be a little way away from my parents. That's normal Outside;

people say they need to fly the nest. It's less automatic in Nossex. In theory I could go and live with my partner Outside, but he's a professional classical musician, travelling the world, so it suits him to have a flat near Heathrow, and he's hardly ever there. For me, there's nothing attractive about the flat or the area if Rob's not there, and I didn't find any interesting work nearby. Nor did the prospect of commuting into central London appeal much. Here in Nossex I've always got friends and enjoyable work, and in many ways I love the place.'

Partner, I thought. *I wonder how that goes down in Nossex.* 'So teaching EFL might give you more options Outside?' I suggested.

'I was thinking along those lines, yes.'

At the base of the tall curved façade was a broad patio, which turned out to be the flat roof of a large hall at a lower level. A winding staircase took us down into it, and I saw that Megs had expertly timed our arrival for lunch. Once again this was frugal soup and bread, though I wasn't grumbling, given a free choice between carrot and fennel, or mushroom and pea, and a chance to come back and try the other as a second helping.

As folk took their seats for lunch, Megs introduced me to her parents, Philip and Anna, and her grandmother Margaret. When I saw how old her parents were, clearly of my generation, I revised my guess at Megs' age upwards. She might well be in her mid-thirties, which would account for her air of assurance, somewhat at odds with her youthful appearance. But then I've reached the age at which young people often look younger than they really are. Her grandmother, on the other hand, really did look younger than she must be. She could scarcely be much less than ninety, but was spry, nimble and alert, small and slight like her granddaughter. She asked Megs 'how's Robert?' but didn't follow up on the terse reply 'fine – he's in Bamberg.'

She was also interested in where I had come from, and I fielded questions about Manchester, where it seemed both she and Anna had spent time on their respective Years Out, a generation apart.

After lunch Megs disappeared up a staircase to her music teaching, while I found plenty of honest work in helping Philip and Anna clear weeds from the cracks in the flagstones on the patio: a most extensive patio, which seemed bigger as I battled on, flagstone by flagstone. There was also moss to be cleared from the surfaces, and I followed Anna's example of conscientious thoroughness, scrubbing every last trace away, leaving little chance of immediate regrowth. She and her husband worked steadily, unhurriedly, giving the impression they could go on all afternoon without a pause, though they were much the same age as me, and I was sweating and dry-throated, and thankful that the afternoon was cloudy and relatively cool.

Eventually some teenagers hurried out of a side door with a table and jugs and mugs of what proved, when I hastened to try it, to be elderflower-flavoured water. 'This isn't really for us,' said John, though he was also taking the chance of refreshment. I followed his gaze to where a number of runners were arriving at the far end of the terrace. Without any command or discussion, the three of us took a jug

44

each and stood ready to serve the runners; meanwhile three of the youngsters that had brought out the drinks went and picked up our tools and continued the weeding.

The runners, all in shorts and singlets, came on in groups, half a dozen together; it appeared to be more of a fun run or training run than anything competitive. As I was mechanically pouring and serving, I heard a surprised voice say 'Steve?'

Looking up, I saw a face from the distant past; a rather older face now, but still recognisable, and a figure still lean and fit, possibly even leaner than I remembered it. 'Martin?' I said in surprise. 'What are you doing here?'

'I live here,' said Martin. 'That is, not *here* here; over in Pinisk, in East Nossex. Are you here for a few days yet? Will you be at the Gathering?'

'I hope so.'

'Catch you there,' and he trotted off to catch up his group of runners, who were scampering back down the path they had just panted up.

'An old friend?' asked Anna.

'We were at Durham University together. I haven't seen Martin since the year after we graduated. I'll have to make sure I'm at the Gathering now.'

'You wouldn't want to miss it anyway,' said Philip.

Cilla, the skinny girl from Pinrose, came by, looking fresh and as if she could have run harder; but she was busy encouraging a friend who was quite the reverse of skinny. Guy was in that group as well, keeping up without difficulty. He grinned and said 'Hi, Steve!' as I served him.

Soon all the runners were gone. The three young folk that had taken over our patio-weeding showed no sign of wanting to stop, so we helped take the table and refreshments back in and washed up the crockery, a task that led seamlessly into laying up for the evening meal. We then stood by ready to serve.

As people took their places at the long tables, I did a rough head-count. Numbers here appeared to be higher than either Pinrose or Icclescombe: there were a good bit over two hundred here, as well as a number of laid but empty places on the end of one of the tables. A considerably higher proportion seemed to be of secondary school age, and there was a livelier buzz to the atmosphere, though not the boisterous bedlam that I would have expected Outside.

Food, oddly enough, was conspicuous by its absence, and as I was about to ask what was happening, a group of some twenty children and a few adults of all ages filed in and lined up ready to sing. Megs followed them out and faced them as conductor. There was a hush, and the piece began.

Soft notes on two tenor recorders opened the performance, followed by an adult countertenor with a beautifully clear and effortless tone, before the choir joined in after the first section. The quality was remarkable, and the acoustic in the hall gave me gooseflesh, just as the singing at Pinrose had. I found out later that it was a setting of part of Psalm 39, by Orlando Gibbons; Megs had rearranged the organ part for recorders. It lasted only a few minutes, but fully deserved the thunderous applause it received.

45

The choir hastened to their reserved places and the food suddenly appeared for us to serve. It was a pleasant novelty to be part of the team hurrying plates of food out to the tables; it reminded me of church lunches back in Manchester. The meal was lasagna and salad, and as one of the last to be served, I was able to beg the corner of a tray, where it was deliciously caramelised. I thought at first that it was a vegetarian recipe, but after a few mouthfuls I realised that there *was* meat there, just not very much. The flavour was rich and interesting, not quite like anything I remembered trying before. I wondered whether semi-veggie was standard in Nossex. Obviously it wouldn't be from vegetarian conviction, but it might be on the grounds of a balanced and frugal use of resources.

The choir had been served first, and by the time I and the other servers had almost finished eating, they had formed up again, and a hush fell as they performed another of Gibbons' anthems.

As the applause died away, the table-clearing began. Almost everybody seemed to pitch in and the debris was whisked out to the kitchen in no time. Megs was hugging her parents in turn; she had her bag on her shoulder and seemed ready to return to Icclescombe.

Philip guided me up several flights of stairs to a small spare bedroom, where I left the rucksack, and then to a large library nearby, occupying a galleried space two floors in height, well lit by tall windows that were catching the last rosy light just after the sunset. I drifted over to the window and looked out over the valley of the South Brook. Far below, the tiny lonely figure of Megs was crossing a stone bridge on the direct path back to Icclescombe; Nossex was clearly somewhere that a young woman could be out alone in the gathering dusk without anyone being in the slightest bit worried.

'We usually show visitors a copy of this,' said Philip, handing me a finely-bound picture book that showed detailed drawings of the building of Quarrytown. 'If you're all right, we'll see you in the morning; breakfast at seven in the hall downstairs.'

I settled down in an armchair with the book, which gave some of the history of the settlement: that it was less than three hundred years old, in contrast to all the other Nossex settlements, whose origins were lost in pre-history, but which certainly pre-dated the Romans. I learned that the old quarry face formed the back wall of the buildings, and drawings at different stages showed the gradual conversion of first one quarry, and then the other, over a period of nearly fifty years.

I put the book back where Philip had taken it from, and browsed in a biography of an eighteenth-century Bishop of Noaster, who had made sure, on his Wandership, to hear both Wesley and Whitefield preach.

The daylight had long gone. Someone had drawn the curtains and switched on the standard lamp beside me. The library had no large central lights, merely a few scattered reading lamps like the one I was using, which held a low-energy bulb. Quarrytown was clearly aimed at low energy consumption, and another early night beckoned. I was tired enough to sleep even as early as this.

46

However, once again I woke very early, and once again I guessed that someone would be up and at work in the kitchen, so I went down to see whether I could help.

It turned out to be Brother Alan from Pinrose, together with another young man, and I found a task in peeling potatoes. They'd decided on a bit of a fry-up – 'we've had plenty of super-healthy meals recently' – and were cracking eggs into pans, together with plenty of parsnips and potatoes.

'I could take you to Caermorgan after breakfast,' said Alan, 'if that's your plan.'

'I guess it is, if I want to see everywhere; but I could happily stay longer in all of these places.'

Before long, others came to help in the kitchen, and we went out to the dining-hall with the first and freshest breakfasts. After a few minutes, Philip and Anna came to join us, and Margaret was close behind. They all preferred the healthy alternatives to the fry-up.

'How did you meet Megs?' asked Anna.

'I just found myself next to her at Icclescombe,' I answered, 'but then she wanted some advice on teaching English, which is what I used to do before I retired.'

'Yes, that's her latest plan for seeing the world,' said Anna, more to the others than to me, 'since Robert won't come near Nossex.'

'Gossip,' said the old lady warningly.

I took this to mean that such personal matters were not open for discussion, and said: 'Maybe I can ask a couple of general questions? This is the third Nossex community I've been in, and they all seem to be Christian communities. What proportion of Nossex is Christian?'

'Nobody's keeping statistics,' said Anna. 'But it's not so different to a church Outside. Think of a big thriving evangelical church – your own, if you like – what proportion of the congregation is Christian?'

I thought for a moment. 'Most, I suppose; you couldn't say more precisely than that. There will be children that have not yet made a personal commitment; adherents who are still thinking through whether they believe or not; and a few family members or friends of believers who are just coming along to humour someone, but aren't really interested. So there will be a certain number of unbelievers or not-yet-believers among the fellowship.'

'So it is here. Nossex is a county of ten Christian communities: ten churches, if you like. But it's not a condition of Denizenship that you become a Christian. Nobody's thrown out of Nossex for unbelief.'

'So my other question is: how difficult is it to be an unbeliever in Nossex?'

They glanced at each other, probably guessing that my purportedly general question had been formed out of curiosity about Megs' situation.

'Less difficult than being a believer in a secular setting Outside,' answered Anna. 'In a classroom or an office Outside, or on the factory floor, a Christian can encounter ridicule, ribbing, or outright hostility. Either that or they keep their heads down and don't advertise their faith. Here in Nossex we wouldn't allow believers ever to make fun of, or show hostility to unbelievers – there is a specific law against that sort of behaviour – and we would encourage anyone with doubts or who absolutely doesn't believe, to be open and honest about where they stand, which means we have to make sure they don't suffer any discrimination as a result.'

'But knowing you're in a minority is still psychologically challenging,' Philip pointed out.

'I can think of one or two who quite enjoy being different,' said Anna.

'Yes, but most don't,' Philip persisted. 'Quite a few of the youngsters who stay Out after their Years Out, it's because they're not believers.'

'You don't *know* that,' said his wife.

'It's a fairly safe assumption,' Philip responded. I wondered whether the slight tension in their disagreement was prompted by their feelings about Megs not being a believer.

'Can I help wash up?' I suggested, not expecting the answer no, as I gathered a stack of plates and headed for the scullery. Somebody was already in both sinks, but I was able to help as the last in the team, placing crockery in the drainage racks, until Alan came to say he was ready to leave.

A few minutes later we were leaving from a small door at the top of Quarrytown, which gave access to a flat roof that carried an array of solar panels.

'How much energy do they give?' I asked.

Alan wasn't sure, but said they probably meant that less wood had to be burned for hot water. We were almost at the top of the hill here, and a path led away towards the sun, climbing the sky in the south-east. Just over the brow, where the hill fell away steeply below us, Alan paused.

'Here's a good view of East Nossex,' he said. A busy dual carriageway sliced from left to right across the landscape below, bridging a winding river immediately ahead. The drone of traffic was an unceasing irritation, even some hundreds of feet below us and more than a mile away; the more so, I found, from having heard no traffic in the previous three days.

'The river forms the southern border of Nossex,' he explained. 'Where the road crosses the river is the pinch point between West and East Nossex. The whole county is shaped like a butterfly, and the only connection is actually under the bridge.'

I asked the obvious question: 'What happens if the river floods?'

'East Nossex is cut off,' replied Alan. 'Though in East Nossex, they'll say West Nossex is cut off, and pray for us. It doesn't happen very often,' he went on, 'if you look on the far side of the river and beyond the road, that great flat area is the South Moor, water meadows with many drainage channels, and beyond that are the New Marshes. Further still, there are the East Marshes. So if the river does rise a bit, there's a lot of scope for it to spread sideways before it rises much further. Although it's technically Outside, we have *de facto* control over the sluices and channels. The

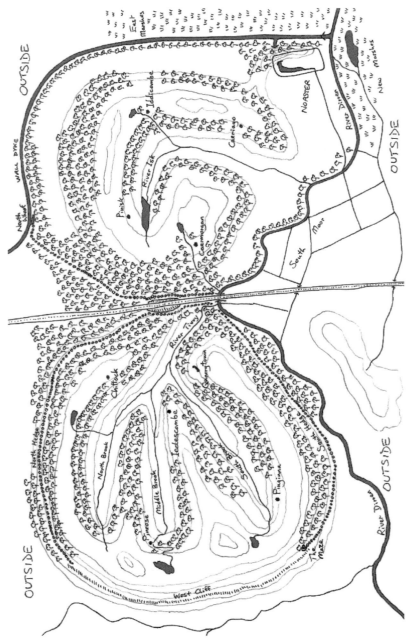

Map of the whole County of Nossex

49

whole area's managed by the Wildlife Society in the neighbouring county, and we have quite a few moles among the membership, and on the committee.'

'What *is* the neighbouring county?' I asked casually.

'Ah,' said Alan, 'that would be Loamshire. And round *there* is Southumberland, and in *that* direction is Barset, and then *this* way is Midsomer.'

'OK,' I said, 'I get the message. Curiosity killed the cat.'

'The river's called the Dirren,' he added, 'but that won't help you much, it's the Nossex name for it, or to be more precise, the original Nemsh name. It has a different name downstream, and I think a third name near its source.'

'Anyway,' I said, 'I daresay you'll modify my memory before you let me leave Nossex.'

'Mmm, and since we don't have magic wands here, we might have to use a large mallet instead... only joking,' he added, seeing my expression, 'you know we don't do violence. On the other hand, we might not let you out at all. Many stumble in from Outside...'

'...and few return to the bright lights and the roar of machinery,' I finished.

He laughed. 'I like that. Where did you hear that?'

'I just made it up,' I admitted.

'I'll remember that,' he said.

'Where's Caermorgan?' I asked, wondering how far it was to our destination.

'Just beyond the bridge,' Alan pointed downwards, then up again, 'there's a steep valley in the woods – three-quarters of the way up – you can see a couple of houses peeping through the trees. That's Caermorgan. Now look a little to the right of that, and on the further hillside you can see a tower...'

'Yes.' I could, or at least I could see the top of a stone tower, protruding from the green trees that covered most of that further hill.

'That's the Purse Tower, home of the Nossex Purse, in Caeriago.'

'Oh, right. Young Guy told me he was going to work there.'

'Yes. I hope he enjoys it. Still, plenty of time to change his mind if he doesn't.' And further right again, beyond the second wooded hill, is the City of Noaster.'

I saw, downriver in the distance, tiny stone houses peeping over a high stone wall. 'How do you spell that?' I asked.

'N-O-A-S-T-E-R. It's from the Latin *Nova Castra*, so we could have spelt it N-O-W-S-T-E-R, but people might have pronounced it 'now stir', which sounds all wrong. Noaster rhymes with much more. You know the Noaster Toaster?'

'No?'

'It's a special kind of toasting fork. We set up a company to market it Outside, and employed a salesman – they called him the Noaster Toaster Boaster. But then he embezzled the account, so they put up Wanted notices, or Noaster Toaster Boaster posters, and then they reproduced them as beer mats, or Noaster Toaster Boaster poster coasters.'

'Really?'

50

'No, I just made all that up.'

'Are you ever serious?' I asked.

'Of course,' he said with an injured expression. 'Often. Well, fairly often.'

He led the way downwards towards the road, but soon the path ran into thick woodland, and the sound of traffic faded. The trees on either side were quite densely packed, elder and holly and hawthorn, and taller trees above that. White, red, and orange butterflies flitted to and fro, mostly out of identification range. A coal tit posed for a moment on a bush, and the continual cooing of wood pigeons could be heard.

The descent seemed lengthy, but eventually we came to the top of a slope, and in a clearing below, saw two groups of people facing each other. Neither group looked quite like typical Nossexfolk, according to the image I had begun to form, which of course was as yet very incomplete. To the left were perhaps a score of men, women and children, all ages from infants to old folk, dressed in a style that reminded me of old-fashioned gypsies. To the right was a smaller group, including only a couple of kids, in appearance what might have been unkindly called 'neo-hippy' – New Age Travellers, I guessed.

I sensed a tension, or hesitancy, about the tableau below; but in much less time than it has taken to describe the scene, Alan had reacted. He fired one word at me: '*Pray!*' with an intensity unlike anything I had seen from him so far, and headed down the slope so hurriedly and decisively that I assumed I was not meant to keep up with him. I compromised by following at a leisurely pace, praying as he had instructed, asking the Prince of Peace that this encounter would be peacefully resolved, and that Alan would be given the right words to say.

As I prayed, and Alan hurtled downwards, a pair of figures from each group detached themselves and approached each other slowly. I couldn't hear what was said, but saw a big moustachioed man from the gypsy group, and a small white-haired chap from the other group, exchange a few words, then shake hands, then embrace each other – not quite unreservedly, I thought. Each was accompanied by a woman, and the two women embraced as well, and here I thought there was no reserve.

At this point Alan, by now at the bottom of the slope, was trying to slow down, and almost crashed into the four of them; they turned, and the big man laughed and clapped Alan on the shoulder, and there seemed to be a release of any remaining tension. The two groups came together and there were general hugs and handshakes and much happy chattering, including Alan, who seemed to be having his leg pulled about his high-speed approach.

As I approached, Alan detached himself from the gathering and joined me, pointing our way down and to the right; almost at once we crossed an old bridge over a small river. 'We'll leave them to get on with it,' he said. 'What a piece of news!'

The dual carriageway we'd seen from above was now very close, though invisible behind thickly packed conifers, which largely damped the traffic noise. As the path dropped a little lower, we suddenly came out of the trees and were confronted with a wall of sound, a near-deafening growling roar from the road, just above us on

51

our left. Huge lorries hurtled by at what seemed breakneck speed. Straight ahead was the River Dirren, that Alan had pointed out, and the path we were walking along ducked under the road, taking advantage of its bridge over the river. Under our feet was beaten earth; on our left and over our heads, grey concrete; to our right, a broad winding river. The small river we had just crossed flowed into this larger one, creating a variety of eddies and whirlpools. I saw a water wagtail, smart in grey and yellow, bobbing on a rock on the far side, oblivious to the din; and beyond it, yellow flowers decorated the far bank of the river.

Coming out from under the bridge, the path quickly twisted aside and was once more screened from the road by dense rows of fir trees. Almost at once we took a left turn off the main track, and began climbing along a narrower path.

'Who were those two groups of travellers?' I asked, now that we were well out of earshot, on the far side of the roaring traffic.

'The big chap,' answered Alan, 'the leader of the left-hand group, as we saw them, is Hezekiah Hughes, and as far as I know pretty well everyone in that group is related to him, directly or indirectly, including his mother, brothers, sisters, children, grandchildren, nephews, nieces, uncles, aunts, in-laws or cousins. We know them as the Hughes clan, or tribe, and they've been coming to Nossex, passing through at unpredictable intervals, for generations.

'Their roots – as far as travellers have roots – are in Wales, and they've always been brilliantly skilled: not just traditional Gypsy clothespegs, or whatever, but woodwork, metalwork, farrying, leatherwork, every kind of craft using natural materials: baskets, tools, you name it. They know how to manage woodland, and they're great with animals, particularly breeding them, but also training or doctoring. And on top of all that, many of them are fine musicians, fiddlers and harpers.

'So in the old days they could almost always earn themselves a good living in rural areas Outside, and they didn't come to Nossex all that often, because there wasn't much money to be made directly here, since we don't do cash. They could barter, of course, and they were interested in our breeding stock, and our musical instruments, and they sometimes took things and sold them Outside for us; we trusted each other, and they liked to be trusted, and they also found less hostility here. They have a special connection with Caermorgan, where they're always welcome, and in the last forty or fifty years things have got much more difficult for them Outside: more hostility, more regulation, far fewer places to go, much less demand for the skills that they trade on. So these days we see them rather more often, though it's still hard to predict when they'll appear, or decide to move on.

'For quite a long time the Hughes clan have been known as keen Christians: Hezekiah's father and grandfather were very godly men, and great preachers – I remember hearing his grandfather Isaiah in Noaster Cathedral, and he was amazing, you could have heard a pin drop. But Hezza himself didn't seem to take after them; he was a very hard man – straightforward and honest, you could do business with him safely – but proud and quick to take offence at any lack of respect. He was a great bare-knuckle fighter in his youth, though he never fought in Nossex.

'Some of his brothers and sisters, and others in the group, I think were believers, inspired by his father, but as long as Hezza was uninterested, they probably had to keep a low profile; he was a very dominant character, domineering perhaps. Anyway, it's different now, he's a different man, I've never seen his face like that before.'

'He did seem to radiate goodwill,' I said.

'I'm looking forward to hearing how that happened,' said Alan. 'I could have wished that our witness here in Nossex had got through to him, but it must have been something or someone Outside.'

'And the other group?' I prompted, as our path forked right and crossed over the lively brook, using a couple of large stepping stones. The moss and ferns that framed the rushing water were a lush rich green.

'Now the Sprat Collective,' Alan went on, 'are quite different. Jack Sprat – the little chap with the white hair – is largely of Romany descent; at least, he maintains that three of his grandparents were gypsies. But his parents left travelling completely, became suburban and settled, and gave Jack and his sister a good education.

'They tried to discourage Jack from any contact with his travelling relatives, and the area they lived in wasn't one that travellers frequented, so it was only once he was old enough to be independent that he could find out about his roots. Before that he could only guess what the life was like; his parents wouldn't even talk about it, which just made it seem more mysterious and alluring. Towards the end of his schooldays, he more or less ran away one summer "to be with the wraggle-taggle gypsies-O".

'It turned out a lot less romantic than he'd imagined; his cousins made fun of him, and he put his foot in it culturally all over the place, because he'd never been told what was done and not done, clean and unclean. But he was still fascinated; it was intriguing, if not so carefree as he'd thought, and he learned quickly, because he was always pretty sharp.

'It led to him studying Anthropology at University, followed by a master's and PhD in Ethnography, specialising in Romany culture, so he's now Doctor John Sprat, and a real authority. At the same time, he was an active Christian at the University: just as he reacted against his parents' rejection of their heritage by becoming a gypsy-specialist academic, so he reacted against their uninvolved and limited middle-of-the-road Anglicanism by becoming a zealous evangelical, with a particular concern, of course, for taking the Gospel to the Roma, and travellers in general.'

'That wouldn't sit well with a strict ethnographic approach,' I said, a little breathlessly, as we continued up the steep slope. Alan seemed unaffected by the exertion, but he was a lot younger than me, I reminded myself.

'Spot on – as long as he was researching their culture as an academic, he had to keep his own beliefs under wraps, and merge into the background as far as possible, so as not to affect what he was observing. But his burden for their conversion grew, and in the end he gave up his academic career in order to be free to preach the Gospel.'

'And how did that go?'

53

'Not quite as he imagined it would,' said Alan. 'He had his contacts, both cousins and others, but they didn't really accept him as one of themselves. They tolerated him as a harmless outsider, if he didn't say too much, but once he started speaking of spiritual rather than cultural matters, the defences were up, and he couldn't get through at all. The people he eventually succeeded in leading to faith weren't true Roma at all, but New Age travellers, folk who were much more intellectual, full of ideas on ecology and sustainability. They enjoyed arguing with Jack, and they were open to new ideas and ready to rethink what life is all about.'

'So that was who was with him?'

'Most of them. His wife Rachel is actually a Nossexwoman – that's his connection with Nossex, and that's why we see them here quite often – she's from Chittock. At the outset they lived in a traditional horse-drawn gypsy wagon. Bad move.'

'What was the problem?' I asked, looking around at the scenery as the path wound upwards alongside the mossy boulders of the tumbling brook. Caermorgan seemed a longer climb than I had thought, when spotting it from the hill above Quarrytown.

'They didn't have enough skills to make a living that way; they were still partly supported by the congregation Jack Sprat had come from. And then as the Collective grew, they needed more wagons, which meant more horses, and they weren't all that clever with horses. So they ended up further than ever from breaking even.

'The crucial move was to sell the horses and wagons and invest in a couple of narrowboats. This suited the skills they had in the group much better – Jack can at least steer a boat, even if he's not very handy otherwise – and the canal network was a better market for their watercolours and craft work. Now they're self-sufficient with a not-for-profit chandlery/craft/art business. It means that they have far less contact with the Roma, the people that Jack originally felt a burden to bring the Gospel to. On the other hand, he's built up what is in effect a travelling church.'

'Church floating,' I suggested, 'rather than church planting.'

'Very droll. Anyway, here in Nossex he met the Hughes clan, who had known his wife Rachel from way back. She managed to restrain Jack for a while, but in the end he *would* go and try to convert Hezekiah Hughes, who is one of the contrariest people around if you try and push him in any direction. What started as a sharp exchange of words ended up as a massive falling-out.'

'Which seems to be over,' I suggested.

'Yes, praise God. It'll be a good story.'

'Nossex is full of stories,' I said. 'Yesterday I heard the second of two stories of Alain Fisbos.'

'Let's pause here, then,' Alan answered, indicating a large moss-covered lump of rock that would serve as a bench. 'I'll tell you a tale of his two children.'

I shrugged off the rucksack and we settled ourselves, the rushing of the brook and the warbling of many small birds in the oak trees overhead providing a background to Alan's voice.

Eight: The Tale of Leo TwoFisBos

In all his thoughts there is no room for God. His ways are always prosperous;
he is haughty and your laws are far from him. Ps 10:4

Alice FisBos was nearly nine when her half-brother Leofrith was born, and she loved him dearly, served him willingly, and played with him whenever he had a mind to play with her. For his part, little Leo found his big sister useful, on occasions, but appeared to give his unconditional love to none.

He was razor sharp, lightning fast at his lessons, so that teachers had difficulty keeping him occupied, and he was interested in very many things, a great wanderer and explorer of the woods as soon as (even before) he was allowed out on his own.

Being formally adopted according to the best law of Nossex, his right name was Leofrith FisBos; but since everyone knew he had been conceived out of wedlock, and the Countess was not his true mother, he came to be referred to as Leo Fitz FisBos or FisFisBos, at first as a joke, but later as a habit, finally turned into TwoFisBos, which was easier to say.

The time came for Leo TwoFisBos to go on his Years Out, or Wandership, as it was called then, and he took service, under the name of Leo FitzEarl, in the household of a wealthy man in Lincoln, working as clerk-administrator, librarian, and part-time poet. Five years he stayed, either in Lincoln or travelling with his master, and as long as there was something new to see or do, or a challenging task to undertake, he was well content, and missed Nossex not at all.

When Leo finally returned to Nossex, he found it dull and limited. He did not feel that his father, as Earl, was sufficiently respected by the people; and the fact that Alain was humble enough not to demand any show of deference, and was actually deeply loved, and therefore respected in a far more valuable way, passed Leo by entirely. He tried to behave with even more dignity himself, to compensate. The Nossexfolk were at first amused, but then repelled, by Leo's airs and graces; Alain and Judith, meanwhile, were disappointed and mortified.

Alain had intended, on Leo's return, to declare him heir-presumptive and the probable future second Earl of Nossex, but the young man's attitude made him pause and inquire discreetly of public opinion. He was not surprised to find that many folk were dismayed at the prospect of Leo as Earl; they loved Alice, and thought she would make an excellent Countess. Alain spoke to Judith, and they agreed to be patient awhile.

Within two years, Leo left Nossex again, and found his way to the court of King William Rufus. There he used the money he had saved during his years in Lincoln, and a certain amount of bluff, to pass himself off as a nobleman of substance. Leo was handsome, taller than his father and with little of that great bulk, though his shoulders were certainly broad; and he had the yellow hair and blue eyes of his mother.

Thus he caught the eye and favour of William Rufus, who liked handsome young men; but Leo was clever enough to keep just beyond the king's clutches, and meantime he also caught the eye of a young heiress. It seemed to him that his fortune would be far brighter Outside than in Nossex.

Back in Nossex, meanwhile, this further desertion made Alain's mind up, and he spoke to Alice about becoming Countess. But here there was an unexpected snag: although she appreciated the honour, and the goodwill of the Nossexfolk, Alice FisBos had no wish to become Countess, in fact a strong wish *not* to become Countess. She was approaching middle age, happily married to a humble forester, and she wanted no responsibilities beyond her four growing children.

Alain retreated in despair; he had seldom been able to change his daughter's mind, and indeed he sympathised with her feelings. So nothing was done, and the next year Leo re-entered Nossex in fine style, with the young heiress, now his betrothed, Beatrice de St-Clair, and three serving-maids for her, and a squire for himself, all expensively mounted on fine horses richly caparisoned.

The Nossexfolk were extremely unimpressed by this show, but they were not unamused, and they were not always able to keep straight faces and neutral voices when giving Leo and his retinue the required deference. Leo was angered, but not surprised, and he bided his time.

Beatrice was less perceptive, and quite unprepared for a lack of respect, so it took her some weeks to realise what the people thought of her. It took her longer still to realise that there was no-one, other than Leo, who would be prepared to enforce the rigid hierarchy she was used to.

Once she fully grasped the situation, however, she was determined. She had found little in Nossex to attract her, and she saw no incentive to teach the Nossexfolk manners when she could enjoy her status without a struggle, elsewhere in England. Leo found himself with a choice between an uncertain inheritance in Nossex, or holding on to Beatrice and her money. The dilemma did not detain him long, and the TwoFisBos / St-Clair party departed, leaving behind one serving-maid, dismissed on the eve of their departure for unmarried pregnancy.

The unfortunate maid, Maud of Bow by name, was left destitute, and surprised and grateful to be taken in and cared for by no lesser persons than the Earl and Countess. It became known that they would in fact soon be caring for their fifth grandchild, for Leo was named as the father. Maud insisted on taking full responsibility for the sin, refusing to blame Leo, instead blaming herself for being led astray by his good looks and charm, and maintaining that she still loved him. At this, Alain and Judith muttered under their breath, but when the boy was eventually born they allowed Maud to name him Leo.

Maud found no husband before the birth, so it was inevitable that the boy would become known as Leo ThreeFisBos; the joke was too obvious to pass up, and in fact the growing boy was most unlike his father, full of laughter and totally lacking in dignity, enjoying the joke of his odd surname more than anyone.

Alice loved her nephew as much or more than she had her little half-brother; a more rewarding love in that it was fully returned. Leo remained in Portervert Castle with Maud as part of the household, and he loved his aunt, and of course his cousins and most of all his grandparents. Countess Judith was overjoyed to find the son she had longed for, and who had proved such a disappointment when granted, finally arriving in the shape of a grandson after her husband's heart, a great hulking happy rollicking lump of a boy who won all his wrestling bouts and was everybody's friend.

Outside, meanwhile, Leo TwoFisBos took his wife's name of St-Clair when he married, and his formidable intelligence found sufficient employment in a key role in Henry I's administration, where he worked efficiently to enrich his king and himself. He never met his natural son.

A few years into the twelfth century, Alain FisBos died suddenly of a heart attack, and finally Alice submitted to the wishes of all Nossexfolk and became Countess. Unwilling as she had been, she filled that role for almost forty years until her own death, and many sensible innovations, customs, and traditions are credited to the days of Countess Alice. Her children all following their mother's first reaction in declining any such honour, Leo ThreeFisBos eventually became Earl of Nossex when his aunt Alice died, taking the responsibility in his mighty and jovial stride.

Nine: Overnight in Caermorgan; walk to Caeriago *(5 miles)*

'That's a nice happy ending,' I commented. 'When I heard the Tale of Alain FisBos, I was told there are many descendants alive today. But they're not FisBos, because his only son was Leo TwoFisBos, and they're not TwoFisBos, because Leo changed his name. Are they ThreeFisBos?'

'Funny you should ask that,' said Alan. 'No, they're not. Firstly, Countess Alice's descendants are the Foresters and the Williamsons, and through them many other families. Secondly, Earl Leo ThreeFisBos never married, but he had fourteen children.'

'That sounds like another Tale,' I said.

'Not really, because we don't know the full details, and what we do know isn't enough for an interesting story. He made some kind of promise to a girl Outside, when he was on Wandership, though nobody knows what the promise was. Anyway, he felt he was bound somehow, but when he came back to Nossex he found his life's partner. They stayed together forty years, faithful till death, and he never saw the girl Outside again, but he felt he couldn't marry, despite what anybody said. So of course the children were all FourFisBos, and that's one of the commonest names in Nossex today. I'm a FourFisBos myself.' Alan stood up and puffed his broad chest out in mock pride.

'And who is the present Earl?' I asked, rising and hefting my rucksack from where it had been leaning against an old log, admiring as I did so the stripy bracket fungus growing along the log in horizontal rows. We set off up the winding path.

'*Countess* Mary is a Forester by birth, though her married name is Smith. You see, the earldom didn't necessarily descend parent to child in the same family. Many heirs, like Countess Alice, didn't want the job; and sometimes, like Leo TwoFisBos, the people didn't want *them*. In the end the earldom came to be offered to whoever among the descendants of the first Earl was both acceptable and prepared to accept the responsibility.'

'Is there much competition for the honour?'

'You're joking. People try to avoid being chosen – if they see it coming. You should have seen Mary Smith's face when they invited her to be Countess. She was so taken aback, she had a mental block and couldn't think of a good reason to say no.'

'It's a pity if she has to take on a responsibility she's not happy with.'

'Don't worry, she grew into the role very quickly. She's brilliant. I'm sure the Lord made her mind go blank because she was the right person for the job. People didn't pick her at random, you know.'

As I thought this over, we suddenly came upon the village of Caermorgan: very much a woodland settlement: there were cottages in between the trees, and fruit trees and bushes in between the cottages. The path petered out, and grass ran right up to the very walls and doors: short turf in some parts, and long rough full of docks and sorrel in others.

An old woman was sitting in a rocking-chair outside one of the cottages, knitting: a woman of considerable size and stature, I saw as she laid her knitting down with a happy smile and came to meet us, her stride steady and strong despite her obvious age.

'Welcome, Alan,' she said.

'Thank you; it's good to be here again. This is Steve, a stray visitor from Outside. Steve, this is Delyth, head of the Coppersmith family, who have been here for two thousand years or more.'

'Pleased to meet you,' I said. 'Do you still work copper here?'

'Indeed we do. Tinkers and woodwards, shepherds and colliers, those are our occupations in Caermorgan.'

'You have coal mines in Nossex?'

'*Colliers*, in Nossex,' said Alan, 'means charcoal-burners – as it used to do Outside. Delyth,' he went on, 'the Hughes clan are on their way; and they're reconciled with the Sprat Collective; and it seems Hezekiah's come to faith.'

'Praise the Lord!' she cried, her face lighting up. 'That's great news, if it's true. We'll need to clear their site,' she added, with a momentary frown. 'But that won't take long, if plenty of folk pitch in.'

Lunch gave me the opportunity to admire the Caermorgan hall, another long cruck-beamed building like the one at Icclescombe; though this seemed older. The meal was a light salad with warm garlic bread; Delyth announced the impending arrival of the Hughes clan, and I noticed that most folk ate fairly frugally. Perhaps there was the expectation of a feast later.

Clearing the site involved gathering windfalls from under fruit trees: plums, cherries, apples and pears; and a good number of happy children climbing the trees to pick all fruit remaining on the branches. Ladders were in use as well, and in the end several large baskets of fruit were lined up by the nearest cottage. Men with scythes moved in to deal with some of the longer grass; others with rakes cleared the mowings away. Some low-hanging branches were pruned off here and there; and a fireplace was tidied up, with a stack of firewood piled nearby.

I noticed that most communication was in a language that sounded like a rather nasalised version of Welsh; presumably it was Nemsh, though folk that spoke to me used English. The work took a good part of the afternoon, and I managed to be involved in most of the tasks; though I didn't attempt to handle a scythe. Once everything was virtually finished, cider was served, and I was glad of the chance to sit and rest a bit.

As more jugs of cider were brought out, and refills offered, Hezekiah Hughes and his clan came up the path into the village. I was struck by the contrast between the broad bearded faces of the Nossexmen, and the lean, mostly clean-shaven gypsies, though some sported moustaches like Hezekiah. Among the group I saw Guy, to my surprise; later on I learned that he was Hezekiah's grand-nephew. Delyth stepped forward and welcomed them formally in three languages; the third was English; the second sounded like Nemsh, so I guessed that the first might have been Roma.

A couple of the clan began to lay a fire, while the rest pitched tents in a semi-circle facing the village. The residents meanwhile returned to various tasks, and I found myself in the kitchen preparing vegetables. Meat of some kind was already stewing slowly in large pots. The smell was tantalising, and the time it took to get everything organised seemed rather long, but eventually we were all seated in a wide circle three rows deep around the fire, and everyone had food.

Music was playing continuously: fiddles, concertinas, mandolins and a harp. There seemed to be enough musicians to allow some to break off and get some food in rotation. Once I'd had a first helping of the stew, which this time contained plenty of excellent lamb, I went to fetch my whistles in the hope of joining in. As I returned, however, someone called on Hezekiah to play, and the noise level fell as everyone looked at the big man. I wondered what kind of a player he was; he seemed an unlikely musician.

Hezekiah took the harp from the harpist, settled it under his beefy hands, and slowly and with amazing delicacy, he played a Welsh air that I recognised:

Lliw Lili Ymysg Y Drain

There was no applause after the sound of the harp died away, but a silence that was even more eloquent of praise and thankfulness. After a long pause, Delyth turned to the big man, as he passed the harp back to the harpist. 'Hezekiah,' she said, 'you seem a different man. Is there a story to tell?'

'Well, yes,' he replied. 'It was my eyes, see?' He took off his black-rimmed glasses and flourished them, then replaced them slowly. 'The eyes explained a whole lot of things, once we realised the eyes were a problem.'

There was a hint of a Welsh lilt in his voice, but no trace of the Nossex nasalisation. He paused, taking his time, then went on quietly: 'I never learned to read, see. Now that's not so unusual among travelling folk, you might say. But my father and my grandfather were great readers, especially the Bible and what they called good solid books, and my brothers and sisters, they all learned to read, most often reading the Bible at my father Jeremiah's knee. It was only me that couldn't make out all those little black squiggles, rows and rows of them, marching across the page. I felt so stupid, and I could feel my father's disappointment, and yet his patience and sympathy, as if I was handicapped or something and needed looking after.

'It made me angry, and I found other ways to show I wasn't stupid, so I became sharp and crafty, and quick to punch anyone who I thought might be looking down on me. I didn't realise it then, but my whole prize-fighting career grew out of not learning to read.

'I had to feel I was the leader, the one people could look up to. Standing over a fighter I'd just knocked down, I felt all right, God forgive me.

'And the Bible, that big heavy book on my father's knee, I grew to hate it, and so I hated what was in it, and turned away from its teaching. All because I couldn't read, and that was all because of my eyes, though I didn't know that till this year.'

'How did you find out?' Delyth prompted.

'Well, there was this gordja, see, who specialised in teaching reading. We were on a local authority site, not so free and easy, though there are worse, but to keep the authorities sweet it was best to let them feel helpful, feel they were doing you a favour, yes ma'am, thank you, sir, that's really useful, ma'am, and so forth. And this woman thought she could teach me to read, which my father Jeremiah had failed to do; but it seemed best to humour her.

'And before we even began the reading lessons, she insisted on going and getting my eyes tested, because, she so diplomatically put it, I'd reached the age of wisdom, where so many people that never used glasses before find they now need them for reading. Well, I went along with that as well, and a right technical rigmarole it was, too. Looking right inside your head, they seemed to be, putting you under the microscope, coming right into your personal space, though I didn't mind that in one way, the optician being a most fragrant young woman, yet at the same time I'm thinking I had a pickled onion with my lunch, poor girl.'

I saw Guy, his face lit by the flickering fire, trying not to smile.

'Well,' Hezekiah continued, with a dramatic pause, 'the optician didn't know whether to tell me it was good news or bad news. It seems my two eyes each had a completely different problem to the other, and they couldn't work *together* at all at all. So the dominant eye, which was the left one, had taken over, and that wasn't one that could do any close work, though the right eye wouldn't have been much help with that anyway, because that one was just generally useless with its stigma.

'Anyway, they could fix all that, she said, and I couldn't believe how sharp and clear everything got when they found the best lenses. However,' and he paused again, 'that wasn't the only problem, it seemed. She'd found something else, something that wasn't just the way my eyes were made, but a growing problem that needed fixing. And fixing it would be a simple matter of an injection in the eyeball.

'Well!' He puffed his cheeks out. 'The optician talked as if it was no big deal. It wouldn't hurt, she said. I thought *that's not the point*. But I wasn't going to show I was scared, so I made the appointment, and came away in a cold sweat.'

'My brother Outside had one of those injections,' said Delyth.

'Good for him,' answered Hezekiah. 'I once faced a man who was holding a knife, and knocked him cold because my fist was quicker than his knife hand. That needs a little bit of courage, I think; but then to face a doctor with a needle, and you know that needle's going into your eye, and you can't use your fists to defend yourself, but you just have to stay still, well, that needs courage of a whole different magnitude.'

61

'It needs trust,' said Delyth.

'Maybe. It's not easy for a gypsy to trust a gordja. But this reading teacher surprised me, because she understood how afraid I was, and she didn't try to patronise me, or jolly me out of it, but said she'd pray for me. I thanked her for that, and I meant it; and I asked her why she cared about gypsies anyway. She said she'd felt a call from God, but she also said she'd been fascinated and inspired by a book by Dr John Sprat.

'Well, I didn't like to say that I knew Jack Sprat, and that I'd recently fallen out with Jack Sprat, and called him all sorts of bad names, because I felt he was a pompous disrespectful know-all who would never truly understand the travelling life if he lived to be a hundred and fifty. His blood might be as Romany as anybody's, but he wasn't born to the life; he didn't grow up with the life. He's outside looking in.

'So I said nothing, and came away, and in the dark of the next night I lay awake, trying not to think about needles, and I thought *she's praying for me*, and I felt comforted, and I thought the least I could do was pray for myself.'

Hezekiah looked at Guy. 'Let me warn you, lad,' he said, 'don't talk to God if you're not ready for what He might say to you. I got a shock. I didn't hear a voice; I didn't see anything. But I was shown things. I was shown how I hated to be looked down on. Then I was shown how I looked down on everybody else. I looked down on gordjas that were only trying to help, that were even ready to pray for me. I looked down on Jack Sprat because he had a bit of an ego, when mine was three times as big. I looked down on travelling men that wouldn't fight, when actually they were better men than I was. I looked down on people that obeyed God, when they had more reason to look down on me – yet they probably prayed for me, too. The more I was shown, the more unforgivable everything seemed.'

Guy gazed wide-eyed at Hezekiah, moving not a muscle.

'There was no hope for me,' the big man went on, 'unless God could take me as I was. But that thought reminded me of all that my father and grandfather had said, that God loves a broken heart, and takes in those that come to Him with absolutely nothing. So I did. I admitted I'd been wrong all these years. And I prayed for forgiveness. And now I am born again.'

Delyth wiped away a tear. 'Hezekiah,' she said, 'it wasn't actually your eyes that were the real problem, was it?'

'No, Delyth, it wasn't. Of course, it was my heart. A proud heart, that wouldn't ask for help right at the beginning, when I needed it. A heart full of anger and resentment and self-justification. A heart of stone. But you know what God says? *I will give you a new heart and put a new spirit in you; I will remove from you your heart of stone and give you a heart of flesh.*[1] And He is doing, though it takes a little time. Part of that is being reconciled to Jack Sprat. Before, I couldn't even like him; now, I love the man! That can only be from the Lord, that's not the old Hezza Hughes.'

For a little while there was silence among those nearby, who had been listening to Hezekiah. Elsewhere in the circle there was chattering and laughter. Hezekiah

[1] Ez 36:26

took a swig of his cider and looked round the wide circle of faces, shining in the firelight. 'You know, Delyth,' he said, 'sometimes I used to find this quite irritating, all these folk coming out to have a romantic evening with the gypsies, as if we only existed to entertain them. Now, I look at happy faces, and I think, what a privilege, to be here to make people happy. That's our *birinn*, our task. I'm looking at the same scene, but I'm seeing it quite differently.

'It's like my new glasses; I can see things more clearly. And to think, just as I could have had my eyes corrected many years ago, so I could have had a new heart long ago, if I'd only accepted that the old one was no good. Things would have been very different.

'Mind you,' he went on after a pause, 'I might be lacking a few good memories, too. How much fighting would I have done if I'd been a believer from a boy?'

'None, I hope,' said Delyth.

'Well, the funny thing is, even before I was born again, I would have said that the best memory was the one fight I lost – to Billy Boswell. It was a privilege to stand toe to toe with that man, and afterwards I was glad to call him my friend. Strange – that you gain so much more by losing than by winning! I learned respect for a better man when I lost. When I won, I often felt contempt for the man I'd just knocked over. Of course, it all makes much more sense now.'

Softly, the harpist began playing again, and gradually others joined in until music was dominant once more, and conversation would have been an effort. I played along where I could; many of the tunes were relatively uncomplicated, and in the usual keys for folk music.

At a pause, I was invited to lead off a tune myself, and swithered between something generally popular, that they might know, or something that would definitely be new for them. Deciding on the latter, I announced *Barefoot Bethany*, one of my wife Ishbel's tunes, and a dark-haired girl of perhaps eight or nine jumped up and said that she was called Bethan, and she was barefoot. As I played she improvised a dance around the fire – well away from the flames, I was glad to note.

All too soon the fire was dying down, and at our backs we could feel that the temperature was dropping. There was a light but chilly breeze, and it promised to be a coldish night. Folk were slipping away; Guy went off with his cousins, presumably to sleep in the open or in one of the tents. I didn't fancy sleeping out, suddenly feeling quite shattered, and I took up the offer of a bed in one of the cottages.

There was a certain amount of coming and going in the main hall, as I collected my rucksack on my way to my quarters. A middle-aged man had apparently just arrived, and his arrival seemed to have put people in something of a rather un-Nossexlike fluster. He was hustled away to a different cottage to the one I was headed for, and before long sleep swallowed up my mild curiosity.

Friday 26th September 2014

The next morning I slept longer than previously. Although I wasn't late for breakfast in the hall, it was in full swing with a few folk already eating. Old Sarah Hughes and Delyth Coppersmith had their heads together, conferring.

'Don't let Hezekiah meet that man yet,' said Sarah.

'He'll have to accept him soon,' said Delyth. 'They might well be baptised together on Sunday.'

'That gives me time to talk him round. But if they met face to face this morning, there's no knowing. The old man isn't all gone yet.'

Delyth seemed to come to a sudden decision, and called Alan over. 'Can you take John with you to the Blackfriars, right away? The Abbot'll take charge of him; he needs a listening ear.'

'Fine,' said Alan. 'Can someone point Steve in the direction of Caeriago, then?'

'Guy can do that – they can go together. Are you happy with that, Steve?'

'Perfect,' I said. 'I know Guy; I've lost two games of chess to him already.' Polite acceptance of Delyth's suggestion came automatically, but in fact I felt another momentary stab of paranoia at being unable to make an independent decision. Was I being set up, or taken for a ride? With a deep breath and a little reflection, common sense reasserted itself: they were only trying to be helpful and hospitable, and Guy would be good company.

After breakfast there were various tasks I could help with; preparations were under way for lunch before the last of the breakfast washing-up was done, and I found useful employment in scrubbing vegetables that were to go in a stew that would cook slowly through the morning. It kept me busy until it was time to leave.

Guy led the way out of the highest part of the village, where a path ran uphill, past the last of the trees and out onto a bare hilltop, on the crown of which was a cairn. We paused there, and I looked back, to see the long hills of West Nossex all pointing towards us like four digits of a claw. Looking above the valleys, the high perimeter ridge behind made a wide horseshoe with its open end facing us.

The hill we were standing on was also part of a horseshoe-shaped ridge, a little lower than the West Nossex hills; and this horseshoe had its open end to the south. From our vantage point Noaster was invisible, but Guy pointed out three other East Nossex settlements, first Pinisk to the north, stone quadrangles high on the hillside.

'That's the Blackfriars School, where I'll be three days a week,' said Guy. 'After they're twelve, most people go to either Quarrytown, Blackfriars, or Noaster.

'Quarrytown's best for music and languages,' he added, 'Blackfriars for maths, engineering, and philosophy; Noaster for theology and medicine. But they all teach just about everything.'

To the north-east was Iddicombe, high in a steep little side-valley; and eastwards the Purse Tower was prominent. From this angle we could see all of it through a gap in the trees, and the small houses of Caeriago clustered round its base. Here on the open hilltop a few sheep and goats wandered about, cropping the grass.

From the cairn the path took a direct line towards the Purse Tower, and gradually we began to descend, re-entering woodland as we came to the steep drop into the valley that lay between us and Caeriago.

'Did you like Grand-Uncle Hezekiah's story?' asked Guy.

'Amazing,' I said.

There was a pause, then Guy said, 'Can I ask you something?'

'Of course,' I answered, wondering what was coming.

'Do Christians have to be born again?'

'Yes,' I said, 'Jesus said so, and if you believe Jesus is the Christ, you have to accept what he said: *no-one can see the kingdom of God unless he is born again.*[1] If you don't believe Jesus is the Christ, you're not a Christian.'

'Can you say an exact day when you were born again?'

'December 31st, 1961,' I said, without hesitation. 'That's when I became a Christian.'

'That's a long time ago,' said Guy. 'That's more than *fifty years* ago.'

'Yes. I was quite young at the time – just twelve.'

'That's how old I am.' He thought for a moment, as a few early-fallen leaves rustled under our passing feet. 'Did you not believe before then?'

'I believed, in the sense that I knew Jesus died for my sins, and I knew I needed His forgiveness. But before that date, I was holding something back; I hadn't given my whole life to Jesus. I was scared of what He might ask me to do; I wasn't prepared to lose control of my life and let Him decide. In the end I knew I would have to take a deep breath and jump; I was just putting it off, telling myself I was too young.'

'*Was* twelve too young?' he asked.

'Once I was old enough to understand that the decision had to be taken, I was old enough to take it. In fact, every day I was putting it off, I was actually deciding not to follow Jesus. *Not yet* is the same as *No.*'

Guy said nothing for a while, as we came to a stone bridge over a broad brook, or a very small river, that wound lazily between willows and alders. We paused and leant on the parapet, looking up the valley towards low hills. Like the other Nossex valleys I'd seen, the floor of the valley was meadows, but the sides were wooded almost to the top, and then the hilltop ridge was open to the sky. In the middle distance, the valley curved away left and out of sight. Close at hand, a Blue Emperor dragonfly dodged to and fro catching midges.

[1] John 3:3

65

'What am I scared of?' he said quietly.

'You tell me,' I said.

'I don't know. That is, maybe I'm scared of Outside. He might send me there.'

'But you'll have your Years Out anyway, won't you?'

'Yes, but we can come back after three years, if we want – though a lot of people take a bit longer. If I become a Christian, God might call me to *stay* Outside. I've been Outside; I've got an uncle in Leamington Spa. It's fun in some ways, but I wouldn't want to stay there for ever.'

'And if you don't become a Christian?'

'I can't not become a Christian,' he said. 'I will; I'm just putting it off. Like you were fifty years ago.'

'In 1961,' I said, 'I was scared of Abroad, rather than Outside, but it's pretty much the same thing. I was afraid of being sent where I didn't want to be. In fact, God didn't send me abroad until I was ready for it, and then He gave me a love for each of the places He sent me. There were irritations, and things that were inconvenient, and things I was nervous about, but nothing *really* scary.'

'Why December 31st?' he asked.

'It happened to be a Sunday,' I said. 'The speaker at my Bible class said: "Maybe there's someone here who's been putting off becoming a Christian. Well, tomorrow's a new year. Start 1962 as a Christian." I thought, *that's me.*'

Guy turned and looked up at Caeriago, clustered round the tall Purse Tower, more prominent now we were closer, not quite looming over us, but impressive nonetheless as it rose out of the trees on either side. He caught my eye, and gave a slight nod and a smile.

66

'It's a new start for me now,' he said. 'New job, new school, new home.'

'Scared?'

'No way, I'm looking forward to all three. Today's no problem, it's four years from now I'm not sure about.'

'In my experience,' I said. 'God doesn't give strength or courage four years in advance of when it's needed. But He definitely *does* give it when it *is* needed.'

Guy half smiled, as if to say *if you say so*; and we set off up the hill towards the Purse Tower. The slope grew increasingly steep, and I found myself breathing quite heavily; though Guy still had a spring in his step when we came to the Tower.

There we were met by a large grey-bearded jovial figure of my own age or near it, who must have seen us approaching, for he came out of the broad wooden door just on cue. He introduced himself as Joseph Beniuda, but told me to call him Joe, and Guy to call him Uncle Joe – which I later found was his near-universal nickname, even to his contemporaries.

Before we did anything else, he led the way into a nearby office, said something to one of the workers sitting at a computer, and beckoned Guy forward. After a few clicks of a mouse, the worker sat back.

'Press Enter,' said Uncle Joe to Guy, who hesitated for a moment, then did as he was bid.

'You've started work now,' Uncle Joe said. 'We'll show you things properly next week; but now you've started, you're a Purser.'

'I thought you were the Purser,' said Guy.

'I'm the *Chief* Purser,' was Uncle Joe's reply. 'Or, to claim my full title, the Keeper of the Nossex Purse. But everyone who works for the Purse is a Purser.'

We went through to a long room at the back of the Tower, where folk were laying tables for lunch. It was another fine meal: a chunky beetroot soup with raisin bread and butter.

After lunch, while Guy was being shown around by one of his young colleagues, Uncle Joe took me up to the library. It was smaller than the Quarrytown library, but similar in being high up and well lit by a tall window with a view over the valley. We settled in armchairs facing out of the window, and he poured two cups of pseudo-coffee, different again from other Nossex brews, dark, powerful and bitter, not so very unlike the real thing.

'Have they been telling you the Tales of Nossex?' he asked.

'Yes,' I said, 'I've heard four so far. Are you going to tell me another one?'

'There's only one story you should hear under this roof. Let me tell you the Tale of my remote ancestor Judah ben David, the founder of the Nossex Purse.'

Ten: The Tale of Judah ben David and the Great Murrain

Surely he will save you from the fowler's snare and from the deadly pestilence; he will cover you with his feathers and under his wings you will find refuge. Ps 91:3

Judah ben David was born in 1275 in London, the seventh son in a prosperous family of merchants and moneylenders; still wealthy, though less so than they had been, because of the increasing restrictions on the activities of the Jews, and the heavy tallage that was levied in the year he was born. Moreover, much of their liquid capital was loaned to the king, and there was no certainty of its return in the foreseeable future.

When Judah was fifteen, Edward Longshanks king of England finally decided to expel all Jews. They had a little over three months to prepare themselves to cross the Channel with such of their worldly goods as could be carried with them. Judah's family planned to join relatives in Rouen, but he was dismayed at this, because Naomi, his second cousin in Stamford, and the one person he felt really understood him, was going to take refuge in Nossex.

His parents poured scorn on the Nossex plan, but they had too much else to worry about to take time to talk him out of his determination to join Naomi. A week before they were due to take ship, he travelled north to Stamford, and the joy in Naomi's face when she saw him was enough to reassure him that he had made the right decision.

Within two days they were in Noaster, where Judah was surprised to find a community of Jews who had accepted Jesus of Nazareth as Messiah, effectively becoming Christians, but who took no trouble to deny their Jewishness, in fact insisted that it was intact. Naomi's family, however, were not tempted to join them, instead settling in Pinginna, in the other Jewish community, one that rejected Christianity, yet somehow remained on good terms with the Christians around them, as had been the case all over England two centuries earlier.

It was a relief to be safely in Nossex, where even if there was little chance of attaining prosperity, there was freedom from danger, opposition and hostility. Judah and Naomi were married not long after, neither of them quite seventeen, and within a few years had swelled the population of Pinginna through the addition of five healthy children.

In the autumn of 1299, as the days were lengthening and the new century approached, a milestone that moved more folk to pessimism than optimism at that time, young Judah stood in the synagogue in Pinginna and proclaimed:

Seven weary winters shall the snow lie and the icicles lengthen;
Seven sorry summers will the clouds roll and the corn rot;
Seven evil years must the beasts sicken and be buried in haste.
Yet the Lord has compassion on the afflicted,
And the prudent see danger and take refuge.

He was quite out of order, too young to speak in this way; yet he already had a small reputation as a prophet, after a fashion, and men were divided over whether to dismiss the prophecy or take it seriously. The dark words gave rise to much debate all over Nossex, as they passed rapidly from mouth to ear.

Cross-examined on his own interpretation, Judah refused to be more precise. He said the words had come to him unbidden, all at once together, but he had no clearer idea what they might mean than the next man. Pressed still further, he would say no more than that he had certain vague but strong feelings: that this calamity was not immediate, but that most folk would yet live to see it; and that it was not so much in the nature of a judgment or punishment, but more like a test, a refining, or perhaps a winnowing of the faithful.

He could shed no light on whether the three sevens were separate, consecutive, or concurrent. Wise and logically-minded folk saw that the bad weather might lead to the pestilence, suggesting a succession of events, but the question remained over the meaning of 'take refuge': should they simply prepare for the worst, or like the king of Nineveh, *'call urgently on God'* in hope that he *'may yet relent and with compassion turn from his fierce anger'*?

Bishop Mark put it simply: 'Is this a challenge to practical action, or to prayer and repentance?'

'Why not both?' said Judah. 'Prayer is not an alternative to action. Your monks and nuns, indeed all Nossexfolk, work with their hands, pray with their lips, and in both direct their hearts to worship God. There is no either-or in this.'

'Then if all should work and pray,' said the Bishop, 'let each one both work and pray. Let us have no workers that pray not, nor any that pray and work not.'

'And at first the work should be planning work,' said Naomi, who stood nearby. 'If the catastrophe is not yet upon us, as Judah feels it is not, then we have been given time by God: time to use the wits He gave us, His gift of the ability to order our future actions, to use the wisdom and experience of the old and wise.'

Judah looked at his wife with a blend of pride and irritation. Wise words indeed, but was it her place to speak just then? He had adjusted to some extent to the apparently equal status women had in Nossex, and in private often deferred to his wife's practical wisdom, but he sometimes struggled when Naomi took the initiative in public.

Naomi was short in stature, and broad in every way: broad-minded, broad-smiling, and broad in the beam. She was formidably well-organised, with a knack of overlooking nothing, and an ability to persuade others to do what was needed. Judah was lean and serious, with sunken cheeks and furrowed brow, a dreamer of dreams and author of surprises.

Together with Bishop Mark, Countess Maud, Abbot Dominic of Pinisk, and Abbess Anna of Pinrose, they debated ideas, prayed, made plans, prayed, and organised teams of willing hands. As the early part of the fourteenth century went by, and the evil years apparently held off, they put in hand a multitude of works.

Most of these projects, as Naomi was quick to point out, were well worth doing anyway. Every year they harvested reeds from the marshes east of Noaster, and gradually, roof by roof, they replaced the thick slate slabs with thatch throughout Nossex. The slabs were used to pave footpaths in all the dampest and boggiest sections. Wooden shutters were made, both inside and out, for almost every window. Firewood was stockpiled in every corner, and more tracts of woodland were coppiced and pollarded than before. Mindful of the greater risk of fire from the thatch and the firewood, the Nossex Fire Quenchers were founded and trained, a noble order that exists to this day.

Drainage was improved wherever possible, and thirsty trees, chiefly willow, poplar and alder, were planted along the brooks and streams, and in any other places that seemed hard to drain. The tarns, ponds, and reservoirs were stocked with fish, and new reservoirs were constructed, including some small ones, almost large tanks, near each community, roofed with straw bales to ensure water supply in freezing temperatures.

The borders were strengthened and secured, and the Watch was expanded and encouraged. Through all this activity, lasting well over ten years, Naomi noted that those that worked hardest and most willingly at the practical tasks were also to the fore in fasting and prayer and encouraging others, though as Bishop Mark said, the fasting had a practical application in preparing the digestive system for hard times, as long as you didn't overdo it. Judah and Naomi repeatedly found themselves part of Christian prayer groups, not wishing to separate themselves from those they were planning and organising things with. Judah became intrigued by the differences in the style of prayer, in some ways so similar to what he was used to, and yet not the same. He began discreetly studying the scriptures with Abbot Dominic.

In June of 1315, when Judah and Naomi were forty years old, and had been grandparents two years, the rain began in earnest. Young people returning from Wandership brought news of a sheep murrain that was culling nine out of ten in some flocks.

'It has begun,' said Judah.

At first the borders were closed to all but returning Nossexfolk, and no youngsters were released to begin Wandership. Later, as tales were heard of disease and famine raging Outside, it was decided to allow in any sick or starving that happened to stumble across a way into Nossex. A Quarantine building was cleared and organised, where they could be nursed and fed by the Grey Friars, and most were fit enough after forty days to be found a place in one of the communities. Hardly any chose to return to the dearth and murrain Outside.

As icy snowbound winters succeeded drenching wet summers, the Nossexfolk endured, and indeed found the years less evil than they had feared. Of course much of this was due to prudent preparation, and many blessed the foresight and hard work of their leaders.

'Bless the Lord, rather, who warned us, and in whom we take refuge,' said Judah. 'He has compassion on the afflicted, and maybe we should do more in that direction.'

A few experienced folk were sent out, taking small amounts of food that could be spared, and selling it at astonishing prices. They returned with money, news, and more starving refugees. The money was taken charge of by Judah, but reckoned as the property of Nossex as a whole; and this was the beginning of the Nossex Purse, so essential today for investment and education.

With the usual contrariness of English weather, and the new malevolence that was now so often seen in the winds and the skies, the summers of 1318 and 1319 brought drought and blazing sun, so that little grew, and even that was shrivelled. Then the rain returned, and news filtered in from Outside of a new plague: a murrain of cattle this time, which was even more deadly than the disease the sheep had suffered from. Beasts died in a day or barely two, and rotted at once, stinking of rancid butter, said the report; even the ravens that nibbled at the corpses had sickened and died, so that men hastened to bury both cattle and birds.

At first, while the murrain was still in the far south of England, some local gentry near Nossex were selling whole herds of healthy cattle in a panic at knock-down prices, since few wanted to buy. Naomi, usually cautious, saw this as an opportunity, and a Quarantine field was quickly prepared. Two herds of twenty and then thirty beasts were successively purchased for a very small part of the new Purse's capital, and passed through quarantine safely; but the third purchase was one too many. At the first sign of sickness in the first heifer, the order was given, and the entire herd killed and buried by sunset, with a team of forty, men and women together, digging and hauling, tipping and covering with quicklime and then fresh earth.

Before the burial pit – by now a mound – was finally covered, it is said, though it is hard to believe, that they took the ropes they had used and added them to the pile, then every stitch of clothing they wore was thrown in, and finally they left the shovels and spades on top of the mound. Naked and empty-handed they went down to the river, men and women together, and washed themselves clean from head to foot, and came out on the other side to fresh clothing hastily brought.

There was some laughter, yet it is said none felt any shame, though perhaps most were too tired and too apprehensive to care about the normal proprieties. The more entertaining versions of the story also relate that two men and two women felt a sudden call from the state of celibacy to matrimony. Records do show two marriages very soon afterwards, but this may be coincidental.

After this shock, the borders were closed again until 1322, when it was reckoned the seven evil years were past, since all the ills predicted had been fulfilled. The Quarantine field was left unused and untrodden for many generations, but the Quarantine building became busy again, as stray starving folk from Outside began to trickle in once more. Beyond the borders of Nossex the after-effects of the famine and plague were still severe, and disease, mostly the sicknesses of extreme poverty and lack of shelter, was still rampant.

One night Naomi had a dream of an apple tree, a largely unremarkable dream that she would surely have quickly forgotten, if it had not been that her daughters, and her daughters in law, had had the same dream on the same night. This convinced them all that the dream must be of great significance at least to their family, for cautious inquiry established that only the women of their family had dreamed of the tree.

There was a gnarled old tree in the middle of an orchard. It produced a crop of big green apples: sour to taste, but good for cooking. Although the branches were many, the crop was rather scanty. The gardener came, and pruned off many unproductive branches, but still there was not much fruit. Now the tree was rather lopsided, so the gardener grafted in a different variety on one side of the tree, and the graft took well and grew. Soon the tree was producing an abundant crop of smaller, yellow apples on one side. They were sweeter, and good to eat, though for cooking some held that a mixture of the two fruits gave a very tasty pie.

The new side of the tree grew fast, and the gardener pruned it back hard, and also pruned the older branches again, so that now the new side was bigger than the old. High in the middle of the tree, the old and new branches intertwined, and the yellow and green fruit appeared together, a pleasant sight. But what was puzzling was that here and there yellow fruit was clearly growing on old branches.

Now you might think the meaning of the dream is very obvious, but to the dreamers, and to those who heard the tale of the dream, it was by no means so clear at first. Only when Naomi spoke to Judah did a possible interpretation appear, one that they hesitated to share outside the family. Much discussion, and study of the scriptures, followed within the household, and eventually Naomi and Judah, and their children and grandchildren, took the decision to be baptised, moving out of Pinginna to a new house in Caeriago, which also housed the Nossex Purse. Together they went down to the river, were symbolically washed clean, and came out on the other side to new clothing.

Eleven: Caeriago to Noaster *(5 miles)*

'Naked and empty-handed,' I quoted. 'It's how we should come to Christ. You told that as a deliberate metaphor for conversion and baptism.'

'It's how the Tale was handed down,' said Uncle Joe. 'I first heard it – in simplified form, because I was very young – from my great-grandfather. After that, I heard it many times, being told to others. I tell it in my own way, but I haven't added anything, and much of it is memorised word for word. I believe it's what actually happened, and the metaphor of naked cleansing, and a new start in fresh clothing, was the Lord's way of prompting Judah towards a decision. Perhaps, too, the slaughter of an entire herd at once, all that blood, made him think of the words of Isaiah, *I have no pleasure in the blood of bulls*, which he would have known for sure, and maybe the verse in Hebrews: *it is impossible for the blood of bulls and goats to take away sins*,[1] which he probably heard from the Bishop or the Abbot.'

I thought about this for a while, sipping the coffee, looking out at the superb view from the bow window. A buzzard floated in lazy circles high above the valley, and closer to, swifts were sweeping round the Tower, zipping sharply past the window.

'How did the Nossex Purse develop?' I asked. 'And what is it used for now? I get the impression Nossexfolk aren't much interested in money.'

'They aren't, that's why you need an institution to keep an eye on it. Money – hard currency, that is – is needed for everything connected with Outside, and we're not totally cut off, we actually interact with Outside in countless ways, once you start to monitor things. And it's money that makes the rest of the world go round, even if Nossex manages without it internally.'

'Is all the hard currency held in common,' I wondered, 'in one big Joint Account?'

'Oh no,' Uncle Joe smiled. 'It would all be very simple if it were. But each individual has an account, though some married couples prefer to have joint accounts, and then each community has an account, and there's a Nossex account, technically called the Council of Nossex Account, because the Council decide on any substantial or unusual outgoing payments.'

'And where does the money come from? Can anyone get rich in Nossex?'

'You have a knack for asking two different questions at once, it seems. The money might come from sale of produce or sale of artefacts; I'll give you a couple of examples. Let's say Icclescombe have a very large crop of sunflower seeds, and they decide to sell some surplus Outside.'

'I picked some the other day,' I put in.

'Glad you got a chance to help. Well, the money would go first into the Icclescombe account; then 10% would go into the Nossex account, and the other 90% would be distributed between the individual accounts in Icclescombe. Except...' he paused.

'Yes?'

[1] Isaiah 1:11; Hebrews 10:4

73

'There's a limit on how much you can have in an individual account. I think at the moment it's £683.74, or double that for a joint account. That odd figure is what happens when you keep uprating by the Outside inflation rate. So some individual accounts might well be full, in which case the money stays in the Icclescombe account, which answers your second question. However...'

'Don't tell me: there's a limit on the community account.'

'Yes, we wouldn't really want one community significantly richer than others. The limit for a community is £68.37 per community member, so most community accounts are capped somewhere between seven and twenty thousand pounds, though Noaster's account is naturally bigger.'

'What is Noaster's population?' I asked.

'Around one thousand five hundred, I think. Though you'll see more than that there tomorrow, with the Gathering. Going back to our examples, let's say Cennis sells one of her harps Outside. In theory the money goes first into her account, with 10% automatically going up to the Pinrose account; in practice much more, maybe even all the money, probably overflows into Pinrose, who then also contribute 10% to Nossex.'

'Does money flow the other way?'

'Yes, every newborn child has their account started with £50 from Nossex, and every year all Nossex residents get £5...'

'For passing Go,' I said facetiously.

'More or less. Though if funds are tight, that might be suspended. And at their own discretion, a community might decide at any time to put a certain amount in each individual account, if the community was doing OK but some individuals had low balances.'

'There must be a lot of small transfers to record and calculate, then. Do you have a computer programme to do that?'

'We do, though we were well able to cope before computers came along. And we run a manual system alongside.'

'Isn't that rather inefficient?'

'Computer programmes may be very fast and powerful,' he said, 'but they crash. Since we installed the system there have been over twenty glitches or outages of one kind or another, and in the same period the human system alongside hasn't failed once. You need the right humans, of course; that's why Guy was recommended to come here.'

'He's a bright lad,' I said.

'Very, but he's not here as the next Einstein or Hawking. He was recommended for his accuracy. He just doesn't make mistakes, and he's very thorough and conscientious. He'll probably make a good programmer, too, so he should be ideal for both the manual and the computer side of operations.'

'So, going back to using Outside money,' I said, 'individuals have some limited freedom, but ultimately most hard currency is controlled by the state.'

'By the *community*,' Uncle Joe corrected me gently. 'All these practices have evolved gradually through consensus; as far back as anyone can remember every Nossexman or woman has had a say in any changes made. It's only common sense. The rules could be changed at the Gathering tomorrow, if somebody put forward a proposal with which a clear majority agreed. Neither I, nor anyone else on Council, made any of the rules; we only administer them.'

'The community as a whole, then, has agreed to a frugal lifestyle of subsistence and relative poverty. How do youngsters support themselves on their Years Out?'

'Mainly through their own earnings. You've seen how our young people can work. However, in some cases the Nossex Purse makes a grant for someone to study for a university degree. If money is invested in a young person's education, they have a free choice whether to come back to Nossex, or to repay the money and stay Outside, or simply to stay Outside without repaying anything. But if they come back to Nossex, it's clearly impossible for them to repay much. So we're only likely to make grants in subjects where we need expertise.'

'What sort of subjects would they be?'

'Agriculture; engineering; education – most often the student has already been involved with some project here, and the project leader has identified a need to expand our knowledge.'

'And if the student is really interested in something, but the Council of Nossex doesn't consider it useful enough for a grant?'

'One common option,' said Uncle Joe, 'is Studying Alongside. Typically the Nossex student goes and lives in a university town, shares a house or flat with genuine students, perhaps gets an external ticket for the university library, does all the reading and discusses the assignments with their friends. They don't actually enrol on a course, and they won't have a piece of Outside paper at the end, but if they choose, they can enter for a University of Nossex degree and submit assignments and a dissertation to academics back here. In fact you can do that at any time, not just on your Years Out.'

The more I heard, the more questions I wanted to ask.

'When a teenager sets off on their Years Out,' I said, 'they must at least have a small float to set them on their way?'

'Oh yes,' said Uncle Joe, 'and it is small – £50 at the moment. But baptised believers only get half as much as the others.'

'Why are they at a disadvantage?'

'They're not, they're privileged – they get to experience the power of prayer when you don't know where else to turn.'

'Do they pay that float back?'

'No, it's a gift, not a loan. Nossex has no borrowing, no loans, and therefore no interest, no debt problems, and no pressure to make a financial return on investment.'

I looked around at the shelves of books on three sides of the large room, and several folk in armchairs, absorbed in reading, as well as a couple of folk working at solid, well-made desks.

'Is this fine building partly a stronghold for the treasury?' I asked.

'It was originally where Outside cash was kept, though it's never really needed to be a stronghold. And we don't just do accounting, we do statistics, genealogy, some administration as well. Nowadays there's no need to keep much cash in the vaults here. We have a single account in an ethical bank Outside, so that substantial investments can be made by cheque or bank transfer.'

'So if you gave me the account number,' I suggested, 'I could make a payment to the Nossex Purse to cover my board and lodging while I'm here. I don't feel totally comfortable receiving so much for nothing.'

Uncle Joe looked quite shocked.

'I thought you were beginning to understand the Nossex spirit,' he said sadly, 'but you're still stuck in an Outside frame of reference. Fair exchange, reciprocity, be no man's debtor, absolute equality – there's no Grace in any of these concepts. Christians should be used to the idea of receiving undeserved riches, and being utterly unable to pay back what is owed.'

'I'm sorry,' I said, chastened. 'I should have known better – I've commented often enough on the far eastern concept of *giri*, that awful burden of having to pay everyone back for any favour you receive. I've even tried to explain the Christian cascade principle: A helps B, B helps C, C does a favour for D, and so on. In each case the help is given when it's really needed, rather than to shed a burden of obligation.'

'Cascade, yes,' said Uncle Joe. 'We call it the Fountain of God's Goodness, which overflows to everyone in need. So let's have no more talk of your paying for your time in Nossex. You don't need to pay your way in cash, though nobody will stop you contributing labour if you want.'

'No, I'd noticed that,' I said. 'Talking of work, am I keeping you off?'

'No, this is my task just now, my *birinn*, to inform you about Nossexonomics. A curious thing about the post of Chief Purser is that there's very little to do. The routine stuff is taken care of by the regular workers; there's a team working on improving the software, and a couple of folk maintaining the hardware; an archivist keeps the old records in order; and most of the non-routine stuff, like serious decisions about investment, is decided on by the Council of Nossex. So my job is really just motivation and supervision, and the workers here are so conscientious they don't need that at all. I do more harm than good if I breathe down their necks.'

'Jim Callaghan said something like that about being Prime Minister,' I said. 'Unfortunately we haven't had a Prime Minister since who saw things like that.'

'Still, if you've heard as much as you can take in, there is something useful we could do. Would you like a little exercise?'

'Why not?' I said, wondering what was coming.

He led the way down a flight of stairs and into a dim chamber with bare stone walls, lit only by a narrow slit window and the rippling, flickering light reflected up from a channel of water as it flowed in at floor level from an aqueduct outside, into a wide and shallow basin set in the floor. There was an overflow into a circular drain. 'Down there,' said Uncle Joe, as we walked round the drain to the far side of the basin, 'is an inverted Archimedes screw turbine that generates enough power for our computers, and a bit more besides. Modern application of very old technology. And this,' he gestured at the tandem bicycle frame set up to drive a rope-mounted bucket lift, 'is another Nossex marriage of simple technologies.'

The words *Heath Robinson* rose unbidden to mind, as I sat behind Uncle Joe on the tandem, and we began to pedal slowly.

'Take it very gently,' he said over his shoulder. 'We haven't had much rain recently, so the flow in the aqueduct is lowish, and we don't want to stop the flow to the turbine.'

There seemed little danger of that. The buckets were small, holding perhaps only a gallon or two each, and at first the pedalling was easy; but as more and more filled buckets rose towards the high ceiling, it felt more like cycling uphill. Soon the splash of buckets emptying could be heard overhead. We settled into a rhythm, and I was very glad that Uncle Joe had set a slow tempo, for cycling is not normal exercise for me. Within ten or fifteen minutes my thighs were protesting, and I was relieved when a couple of fit-looking girls appeared and wanted to take over.

'Two more minutes!' cried Uncle Joe, and I gritted my teeth and kept going until the girls more or less insisted on pushing us off.

'Do you good,' he said, clapping me on the shoulder as I tried to shake the lactic acid out of my legs. Meanwhile the girls were setting a tempo half as fast again as ours, so that Uncle Joe checked the flow in the drain. 'Take it easy, girls,' he said as we went out.

He explained that this activity was part of the preparations for the Sabbath; here in Caeriago they kept the traditional seventh-day rest, from dusk on Friday until the same time on Saturday, and on Friday afternoon everything would wind down in good time so that the Sabbath wasn't preceded by a frantic last-minute rush.

'Nossex doesn't like rush,' I suggested.

'No, we certainly don't, but in Nossex or Outside, the Sabbath, whether you keep it on the seventh day or the first, should be the antithesis of rush.'

Indeed there was no rush, as the Sabbath meal began well after dark and proceeded in a most leisurely fashion. As in the other Nossex communities I had visited, everyone ate together in one large hall; but here there were many smaller tables, covered with white linen, rather than the usual few long tables and bare wooden surfaces elsewhere. Uncle Joe introduced the meal with a short prayer, but thereafter each table continued the ceremony separately. The only lights were the candles on the individual tables, giving each table the intimacy of a family, while still keeping some awareness of the other families nearby.

Uncle Joe explained afterwards that while youngsters like Guy would spend most of the week in their peer group – in his case one peer group at work and another

77

at school – for Sabbath everybody was attached to a family, and would be considered part of that family as long as they were in Caeriago. As a guest of the community I was part of his family until it was time for me to leave.

The rest of the evening passed quickly as I browsed in books in the library, with many fascinating titles: *Old Nossex Cuisine*; *The Chronicles of Caeriago*; *The English Jewry under Angevin Kings*. Finally I made my way to the bed I'd been allocated in the lads' dormitory.

Saturday 27th September 2014

I slept soundly and only woke as the dormitory were all stirring, yawning, stretching, then dressing with a briskness that reminded me of boarding school half a century before. We clattered down to breakfast as a group, and the noise in the stone staircase raised another echo of my teenage years. The meal was self-service: muesli and milk, a choice of raisin or walnut bread, cheese and hard-boiled eggs. It was all I wanted, and even after sampling both, I couldn't decide which bread was the more delicious.

Guy came by, on his way for a second helping. He grinned at me and stuck his thumb up. There was a glow about him that had not been there yesterday, something different from his usual chirpiness, and I said a silent prayer of thanks.

The thankfulness helped the tasks of clearing away and washing up to go quickly, and it seemed only a moment later that Uncle Joe found me as I was on my way to pack.

'What did you say to Guy yesterday?' he asked. 'He said you spoke to him, and now he's a believer.'

'I answered a simple question, and I gave my testimony. It happened to be what he needed to hear at that point.'

'Well, you'll see him baptised tomorrow. Are you off to Noaster now?' he went on. 'There's a direct path over the hill, not much more than two miles, but you've got plenty of time, and if you want to see a bit more of Nossex, you could go down the valley to join the main track from West Nossex to Noaster. That would be about five miles, I guess.'

'OK, that sounds good,' I agreed, and a few minutes later I set off southwards on a path slanting gradually down under tall sweet chestnut trees. The deeply seamed bark twisted round the broad boles in a slow spiral; underfoot the split cases of the fallen nuts spread out in yellow-green four-pointed star shapes. It was the first time I'd been trusted to roam Nossex on my own, I realised, and I enjoyed the opportunity to soak up the atmosphere without being distracted by conversation. Now and then I paused to gather up a few chestnuts, until I'd filled the sandwich box and one of the pockets of the rucksack.

It was a little puzzling to look around at a woodland scene that contained nothing that I might not see in any other English wood, and in fact I often had walked through woodland like this on the Four Points Ramble: Staveley, Cannock Chase, Hartshill,

Marlborough, the Quantocks, and many other places. All the same, it felt quieter and more peaceful, even more blessed, though I must surely be imagining that from what I'd learned about Nossex society.

I was not on my own for very long, however, to enjoy the peace. Once I had come out of the woodland down onto the flat river plain, and joined the slightly dusty tree-lined track running eastwards to Noaster, I found myself part of a scattered procession of twos and threes and small groups, all going the same way. Overtaking a laden donkey cart, I saw that the carter, walking alongside the donkey, was Martin North, my old friend from Durham days. This coincidence at least, I thought, couldn't have been arranged by the Nossexfolk, so maybe my ramble through Nossex was being directed by a much higher Authority.

'Hullo again,' I greeted Martin. 'Is this your job in Nossex?'

'It is this month,' he answered. 'I'm on a One-in-Twelve. I'm taking potatoes to Noaster. Do you want to put your rucksack on the pile?'

'If the donkey doesn't mind.'

'You don't mind, do you, Chris?' said Martin, ruffling the hair between the donkey's ears. 'He won't notice the weight of the rucksack. If one of us got on the cart, he *would* notice, though he never complains, he's a long-suffering ass.'

I slipped off the rucksack and settled it on top of the rough sacks. We paused to let some bicycles go by, a couple of families with several children, moving at the pace of the slowest. Over to our right, the line of the river was marked by the trees that lined its near bank. Closer to, parallel to our track, ran a smaller watercourse that I guessed was a mill leat, or perhaps Noaster's water supply.

'So what's One-in-Twelve?' I asked.

'One month in the year, you do something completely different. I believe it started with the White Friars and the Grey Friars doing a swap, centuries ago, as a spiritual discipline. The Grey Friars took a retreat from their social service: tending the lepers, caring for the mentally ill, looking after the old and infirm, preaching to the crowds in Noaster, and they went to Pinrose to pray in silence, and to work with their hands in solitude; while the White Friars left behind their contemplation and the peace of the cloister, and came to Noaster to get involved with people and their needs and difficulties, which gave them plenty to pray about in the other eleven months.'

'Could they do each others' jobs competently?'

'Well, they didn't all swap simultaneously, of course, so there was always a majority of experienced people. And we don't all swap at once now. I'm normally a maths teacher at the Blackfriars School. If all the teachers were replaced by non-teachers at the same time, things might get a little *too* innovative; but a couple at a time is refreshing, you often get completely new insights.'

'So how long have you been a teacher in Nossex,' I asked, 'and how did you end up here?'

'Not quite forty years. I met Lydia my wife in my first job, in Bristol. She was on Years Out, Studying Alongside at Bristol University, but after that she wanted to

79

come back here. She brought me here for a weekend, and I loved it. If I hadn't, we probably wouldn't have married.'

'Where is she now?' I wondered, absent-mindedly admiring several butterflies in the low hedges either side of the track

'Baby-sitting some of the grandchildren, who are too young to enjoy the Gathering.'

'How many grandchildren have you got?'

'Eight – six here in Nossex and two Outside. Enough to keep me busy. And you – where have you been since I saw you last – when was it?'

'It would be 1972,' I said. 'I did this, that and the other for fourteen years after graduating, then settled down to TEFL when I was 35, married a colleague, and we taught abroad together for several years: Turkey, Sweden, Hungary, before going to Manchester to get a Masters degree and ending up staying.'

'Family?'

'No, just the two of us.'

'And how do you come to be in Nossex?'

'I just found my way in by accident,' I said. 'I've retired from teaching, I write books now, walking books; not guide books, slow travel books, I call them.'

'They won't let you write a book about Nossex,' he said with conviction.

'Pity,' I said, 'it would make a good story. Anyway, going back to One-in-Twelve, how did it get from a simple friar-swap to everybody doing it?'

'I'm not sure of the exact history,' admitted Martin, 'but first of all the Black Friars and Green Friars got in on the act to make it a four-way swap.'

'*Green* Friars?' Surrounded as we were by green, with grassy meadows on either side of the track, and the willows and poplars that lined the route towering above us, I wondered if green-robed friars would be totally camouflaged. Presumably Friar Tuck had worn Lincoln Green along with Robin Hood.

'It's a Nossex joke with a long history,' explained Martin, 'rooted in the Celtic tradition of Green Martyrdom.'

'What's *that* when it's at home?'

'It isn't at home, that's the point. Red Martyrdom is giving your life-blood for the faith, but Green Martyrdom is giving up your home life in order to travel and preach the Gospel. *Foxes have holes, and birds have nests, but the Son of Man has nowhere to lay his head.*[1] In the Dark Ages, green martyrs set out and simply never came back. Nossex Green Friars aren't an organised body, it's just a name for those who might go on a short mission Outside as their One-in-Twelve, or for Nossexfolk who give their lives to overseas mission.'

'Do many do that?'

'Quite a few. We support them totally in prayer, of course, but we can't give all that much financial support, which is a problem now that many mission organisations expect people to raise their own funding. A hundred years ago, even fifty years ago,

[1] Matt 8:20

80

that wasn't an issue, and a lot of Nossexfolk went out on the mission field. Nowadays they need to find supporting churches Outside, so if young people feel called to mission, they need to test that first on their Years Out, then probably stay Out for some years more, perhaps moving around, because you really need more than one supporting church.'

'It's a problem for everybody,' I agreed. 'But I would imagine potential Nossex missionaries would cope, with the work ethic they have here.'

But Martin disagreed with my description. 'Not sure it's a work *ethic*,' he said, 'more a work culture – or even a work bias, a work tendency. They're not workaholics, not escaping from something else into work, nor driven by guilt or obsession. They aren't necessarily thinking they *ought* to work, they just *love* work, love to be doing something, which is actually a natural human tendency if it hasn't been spoiled by being *forced* to work. But they also know when to stop, and they don't have any hang-ups about leaving a job unfinished. In fact they often say that's good, to have something to pick up straightaway when they start in the next day.'

'So they don't set themselves deadlines?'

'Not if they can help it. Let the task find its natural rhythm, that's what they say. They work steadily, totally absorbed as often as not, in that state that the fellow I can't pronounce calls "Flow".'

'Csikszentmihalyi?'

Martin blinked. 'Is that how you say it? How did you know?'

'We spent a year in Hungary,' I said apologetically. 'I notice, by the way, you say *they* all the time about this work culture, not *we*, but I seem to remember you're a worker.'

'Yes,' Martin admitted, 'but I'm a driven, OCD, guilt-ridden, got-to-get-the-job-finished kind of worker by nature. Outside spoiled me, and although I can appreciate the Nossex way of working, I can't consistently work that way myself. I've even heard one of the Brothers refer to work in terms of self-denial, but in exactly the opposite way you would imagine Outside. He said that just as you should always rise from the table feeling you would have liked to eat a little more, so you should always down tools feeling you would have liked to work a little longer. Of course that presupposes a natural appetite for work, which for most people here is unspoiled.'

'Most people.'

'Well, of course, sometimes someone really doesn't feel like working. But the assumption here would be that the person concerned is unwell – and as often as not, that's the case.'

'So that's why the predominant greeting here is *Can I help?*' I said. 'They can't bear to pass by an enjoyable bit of work.'

'Yes, and the workers will maybe take a five-minute break, which is no bad thing, but their reasoning is that it would be selfish of them to keep their enjoyable work all to themselves and not let someone else have a share.'

81

A little way ahead of us, as Martin gave this startling analysis, two women who were trimming shoots from osiers gave their secateurs to a couple of passing teenagers going the same way as us: on their way to the Gathering, presumably, but taking in a sample of 'enjoyable work' *en route*.

'How far back does this way of thinking go?' I wondered. 'Is it part of the strong Christian tradition?'

'Who knows?' Martin shrugged. 'Actually,' he corrected himself, 'there are people here who might have a very good idea. Nossex history – or Nemet history further back – is very well documented, and the old folk who've found time to study the documents could take a good guess at where it comes from. I would think the tendency was pre-Christian, but of course Christian teaching wouldn't *dis*courage work, except on Sundays, and I haven't heard that that was ever contentious.'

'So what is a Nossex Sunday like?'

'Well, you'll find out tomorrow, won't you? Though with a Gathering, it won't be absolutely typical.'

The track we were strolling (or in Chris's case, plodding) along was becoming quite crowded. I looked back, and saw that many more folk were following us. It gave a sense of anticipation that reminded me a little of heading for a football match.

'When did the Christian tradition begin?' I asked. 'The earliest I've heard of so far is Gaius, who built the villa at Pinrose in the fourth century, but Sister Christina said the village was already Christian before that. When did the Gospel come here?'

'Very early, in the late fifties of the first century, soon after the Roman invasion. Have you heard of Quintus of Cyrene?'

'No,' I said, focusing on the brownish-gold walls of Noaster, that were looking more substantial as we approached at donkey speed.

'What Tales have you heard?' asked Martin.

'Cennis,' I said, counting on my fingers, 'Alain FisBos, two more Tales about his family, and Judah ben David.'

'Of course,' smiled Martin, 'you'd be bound to hear that in Caeriago. It's a great Tale. I'll tell you the Tale of Quintus of Cyrene, then, and you can spot the connection.'

82

Twelve: The Tale of Quintus of Cyrene

You will be given what to say, for it will not be you speaking,
but the Spirit of your Father speaking through you. Mt 10:20

Nemet welcomed the Romans. They had had some trading contact with the Roman Empire well before the invasion of Britain, and from afar they rather admired Roman civilisation – or at least, the idealised image they had of it. So when the invasion came, the Romans judged they would have no trouble from the Nemetians, and they built a small fort alongside the main Nemetian settlement, which became known as *Nova Castra* – Noaster, as it's called now.

Another reason the Romans expected no trouble was that the Nemetians were an astonishingly peaceful tribe, considering that they appeared to be genuine Celts. While the other tribes liked nothing better than fighting among themselves, the Nemetians thought this was totally stupid. Axes, they said, were made for cutting timber, not flesh, and they had no desire to beat their ploughshares into swords.

Before the Romans came, the defences of Nemet were aimed at making it too much trouble for the other tribes to come here and fight. Once the Romans arrived, the Nemetians heaved a sigh of relief, as they believed these civilised folk would keep the peace – and indeed they did: the Romans never wanted to fight just for the sake of it. They only wanted to maintain order so that trade and commerce could flourish.

So Nemet was more open to the outside world during the Roman occupation than ever before or since. Nova Castra flourished quietly and peacefully, and the smallish Roman garrison treated it largely as a place for rest and recuperation, away from the more troublesome parts of Britain. In the very early days there was a soldier here by the name of Quintus of Cyrene.

Cyrene, of course, is in North Africa, but Quintus wasn't African, even if he was born there; he came from a Roman family that happened to be settled in Cyrene. As the fifth son, he had to make his own way, and he joined the Roman army, serving in many far-flung parts of the Empire.

It seems that he was in Judea as a young man, perhaps no more than twenty years old, at the time of Christ's crucifixion and resurrection, and of the first Pentecost, and although he possibly didn't witness any of that first-hand, he certainly spoke to fellow-soldiers who did. At that stage he was sceptical and scornful of the new cult, as he saw it; but some years later, in Antioch, it is said, he met and befriended some mature Christians, and was converted then or soon after.

Roman soldiers who were Christians had to be fairly discreet about their faith, but he came across others, here and there, and also in his various postings he could find local believers for fellowship. For some years in Lugdunum (modern Lyons) he was part of a little fellowship of a dozen believers, including Romans, Gauls, and Jews.

But when Quintus came to Nemet, as far as he knew, he was the only Christian in the area, and he realised with nervousness that the task of spreading the Gospel here was in his hands.

Where should he start? How should he pitch his testimony? And what would the Nemetians make of the concept of sinfulness? As far as he could see, they were the best of men and women, with hardly a malicious thought or a thoughtless deed among the whole tribe. What need would they feel of atonement?

For a week he prayed, whenever his duties allowed, and although he didn't intentionally fast, he was nervous enough to lose much of his appetite, and skipped meals here and there without realising it. Then one day the local priest, or holy man, said:

'Quintus, may I ask you a rather delicate question?'

'Go ahead,' answered Quintus, hoping he had understood correctly. Nemsh was very similar to Gaulish, but not identical, and already he had made one or two hilarious mistakes.

'Do you really believe in all those Roman gods?'

'Absolutely not,' said Quintus, startled out of his usual caution. 'There is only one God.'

The old man beamed. 'Yes!' he cried. 'One God, who made everything, knows everything…'

'Sees everything,' put in Quintus, 'is everywhere, can do anything – and loves everyone.'

'Everyone?' repeated the old man softly. 'Can he really love us all?'

'Why would He not love you?'

'We are so proud,' came the sad answer.

Quintus was dumbfounded. Of all the tribes he had come across, the Nemetians were far and away the humblest; there was no hint of strut or swagger even among the strong young men.

'How do you mean, proud?' he said. 'What is proud about you people?'

'God is so great, so magnificent and wonderful, and we are so little, so weak, so helpless. We should consider ourselves nothing. But we look at the other tribes outside Nemet, fighting each other, and losing their best men; stealing cattle from each other, then stealing them back again, so that the cattle are thin from being driven back and forth; burning each other's crops, so that both go hungry, and we think: how stupid they are – and how wise we are, how sensible! Only today, I was listening to stories of how the so-called gods of Rome behave, without shame or decency, and I thought, what fool made up these stories, and what fools believe them? And how wise I am, who can see the absurdity of these stories. I am puffed up with loathsome pride!'

'Is it not a wise man that knows he is not wise?'

The old man smiled, but countered: 'Is it wiser to be proud of being wise, or proud of knowing you are not wise? In either case the pride remains. And how, then, can you know that God loves us?'

'He came to live amongst us,' said Quintus, and went on to explain the good news of Jesus as best he could, while the old man listened intently, until the tears ran down his cheeks and into his beard.

'You must tell this to our people,' he said finally. 'At least, the heads of the families at first. Will you speak to a meeting tomorrow night?'

Quintus agreed a time, and spent the intervening day in a daze of hope, continually gnawed by pessimism, yet ever renewed, until he found himself in front of three or four dozen expectant faces: broad, tanned, lined and ancient faces, at least three-quarters of whom were women, to his surprise – though it occurred to him that women live longer than men, so perhaps in Nemet the 'head of the family' was automatically the eldest member. Nevertheless, his listeners showed no sign of any loss of faculties, their intent expressions telling of full and thoughtful understanding.

They listened in silence at first, then began asking questions, questions that showed an awareness of the issues. He had the impression that they were hearing news that they had somehow anticipated, and one by one, like the priest the day before, the tears began to flow, until he was so moved and reminded of his own surrender, ten years earlier, that he too began to weep.

Before they left, one by one they embraced him, and each said 'God bless you, Quintus,' as they left.

Two days later, the priest met him again, and said: 'We believe. You must baptise us.'

'All of you?'

'All of Nemet, except some few that are not sure, and prefer to wait and see. The heads of families have spoken to their families, and the families believe.'

Quintus took a deep breath, said a silent prayer, and arranged to meet two days later at dawn by the riverbank, some ten miles away from Nova Castra. To cover himself, he spoke to the senior decurion, saying that he had been invited to a native gathering, which he was sure would be peaceful, but that perhaps he would take two soldiers with him as witnesses.

This was agreed, partly because he emphasised that he would probably learn more about who were the people with real authority among the natives. Everything was so new that the local native-run administration was still in the process of being organised and appointed. As experienced men, they knew that confirming the existing power structure was the most effective strategy.

The two 'volunteers' were not overjoyed to find that they had half a night's march to arrive at a mysterious native event at dawn. They were surprised at the large number of natives peacefully waiting, and amazed to see the veteran Roman soldier, who had brought them all this way, go down into the shallow river and begin sluicing water over a few old men and a number of old women, repeating the same few words: 'In the name of the Father, and of the Son, and of the Spirit.'

After a little while, Quintus came out of the river, and the heads of the families, that he had baptised, turned to the next generation in their own family and baptised them, who then in their turn baptised the young people.

'What's this all about, then?' one of the soldiers asked Quintus.

'Are they Christians?' asked the other, with disapproval in his tone.

'They are now,' said Quintus. He took a deep breath and told the two hard-bitten men about his own journey to faith, and then the incredible readiness of the Nemetians to accept this new religion.

'From the moment I came here, I thought they were soft in the head,' said one; but the other said nothing, as the sun came over the hill and turned the scene golden. A few weeks later, he spoke to Quintus again.

'There is a glow about these people,' he said. 'Tell me more about this new religion.' Before long he was added to the Nemetian fellowship, though he struggled with Nemsh, and Quintus had to interpret for him, in addition to other responsibilities. He wished there were more experienced Christians there to help with the teaching, for the Nemetians asked many deep and crucial questions, which were not always easy to answer.

Moreover, there was always the chance that he would be posted away from Nova Castra, and who would teach the Nemetians then? He wrote to the church in Lugdunum and shared his concerns, and after some months a letter came back:

Phoebe of Cenchreae to Quintus of Cyrene and the Nemetian Church, greetings in the Lord! Peace be with you all. I praise God the Father when I hear of your faith and joy and love for each other, which is given by the grace of our Lord Jesus Christ. Hold fast to that faith, and encourage each other to maintain every kind of good work, not thinking, however, that in this way you may earn salvation, for we do not do good deeds in order to be rewarded, but rather we delight in doing what is right because we have been rewarded with eternal life, which is already ours in Christ Jesus before we can do any good thing, for the Father had compassion on us and sent His son into the world while we were still spiritually dead.

Quintus, my fellow-worker, use the scriptures, which I know you have because Publius told me so, to instruct the believers, for all that is necessary for salvation is to be found there. I must now return from Lugdunum to Rome, but Persis my sister in the Lord is intending to come to you as soon as she can, and I know she will be able to help you greatly.

Publius and Helena greet you, as do Maria and Simeon, and Cornelia, and Benjamin, and Gesataia and Ivorix. May the God of all peace keep you, as I am sure He is able.

It was a short letter, but reassuring, and it helped Quintus to feel that help was on the way; but more months passed, and eventually he received notice that he was to be transferred away from Britain, in fact back to Gaul, and still Persis had not arrived. With very little hope, he prayed one last time, and as he was clearing his table and handing over duties to his successor, on the very evening before his departure, a little shrimp of a woman, painfully thin yet heavily pregnant, arrived in Nova Castra and asked for him.

He went to her, and finding that she was the longed-for advisor and teacher, and seeing her state – her time was very near – he sent for Cara, who was not only a wise leader in the church, but the best midwife in all Nemet. He knew each would be of great value to the other, which was a comfort, for Persis was too tired to tell her story, and he had no chance to stay until she was sufficiently recovered to tell it at leisure.

Quintus of Cyrene never returned to Nemet, or even to Britain. There is a rumour that he was martyred under Nero, but we have no clear evidence of that.

Thirteen: Overnight in Noaster

'So what was Persis' story?' I asked.

Martin smiled. 'Someone else will tell you that. There are twelve Tales of Nossex, and there's a tradition that you should hear each one from a different person.'

'Why?'

'I don't know. Maybe because it's more fun that way. Maybe to ration the kids, who given the chance would pester their family for all twelve at one go, and then be disappointed that there weren't any more.'

'And you said, spot the connection. Would it be the baptism?'

'Yes, the tradition is that the baptisms in both stories took place in the same pool on the River Tivvy.'

We were now close under the walls of Noaster, approaching a smallish and rather plain gateway with a round arch and two wooden doors that stood wide open. On either side the stone walls stretched away north and south; the gate faced due west, and I later found it had the prosaic name of West Gate. The walls were not crenellated, and were quite plain apart from a number of narrow windows, that from a distance I had taken to be arrow-slits, but on closer inspection were clearly fully glazed.

We passed through the arch, which felt almost like a tunnel, for the walls must have been twenty feet thick at least. Beyond the arch, we found ourselves at the corner of a wide open space, in the centre of which was a harbour, or canal basin, or wharf, with broad pavements on both sides, partially decked with tables and chairs. Two long narrowboats were moored on the near side; for a moment I was surprised, and then I remembered Brother Alan's description of the Sprat Collective. These must be their boats, I realised.

'We start unloading here,' said Martin, interrupting my gazing around. He waved a hand at the building immediately on our right, tucked against the wall by the gate. It was clearly a café or restaurant; some of the nearest tables and chairs outside were presumably served from it, and there was space for many more inside.

We hefted a sack of potatoes each and made our way inside, walking through to the kitchen at the back. Two young women that were working there returned with us to the cart, so that we could take four sacks in next. They were stocky and broad-shouldered girls, of the build that I was already recognising as a Nossex type, common if not universal, and they handled the sacks as if they contained cotton-wool rather than potatoes.

An older man, apparently in charge of the establishment, came out to the cart with us for the next turn, and tutted in dismay as we saw that the patiently waiting Chris had not waited in every sense, but had watered the flagstones with a gallon or so of donkey wee.

'Sorry,' said Martin.

'I suppose we have to let you off, since you're on a One-in-Twelve.' The man's smile had returned, and the rebuke was clearly not serious, though he continued: 'Pity it doesn't seem likely to rain in the near future.'

'No, I've no excuse,' admitted Martin, 'I know how to persuade him to go before we come into town, I just forgot.'

Meanwhile one of the girls had already nipped back inside for a bucket, and filled it from the quayside, and was sluicing down the area, having persuaded Chris to back up a couple of yards. The other girl hoisted another sack on her shoulder.

'That's seven sacks,' said Martin. 'Do you need more?'

'No, that'll do us a few days.'

I suddenly remembered the chestnuts, and retrieved my rucksack from where it had been propped against a chair, luckily out of splash range.

'Would you like a few chestnuts?' I said, and the man's smile broadened.

'Stuffing,' he said thoughtfully. 'Yes, please.'

As I offloaded the chestnuts, Martin turned Chris to the north, and we headed along the waterfront, past the two seventy-foot narrowboats, former working boats by the look of them, gaily painted in green and red, a motor and a butty, *Esther* and *Maud*. The butty was largely unconverted, still ready to carry cargo, and the little cabin could only have slept two or three, or maybe four if two were kids; I guessed most of the Sprat Collective must live on *Esther*, which appeared to have been converted for passenger use.

In the north-west corner of the city, beyond the corner of the basin, more tables were out on the pavement. A large and jolly woman in late middle age came bustling out to meet us.

'At least Chris didn't decide to widdle here,' muttered Martin, while she was still a little way off. 'My ears really would have been burning.'

'Praise the Lord, just in time!' the woman exclaimed. 'Can you let us have three hundredweight?'

As we took the first two sacks in, I saw Megs, looking as stunning as ever, sitting alone with an empty tankard in front of her. She flashed me a smile, and I smiled back, though it might not have been the most relaxed smile with a sack of potatoes on one shoulder. Once more, a couple of the workers came out to help carry, and two youngsters also got up from one of the tables to help, momentarily surprising me, until I remembered that the distinction between employee and customer was hardly relevant in Nossex.

That took care of all three hundredweight that this establishment wanted, and the small cart was suddenly almost empty. Three more youngsters arrived panting, having run down from the highest corner of the city, and begged the remaining sacks 'for the Palace'. Meanwhile two enthusiastic young girls, who obviously knew Chris, had come and greeted their friend. He twitched his ears and seemed happy to be made a fuss of. Martin agreed to let them take care of Chris, once he had unhitched and parked the cart.

89

'Do you fancy a tour of the walls?' said Megs, startling me; I hadn't seen her get up and approach us.

'Steve, you should take her up on that offer,' said Martin. 'It's a good day for it. I'll take your rucksack up to the palace and bag us a bed each in the dorm. We'll meet up sooner or later; there'll be music at Priscilla's later on, if you fancy listening. Megs can tell you where that is as part of the tour.'

'OK, thanks,' I said, and as Martin and the girls released Chris from his cart, Megs and I climbed a flight of well-worn stone steps to the top of the wall close by.

'I'm glad you turned up,' she said. 'I was just thinking of taking a turn round the walls on my own; I'm not in Noaster all that often. But it's more fun to have someone to show round who's here for the first time.'

We turned left, and immediately left again, as we passed the north-west corner. The top of the wall was very broad and well-paved; there was a low parapet, about waist-high, on the outer side, and a plain iron railing of similar height on the city side, so that views of the city were unimpeded, but walkers were safe. I guessed that the railing was much more recent than the walls, and asked for confirmation.

'Yes,' said Megs, 'Noaster is Roman – *Nova Castra* – and the city walls are first century in origin, though they've been repaired and rebuilt and renovated umpteen times over the centuries, so they're not as original as it might seem. You see all those windows on the inner face of the walls – there, and there, and there?'

I did; I'd already noticed them, and wondered what lay behind.

'The original walls were mostly earth and rubble. The Romans built them with an outer and inner skin of a single course of well-squared blocks, and filled the space in between with rubble, covered at the top with these flagstones. It looked neat, and it was very strong. But much much later, when part of the wall needed fixing, somebody realised that the walls didn't need to be artillery-proof any longer, because we were relying on secrecy rather than defiance. So they cleared the rubble out of that section, and turned the space between the outer and inner skin into dwellings.'

'So some people live *in* the walls.'

'Exactly. Over time, quite a few parts of the wall, maybe most of the wall, I'm not sure, has been converted in this way. It meant that the population of Noaster could increase a bit without having to build outside the walls. All the Nossex communities like to be compact; you may have noticed that there are no isolated dwellings anywhere in Nossex.'

'Not consciously,' I admitted, 'but now you mention it... Is that a tunnel?' I changed the subject, as we were about to pass beyond where this feature that had caught my attention could be seen. The canal basin or wharf curved round ninety degrees and seemed to disappear under the small hill on which the far side of the city stood.

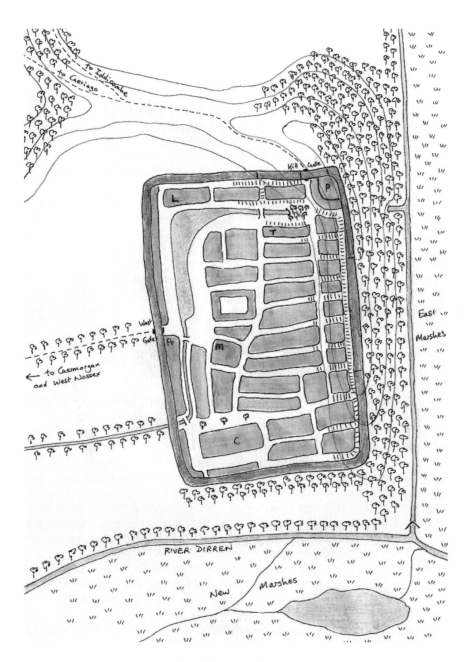

Plan of the City of Noaster

'Yes,' she answered. 'There was a cave there, quite a big one, when the Romans came. You see the odd way the city walls go up almost to the top of that little hill, so that two-thirds of Noaster is flat, but the other third is rather steep? Well, the original Nemsh village was on that hillside, beside the cave, and the Romans decided to enclose it within their town. They put all their principal buildings down here on the flat, and this part of the city was constructed on the usual grid pattern.

'Here, where the wharf is now, there was a largish pond or mere, and instead of filling it in, they incorporated it into their sewage system, which meant that they needed an inflow and outflow. They built the mill leat over there as an inflow, and lowered the floor of the cave and then knocked through a short way to the far side of the hill, where it joins the canal, the Wall Dyke.

'That was built by the Romans too; it joins the Dirren to another river a few miles away, and enabled them to move goods in two directions to and from Noaster.'

We moved on, strolling southwards until we passed over the West Gate where I'd arrived less than an hour before. There was a good fresh breeze up here; now and again Megs had to push her blond hair away from her face.

'That's Priscilla's,' she pointed down at the café where we'd first unloaded, and where the damp flagstones were already drying out. 'Where you picked me up is called the Lazaretto; it used to be a leper house in the middle ages, run by the Grey Friars.'

'I thought *you* picked *me* up,' I said. 'I wouldn't want my wife to think I go round picking up young women, which reminds me, I need to contact her today.'

'You should get a reasonable signal here in Noaster.'

'I don't have a mobile.'

'Oh. Well, in that case, we can finish the tour at Tunnel House – it's as near as Noaster gets to an internet café.'

We moved on, passing over where the mill leat came into the city, powering an invisible waterwheel somewhere within the wall; we felt the vibrations through the soles of our feet, and heard the remorseless grinding. To our left was a large hall, which Megs pointed out as the Cathedral, although its shape and architectural style were more reminiscent of a Roman administrative centre.

Turning again at the south-west corner, we now had the river fairly close on our right; but it was screened by trees, and as we went forward there began to be trees closer against the walls as well, tall trees towering above us, so that we were in their shade, and less affected by the wind.

'Around here,' said Megs, pausing halfway between the south-west and south-east corners, 'there used to be the main gate, and a Roman road heading off south-wards to join one of the main roads to London.'

'What happened to the gate?' I asked.

'I can't tell you that; it's one of the Twelve Tales of Nossex, and I've already told you one, so I can't tell another. I don't want to spoil it for whoever tells it to you.' She smiled. 'Ask for the Tale of Gaius the Youngest.'

At the south-east corner the wall began to ascend the small ridge. Outside was still tree-screened; but inside we gradually gained an increasingly fine view of the layout of Noaster, the pattern of its narrow alleys on the hillside, with many steep flights of steps crossing a couple of alleyways running horizontally along the contours. The overall impression was of warm brown stone, the tints ranging from golden to tawny to grey-brown, and the roofscape a curious hotchpotch mosaic of stone and thatch, some of the thatch old and brown, some new and straw-coloured.

'It's an odd mixture of thatch,' I said.

'Quencher Regulations,' Megs explained. 'No thatched roof may be either next to another, or opposite another. They're extra fanatical about fire prevention in Noaster. There's never been a major fire, which is a remarkable record; and that's partly because after every minor fire there's a major inquest, and lessons are learned. Each of the other communities has a gang of Quenchers; but in Noaster there are four gangs, and there's a friendly rivalry to make sure their quarter is the safest. Any fire, however small, is an embarrassment for the Quencher gang in that quarter.'

'Do they double as chimney-sweeps?'

'Too right they do. If you want a job done properly, do it yourself, and the Quenchers have a special interest in making sure every chimney's regularly well swept.'

Smoke was issuing from several chimneys as we spoke, and the breeze from the south-west was bringing smells of woodsmoke, as well as delicious aromas of roasting or baking, stewing and frying. I was looking forward to a meal; Nossex, and the exercise Nossex life always seemed to involve, was a great appetiser. As we ascended the gradual slope of the long eastern wall, the view to the west, beyond the city, opened out: the river glinting here and there through the trees that lined it; further off, the busy road, tiny vehicles whizzing along, and the faintest hum still audible even at this distance; to the left the flat green expanse of the South Moor; to the right the wooded hills, one behind another, that held the hidden settlements of Caeriago, Caermorgan, and Quarrytown. I could see the bare hilltop above Quarrytown, from which Alan had shown me my first view of Noaster.

Megs drew my attention back into the city below, pointing out a building that formed a hollow square, more or less in the centre of the city.

'That's the original Roman forum,' she explained. 'Nowadays it's sometimes a market, though there's very little buying and selling, more exchange and barter, and that doesn't last long. Part of it is a school, and another part does pre-school childcare.'

We went on upwards, the gradual slope twice interrupted by flights of steps to a higher level. Below the wall, a series of narrow alleys plunged downwards into the heart of the city. The stone houses lining each alley presented a fascinating array of narrow balconies, little roof terraces, and flower-filled window-boxes above deep shadowy yards that nevertheless held some greenery in pots and tubs. Megs said that the deep yards were well sheltered, and some had glass covers that could be closed at night and in winter, giving a chance to grow exotics.

93

Soon we were up at the highest part of the wall, buffeted by a wind that was quite powerful; Megs was probably glad to be wearing trousers today. House martins appeared to be enjoying the wind, flashing white rumps as they swooped over our heads and down to the eaves of the tall houses lining the alleyways.

The north-east corner of the wall was filled in with a stone bastion making a substantial quarter-circle, the upper part just a little higher than the wall, but not high enough to be visible from the east, over the tree-tops. The lower part of the bastion was a considerably wider quadrant, its flat roof forming a wide terrace with a superb view of the city. There were many tables and chairs out, and some folk were already eating lunch.

'That's the Bishop's Palace,' said Megs, 'though we just call it the Palace. It's not just the Bishop's residence, it does accommodation and food; you're there tonight, aren't you?'

We turned the corner again and began a descent that was much steeper; the view directly down the north wall would have troubled anyone with vertigo. Fortunately this is not one of my phobias, and clearly wasn't Megs' either, as she led the way confidently down the steepest part, and then down another flight of steps off the wall, before crossing a neat little stone bridge over the deep cutting close to the tunnel.

'I'm ready for something to eat,' she said, 'are you?'

I certainly was, and we went into a tall narrow building in between two flights of steps. Over the door was carved 'Tunnel House'. Once inside, Megs took me up to the second floor, bypassing two levels where a few folk were already eating, because, she said, the best view was higher up, and indeed the view from the window was very impressive.

The lad who served us was perhaps in his early teens, very attentive, and able to rattle the short menu off by heart. I opted for goose and bean pie, while Megs preferred a goat's cheese salad. We then watched as the lad pinned the order inside a dumb waiter, and spun the rope through his hands to send it down to the kitchen. Only a few minutes later the rope began to move, and our two lunches arose from the depths at a more sedate pace than the empty dumb waiter had descended. Water was available from a jug on a sideboard.

A typically Nossex creation, the goose and bean pie would have been more honestly described as 'beans, a soupçon of goose, and a lot of other things pie': the goose was really quite elusive. But I wasn't going to grumble; it was as tasty as everything else I'd eaten in the last five days, with some sharpish unfamiliar flavours and excellent savoury pastry.

As I devoured the substantial plateful, my attention was divided between the view of part of the wharf area of the city, with people strolling about, and the interior of this upper room in Tunnel House, all plain well-worn unvarnished wood, quite bright from the tall windows facing south and west. Along the far wall, furthest from the windows, was a rather incongruous array of five computer terminals, two of them in use: an apologetic intrusion of the 21st century into these very retro surroundings.

I became aware that I was ignoring Megs.

'Sorry,' I said, 'I'm not good at talking over a meal.'

'Don't worry, I'm used to it. It's a man thing.' There was a smile in her eyes, which were not, I realised, brown, as I had casually assumed because they looked dark against her pale complexion, but ginger-orange, pretty much the colour of the chewy bits in thick-cut marmalade.

I managed to stop myself staring, and thought of Ishbel's eyes, sea-blue with tiny brown flecks that could only be seen very close up. It was time to try and make contact, so I asked 'can you just log on to one of those computers?'

'Yes – the instructions are on the card by the keyboard.'

It was simple and obvious, and in a moment I was logging onto Facebook, to avoid staring at the dozens of unread messages there would surely be in my email inbox. And providentially, there was my wife's icon over to the right, suggesting she was online, so I opened up Chat and typed 'How's it going?' To my relief, an answer appeared almost at once: *OK – the usual stuff.*

'Students behaving themselves?'

Yes – Good bunch of hard workers. Seen anything interesting?

'Lots,' I typed. 'Too much to tell you now. I'm in Noaster, a walled city in Nossex.'

Nossex? Where's that?

'I'm not quite sure. I got kind of lost.'

I hope you can find your way back!

'I'll go back the way I came, and I'll have a lot to tell you about by this time next week. Nossex is magic.'

Could I visit it with you sometime? This made me pause for a moment, as I realised I was unsure whether a second visit to Nossex would be welcomed by the Nossexfolk. I typed 'Hope so,' and we rounded off our online conversation with an exchange of endearments.

As we left the restaurant, there was a cry of 'water for the Palace!' and Megs asked whether I fancied a bit of work. It seemed like a good idea, so we followed a couple of youngsters into the interior of the steep part of the city wall, which proved to be a shadowy chamber sloping upwards, in shape something like the space enclosing a long escalator on the London Underground.

But here there were no moving staircases, and the walls and arched roof were of bare stone. As in the Purse Tower at Caeriago, a leat flowed in through the outer wall, and here too there were bicycle frames to provide pedal power. Rather than a vertical bucket lift, here ingenious gearing allowed cyclists to operate successive Archimedes screws to raise water diagonally upwards through a series of basins.

Several volunteers had answered the call, and Megs and I stood by to take over when any of the first batch might have had enough. Once our turn came, it proved rather hard work. In my case the relevant muscles were still feeling the effects of the day before.

Megs managed to keep pedalling for more than twice the time that I did, and I had to remind myself how much older I was. At least there was no shortage of folk willing to take over as I tumbled off to get my breath back and massage my aching thighs.

'It'll do you good,' said Megs unsympathetically as we went out into the bright afternoon. 'There'll be music down at the quayside,' she went on; 'I'm going to fetch a couple of instruments. Where are your whistles?'

'In my rucksack, which Martin said he would leave at the Palace to bag me a bed.'

'That's more or less where I'm going; I'll show you the way.'

She took me up to the Palace, in through an open door and up a winding stone stair, before pointing me towards the 'men's dorm', which was something like an old-fashioned youth hostel dormitory on a grand scale: a broad room with three windows in a curving outer wall, and several triple bunks that took advantage of the high ceiling to allow the room to sleep twenty-seven.

I looked up at the top bunk, remembering sleeping at that height in the Tunnel Mess on the Festiniog Railway Deviation. But that was forty-five years ago, and Martin had realistically bagged a bottom bunk for a sexagenarian. I extracted the whistles and went out to wait for Megs, who soon appeared, not with a hurdy-gurdy this time, but a small round-bodied mandolin and a couple of recorders. She led the way down to the quayside, where musicians were already clustering around the narrowboat *Esther*.

One of the Sprat Collective women was sitting on the roof with a concertina, leading a selection of well-known tunes, mostly but not exclusively English. Chairs were borrowed from nearby café tables and we found ourselves spaces in the circle, and joined in. As I played, and enjoyed the warm sunlit scene, narrowboats in the foreground, and the intricate jumble of brown stone houses rising to the Palace and the high east wall in the background, I thought that this was one of the good moments in life, and was only sorry that Ishbel wasn't with me to share it. Every now and again a tune cropped up that was completely unfamiliar, and I wished I had a better, or faster, musical memory.

In a break in the music, I wandered up to the concertina player and asked: 'What was that you played after the *Horses Brawl*? Was it a separate tune, or just a minor mode variation?'

'Good question,' she said. 'Maybe both – it's the *Branle des Buffes*, or Buffaloes Brawl, supposedly from the legendary 1586 edition of *Orchesographie*.'

'I thought that was 1589,' I objected.

'That's the edition everyone knows. The earlier 1586 edition was lost.'

'Oh. Is that why it's legendary?'

'Exactly.'

It seemed likely that this was a spoof history for a modern composition, but I begged a copy of the tune anyway.

Buffaloes Brawl

Some time later, I began to think that more food would be quite a good idea. Megs said she wasn't hungry, so I took my chair back to the Lazaretto where it had come from, and saw Brother Alan there, who was happy for me to join him. He recommended one of the pizzas, which came in a half folded over form that reminded me of Turkish *pide*. In fact it wasn't quite the same, but it certainly justified Alan's recommendation.

'It's quite a café culture in Noaster, isn't it?' I said between mouthfuls.

'In the summer, maybe, and in the dry weather we're having now, but today's unusual, because we've got the Gathering coming up, and probably twice as many people here as on a normal Saturday evening. There aren't usually this many tables and chairs outside, and in cold winter weather there'll be none at all; everyone will be inside, which puts pressure on capacity, so not everyone eats at the same time.'

'That's different from the other communities,' I suggested.

'Yes, everywhere else the whole community eats together, for main meals anyway; breakfast's often in the nuclear family. Here, it's a bit more fragmented. Still, even in Noaster, everyone knows everyone; you're not eating among strangers, except perhaps at weekends like this one, where folk come in from all the communities.'

'Do you get to meet most Nossexfolk, or are you a bit isolated in Pinrose?'

'Most of the time fairly isolated, that's our choice, but every year there's the chance to get around on One-in-Twelve. Do you know what that is?'

'I found out this morning, yes.'

'This week I'm starting a month with the Stone Surveyors, checking that buildings and structures are in good order, and doing minor repairs on the spot, or putting in reports calling for renovation. That'll take me all over Nossex, it'll be fun.'

We sat for some time, as Alan recounted some of the other One-in-Twelve experiences he'd had, and I thought how the same idea Outside could give even wider variety to people's lives. But then perhaps the infinitely greater complexity of society there would make the scheme unworkable. Maybe it could only succeed on the small and very human scale of Nossex.

The evening was cooling rapidly as the sun dipped behind the west wall. It was not exactly cold, but becoming less comfortable to sit out, and as I thought this, the musicians were moving *en masse* to an upper room inside. I said 'see you' to Alan and joined them. Some were taking a break to eat, but there was a quorum who were carrying on, including Martin with his guitar. He was gratifyingly impressed that I could now play an instrument, which hadn't been one of my skills in undergraduate days. As at Caermorgan, I was invited to lead off a tune, and this time I ventured one of my own:

Ursula

Some time later, there was suddenly a general consensus that the evening was over, and folk were dispersing. Martin and I were part of the largest group, who made their way up to the Palace, men and women separating to their respective dormitories. I found my bunk again by identifying the rucksack; as I did so, I was tapped on the shoulder and an ample figure of about my own age shook my hand.

'Welcome to my magnificent palace,' he said, glancing ironically at the utilitarian surroundings. 'I'm Matthew.' I noticed that he was wearing a purple shirt and a white enamel pendant of a descending dove. Presumably this was Noaster episcopal attire.

'Steve,' I said. 'Thank you.'

'Matthew's slumming it with the rest of us,' said Martin. 'And Eva joins the girls in the other dormitory. Meanwhile one lucky young couple get to sample the Bishop's four-poster bed.'

'Very self-sacrificing,' I said.

'Not really,' said Matthew with a laugh. 'It's only three or four weekends a year. We have our privacy most of the time, and on occasions like this it's fun to meet different people.'

It had been a long and tiring day, and despite the number of men and boys in the room, and the amount of creaking, whispering, snoring, and other general disturbance, I had little difficulty in sleeping solidly most of the night.

Sunday 28th September 2014

We were all roused at first light the next day; Martin told me that the bunks would be wanted for the Jews from Pinginna, who had walked the fourteen miles through the night, because of course they would not travel on the Sabbath. They would now have the chance to sleep through to the Gathering in the afternoon.

Breakfast on the terrace was pleasant; it was a cool bright morning, and the dry weather seemed set to continue. The view of the city was fascinating, and beyond the western wall, walkers and a few cyclists could be seen approaching.

I managed once more to get involved in washing up, and once that was done folk were already making their way down to the large Cathedral building in the far corner of the city. Inside it seemed bigger than it had looked from the outside. There were broad galleries round three sides, all focusing on a raised section of the ground floor, a configuration like some big non-conformist churches I'd known.

I wondered whether the curious external stone staircases had been specifically built as fire escapes. On the ground floor there were broad doors on all four sides. It all looked likely to predate any Outside concerns about fire safety, but from what Megs said, the Nossex Fire Quenchers had been enforcing sensible regulations for a long time.

My thoughts were interrupted by the beginning of the service. It was informal in style, not using any set liturgy, but clearly structured and prepared rather than improvised. At an early stage there was a choir performance. I recognised Guy, remembering that he had said he was going to sing in a choir. Cilla, the girl from Pinrose, was there, and a couple of other familiar faces of people I hadn't had the chance to get to know. Megs, who had presumably rehearsed the choir, gave them a start note on a pitch pipe, but then stood aside and left them to it.

The anthem was short, but very well sung. It was followed by the baptism of a dozen or more candidates of various ages. The oldest, and tallest, was Hezekiah Hughes; then there was the man who had turned up at Caermorgan and been whisked off to Pinisk, looking small and a little shrunken between the big gypsy and another immense figure. This third man was not tall, but broad and deep-chested, with massive shoulders that sloped up to his head, leaving no visible neck. I wondered if he was a descendant of Alain FisBos. The remaining nine or ten were young adults and teenagers; Guy was among the youngest, but not the only young one.

I saw Cilla and Titus among the supporters holding towels at the ready. The candidate Cilla was supporting might have been the same girl she had been encouraging on the run. It was difficult to be sure, for today the girl was cool, radiant, and elegantly dressed, rather than beetroot-red, sweating, and gasping for breath. Titus was supporting one of the other English learners I'd met, Ardil, a Kurd from Iraq.

Baptism here was clearly not by immersion; there was no baptistery, but a section of the floor just a little lower than elsewhere, sloping to a drain in one corner, and an ancient stone font of considerable capacity.

99

The brass jug that the Bishop used to pour water over each candidate's head held enough to make them very wet, as well as his own sleeve when he had to reach high enough to baptise Hezekiah. The formula was brief: 'Hezekiah Hughes, I baptise you in the name of the Father, and of the Son, and of the Spirit. Rejoice that your name is written in the Lamb's book of life.'

The newly baptised were quite damp, and the towels of their supporters were well used, but they made no move to go and change, remaining to dry off gradually in the warm cathedral. I regretted the absence of a brief testimony, such as would have been normal in my own church back home, but perhaps it had been judged too time-consuming, with that number of candidates. At least I had already heard Hezza's testimony, and knew something of Guy's and Ardil's stories.

A sturdy dark-haired girl stepped up to read from the Bible. She looked familiar, and I realised I had last seen her carrying sacks of potatoes and sluicing down donkey-watered flagstones. Her voice was strong and clear, as she read Colossians 3:1-12, before the Bishop stood up to preach.

'Nossexfolk,' he began, 'of course this passage applies to us all, but let me address particularly those leaving at the beginning of their Years Out, and among them, those who are believers: the majority, I know. Remember verse two; it's short, you can learn it by heart: *set your minds on things above, not on earthly things.*'

'You'll have heard it before, perhaps many times, but I'll say it again: your Years Out are not designed for you to sample pleasures that are frowned on here in Nossex. If you want to take up rugby, which we don't do here, well and good; rugby's not sinful, though we hope you won't come back crippled for life. But if you're looking forward to opportunities for casual sex, being Outside doesn't make that all right. Let me stress that the sin is not primarily in the sex, but in the lack of commitment. As Nossexfolk, you are likely to find it hard to commit permanently to anyone Outside, unless and until you are absolutely sure you're not returning.

'This goes of course for any other kind of sinful behaviour as well: God may seem less present Outside, but that's not the case; there's nowhere you can go to avoid Him. *Am I only a God nearby, declares the Lord, and not a God far away? Can anyone hide in secret places so that I cannot see him? declares the Lord. Do not I fill heaven and earth?*[1] So nothing that is wrong in Nossex can be right Outside.'

He went on to warn them of the attractiveness of limitless amounts of material goods and fun activities, before applying the passage to the Nossexfolk in general: the majority who were staying rather than leaving, and who hardly needed to be warned against materialism…

My mind wandered, as so often in sermons, however, and although I did take in some of the remainder of Matthew's sermon, when I got round to making notes on it a day or two later, I could remember little that was coherent. Before I knew it we were heading out of the cathedral, and I was invited to join the Bishop's table at Priscilla's. It was warm and sunny, late summer weather rather than early autumn.

[1] Jer 23:23

Cold soup and cold pizza with a choice of toppings, along with a generous help-yourself salad bar, was actually very satisfying, if not quite like a traditional English Sunday lunch. Presumably the idea was to minimise the work anybody had to do on the Sunday; the bulk of the preparation might well have been done the evening before. I particularly liked the cucumber and walnut salad, and was just wondering if any of the potato salad had come off the donkey cart we'd unloaded the day before, when I reminded myself to be a bit sociable, rather than just eating.

'How long have you been Bishop?' I asked Matthew.

'Nearly fifteen years now,' was the answer after a pause for calculation. 'The years fly by, don't they, dear?'

His wife Eva smiled and agreed. 'It seems only last week they were enthroning you as Matthew III, the 117th Bishop of Noaster.'

'And very nervous I was, I remember it well,' he added.

'What a lot of bishops,' I said without thinking.

'For nearly two thousand years, it's actually not a huge number,' Eva pointed out. 'Many bishops have served long periods, though Persis still holds the record at sixty-six years, and that's not likely to be broken.'

'Is that the Persis who followed Quintus of Cyrene?'

'Yes, we count him as the first bishop, and Persis as the second. We don't know that either of them claimed the title, but they certainly filled the role, and early records refer back to them as bishops.'

'I've heard other bishops mentioned in some of the Tales of Nossex,' I said. 'Who was the most famous bishop?'

'Andrew Breeze,' suggested Eva.

'I could tell you his Tale,' said Matthew, 'if you haven't heard it already?'

I shook my head, and he began.

Fourteen: The Tale of Bishop Andrew and the Dark Veil

He lifted me out of the slimy pit, out of the mud and mire,
he set my feet on a rock. Ps 40:2

Andrew Breeze was born in Chittock in 1622, and as quite a young boy, maybe ten years old, had a very clear call from God: 'Andrew, as you will handle wood, so handle my word with care, for you will walk far and preach to many.'

From that day Andrew set himself to learn the Scriptures, and although like any Nossex boy he could turn his hand to most tasks, he specialised in carpentry, like his Saviour. He could be merry and enthusiastic, and loved to play dance music on bagpipes that he had made himself; but at times dark thoughts took him, and he found himself weeping for no reason he could put into words, and struggling to find the energy to keep working like normal folk. It felt, he said, as if there was a dark veil between him and the world, dimming even the sunlight, and God was somewhere beyond the veil.

The folk of Chittock were sympathetic, diagnosing the Dark Veil as a sickness of the spirit, rather than laziness or weakness, and they would sit him close to the fire (for the Dark Veil more often descended in the cold and the dim light of winter), and ply him with herbal tea. If he looked particularly downcast, a musician might come and play for him. At first his tears would flow with the music; but when he felt able to pick up his pipes and join in, then all rejoiced, because by degrees his spirits and his strength would return as he played.

Because they were concerned for his equilibrium in the tempestuous world Outside, the Chittock elders discouraged Andrew from beginning his Wandership until he was nineteen years old, three years later than was usual in those days. In the end he insisted, saying 'With God's strength and your prayers, I will take the road, and accept whatever He sends me as part of my Green Martyrdom.'

He travelled first to Cambridge, and then on to London, taking the opportunity to listen to a variety of Puritan preaching, and settled at first in the City of London, where he lodged with Sam Bullock, a very godly old carpenter, whose hands were beginning to suffer from arthritis, so that Andrew was a great help to him. In return young Andrew learned much about joinery, but more about prayer and Christian discipline amid the growing ferment of the times.

They went together on Sunday evenings to sit under the preaching of Jeremiah Burroughs at St Giles, Cripplegate; but in the mornings Andrew made the most of the opportunities to hear many other fine preachers in the numerous churches that were within walking distance. When the 7am 'morning exercises' began, preaching and prayer out in the street in Cripplegate, old Sam and young Andrew were in the gathering more often than not.

However, life was not all work and prayer. On weekday evenings, especially when the days were shorter and the nights longer, Andrew would often be found in one of the taverns in Cheapside or on Ludgate Hill, playing his pipes.

And if he was not playing, he was talking, discussing the many new ideas of the time concerning society, justice, education, and ethics. For more than two years this busy life continued, and he seemed to be given renewed energy day by day, soaring as on eagle's wings, so that he hoped that he had left the Dark Veil behind with childhood, or that he had found a way of prayerful living that would keep his spirits bright and clear.

One day he heard a fiery young Welshman preach, Vavasour Powell by name. It was a stirring sermon, but there were certain bold statements he did not quite agree with, and at the church door after the service he plucked up courage and challenged the preacher. This led to a discussion that adjourned to a nearby house; at one point, hearing Andrew's accent, Powell spoke to him in Welsh, and Andrew answered in Nemsh. They could understand each other up to a point in these related dialects, and this helped bond a friendship that endured despite many differences of opinion.

Before long Powell was returning to Wales, and he persuaded Andrew to go with him as an extended preaching trip to the villages, where many godly folk were starved of good preaching. They began far in the south and travelled north, over bleak hills and along narrow valleys, preaching turn and turn about, sometimes to large congregations in the little towns, sometimes to mere handfuls of folk in remote hamlets.

Powell's energy was relentless, and whatever the weather, day after day he walked on, always hearing of some other small gathering or fellowship that longed to hear the Word preached. Andrew was borne up on the joy he saw in people's faces, and on the conviction of being of service in the spread of the Kingdom of Heaven, and he felt well able to walk stride for stride alongside his Welsh friend.

One day, however, Vavasour Powell fell sick of a chill, and lay in a fever for days in the little cottage of an elderly couple who nursed him lovingly. Andrew found himself redundant; he had no contacts or introductions to enable him to go forward without his friend, and in the sudden idleness he felt the first shadow of the Dark Veil approaching. Tired and homesick, he prayed for guidance, and it seemed time to return home, at least for a while.

He set off eastwards, back into England on what he hoped was the shortest way to Nossex. It took him through Kidderminster, where he stayed two days, marvelling at, and gaining some encouragement from, the revival under Richard Baxter, though that remarkable man was actually away at the time, with the Parliamentarian army in Coventry. Andrew took a slight detour, in hope to hear Baxter there; but he was out of luck again, for there was warfare afoot, and Baxter was with the forces in the field, as chaplain, of course, rather than combatant.

Finally Andrew stumbled into his homeland, and collapsed in Chittock with a doubly Dark Veil shutting out all happiness forever, or so it felt. Music did nothing for him, at least at first. He sat outside under a tree and looked blankly at the tedious sunshine, the little birds hopping fatuously around, and the ridiculous yellow flowers nodding in an irritating breeze, and wondered why he should continue to exist.

His mother brought him herbal tea, and sometimes sat with him a little, but did not try to talk. On another day, a teenage girl came and asked him about London; she was due to start her Wandership soon, and wanted to hear about the famous preachers there. Andrew forced himself to speak. The girl was beautiful, with long dark hair and shining dark eyes, and something of that beauty shone through the Dark Veil and touched his spirit. But he found he could recall the teaching of Cripplegate with much less clarity than he would have liked, and he regretted the lack of books and pamphlets to help him retell the words of others. Back at Sam Bullock's, he had begun a small collection of the new printing, but he had not taken any of it with him to Wales.

The thought of going back to London, just to collect his books, roused him a little; and then he remembered the taverns and the music, and melodies began to run through his head: Watkyn's Ale, Packington's Pound, Quodling's Delight, and most often Cam Ye Not From Newcastle.

He found himself humming listlessly, and his mother heard it, and smiled. The next day, the dark-haired girl came again, and brought with her a set of bagpipes. Andrew tried them, found them good, and thanked her, asking her name.

'I'm Esther,' she said. 'And now you must play for me.'

He did so, and with each tune the Dark Veil thinned a little, a very little. Within a couple of days he was back in his workshop, wielding spokeshave and auger, mallet and chisel; and the hard work pulled his spirits up by the day. In the evenings he played with other musicians; the girl Esther was there too, a skilled fiddler, he realised.

Soon he was able to return to London, and rejoin old Sam Bullock, who had begun to go more often to St Stephen's Walbrook, to sit under the preaching of Thomas Watson. Andrew became a firm friend of this young minister, who was much the same age as himself, and Watson's steadiness was an anchor for him in the turbulence of the times. New ideas and philosophies seemed to multiply daily, and every tavern was full of the wildest talk; religious discussions, too, embraced every hitherto taboo possibility.

There were Ranters, Quakers, and Baptists; Diggers and Levellers, and all shades of opinion in between the extremes. It was disconcerting to hear folk passionately pleading for freedoms that had existed in Nossex for centuries, and part of the stress of the discussions, for Andrew, was the need to remain silent about the existence of his homeland.

He was at least able to argue with conviction that money was unnecessary, that land should not be owned, but available to all for common use, and that all were equal in the sight of God, and none should be too proud to earn his bread with the work of his hands. The belligerent means by which men sought to achieve these ideal ends, however, utterly repelled him.

His original plan had been that this second stay in London should be short, just to earn a little money and lay it out in purchasing a selection of the many fascinating books and pamphlets that were appearing by the day, and then to take his whole collection back to Nossex.

He set about this with enthusiasm and energy, but soon realised it would need more than one trip home. On his first return to Nossex, the Blackfriars School asked him to organise a discussion group (soon dubbed the Blackfriars Inquisition), to debate the new writing and the new ideas. It went well, but he realised at once that much more material was needed, and also that the worst ideas as well as the best should be represented, so that they could be dissected and dismissed through reasoned argument, not rejected in ignorance and prejudice.

So through the late 1640s and early 1650s, he settled into a pattern of spending much of the year in London, and then returning to Nossex in the heat of the summer, when London stank the most, taking with him much new writing, and joining the Inquisitions at the Blackfriars. They analysed and argued over Milton, Descartes, Hobbes, Comenius, and anonymous publications such as the *Kingdom of Macaria*, and *Tyranipocrit Discovered*.

He took young Esther back to London with him after the first summer; she lodged with an old dressmaker in Watson's congregation and earned her keep by her deft needlework. They often saw each other at church services and prayer meetings, but did not sit together; however, Andrew thought it wise to stay closer when she came to play music in the taverns. Her striking looks attracted many men, and it was safer for her if she was seen as Andrew's girl, though he tended to refer to her as his sister, which was more or less how he thought of her. They played together well, and were in demand for informal dances.

Andrew Breeze

Thomas Watson

105

His spirits dipped sometimes, typically in the depths of winter, but the prayers and support and friendship of old Sam, of Watson, and of Esther, all of whom knew about the threat of the Dark Veil, brought him through into each spring on a fairly even keel, until February of 1651, when Sam Bullock died.

This blow came on top of a series of events, each of which Andrew found profoundly upsetting: the beheading of the King, the suppression of the Levellers, and the collapse of the Digger communities. Everything seemed to be turning away from peace, justice, equality, and godliness, and towards a choice between dark oppression or violent chaos.

He took to his bed, at first with a heavy cold, but as time went on and nursing brought no return of energy, he had to admit to Watson, who visited faithfully, that the Dark Veil had overcome him completely. Watson spoke to Esther, and she too began to visit regularly, bringing herbal tonics, and playing gentle tunes for him on her fiddle. After many dark days, he got up shakily, and that year he returned to Nossex early, and stayed longer.

Spring in Nossex finally restored some zest for life, and he was able to teach a course in philosophy at the Blackfriars School, which stimulated a desire to acquire yet more books. So he continued to split his time between London and Nossex for some years more. Esther ended her Wandership, and became a teacher at the school, starting a fresh inquiry into botanical science, based on Culpeper's new *Complete Herbal*. The plan was to identify and catalogue every plant found in Nossex, and to prove its uses. Andrew was delighted with the project, and led groups that helped collect specimens. Meanwhile he reorganised the school library, and saw to it that copies were made of many of the materials. He was much in demand as a preacher, too, putting into practice the plain Bible exposition he had enjoyed so much in London.

In the year that Oliver Cromwell died, Andrew's energy ran out, and the thick Dark Veil once more shut out the light. The political events Outside were only the trigger for a collapse that was coming anyway, but it was certainly depressing to see an invisible crown handed down by the old foolish hereditary principle, to a son clearly unfit for the responsibility.

Andrew's community rallied round and cared for him, and again it was Esther who helped his gradual recovery to begin, knowing as she did the blend of patience and gentle nudges that could make it possible. She was nearly thirty years old by now, still single, though in Nossex that was a choice that quite a few made, and nobody looked down on anyone for that reason.

A little later, as he was beginning to smile occasionally, and to hum the odd tune or two, she asked him quietly:

'Andrew, if you were to marry, what manner of wife would you wish for?'

He thought for a moment, as if pondering a riddle. 'Why,' he said, 'someone not unlike you, I suppose. But the question is hypothetical, for I have no plans for marriage.'

'Andrew,' she said again, 'look at me. What manner of husband would be good for me to have?'

He looked into her eyes that were dark as sweet chestnuts, and considered again. 'Someone in need of loving care and much patience,' he said, adding firmly 'and I pray that God will grant you one who is worthy of you.'

'Perhaps He has,' she said, 'but truly, it seems much patience is needed.' She went out, softly singing the chorus to Cam Ye Not From Newcastle:

Why should I not love my love?
Why should not my love love me?
Why should I not love my love?
When love to all is free?

She might never have come any closer than that to the man she loved, but four years later Andrew Breeze was chosen as Bishop of Noaster; and God told him *most* clearly that he would need a good wife to support him in the job.

Fifteen: The Gathering; second night in Noaster

'And how did he get on as bishop?' I asked.

'Very well,' said Bishop Matthew. 'He didn't just sit in the palace in Noaster; he did the rounds, visited every community three or four times a year. He knew everybody and people felt able to speak frankly to him, so he knew what was happening.'

'He and Esther were a team,' added Eva. 'They supported the continuing revolution in the teaching at the Blackfriars, putting Comenius's ideas into practice. She was involved in all sorts of projects, she wasn't just a bishop's wife; her story's worth hearing as well, even though it overlaps with his. They both encouraged much more focused Wandership, and often much longer: youngsters were urged to gain as varied experience as possible, to bring back skills and knowledge and even dubious ideas, so that they could be debated.'

'Is Wandership the same as Years Out?' I asked.

'That's right,' said Eva. 'We only started calling it Years Out sometime in the twentieth century.'

'Andrew still did plenty of preaching,' the Bishop continued, 'but he was more concerned to enable youngsters to develop a preaching gift. There's always been great respect for age and experience in Nossex, but Andrew persuaded people to give youth a chance, let people make a few mistakes.'

'What time does the Gathering start?' prompted Eva.

'About now,' the Bishop admitted, 'but it's all right, they can't start till I'm there.'

'Exactly,' said his wife. 'People are waiting for you,' and she stood up.

We also hastened to rise, and hurried back along the mill stream, then across the square to the cathedral. We were not the only scurrying figures, but when we got inside, most seats were taken. Matthew, of course, had the bishop's chair. I looked around, and saw that Martin was keeping me a seat. Within a few moments most latecomers were seated, and the Bishop rose to open the Gathering in prayer.

The first few items seemed fairly routine; they were dealt with most briskly, and my mind wandered a little as I looked round the packed hall and the well-filled galleries, spotting a few familiar faces. Megs was over on the far side, facing our way.

Countess Mary was chairing proceedings. I began to pay closer attention when she made the following announcement, something in the tone of her voice suggesting that this was not routine: 'The Council of Nossex has received a petition from the twelve-year-old children, with the support of many older ones, under threat of a Helping Strike.'

There were a few chuckles around the hall, and everyone sat up a little straighter. I saw Megs smile.

'Leah FourFisBos will now present the petition with brief supporting arguments.'

A sturdy girl with black curly hair and a confident air stood up and spoke in a clear high voice: 'Mobile phones are now allowed only to thirteen-year-olds. We ask

Council to change the age to twelve, for three reasons. First, twelve-year-olds can easily operate mobiles, more easily than most adults. Second, many twelve-year-olds move when they start work and change schools, so they want to keep in touch with their families and home community. Third, modern smartphones are very useful for education, so children should be able to use them as early as possible.'

'Thank you, Leah, that was beautifully brief. Before we vote, Abbot Peter will give some counterarguments – also briefly.' The Countess emphasised the last two words, looking directly at the Abbot, who smiled and rose.

'Nobody doubts that twelve-year olds can operate phones skilfully, that is not why they have not yet been allowed them. As to contact with home, our experience is that homesickness persists *longer* if very frequent contact is allowed. As to education, teachers prefer children to learn self-reliance, and non-electronic research skills, before too much dependence on electronic aids develops. There is also an issue with smartphones, as they can receive live television, but here in Nossex we have no licence. It would be impossible to ensure that no child was ever watching live television.'

'Solid arguments on both sides, then,' commented the Countess. 'Before we vote, may I remind you that any change would be for a trial period of one year, so it would be reviewed at the next Autumn Gathering. As this matter particularly affects children, we will take the youth vote first.'

Predictably, the children and young people were very strongly in favour.

'Nossexfolk,' said the Countess, 'now that you have seen the judgment of the children, including the older and more mature young people who have no personal motivation, who is for yes?'

That wasn't quite impartial, I thought, as the assembly voted in favour by roughly two to one.

'A year's trial, then,' said the Countess, and glancing at the clerk, 'on the agenda for review next autumn.'

A couple of reports followed. Although they also conformed to the pattern of brevity to the point of terseness, I found little to take a close interest in. I wondered when there would be a break.

'Refreshments outside in a few minutes,' whispered Martin in my ear.

'The next item,' said the Countess, 'is the Confirmation of Council. No community has indicated a wish to change their representative. Does anyone wish to object to Council continuing in its present membership?'

A tall young man, maybe no more than a teenager, lean and dark-eyed with long wavy hair, leapt to his feet.

'Yes!' he cried. 'Every year we have this charade, and nobody challenges any member of Council, and nothing ever changes. I propose a motion of no confidence in whichever member of Council is oldest. We need younger blood on Council.'

There was a general murmur, which sounded like a blend of annoyance, interest, and amusement. The Countess glanced around the hall.

A voice was heard from somewhere at the back: 'That would be me, then.' It was Sister Christina, I saw.

'Thank you for the suggestion, Ben,' she went on, 'I would love to stand down; I've been feeling for some time that I should be doing a little less going to meetings and more praying. So we can save Gathering the bother of a vote, and now that the folk of Pinrose have heard your comment, I dare say they'll select a much younger representative to replace me.'

There was another wave of murmuring.

'As the Abbess says,' observed the Countess, cutting across the murmuring, which quickly died away, 'if she is standing down, there is no point in a vote of confidence. However, her resignation as Pinrose's representative on Council is not for this Gathering to accept or reject, but solely for the community of Pinrose. So I'm sorry, Ben, unless you propose another motion of no confidence in someone who actually wants to stay on Council, you don't get your chance to vote somebody off. But we will now vote to confirm Council, with the exception of Pinrose's representative, who will be confirmed at the Winter Gathering. Who is for yes?'

It was virtually unanimous, though I noticed that Megs abstained.

'And just before we break for refreshment,' said the Bishop, 'one more item: the betrothal is announced of Carys Williamson of Pinrose and Howell Thatcher of Iddicombe.'

I had glanced at Carys as soon as I heard her name, and her reaction to this announcement was puzzling: first her eyes widened and her mouth dropped open, then her hands flew up to cover her mouth. Clearly the announcement was as much news to her as to me or anyone else; but then a smile came into her eyes and she lowered her hands, showing her lips now set in an expression of determination.

As folk rose and headed outside for the refreshments, I saw Carys walk slowly towards a young man who stood and smiled at her, while his body language suggested considerable apprehension. I couldn't hear what she said, or indeed if she said anything. For a moment it looked as though she was setting herself to clout him round the ear, then she suddenly seized him round the waist and lifted him off his feet, before dumping him roughly down again and kissing him.

The crush of people prevented me seeing any more of that intriguing story unfold; meanwhile Martin was working his way through the crowd towards the young firebrand, who I guessed might be one of his pupils. I followed to learn more of another story.

'Well, Ben,' said Martin, 'you've made a difference there.'

Ben didn't look pleased with himself. 'There wasn't a vote,' he muttered.

'Bonehead!' Martin sounded affectionate rather than contemptuous. 'If there *had* been a vote, you'd have been absolutely slaughtered. But because Abbess Christina was gracious enough to stand down, the Council *will* end up looking a bit younger.'

A teenager poured us mugs of apple juice from a big stoneware jug.

'I thought the Abbess seemed a very wise woman, when I met her,' I said.

'Ben,' said Martin, 'this is Steve; we were at Uni together, aeons ago.'

Ben momentarily shed his angry-young-man pose, smiled and shook my hand. The Abbess appeared at my elbow. 'Thank you for that, Ben,' she said. 'A little dramatic, perhaps, but a bit of drama spices up a Gathering. You helped concentrate my mind, and better to stand down while people are still saying nice things about you – thank you, Steve – than after they've started saying *silly old bat.*'

'It wasn't aimed at you.' Ben looked embarrassed.

'I know it wasn't,' she said. 'Youth needs to be heard – a fair point.'

The refreshment break was relatively soon over, though it took quite a few minutes for everyone to get back into their places. The bishop began with a brief prayer and a reading from Colossians:

> *But now you must rid yourselves of all such things as these: anger, rage, malice, slander and filthy language from your lips. Do not lie to each other, since you have taken off your old self with its practices and have put on the new self, which is being renewed in knowledge in the image of its Creator. Here there is no Greek or Jew, circumcised or uncircumcised, barbarian, Scythian, slave or free, but Christ is all, and is in all.*
>
> *Therefore, as God's chosen people, holy and dearly loved, clothe yourselves with compassion, kindness, humility, gentleness and patience. Bear with each other and forgive whatever grievances you may have against one another. Forgive as the Lord forgave you. And over all these virtues put on love, which binds them all together in perfect unity.*

'Nossexfolk,' he went on, 'we will now see love and forgiveness in action, and to the words *no Greek or Jew* we can add: no Roma or New Ager, no Gypsy or Gordja, no Travellers or Nossexfolk, but all are one in Christ. The Hughes tribe and the Sprat Collective have each forgiven the other and are reconciled; and they have undertaken to respect the peace of Nossex.'

The two leaders, whose handshake and embrace Brother Alan and I had already witnessed by the Tivvy, stood up and approached each other, the tall figure of Hezza Hughes magnificent in a gold embroidered waistcoat and royal blue neckscarf. He towered over the wiry, but slightly stooped Doctor John Sprat, who had considerably smartened up for the occasion, though less flamboyantly than his counterpart. They smiled at each other, and this time the embrace appeared unreserved.

Behind each came a woman: Hezekiah's mother and Jack Sprat's wife. They were similar in age and less of a mismatch in size; but old Sarah Hughes exuded a far more formidable air of authority than Rachel Sprat. Their hug also seemed genuinely warm.

'In joy and thankfulness at this reconciliation,' the bishop continued, 'and also because the time is long overdue, the Council of Nossex have determined to offer – subject to ratification – Denizenship of Nossex to these two communities. Countess Mary will now go through the formalities.'

The four leaders withdrew, each pair to stand in front of their community, who rose and stood behind them. The Countess also rose.

'The family of Hughes,' she began, 'have been known to Nossex, and visited frequently, time out of mind, and have been accounted Friends of Nossex for generations. They have indeed been offered Denizenship before, but have preferred a looser and freer association; but now that Outside is becoming increasingly unhelpful to Travellers, they are willing to accept.

'The community led by John and Rachel Sprat have been known to us for over twenty years, and have been Friends of Nossex for almost as long. They too would be happy to accept Denizenship.

'It is proposed,' the Countess went on, 'that the Hughes family be attached to the fellowship of Caermorgan, where they are well known, and the Sprat Collective to Chittock, where they too have friends and relatives. Both groups have agreed to pitch their tents within sight of their respective communities, and not to set up any new community site in Nossex – with two exceptions – that tents may of course be pitched temporarily as convenient for remote jobs; and that the Sprat Collective may moor their boats here in Noaster or at the North Wharf on the Wall Dyke.

'Older children may attend the Noaster, Blackfriars or Quarrytown schools, if they so wish; and the younger ones their community schools, again if they so wish. There is no compulsion. Both groups will continue their travelling lifestyle, and their Denizenship does not entail any commitment to being in Nossex at any particular point in time, or any minimum period of residence.

'This Denizenship extends automatically to any future children, but not grandchildren, of those receiving it today; however, future spouses or new members of these communities who join while Outside will need to have their Denizenship approved by a future Gathering.

'Nossexfolk,' she concluded, 'Council recommends that you ratify this offer, but the ultimate decision is yours. We will now take two minutes for each person to pray about their decision.'

The cathedral fell eerily silent.

'Who is for yes?' the Countess's voice finally rang out.

A forest of hands were raised.

'Who is for no?'

I noticed that the two groups 'on trial', as it were, kept their eyes firmly forward, not looking round for the handful of dissidents.

'Ratified,' said the Countess. 'Any issues or worries, please speak to Council afterwards. And now another item that needs careful thought.' She glanced sideways, and the man I had seen at Caermorgan, who had caused such apparent concern, walked across to an empty chair, diagonally across from the bishop's throne.

He settled himself in the chair and looked up. There was apprehensiveness in his eyes, but an air almost of relief in the sag of his shoulders.

The Countess spoke: 'Your name?'

112

'John Smith.'

'Place of birth?'

'Caermorgan.'

'Can any here confirm that this is John Smith of Caermorgan?'

Many hands were raised.

'When did you leave Nossex?' continued the Countess in the same neutral tone.

'1998.'

'And when did you return?'

'Three days ago.'

'Where have you been in the meantime?'

'A lot of places, but most of the time in London.'

After a pause, the Countess said slowly: 'And why have you returned?'

'To seek sanctuary, supervision, and by God's grace, healing.'

'Why do you ask for these things in public at this time?'

'Because the people of Nossex should be on their guard against me.'

There was a faint sound, almost a collective sigh, like a breath of wind across the packed hall.

'Why is that?'

Another pause, and I wondered if the obviously prepared script ended at this point. But the defendant – or was he an appellant? – continued:

'I am attracted to under-age girls.'

Again the stir in the hall, this time less faint.

'Have you followed that attraction?'

'I befriended a teenage girl.' The silence was tangible. 'Nothing inappropriate occurred, but I was aware that my motives were wrong. And during the same period, I was accessing indecent images online.'

'How have you addressed these issues?'

'I am no longer in contact with the girl. I have cleaned the computer's memory and afterwards destroyed the hard disc. I have prayed to God for forgiveness and given my life to Christ. And I believe He told me to return to Nossex and seek guidance.'

The Countess looked over to the Bishop, who stood up as she sat down.

'John Smith,' he said, 'the Council of Nossex has deliberated your case, and we propose as follows: that you remain in Nossex and never leave it until the end of your life. We offer supervision and counselling for the rest of your days. We also stipulate that the people of Nossex be made aware of your orientation, as indeed they now have been. We offer full protection under Nossex Oppression Law against any harassment or ill-treatment of any kind, by anybody, old or young, on account of that known orientation. You, for your part, should take care not to be alone, nor almost alone, with children; but so long as other adults are present, we counsel you not to cut yourself off completely from the company of children, and we would ask adults to co-operate in this.

'As for healing, we will pray for it, but it is not in our power to grant it, and even if it might appear to have been granted, we believe that this judgment should remain in place.

'This judgment,' the Bishop continued, 'is subject to ratification by the people of Nossex.' Turning to face the hall, he went on, 'Nossexfolk, before you indicate agreement or rejection, I would say a few words more. It may be that John Smith is no longer a danger, but we need to be wise and act as if he is. Outside, if his orientation became known, he would be driven from place to place by vigilante groups until he was forced to go underground for his own safety. Lonely and hunted, he would be at great risk of falling back into evil. Here in Nossex, we can protect both him and ourselves relatively easily. You saw him baptised this morning, an indication that we believe his repentance and new life are genuine. The risk must be small, and even if a small risk exists, John Smith is one of our own: we should bear the risk and the responsibility ourselves, not export it. We will now take two minutes for each person to pray about their decision.'

There was a momentary shuffle, then what seemed a long silence before the Countess rose to her feet again. 'Who is for yes?' she asked.

'You can't vote!' hissed Martin in my ear, as many hands went up all around, and indeed, I had become so wrapped up in the drama that my hand had twitched.

'Who is for no?'

A few hands were raised.

'It is noted,' said the Countess, 'that some disagree. You may bring your objections to the Council if you wish. But the judgment stands, if John Smith accepts it. Do you, John?'

'I do,' he whispered, almost inaudible from emotion, stood up trembling and went unsteadily back to his seat.

'And now,' said the Countess, 'for a less dark and serious matter, but still one touching our security. Steve Saxton!'

I jumped.

'Your turn for the hot seat,' said Martin.

Completely unprepared, I stumbled and almost tripped over Martin's foot as I set off towards the solitary chair, wondering if this felt more like Harry Potter's hearing in front of the Wizangemot, or the spotlit walk to the black leather chair in Mastermind. In fact the Mastermind theme rang in my head above the beating of my heart as I attempted to walk calmly and sit confidently. Whatever the questions, I presumed at least I would not be answering them against the clock.

'Your name?'

'Stephen Saxton.'

'Place of birth?'

'Paignton in Devon.'

'Can any here confirm that this is Stephen Saxton of Paignton?'

Martin raised his hand.

'From where do you know Steve?'

'The Christian Union at Durham University.'

The Countess turned to me again, and I felt a momentary warmth, somehow sure that she was on my side, whatever the real questions might be once we had got through these preliminaries.

'Your current church?'

'Holy Trinity Platt, in Manchester.'

'Is this church known to any here?'

A scattering of hands went up and, slightly comically, the Countess raised her own hand in answer to her own question. Among the raised hands I saw at least one vaguely familiar face, a young woman I thought I might have seen among the hordes of students a few years back; she might even have been to Sunday lunch with Ishbel and myself.

'Your *current* occupation?'

Now I could guess where this was going.

'I'm retired: househusband duties; church activities; proofreading; and I write books.'

'What sort of books?'

'Slow travel books. I'm walking around England, writing about what I see and hear on the way: wildlife, local history, local specialities and so on.'

115

'Who benefits from these books?'

'Each book is sold in aid of four charities.'

'Has anybody read any of these books?'

Good question, I thought, then realised it was directed to the present company rather than wondering whether my books sat on shelves unread. To my surprise, three or four hands were raised, including once more the Countess's own hand.

'Were you contemplating writing a book about Nossex?'

Once more the faint intake of breath whispered around the hall.

'I can't say the idea never occurred to me,' I said carefully, 'but I assumed it would not be permitted.'

'We certainly reserve the right to forbid it,' said the Countess firmly. 'But if it *were* permitted, how would you safeguard the security and hiddenness of Nossex?'

'Nossex society,' I said, thinking as I spoke, 'might well appear utopian, or at least an attempt at utopia, to readers Outside. Utopia is a well-stocked and familiar genre, where a fictional place is described in the guise of a factual travel narrative. I could write a 'Ramble Through Nossex' as a double bluff: fact masquerading as fiction masquerading as fact. Readers would assume that the place didn't really exist, and would hardly think to look for it.'

'But supposing a few literal-minded readers did look for it?'

'I would certainly be very vague about the location, and such clues as I gave could be misleading rather than helpful. Names of living people would be changed, since I believe most if not all of you have links Outside.'

'What would be the benefit of such a book?'

'I think you have something very special here in Nossex: a functioning Christian community which is unique in a number of interesting ways. I think it would be helpful for Christians to read about it. If I wrote the book, it would be a much more Christian book than any of the first nine, so I would choose Christian charities as beneficiaries.'

'And would you submit the final draft for our approval, and accept modifications if asked for?'

'I would certainly submit the final draft, and be prepared to negotiate over any requested modifications.'

'*Negotiate*,' said the Countess, 'suggests that you might not accept the requests.'

'I would accept them,' I said quickly, 'what I mean is that I would want the revised text to be written by me. I wouldn't want even a small part of my book to be written by somebody else. I'm sorry if that sounds selfish.'

The Countess glanced at the Bishop, who rose. 'Nossexfolk,' he said, 'much has been written about Nossex already, but so far all that writing remains in our own archives or on our bookshelves. As far as we know, nothing has been published Outside. You have heard the possible benefits of this proposed book. You have also heard the safeguards Steve proposes. If this man is trustworthy, then the potential risk is no more than we run through the many contacts we already have with Outside. If this man is not trustworthy, the risk is considerable. Therefore your decision may well come down to: do you trust this man? He is known by one of us; his church is known to a number of us; several of us have met him in the last few days. We will now take two minutes for each person to pray about their decision.'

The pause seemed never-ending.

'Who is for yes?'

I hardly dared look, but a few hands went up at once, and then gradually, more and more hands were raised until it looked a clear majority.

'Who is for no?'

Again, a few hands were raised, but this time there was no gradual increase. Clearly, quite a few folk had abstained.

'It is noted that some disagree,' said the Countess. 'You may wish to take the opportunity to raise issues with Steve while he is still in Nossex.'

I returned to my seat by Martin, and took in little of what remained of the Gathering, which seemed once more to be routine matters swiftly despatched.

As everyone poured out of the Cathedral, the Bishop came over to Martin and me. 'Early night?' he said to Martin.

'Sorry, Matthew, I need to take late shift, I promised some folk I'd join them for the evening.'

Matthew turned to me. 'To help accommodate more people after a Gathering,' he explained, 'some of us turn in really early, after a quick supper, and then we'll get up around two o'clock and go fishing, while the revellers stagger in and collapse onto the bunks we've conveniently vacated. Would you be up for that?'

'I've no expertise in fishing,' I said.

'No need, just come for the company and the experience.'

'OK,' I said.

Monday 29th September 2014

I crawled out of my sleeping-bag at what felt a particularly unearthly hour; Matthew was up and about, shaking Howell by the shoulder, but getting no response other than a faint groan. I blundered around in the near darkness, looking for my clothes. Someone seemed to be waiting to crash out on the bunk I'd just vacated. Matthew gave up on Howell, and gestured to me to follow him, and we headed out of the palace and down a steep torchlit alley to the square.

Down at the quay, a few shadowy shapes were gathering. It was a surprisingly mild night, much milder than the night before, more like high summer than early autumn. I recognised Carys, who was looking hopefully in our direction.

'Sorry, Carys,' said Bishop Matthew. 'We couldn't rouse him. He was pretty shattered when he turned in; he said he hadn't slept much last night, he was so nervous.'

'Poor lamb,' commented Carys with a smile, mocking but affectionate.

117

'You know Steve already, don't you? You could join Eva and me and Tabby – that makes five.'

There was less standing about and more briskness than I would have expected. I was introduced to Tabby 'of the Grey Friars', who was a jolly and energetic woman in early middle age, and indeed her rather plain top and trousers were in matching grey, as far as I could judge in the darkness. We found our places in the boat: Matthew took the tiller, his wife Eva and myself were idle in the bows, while Carys and Tabby used short paddles at first to guide us out through the tunnel to the canal, then exchanged the paddles for an oar each, and pulled us easily the couple of hundred yards to the lock, which was full with the top gates open.

There we waited for other boats to join us, and I took the chance to ask Tabby what she did.

'Whatever I'm asked to,' she answered. 'But I guess Outside you would call me a nurse-cum-careworker-cum-social worker; that covers most of what I do, looking after and helping anyone who needs help or support. I do a certain amount of gardening too. It's a wonderful life: enough routine to be comforting and enough of the unexpected to be stimulating. And it is so rewarding to be needed.'

One by one, three other dinghies glided into the lock, the top gates were closed, and then very slowly the bottom paddles were opened, so that our descent would not toss the boats around in the lock. Once the lower gates creaked open, the four boats dispersed, two across the river to marshland on the far side, while we and a fourth boat drifted downstream and each turned into a different gap in the reeds.

We found a spot that the bishop seemed happy with, and the intricate and patient business of baiting hooks and lines, which I understood hardly at all, and waiting, which I understood well enough, passed the starlit hours. Despite the absence of any moon, the darkness was only relative, once the eyes adjusted. To pass the time during periods of inactivity, I prayed silently for each of the other four in the boat, and for Carys' betrothed, wondering how that would turn out. Between prayers I was mentally digesting the events, conversations, and impressions of my week so far in Nossex. It had been a very full seven days.

The night continued very mild, so that sitting still carried little risk of chill. From time to time there was a moment of excitement, as different fish were hauled in: a couple of eels, pike, carp, bream, or tench gradually filling the wicker baskets either side of Matthew.

'Not a bad catch at all,' he said finally, deftly stunning one last fat fish. 'We could head for home now, I think.'

First with paddles, then with oars, Carys and Tabby got us under way, and now that quiet was presumably less essential, I took the chance to ask Eva if she would tell me the Tale of Esther Breeze. She was happy to oblige, and her narrative was pleasantly backed by the rippling of water under the prow, and the faint ruffling of the light wind in the bent flower-heads of the reeds.

Sixteen: The Tale of the Patience of Esther Forester

I waited patiently for the Lord; he turned to me and heard my cry Ps 40:1

Esther Forester was born in Pinisk in 1629. When she was a teenager, in the 1640s, there was great ferment Outside, war and political upheaval; the world, they said, was being turned upside down. Amid this turmoil there was rumour of great preaching and scripture exposition, and fascinating new philosophy being discussed.

Esther felt drawn to the wider world, and became a little impatient for her Wandership to begin. She asked many questions of her teachers, and one day she was referred to Andrew Breeze, a young man who had been living in London as part of his Wandership, and had just returned.

She was warned, however, that he was suffering greatly from weariness of the spirit; and as she walked the woodland miles, down to the bridge over the Tivvy, and back up on the West Nossex side to Chittock, she prayed, selfishly, that he would feel able to speak to her, but also unselfishly, that the God of grace would grant him healing, and that she would be able to help in the healing process.

On arrival in Chittock she was directed to Andrew's mother, who encouraged her to speak to him. 'The time might be right,' she said. 'Be patient; don't hurry him.'

Andrew was sitting under a tree, pale and listless, staring at nothing in particular on a beautiful spring day that ought to gladden any heart. But she saw the hopelessness in his eyes, sensitive grey eyes that seemed to gain a tiny hint of animation when he began to tell of the preaching of Jeremiah Burroughs, and the godliness of his landlord Sam.

Her heart went out to this thoughtful young man, and she longed to be able to alleviate his despair; but she thought it best not to prolong this first conversation, sensing his weariness. She thanked him for his news of London, and went back in to say goodbye to his mother.

'Wait here a moment,' said Andrew's mother, and took another cup of herbal tea out to her son. 'You've done him good,' she said when she came back. 'If only he had his music! Do you play anything?'

'Fiddle,' answered Esther. 'What does he play?'

'Bagpipes – but his pipes are in London. Can you come back tomorrow, and play for him?'

'God willing,' said Esther, and set off briskly back down the path to East Nossex. When she crossed the Tivvy again, however, instead of turning up the path to Pinisk, she walked straight on, along the long level track to Noaster. It was a glorious day, and she prayed as she went, alternately praising God for His creation, and interceding for Andrew, asking that he would have joy of music again, like the fat thrush that was singing just then from a willow tree. She prayed, too, that she would find what she sought in Noaster.

Esther Forester

It was late in the afternoon as she entered the city, hungry, thirsty, and leg-weary, but her prayers were answered: the woodturner's workshop was on the point of closing, but he was still there, he had more than one set of pipes not yet spoken for, and he knew Andrew and was happy to recommend the right instrument for him. Clutching the pipes, Esther was able to find food and water in one of the Noaster dining-halls, sufficient refreshment to sustain her on the remaining miles back to Pinisk through the gathering dusk and the early part of a moonlit night.

She was tired but happy when she arrived; Nossexfolk are great walkers, but the thirty miles or so she had covered in the day was the furthest so far in her fifteen years.

'Where have you been?' was the greeting she received from a boy her own age, a handsome lad with a confident air.

'What is that to you, Augustine Coppersmith?' she responded wearily.

'You're exhausted,' said Augustine. 'I'm concerned about you. You should look after yourself more.'

'I'm concerned for someone who needs help more than I do,' she retorted. 'These pipes are for Andrew Breeze; he needs a new set.'

'You don't want to bother with that lazybones,' was the dismissive rejoinder. 'He'll never count for anything.'

Esther held her tongue and turned away. She knew, as a Christian, she should not hate her fellow-student, but really, Gus Coppersmith was impossible. They were the same age, in fact she was a couple of months older, but he treated her like a younger sister, and as if she was ignorant and helpless. More than that, she had the distinct impression he saw them as a future couple, whereas she would rather stay single all her life than marry Gus.

She counted the miles she had walked well worth the effort, when she saw the effect on Andrew the next day. He actually smiled; he seemed glad to see her; he asked her name, which he had been too turned in on himself to do the day before; and he played for her. It was gratifying to feel that he played *for her*, and for the first time in her life she praised God for making her good-looking.

She had known for a while that she was beautiful (though she would have preferred to be a few inches shorter), but so far that had seemed more of a nuisance than anything, just attracting unwanted attention from the likes of Gus. Now she actually wanted someone to find her attractive, and she could tell that he did. Of course he would consider her far too young at present; but she could wait, and meanwhile it was good to hear the warm buzz of the pipes, as he played slowly and reflectively through Packington's Pound.

She saw Andrew two or three times in the weeks that followed, when he came to play at sessions, and once at a dance. Clearly he was recovering rapidly, and was happy to talk about London, the music as well as the church life.

Soon he was gone, back to London, and the long year before she could leave Nossex crawled by. The next summer, when he returned, she took courage and asked if he would take her with him and help her begin her Wandership. Now her youth was an advantage, for it was natural that she should depend on him, and therefore seek his company. And if he was a little protective, that was acceptable, for he knew the dangers of London, and he always respected her intelligence and judgment. In the process, she found herself in the role of younger sister, but with Andrew that was pleasant, and she could wait.

It was good to share in the life of the church, and in music, and in exploring the ideas that London had to offer in those years. Andrew was drawn to the ideals of the Diggers, convinced of the deceitfulness of riches and the corruption of power; Esther, meanwhile, was more interested in the educational ideas of Comenius and his followers, and also empirical observation rather than abstract theorising as a means of advancing knowledge.

121

They had many long discussions with others, but sometimes just the two of them, and Esther had the satisfaction of knowing that Andrew valued her opinion. She was there for the inaugural Blackfriars Inquisition, and showed herself skilled in asking questions that stimulated the youngsters to deeper thought and further research.

But as the years went by, and she was no longer a teenager, he seemed not to want any greater intimacy than close and warm friendship. Meanwhile, it was all Esther could do to keep count of the offers of marriage she received. Augustine Coppersmith, of course, had asked her at the beginning of their Wandership, and unabashed at the firmness of her refusal, asked her again almost annually. It became so boring that on the fifth occasion, she was prepared, and took out a scroll on which she had written *The Answer is still No*.

There were others, of course, young Nossexmen who knew Gus was getting the brush-off, and young men in the London churches who found out that there was no betrothal between her and Andrew. In some cases, these boys were not emotionally involved; they simply saw her as a girl likely to make a good Christian wife, and it was not hard to say no, knowing they would move on and ask another. But others were desperately unhappy at her refusal, and she found this distressing, wishing that her Andrew would wake up to the fact that he needed her. She prayed about it, and the answer she seemed to hear was *He is mine, for now; have patience*. This seemed to hint that her heart's desire might yet be granted; but she feared her own tendency to optimism and hopefulness, which could be deceiving her into wishful thinking.

After seven years, she gave up going back to London, and settled down in her home community of Pinisk, as a teacher at the Blackfriars School. Two London publications that prompted school courses were Playford's 1651 *English Dancing Master*, which she used, supplemented by her own compositions, to teach musical theory and practice, dancing, and composition; and Culpeper's 1653 *Complete Herbal*, which gave rise to the Nossex Survey, and in the process training in scientific observation, as well as medicine and cookery.

She founded the Society of Experimenters, a title borrowed from an anonymous publication, *A Description of the Famous Kingdome of Macaria*, which she and Andrew had read together, though they decided it offered no improvements on Nossex society. She also helped with the rapidly expanding school library, when Andrew was away. He continued annual visits to London, though these were shorter as the years went by.

Eventually, after twice more nursing him back to sanity with all the wisdom and patience she possessed, she dropped the heaviest of hints about marriage, even coming close to proposing herself. Now at least he was not unaware of her hopes, and she guessed that he felt himself unfitted for the role of husband. She would not have been too proud to beg, plead, or argue, but she suspected that this approach would have driven him away, so once more she reminded herself of his mother's words, long before: *Be patient; don't hurry him*.

During her years as a teacher at the Blackfriars, Esther became aware of steady and implacable opposition from Augustine Coppersmith, who was also on the staff, teaching Latin and Theology. Their approaches were incompatible: she followed Comenius and others in holding that learners needed to be happy, unthreatened, unpressured and interested for lasting learning to occur, while Gus (as the students called him behind his back, though even his friends did not venture it to his face) thought that humankind was naturally lazy, and needed to be stimulated by fear.

He even used a cane in the classroom, which was almost unheard of in Nossex, and the Abbot would have forbidden it, but could not deny the existence of the Bible texts that Augustine quoted in support of his practice. Equally it could not be denied that some previously rather noisy boys were impressively quiet and obedient in Augustine's lessons, and in fact the cane seldom had to be used.

Esther and many of her colleagues might suspect that only mechanical low-level learning was happening, bare facts that would be forgotten in ten years' time, but they had no way of proving this, and meanwhile, Gus actually complained to the Abbot about the noise some of her classes made, and wrote to the Council suggesting that she was wasting pupils' time on the many field trips.

These were niggles. The Council and the Abbot had confidence in her, she knew, and Gus could do her no real harm. But it was unsettling, knowing she had an enemy in the school and in the community, an enemy, moreover, who was quite convinced he was right and had God on his side, so was unlikely to give up.

In 1662, the bishop died, and Andrew's name was on the short list to be elected. In those days, the procedure was much as it is now: anyone could be chosen, and every baptised person in Nossex would vote. But to prevent a complete dog's dinner of an election, Council would discreetly sound out opinion, and a short list of those likely to gain a significant amount of support would be put forward.

Augustine seemed particularly upset that Andrew was a candidate, and it appears that he orchestrated a campaign to persuade folk not to vote for him. He had to be careful about how he did this, because in Nossex it's illegal to canvass, or to try to influence how another person might vote. Anything like a political party, a pressure group, or a clique or cartel or cabal, is against the law. You can say what you think in an open discussion, but others must not feel under any pressure to agree with you, and you shouldn't pledge your support in advance.

Although nobody seemed to know for certain where they started, rumours scurried about, exaggerated rumours about the extent of Andrew's mental health problems, and whispers that Esther had been his concubine for many years (*if only*, she thought, and then rebuked herself).

Despite all this intrigue, Andrew was elected, and the following day he came to Pinisk, and asked her to walk with him by the lake.

'Esther,' he said, 'I cannot bear this burden of responsibility alone. I prayed for help, and God told me quite unambiguously that I need a wife, and He actually said that He didn't need to tell me who that wife should be. I've kept you at arm's length so long. Can you forgive me? Will you marry me?'

'Do you know,' she said, 'this is my nineteenth offer of marriage. If I say no once, will you ask me again, just to make up a full score?'

'This is not a matter for jest,' he answered with a pained look.

'Do I not know that? But if I have been kept waiting more than a dozen years, may I not keep you waiting a few dozen heartbeats, as a tiny recompense for all my patience?'

'Is that a yes?'

'Of course it's a yes, you *silly* man,' she said, and they were married a week later. Andrew's mother, normally the calmest of mortals, wept all the way through the ceremony.

As had been anticipated, there were times during Andrew Breeze's 26 years as bishop when his depression returned, and although this became more infrequent as the years passed, so also his emergence from the depths became slower each time, and Esther needed all her patience, and her faith that the Dark Veil would eventually lift.

When Andrew was out of action, she made his pastoral visits on his behalf, a steady round of the Council members to glean news of the different communities, and to enable those with the greatest responsibility to unburden themselves safely. In theory she reported matters back to Andrew for his prayers; in practice, she shared only as much as she thought he could cope with. It was far less important that he should know everything, than that there should be a listening ear for those that needed one. Because she was not the Bishop, only the Bishop's wife, she offered no advice and made no suggestions, but only listened.

As the years went by, people said that she was an even better listener than Andrew, who was himself very non-prescriptive. But Esther was always happy when he was well enough to take back the responsibility, and she could devote more time to her music, the dance classes and the fiddle tuition, and the ongoing Nossex Survey, though by now she was only a humble participant rather than the prime mover.

In 1688, Andrew died of a fever, and Esther began packing her few possessions, to move she knew not where, when Brother Augustine, who had taken the cowl as a Black Friar soon after she married, appeared on her doorstep, two days after the funeral.

'Esther,' he said, 'you are free now. Marry me, I beg you.'

'Brother Augustine,' she answered in exasperation, 'how *could* you imagine you could follow Bishop Andrew?' She ushered him out of the door, and turned back to packing, slowly and with much sidetracking.

But as it turned out, she was not about to move. To her astonishment, her name was on the short list for the next Bishop, and despite a rather nasty and implausible rumour of an affair she was supposed to have had with the Keeper of the Nossex Purse, she was elected.

If only, thought the Keeper of the Nossex Purse, and then rebuked himself.

Seventeen: Noaster to Iddicombe *(6 miles)*

The sky was becoming lighter beyond the marshes as Eva finished her tale. Matthew steered the boat out into the river and Carys and Tabby began the pull upstream.

'Was it normal for Brother Augustine to consider abandoning his vows and getting married?' I asked.

'He wouldn't have been abandoning any vow,' said Eva. 'Nossex friars aren't quite like religious orders Outside. The only lifelong commitments in Nossex are at baptism and marriage. If someone joins the Friars they make a declaration of their commitment, either until further notice, or for a fixed period of time.'

'How long might that be?'

'The fixed periods are usually short; for example, some people join us for their One-in-Twelve, so they'll commit for one month. Quite a few young people sign up as Green Friars for a year at a time.'

'So you're not like the Franciscans Outside?' I asked Tabby.

'No, it's a bit misleading,' she answered. 'We call ourselves Grey Friars because the original ideals of Francis of Assisi are quite close to our way of doing things, but in fact our order in Noaster took something from the traditions of the Hospitallers, before Francis's time, and a little bit from the Celtic monastic tradition, long before that. We've also been influenced by the ideas of the Brethren of the Common Life. The Nossex Black Friars aren't genuine Dominicans, either, it's just a convenient label because they're heavily involved in education.'

'And the White Friars?'

'Again, they wear the colour because they have a lot in common with the Carmelites and the Carthusians, but Pinrose was already a contemplative community long before either of those orders was founded. Anyway, you can be sure no Nossex community would sign up to an order that involved obedience to an authority Outside.'

'Would the current interpretation of the Rule of St Francis constrain you?'

'I'm not sure,' answered Tabby, 'because I haven't studied closely how Franciscans operate Outside these days. But I guess we would find their Rule too rigid, and yet not strict enough. We prefer to be strict, but flexible, focusing on the spirit of the Rule rather than the letter.'

'For example?' I prompted, as the boat swung into the lock, the lower gates still open, and we waited for the other boats to join us.

'Well, we're committed to poverty, as were the Franciscans in the beginning. But they built friaries and churches and collectively received huge amounts of money in endowments and fees. So in practice they were often rich and comfortable, while maintaining a fiction of individual poverty. I'm not commenting on how it is now,' she added hastily, 'because I really don't know. But in Noaster,' she went on, 'there is no Greyfriars building or centre, and individually we're homeless. I don't have even a single room of my own, and I often don't know where I'm going to get my next night's sleep – or day's sleep, if I've been active through the night, as now.'

'That sounds rather scary,' I said.

'It is unbelievably liberating,' she answered with great emphasis. 'You rest totally in the love and care of the Almighty, and you truly feel His arms around you.' I noticed that Carys was listening intently.

'If monastic vows aren't lifelong in Nossex,' I said, 'that puts the resignation of Abbess Tilflæd in a different light.'

'It was her experience that actually focused attention on whether such vows *should* be lifelong,' said Eva. 'That's one reason her Tale is important in Nossex history. It also made us think about the relative importance of motherhood. Of course a mother with young children can still work, and usually does, because in Nossex childcare is shared. But we're reluctant to let a mother with young children take on any heavy *responsibility*, because she would find it difficult to give that responsibility her full attention.'

'Ditto a father of young children,' said Matthew. 'For men, the danger is more that they might focus too much on their responsibility, and forget their children.'

Something else occurred to me, as another boat sculled in alongside us, and the daylight grew.

'How long was Esther Breeze bishop for?' I asked.

'Twenty-one years,' answered Eva. 'She stepped down at the age of eighty, and spent the rest of her life mostly involved in music, encouraging youngsters, especially in composition.'

The other three boats had made their way into the lock, the lower gates were closed, and paddles opened very gently, so that the lock filled as slowly as it had emptied earlier.

'Composition,' I said. That was what I'd heard a few days earlier. 'Was it Esther Breeze that wrote the *Nossex Se'nstep*?'

'Yes, and many other tunes besides. She wrote tunes all her life, from when she was a girl. You might know some of them, if you play English folk music. You know Playford's *English Dancing Master*?'

'Definitely – we play quite a few of those tunes.'

'Well, Esther wrote some of the tunes in the early editions, and Andrew wrote a couple as well. They knew John Playford – London was a much smaller place then. He was collecting dances and the tunes that went with them, and Andrew and Esther used to play for dancing, so they were useful sources for him.'

'Which tunes did she write – and how can you be sure?'

'I don't remember all of the ones that are hers – *Chestnut, Argeers, St Martin's* and *The Slip*, anyway, and Andrew wrote *The Glory of Nossex*, as we call it here; of course, it had to have a different name, so it's *Glory of the North* in the *Dancing Master*.'

'*Chestnut*'s one of our favourites,' I said. 'It's a lovely tune.'

'And as to how do we know, well, Esther's notebooks are in the Blackfriars library, and she kept her own compositions separate from the tunes that she collected.

They're fascinating documents: did you know that *Chestnut* grew out of a street-hawker's cry?'

'No?'

Eva sang softly:

'It was as simple as that,' she said. Esther heard it and noted it down, and then worked it up into a full 24-bar tune, including repeats. It's all there in her notes – if you pass through Pinisk you should ask to see them.'

The lock was almost full, and the paddles were cautiously opened wider to complete the operation. Birdsong filled the air, and there was much fluttering among the trees that fronted and largely hid the walls of Noaster. Away to the east, beyond the marshes, the sky turned a light gold as the sun prepared to show itself.

Having been first in, our boat was first out of the lock, and our two young or youngish oarswomen pulled strongly along the Wall Dyke to the tunnel, which would have been difficult to spot behind trailing willow branches if we hadn't been heading straight in. The rough-hewn walls and roof were picked out in flickering reflected light from the water; the tunnel opening faced due east, and once we were inside, the first beams of the rising sun shone through the green veil of willow leaves, a wonderful sight as I faced backwards from my seat in the bows.

Soon we were disembarking. The wharf was quiet and almost deserted; and Noaster had the feeling of a city asleep. Close by there was evidence of this, for stretched out on the roof of *Esther* was the long figure of Hezekiah Hughes, flat on his back, hands folded over his magnificent waistcoat, which rose and fell as he breathed peacefully. Jack Sprat was curled on his side nearby, his white hair and beard contrasting with the coil of dark rope he was using as a pillow. Further along *Esther*'s roof, John Smith was sleeping on his stomach, head resting on his folded arms, and on the short cabin roof of *Maud* two boys were asleep. It seemed a fair assumption that the berths inside were occupied by the women and girls.

Although the daylight was growing brighter, the sun was still behind the high eastern wall, and the stone cityscape was cool and shady. There were gardens, a few trees and other greenery amid the brown-gold stone, but no bright colours other than a few flowers.

I was struck by how much more attractive an urban scene could be with no garish paintwork, advertising, or yellow lines, no gaudy plastic banners or signs, no TV aerials or satellite dishes, no steel, chrome or concrete. There were trails of smoke coming from various chimneys, and together with the aroma of woodsmoke, I smelt bread baking and something nutty roasting, perhaps, I thought, ingredients for one of the Noaster varieties of coffee.

While Matthew and Eva busied themselves with the boat, Tabby went off on an errand of her own; and so Carys and I had the task of taking the catch to a specific kitchen, a place I hadn't yet patronised. We stacked one basket on the other and each took a rope handle to carry the baskets between us.

'Congratulations, by the way,' I said, 'I should have said earlier.'

'Thank you,' she answered.

'He took you by surprise,' I suggested, as the most discreet way I could think of to ask what on earth had been going on.

'He certainly did, the monkey. I had absolutely no idea.'

'Not even that he might, sometime?' I persisted. 'How long have you been going out together?'

'We haven't been going out together. That was a complete and utter out of nowhere surprise – and he succeeded in his aim – to take me off my guard. It's the most outrageous way of proposing. Don't get the idea this normally happens in Nossex. I don't know how he got the bishop to agree to make the announcement.'

'So have you said yes?'

'Oh, yes – I was tempted to spin it out a bit, leave him in suspense – but time's short; we're both off to start our last Year Out in a couple of days, and then we'll be hundreds of miles away from each other.'

'When did you realise you loved him?' I asked.

'Who said I loved him?' she shot back. 'I haven't promised yet. This time next year I'll promise to love him. So far I've only promised to marry him.'

'I don't understand,' I said. 'You must at least fancy him, and presumably he fancies you.'

'Oh, sure, I guess he does fancy me – that's no big deal, he surely fancies plenty of other girls, and plenty of other men fancy me, even you fancy me…'

'How do you know that?' I squeezed in, but she just rolled her eyes and continued:

'…and I fancy plenty of other men. It's about a lot more than fancying someone.'

'So what is it about?'

'Can we work together as a team; can we serve together; do we have the same attitude. I've known Howell for years, I know his family, he knows mine. Our fathers are friends. By the grace of God, it'll work. He'll do.' She smiled. 'I can handle Howell. We met up in a wrestling match a few years back and I put him on his back twice. Best of three, it was, so he hasn't had the chance to put me down yet.'

'You have cross-gender wrestling?' I asked in disbelief.

'It's not all-in wrestling, it's Nossex wrestling, which has very specific moves and rules, and competition's in narrow weight categories. Men may have a little more upper-body strength, though Nossex girls are strong, and women have a slightly lower centre of gravity. But then of course there are strict rules about where you can't put your hands, and that gives women an advantage, because there's only one small, very small area they can't touch, whereas men have to be much more careful, and the referees watch like hawks.'

'So was he getting a little bit of revenge yesterday?'

'Probably. He'll want more. But I'll be ready for him.'

We came to our destination and delivered the baskets to a couple of very grateful and appreciative cooks. As well as a kitchen, there was an eating area, with tables outside as well as inside. The smell of eggs and bubble and squeak frying made my stomach rumble, and Carys drew a deep anticipatory breath.

'I could go and see if the sleepyhead's woken up yet,' she said with a broad grin, 'but I think breakfast would be a more immediate gratification.'

'May I join you?'

'Of course.'

We were served right away; not so many folk were up and about, and as we found seats outside that gave a view of the quay, Carys explained that the day after a Gathering was always a slower start than a normal Monday. In fact many would take the whole day off from their normal occupations, and the schools would not be functioning.

The rye bread that went with the fried eggs and potatoes was still warm and moist from the bakery, and beautifully crusty. 'Somebody was up and about early,' I commented.

'Well, so were we. The bakers probably took first shift in bed, just as we did. It's one way Noaster copes with the influx.'

The view from our table gave an excellent opportunity to watch the city gradually waking up, as figures began to appear, strolling along the waterfront, often in pairs or groups talking quietly. Scanning the scene, my eye was caught by a wooden sign on a door nearby: Elbow. It seemed an odd name, so I asked Carys: 'Why would a house be called *Elbow*?'

'It'll be the name of what you would call a cell group or house group Outside. Everyone in Noaster worships in the cathedral, but that makes a very big congregation, so they're divided into about fifty *Limbs and Organs*.'

'Oh,' I said. 'So the place I noticed yesterday, that said *Liver*, wasn't a specialist butcher's.'

Carys laughed. 'No. I think the names are a fairly new idea. In the past, the congregation subdivided naturally into the families – extended families, you would call them. But that left out quite a few people, so they reorganised it to include everyone, and someone suggested choosing body parts as names.'

The tables alongside us began to fill up, and as Carys and I finished eating, and moved on to enjoying a particularly nutty type of 'coffee', Howell appeared a little way off, rubbing his eyes and looking around rather hopelessly.

'I'll get him,' I said, suspecting that Carys would have preferred to leave him staring around, just for the amusement of watching him at a loss. I took my coffee with me and after pointing Howell in the right direction, wandered along the wharf to a bench that was catching the early sun, as it rose over the east wall.

The sleepers on the narrowboat roofs had mostly awoken. Beyond the boats, at one of the tables outside the Lazaretto, I saw Hezekiah and John Smith together, the combination that had so worried old Sarah Hughes. Their right hands were clasped across the table, and for a moment, implausibly, I thought they were arm-wrestling. It would have been the most unequal and briefest of contests. Then I realised that in fact they were praying together.

My coffee was soon gone. Missing the caffeine of the Outside brew, I began to feel sleepy, and decided to stretch out on the bench with my hat over my eyes.

****

I was woken by a shadow falling across me, and took the hat off my face to see Ben, the firebrand challenger of the day before, standing over me, with my rucksack in one hand. From how far the sun had climbed, I guessed that I'd slept most of the morning.

'Sorry to disturb your sleep,' he said, 'but I've been asked to guide you to Iddicombe, as I'm heading for home, and I thought you might like some lunch before we go.'

'Good idea,' I said, sitting up, 'and thanks for fetching the rucksack.'

'Martin gave it to me; he got it from the Bishop. Where do you want to have lunch?'

'Ah, sophistication.'

'Sorry?'

'Do you know the *Hitchhiker's Guide to the Galaxy*?'

'No – cool title – is it a film?'

'It was a radio series first, and I thought it was best like that. Anyway, sophistication is the Third Stage of Civilisation. Three stages: how, why, where. Stage One: Survival: How can we eat? Stage Two: Inquiry: Why do we eat? Stage Three: Sophistication: Where shall we have lunch?'

'I like it,' he said. 'That means Noaster is the only sophisticated place in Nossex, because it's the only place where there's any choice. Which places have you tried so far?'

'Tunnel House, Priscilla's, the Palace,' I reeled off, then had to stop and think. 'The Lazaretto, of course, and for breakfast this morning we were at the far end of the quay, over there; we'd just delivered the fish we caught overnight.'

'Marcus's,' Ben identified it for me. 'That's it, you've sampled everywhere in Noaster. And if you delivered fresh fish to Marcus's, most people would recommend going back there; they do brilliant things with fish.'

130

'Most people?'

'Not everyone likes fish, but if you do, that's the place to be today.'

'All right,' I said, 'let's go.'

We walked back along the waterfront and across the square to a table close by where I'd been for breakfast. Carys and Howell were sitting at that same table, and I wondered whether they had been away and come back, or simply sat and talked all morning. I waved to Carys, and Ben gave Howell a smile and a thumbs-up.

'You know Howell?' I asked.

'He's my cousin,' was the answer, and as soon as Ben said that, I saw the likeness, which hadn't been immediately apparent because of Ben's longer hair and sketchier beard.

Rather than going into the kitchen, as Carys and I had done first thing, we sat down and were served by a girl who looked barely twelve, though she proved a very competent waitress. The menu was not extensive; however, the names of the two choices, *Bishop's Rapture* and *Geraint's Special*, meant nothing to me. I looked inquiringly at Ben.

'You just have to try them,' he said unhelpfully. 'The first one is more like a soup, though with a lot of things in it; the second is a bit more solid. Both brilliant.'

I settled for *Bishop's Rapture*, and when it arrived a few moments later it proved well named: a thick broth of fish and mushrooms and all manner of other things cooked in cider. I wondered if Nossexfolk, like hobbits, were addicted to mushrooms; they seemed to feature very often. But of course Nossexfolk used the food available according to the season, so plenty of mushrooms in autumn was hardly surprising. Ben had *Geraint's Special*, and I begged a spoonful in the interests of research, finding it something like a well-spiced kedgeree using potatoes instead of rice, and featuring almonds.

Looking across the table at Ben, I had another paranoid moment. The lad seemed likely to be good stimulating company, but why exactly had I been asked to accompany him, or was it vice versa? Who was taking the decisions? *Yes, yes,* I told myself, *I know God's ultimately in control, but is there some human agent here in Nossex who's pulling the strings?* Maybe getting to know Ben a bit better would clarify the issue, I thought.

'Yesterday,' I said, 'were you just trying to make the Gathering a bit more exciting, or are you really unhappy about how the Council run things?'

'Both, I suppose,' said Ben. 'There's hardly ever any real discussion in the Gathering, and it doesn't change anything. The Council have already decided what's going to happen. Sofa management, they call it Outside – a cosy little huddle with everything stitched up beforehand. The Gathering's just a rubber stamp for the decisions taken by twelve people.'

'And they are…?'

'The Bishop, the Abbess of the Grey Friars, and one other representative from Noaster; and then one each from the other nine communities. The Abbot of the Black

Friars represents Pinisk; the Chief Purser represents Caeriago; the Senior Rabbi represents both Jews and Christians in Pinginna; the Countess represents Chittock; and until yesterday the Abbess of the White Friars represented Pinrose. My grandmother represents Iddicombe; she's head of our family, and the other four communities are also represented by heads of families, so they're pretty ancient too. Nossex is a gerontocracy.'

'What proportion of council is female?' I wondered.

Ben screwed his face up and counted on his fingers. 'Eight out of twelve,' he said. 'A matriarchal gerontocracy. Pinrose might choose a man to even things up a bit, but I wouldn't bet on it.'

'*Do* people bet in Nossex?' I asked innocently.

Ben rose to the bait. 'Of course not,' he said, mimicking extreme disapproval. 'What an idea! Most ungodly and imprudent, if you bet real money, which would be hard to organise anyway.'

He saw my smile, and relaxed. For a few moments we enjoyed Marcus's excellent food in silence.

'The Gathering could reject the recommendations of Council, couldn't it?' I pointed out. 'There were several votes yesterday.'

'But Council only recommend what they know the Gathering will approve,' said Ben impatiently.

'That seems very practical,' I said. 'If every point had been debated from scratch, that Gathering would have taken a week. If Gatherings were long and boring, you might not have a very high attendance, and that leaves the way open for a small minority to hijack the process. You don't know how lucky you are to have a wise Council and a Countess who's a very efficient Chair.'

'Too efficient,' he answered. 'Even when I put my oar in, it didn't hold things up for more than a couple of minutes.'

'Do you *like* chaos and confusion?' I asked.

'Not all the time,' he admitted. 'But now and again it would be stimulating.'

We finished our meals, drained glasses of water, and set off. To me it still felt strange to walk off without paying: the more so here in Noaster where the five eating places seemed more like restaurants than dining halls. We wandered the length of a narrow alleyway, climbed a flight of steps close to the tunnel, then turned left and went through an iron gate in the city wall. The gate had a simple latch with no sign of any way in which it could be locked.

Beyond the wall, a path led a short distance up to the ridge on which the east wall stood: a ridge that curved round to join a spur of the hill on the far side of which was Caeriago. Trees grew on the outer side of the ridge, blotting out any view of the East Marshes where I'd been fishing in the small hours. Equally we, or anyone else walking this path, would not be visible from Outside.

As we followed the path round near the crown of the ridge, we came to a narrow saddle with views on both sides. To the left, southwards and below, were the orchards and walled gardens on the level ground outside Noaster. On the right, northwards, we looked down on a strip of cultivated land stretching away into the distance, with the hill on one side and a line of trees on the other that I guessed marked the course of the Wall Dyke.

Immediately below us on this side was a cluster of pools from which arose a characteristic aroma, explained at once by Ben, though I'd already taken a guess.

'That's where Noaster's shit ends up,' he said bluntly. 'There's a hydraulic ram to help pump it through from the city. In the days of the Romans, it went through the tunnel and into the river, but we can't do that now. The pools move every now and again, to give stuff time to rot down.'

We came to a junction of paths. Ben explained that straight on would take us to Caeriago; in fact the top of the tower was just visible over the brow through the trees. We forked right and headed off towards Iddicombe along a track that ran through forest for part of the way. The day was warm, and carrying a rucksack, albeit not a heavy one, I was glad to be in the shade rather than in direct sunshine. Butterflies were numerous, mostly Speckled Woods, with here and there a Comma or Red Admiral. Small birds twittered and cheeped amid the cooing of wood pigeons, and I heard the occasional squawk of a jay. Grey squirrels ran to and fro in the canopy, proving that the Nossex defences had not been of any use in protecting the red.

'Are you active in politics Outside?' asked Ben.

'Not really,' I said. 'I vote, but I'm not an activist or a member of any party. I don't really like any of the available options.'

'At least you've got democracy.'

'Don't you think you have democracy in Nossex?' I asked.

'What do you think?' Ben's intonation said clearly that he didn't think so.

'You get a lot nearer than we do Outside,' I said. 'Did you vote for your representative?'

'Well, yes,' he admitted. 'I voted for Gran; I know she'll do a good job. I don't have a problem with *her*, I just think Council ought to be less of a closed shop.'

'So,' I said, 'you were able to vote for someone you know well and trust completely, right? And in Iddicombe everyone knows everyone, yes?'

'Yes, but...'

'So out of the whole community people were able to choose the best person for the responsibility. But I won't have that option next May. I'll have a choice between five people I don't know, except for their biased self-presentation in party literature. Four of them are standing for parties I wouldn't vote for under any circumstances. The fifth is a young woman I know nothing about, so I'll be taking a chance if I vote for her, except that she won't get in anyway.'

Ben looked at me a little nervously, less of an angry young man now that he was listening to a grumpy old man. We were crossing a clearing ringed by tall beeches, and in the pause in our conversation the forceful song of a wren sounded across the space.

'Sorry,' I said, 'you got me started. We have this much in common, that we don't like the status quo we're living in. I haven't lived a single day of my life under a Prime Minister I voted for, and I was fifty-five before I had an MP I'd actually voted for, and now I know that *he's* not to be trusted. Where's my democracy? And what's wrong with yours, apart from the average age of Council?'

'Well,' said Ben, 'they're all Christians, apart from the Senior Rabbi, so atheists, or people who just have doubts, aren't represented. There's no place for radical ideas.'

'It seems pretty radical to me, coming from Outside,' I objected.

'No, it's reactionary, going back to a subsistence economy that in some ways hasn't changed since before Quintus of Cyrene.'

'Why should it change, if people are well fed and housed and happy?'

'There's more to life than that, isn't there?'

I had to admit that there was, but said that I didn't think we had any more of life's positive aspects Outside than could be found here in Nossex. This didn't end the argument, as far as Ben was concerned, and he kept it going until the thatched roofs of Iddicombe appeared as the path ran out from under the trees.

It was a picturesque village, with cottages on either slope of a steep little valley. There was an old-fashioned rural aroma about the place, compounded of sheep, sawn wood, and other elements that I couldn't identify, together making up a pleasant but fairly powerful smell. We found ourselves at the head of the valley, with a tumbling stream descending in between the two rows of cottages, and up here by the spring, a larger building that turned out to be the usual hall and kitchen. Ben took me a little way down, to a cottage where he introduced me to his grandmother Cara, a woman in her eighties, I guessed, clearly still active and alert.

'If you're just stopping one night,' she said, 'you can have Howell's bed; he's staying another night in Noaster.' She saw me settled, then left me some time to myself, for which I was grateful, taking the chance to write up some notes for this book.

At the evening meal, I saw that others, like me, were passing through: Countess Mary and Abbot Peter, both of whom I knew lived elsewhere, joined us at one of the tables. It occurred to me that although it now seemed natural to think of the Countess as Mary, and the Bishop as Matthew, I still thought of Peter as The Abbot. It must have been something to do with his air of authority; he was a very abbotty Abbot, clad all in severe black. He tucked into the wholemeal bread and big bowl of stew with gusto; it was a typical Nossex meal in being frugal in concept, but ample in quantity and tasty in execution, quite distinct in flavour from the other stews, broths, and soups I'd already enjoyed.

Afterwards I managed to get involved in the washing up, and as I was finishing, heard the sounds of music beginning: another session, it seemed. Ben, who had temporarily shed his rebellious persona to rinse dishes, explained that in Iddicombe the music was normally on Fridays; this was an extra session for the day after a Gathering, which often merited a celebration.

One jolly and rather simple tune was whistle-friendly and easily picked up, so I asked its name and was tickled by the title: *The Capering Abbot*. This abbot didn't seem very likely to caper, so it must have been named for one of his predecessors.

After a few tunes, there was a pause for mugs to be replenished, and I took the chance to join some of those who had been listening rather than playing. The Countess and the Abbot were sitting with young Ben.

'They've found you somewhere to sleep?' asked Mary.

'Yes, thanks,' I said. 'I'm being very well looked after; I think I was expected.'

'You may not have noticed,' said Ben, 'but you've been watched from the moment you set foot in Nossex. This place is bloody paranoid, they see every stranger as a potential infiltrator, every citizen as a possible traitor.'

'I certainly had noticed,' I admitted, 'and it bothered me a bit at first. But in the circumstances I think it's reasonable. The secrecy of Nossex is precarious, and you need to be cautious. A travel writer like me could have been a big risk, in fact, I still could, I'll have to be very careful with the book and I'm grateful to you for trusting me.'

'I'm being watched too,' he said, sounding half proud and half angry. 'Just because I disagree with the ultra-pacifism, and I don't buy the whole Christian mumbo-jumbo, they think I might betray everything.'

'How might you do that, Ben?' asked the Abbot with a smile.

'Sell the Caeriago valley to a golf course developer. Blow the whistle on the Nossex Purse's lack of transparency to the financial regulator. Apply to English Heritage to have the walls of Noaster listed. Complain to a mobile phone operator about the lack of a signal in Pinrose. Write to the *Daily Mail* about the imposition of communism on an unwilling peasantry.'

'Unwilling?' I queried.

'Not to mention the brainwashing and indoctrination,' he added. 'Of course these are all decoys – I'm not telling you my real plans for sabotage.'

The Abbot was chuckling. 'Our indoctrination hasn't worked very well on you, has it? Nor the brainwashing. We'll have to put your brain back in the sink and give it an extra scrub.'

Ben scowled, but there was a smile in his eyes.

'You don't seem very worried,' I said to the Abbot, 'but surely there is a risk. There must be hundreds of ways Nossex could be discovered.'

135

'But it is discovered,' put in Mary. 'All the time. You discovered it. There are thousands, maybe tens of thousands of people Outside who know about it. Most of them we would count as Friends of Nossex: people who were born here, relatives, visitors who like the place, and all of these will respect our security. But there are some who grow up here and decide they don't really like it or agree with it, and they normally stay away after their Years Out, though some leave later. Any of them could give us away, but they don't.'

'How come?' I asked.

'It *is* brainwashing,' insisted Ben. 'Even if you hate the place, you can't help loving it. I've got all sorts of plans to shake Nossex up a bit, but once I leave here I'll probably miss it, and feel sorry for it. Betraying Nossex would be like stabbing a baby.'

The Abbot winced.

'That might be *part* of an answer,' said Mary. 'Even people who don't agree with the principles Nossex rests on might see that it's unique and valuable and should have the right to continue to exist. But humanly speaking, there's no rational way to explain how it's stayed secret for one thousand six hundred and seven years. It has to be the power of prayer and the sovereign will of God.'

Ben snorted. 'That's two different things.'

'If you don't believe God exists,' said the Abbot, 'then it's only one thing – prayer – and you have to find some other supernatural explanation for its effectiveness. But for Christians, if it's God's sovereign will that Nossex be preserved, then He moves people to pray for that to happen. His strength is made perfect through our weakness.'

'I sensed the prayer as soon as I set foot in Nossex,' I said. 'But you quoted a very exact number of years just now. How can you be so precise?'

'You haven't heard the Tale of Gaius the Youngest and the Breaking of the Bridge?' asked Mary, and as I shook my head, she went on: 'Then I'll tell it.'

Gaius the Youngest

136

Eighteen: The Tale of Gaius the Youngest

You have been a refuge for the poor, a refuge for the needy in his distress. Is 25:4

Gaius the Youngest was the son of Gaius the Younger, and the grandson of Gaius the Elder, the builder of Pinrose. It amused people to continue calling him Gaius the Youngest (*Gaius junissimus* – which was actually bad Latin, but that was part of the joke), even when he was over eighty years old, and it was not until he was at that advanced age that anything out of the ordinary is remembered of what he said or did.

In the year 407, the very last Roman troops and administrators left Noaster, which might have seemed a small change, since for many years it had been a minimal token presence, outnumbered by the retired Romans and their descendants, who had in any case become 'Nemetised'. More serious was that simultaneously, significant garrisons were withdrawn from all Roman forts and towns that Noaster had any sort of contact with. Some said all troops were being withdrawn from all Britain.

Many Nemetians saw no problem with this, but the older folk remembered the great Saxon raid of 367, and were apprehensive. A word from the Lord came to Gaius the Youngest, and he prophesied:

> *Remove the stones of your pride from over the water, and block up the gate of your city. Show a blank wall to the evil that will come; shut out the pillagers, the rapists and the murderers, and keep open only the secret ways that God will allow the hunted and the helpless to find.*

This was in the midst of an Autumn Gathering, and the matter was debated then and there. The bridge was indeed the pride of Noaster, a broad, solid and handsome three-arched stone bridge that was simple and elegant, yet looked good for centuries to come, if not millennia. To a number of speakers it seemed criminal to dismantle something so fine. On crossing the river the road led immediately through a splendid gateway in the curtain wall of the little city, and some were equally unhappy at the idea of blocking up this gateway, as Gaius the Youngest's prophecy seemed to dictate.

Debate flowed back and forth, with the more confident younger folk reluctant to take the prophecy seriously, while the older and more learned were ready to err on the side of caution, if need be.

'The Roman Peace is over,' said one. 'We need to look back at how Nemet preserved itself in the days of tribal warfare – by secrecy and discretion.' Others, learned folk who had read the old records, described how Nemet had once been hedged and fenced and hidden from the outside world.

'Supposing the evil prophesied does not come about?' said Gaius' wife Priscilla. 'We can always rebuild the bridge. It might be a lot of hard work, but that would be much easier than rebuilding the whole of Noaster if the evil days *do* come. If any of us survive to do the rebuilding, that is. The loss of a bridge is a little thing compared to the loss of all Nemet, the loss of peace and freedom.'

Last of all, one of the handful of Saxons that had already settled in Nemet spoke up, haltingly, for his Nemsh was very basic.

'My people say,' he began, 'no... one man tell me... war leaders hear that Romans go back Rome. Big war group come next year, in spring, take land, take cattle, take women. I tell you this because – you not fight our people – you hide. No problem. We hide with you. We like peace too.'

'Do we need more arguing?' said Priscilla. 'Start planning!'

The Gathering was swiftly concluded, and the builders and architects put their heads together. Early the next day a start was made, and leaders organised teams in different places so that the great number of workers did not hinder each other.

First, before the bridge became impassable, teams crossed it and dug up the approach road on the far side of the river, outside Nemet. Not only did they dig up the road, but also much of the low-lying meadow either side of it, taking away the topsoil for use back in Nemet, and lowering the level and cutting channels so that south of Noaster, beyond the river, was on the way to become marshland, just as the area east of Noaster, over the hill and beyond the Wall Dyke, had always been.

Long before this task was finished, the first arch of the bridge was gone, and thereafter boatloads of soil were transported by water; channels were deepened, ensuring in the process that the river would not be fordable, and clumps of reeds and sedges were transplanted from the eastern marshes, to give the new marsh a start.

Meanwhile, much of the stone that was disappearing from the bridge was being used to rebuild the wall. At the suggestion of Gaius the Youngest, rather than merely blocking up the gateway, the towers either side and part of the wall for several yards beyond were all dismantled carefully, and the whole rebuilt with stone selected for a random variety of shades, so that there was no sign in the plain brown wall that a gate had ever been there. When all was done, as done it was before the worst of winter had yet begun, skilled gardeners planted the bare earth outside with all manner of grass, weeds, herbs, shrubs, anything that would grow quickly when the spring came.

Inside the wall, there was a certain amount of stone left over, including blocks specially shaped for the arches. These were used for footbridges over the Water of Noaster, which are there to this day, though of course there has been some repair, and they are probably not in their original fifth century condition, any more than the city wall is.

The following spring, all signs of the works that had been undertaken quickly greened over; wildfowl in abundance began to colonise the new marshland, as did eels and fish in plenty. It was commented that the loss of a bridge would be compensated by good food for many a day.

The day came when, beyond the new marshes, the sun glinted on the weapons and helmets of the feared Saxon warriors, who stood and seemed to be calculating whether this fortified place would be worth attacking. In Noaster the word went round to keep strict silence and to watch without showing oneself.

One young man, however, Rees by name, had planned a more active response. It may be that several had secretly put their ideas together, for the woodworking apprentices had for some time past been constructing a full-size Roman ballista, and this was now completed, though as yet untested. It was given out that this was purely a joinery and engineering challenge, a fun exercise for learning purposes, and the Nemetians were so far from aggressive thinking that this explanation was accepted.

That night the watch-fires in the Saxon camp glowed ominously, but Rees went to a place where he knew of a large wasps' nest, and succeeded in detaching it from the branch on which it hung, and enclosing it securely in a box of thin wood, at the cost to himself, he said later, of only three stings.

At first light the wasp-filled box was placed on the slide, the tension wound back, a prayer offered that the Saxons would depart without a fight, and the ballista finally fired. One observer reported a flash from one of the watch-fires, and faint sounds of commotion were heard across the new marshes.

The cautious older folk, when they learned what was done, were not pleased, and strong words were spoken in stage whispers. But by the following day there was no doubt that the Saxon warrior band had gone, the fires left to burn out.

Only some years later, from a refugee that came in through one of the hidden entrances, did the Nemetians hear the end of the story from the Saxon angle. The box of wasps had indeed landed in a fire and burst, scattering sparks and angry wasps in all directions. When the well-stung men had retreated in disorder and regathered at a safe distance, several voices reported what had happened: the silent fortress had somehow thrown a wasps' nest at them.

'I suppose it'll be a nest of adders next,' commented someone, which was just a poor attempt at dark humour; but it so happened that the leader of the band had a particular horror of snakes, and he at once gave the order to move on, away from this accursed place. And so the prophecy of Gaius the Youngest, and the ingenuity of Rees, preserved the integrity and peace of Nemet, as well as giving birth to the New Marshes.

Nineteen: Overnight in Iddicombe; walk to Pinisk via North Wharf *(8 miles)*

'A great story,' I said. 'So they all lived happily ever after.'

'Not all,' put in the Abbot. 'Up to that point, during the time of the Romans, Nemet had been quite open; people traded, there were shops, of a sort; Roman money circulated. When the bridge was removed and the wall closed, those whose main occupation was trading lost their livelihood, and their money quickly became useless. One or two left almost immediately, to set up in business Outside.'

'Is that when the concept *Outside* began?' I asked. 'It seems a very powerful image in Nossex.'

'Possibly,' answered Mary. 'Though the Nemsh word *hibith* is quite distinct from the words for *outside* in the other Brythonic languages, and it's possible that before the Romans ever came, when the Nemetians very much kept themselves to themselves, it was already a loaded word.'

'Anyway,' the Abbot went on, 'not all the traders left, and within the church it was suggested that their redundant money should be held in common for the benefit of Nemet in general. Most of the remaining folk that had significant amounts of cash agreed, and the money went into the church treasury, which already had a healthy balance. There was some debate as to what to do with it all; some argued for a separate church building, that need not double up as a general purposes space and dining hall.

'Before any action could be taken on this, the problem was solved by a certain Marcus the Vintner, who departed secretly one foggy night taking with him all the gold and silver, leaving only the copper coins of more weight than value. Some were angry, but many were relieved, and Gaius the Youngest said: *Mammon has left us, taking with him the chains that would have weighed us down, and that will be his destruction. The base metal remaining is better as playthings for children than as treasure for grown men and women.*'

'What happened to Marcus the Vintner?' I asked.

'He was robbed and murdered in Leicester, within a fortnight – and his murderers probably didn't live long to enjoy the money either, because the Saxons sacked the place soon after. Meanwhile Nemet settled down to be a cashless society, with the coppers circulating as rewards and pocket money for children, as they do to this day.'

Someone on the edge of the group held up a coin, and it was passed for me to see. Amongst other letters I distinguished the word Constantius.

'Constantius II,' explained the Abbot. 'Mid-4th century. Of course that's very unlikely to be a Roman original. Parents used them as rewards for children, who used them to buy treats or exchanged them among themselves, and in time most of them were worn smooth. The coppersmiths found a few good-quality

140

examples that had been kept as souvenirs, made dies, melted down the worst of the old coins, added some scrap metal, and minted new coins in the resulting alloy. By now that's been done many times.'

'When I was a boy,' I said, 'I had a penny that was a hundred years old, and it was worn almost unreadable. So I guess that's about the limit for a coin in constant circulation.'

'Yes. On the other hand, a coin that's kept safe somewhere, and handed down from grandparent to grandchild, say, doesn't wear at all. So in theory this could be Roman, or a thousand years old, or only fifty years old.'

'And what's this worth in Sterling?' I asked, handing it back.

'Nothing. Nossex Brass isn't convertible. Outside money doesn't buy anything here, and Nossex Brass buys nothing Outside – unless you could convince a coin-collector that it was genuine Roman, which you shouldn't, because you don't know that.'

Someone beyond our table decided it was time for another tune, and led off a Se'nstep; by now I was recognising the shape. It sounded not too difficult, so I hastened to rejoin the session.

Thatcher's Se'nstep

After another half-hour of music, a couple of youngsters brought out trays of coffee and current buns, which turned out to mark the end of the session, though the musicians remained in place, and some of them played for the short time of evening worship that followed the coffee break. It seemed a little strange to have coffee so late on, until I remembered that Iddicombe's version of coffee substitute, which was quite delicately flavoured with something aniseedy (probably fennel, I guessed), would be as caffeine-free as all the others.

The worship was followed by a time of prayer that was largely focused on Outside: missionary families in Africa and South America, and someone in full-time ministry in Yorkshire, all relatives of Iddicombe families; and several young people prayed for people and situations they had met on their Years Out. I commented on this to Cara, on my way to bed, and she said her late husband had made a particular effort to counterbalance the natural Nossex tendency to turn inwards.

'My Howell was a bit of a dissident in his younger days,' she said, 'just like young Ben. But he was a believer, which Ben isn't yet, so his subversiveness was aimed in a much more positive direction.'

'Do you worry about Ben?' I asked.

'Sometimes, of course. He says some dreadful things sometimes. But when I pray for him, I feel an assurance that in time, he'll find the true path.'

Tuesday 30th September 2014

Breakfast the next morning was substantial, with second helpings of scrambled eggs and fried potatoes, and then I managed to get involved in some sweeping and cleaning tasks that reminded me rather of youth hostel duties decades before, followed by a stint turning a mangle (which took me back well over fifty years) before hanging piles of washing out. By the time I was settling the rucksack on my shoulders, ready to walk the shortish distance to Pinisk, I felt I had done my bit for the morning.

The Abbot was setting off too. 'If you're going to Pinisk,' he said, 'would you like to join me on the scenic route? I'm going the long way via North Wharf; I need the exercise, and it would give you a chance to see a bit more of East Nossex. It would mean missing lunch, though, which would be good for me, but you don't look as though you're carrying the excess weight that I am.'

'I had an excellent breakfast,' I said. 'A short fast would do me no harm at all.' I wondered if I was being as truthful as I should.

'I don't want to get back to the school too early,' he explained, as we set off. 'I've no teaching to do today, nothing until the Inquisition. The staff always cope very well if I'm not there, in fact I think they do a better job if I'm not looking over their shoulder.'

'That's funny,' I said, 'Uncle Joe said much the same thing. Is that a Nossex tradition, hands-off leadership?'

'Perhaps. We don't want to interfere with the work motivation. People work so much better if they're pulled along by enjoyment or even love of the task, rather than driven by anxiety or fear. If you're happy in your work you're not wasting any nervous energy on anything other than the job in hand, so you can achieve more. I like to see what the staff and students are doing – it's often really inspiring. But it's best if I wait to be asked for advice or invited to see something.'

'How far back does this enjoyment of work go?' I asked. 'Martin thought it might be pre-Christian, pre-Roman, but he didn't know.'

'It seems likely, but it's hard to be sure. There are pre-Roman writings in the archives, or at least early copies of such materials, but they're in Old Nemsh, and we're guessing at some of the more obscure vocabulary. Even the words that are identical in modern Nemsh probably had subtly different meanings in those days. But there are indications that a couple of hundred years before the Romans came, the Nemetians had a really horrible experience.

'It seems there was a pitched battle, with large numbers killed. From the wording it's not quite clear, but apparently Nemet *won* the battle, virtually wiped out the opposition, and yet the victors were traumatised and full of guilt, and there was a reaction of *never again*.

142

'The principle of non-violence stems from this event, and the honouring of hard work and co-operation is tied up with it: any aggression is channelled into the energy that flows into fulfilling the task in hand.'

'That makes sense,' I said. 'It's difficult to feel aggressive if you're totally absorbed in an activity you enjoy.'

'Unless it's an inherently aggressive activity. We don't pursue many of those in Nossex.'

The path the Abbot had chosen led away from the top end of the steep lines of cottages, curving westwards past a small tarn that I guessed would be Iddicombe's water supply. Swifts were scything to and fro through the air above the water. Beyond that, we were out on the open hilltop, with good views around the interior of East Nossex. Behind us, when I looked back, I could see the Purse Tower a few miles off; and in the other direction away to the left were the buildings of the Blackfriars School, sloping brown stone quadrangles on the hillside above a lake, and the cottages of Pinisk clustering closely round the school.

One track led round the hillside directly to Pinisk, but we took another path, north-westwards over the hill, passing a flock of sheep that were being observed by a sturdy girl in her early teens. She gave the Abbot a smile and a wave of her shepherd's crook. He waved back, then paused to pat the brown collie dog that had trotted over for a more tactile greeting.

'Total devotion,' he commented. 'I think God gave us dogs to show us how to love Him.'

'And cats to show us how He loves us,' I said. 'We have a cat who's a lazy useless nuisance, but somehow we still love her.'

'If you say so. I'm a dog person myself. But then the Pinisk cats are working rat-catchers, rather than pets. We respect them if they do their job.'

'Were those Pinisk sheep?' I asked, as we walked on, crossing the crown of the ridge diagonally. Two skylarks were singing, black dots in a blue sky.

'No, they're from Iddicombe, but the girl is one of my pupils. Some of the children work elsewhere on certain days, and come into school on the other days.'

'Yes,' I said. 'Guy told me about that; he's splitting his time between being a Purser and a schoolboy.'

'Right. But some other children split the day, because we have the farm, the dairy, the tannery, the vet's, the printing press, and other workshops, and so some children will do two or three hours' work and two or three hours' school, on a daily basis. Children assigned to the farm normally stay with that through their school years, and each of the beasts will have two children assigned specifically to them. Cows like to know the person milking them; they yield much better that way, and they need milking seven days a week, of course, which is why there are two children to share the responsibility.'

'Timetabling must be a bit of a nightmare,' I suggested.

143

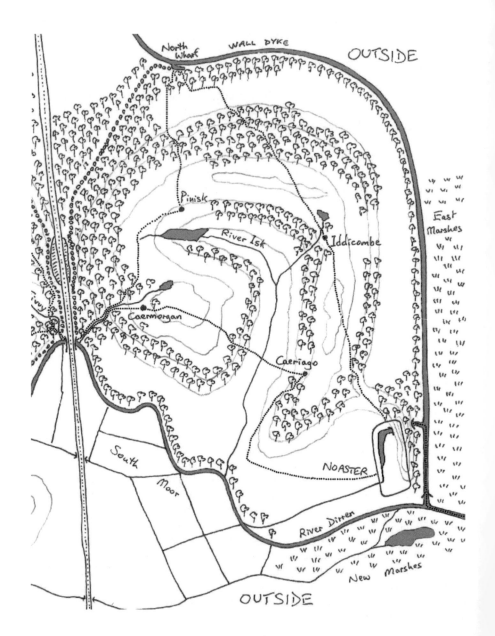

Map of East Nossex with route walked

'A beautifully realistic and challenging task for one of the older student groups. We include it in a course that includes maths, finance, and social psychology: a good preliminary to studying management Outside, should anyone wish to do so.'

On the far side of the ridge, the path slanted down into woodland: tall pines at first, with relatively little underbrush, and good views for some distance on either side. The Abbot began to look about in a more searching way, and soon he turned aside to collect a good crop of cep mushrooms. I helped him in the gathering, checking with him the identity of all my specimens, and commenting on Carys' keenness in gathering fungi.

'She's one of the best students I've had in that field,' he said. 'Intensely curious, wanted to know the name and use for every growing thing. And because she was so keenly interested, she remembered everything. Comenius puts it very well; I've quoted this so often I know it by heart: ...*if a man be hungry, he is eager to take food, digests it readily, and easily converts it into flesh and blood. Thus Isocrates says: "He who is anxious to learn will also be learned." And Quintilian says: "The acquisition of knowledge depends on the will to learn, and this cannot be forced."*[1]'

'Yes,' I agreed. 'I've seen that again and again in language teaching. Motivation is everything, and it has to come from inside the learner. You can engineer a degree of motivation from outside, but it's not as effective, or as long-lasting.'

As well as mushrooms, we found elderberries and rowan berries, and had filled a few bags and containers by the time we came out of the woodland onto level fields that stretched away on our right in a great curve. Here and there groups of workers could be seen engaged in various harvesting tasks.

Straight ahead, the flat cultivated land was perhaps half a mile wide between the woodland we had emerged from, and the long line of trees that marked the course of the Wall Dyke. We made our way directly across, with a break half way to spend twenty minutes helping folk to lift potatoes. The abbot also left the bag of rowan berries with those workers, who promised to deliver them to the Lazaretto in Noaster. I wondered if the Abbot was a particular friend of the formidable woman in charge there.

I was glad to straighten my back when we moved on to the Wall Dyke, where the near bank was crowned with a narrow strip of trees perhaps twenty yards wide, dense enough to prevent any clear view into Nossex. From between the trees there was a fine view of Outside lands northwards, with the deserted Wall Dyke bending round and stretching off into the far distance. On either side of the canal were flat meadows, one or two stocked with black and white cattle.

Away to the left could be seen the line of the dual carriageway, with the tops of the lorries that were droning northwards and southwards visible above green hedges. To the right I could see the near side of the canal, not only lined with trees, but also fringed with reeds that made it impossible for any boat to get close enough to the Nossex bank to moor.

[1] Comenius, JA (1638) *Didactica Magna*

145

But just below us was the exception: a short wharf of two boat lengths, construct-ed in stout timber that looked relatively new. Dense reeds screened this wharf from the canal, and it looked as though there was a narrow channel with an oblique approach that would be difficult for Outside canal cruisers to spot if they didn't know it was there.

Now there was nothing to see. The Abbot explained that the Sprat Collective put in here if they were simply loading or unloading, and not stopping in Nossex.

'That's where mobile phones come in handy,' he said. 'They can tell us their time of arrival pretty accurately, so we can meet them with anything we want them to take away, and collect what they're bringing, without wasting any time at all.'

He turned aside to a massive rampart of brambles that bore a heavy crop of blackberries, and we spent an hour or more filling some of the many bags and containers the Abbot kept producing from the one bag he had been carrying when we left Iddicombe. Eating a small percentage of the biggest and juiciest helped to keep thirst at bay, though they did little to stop my stomach telling me it was high time for lunch.

We didn't only collect blackberries. The Abbot pointed out and gathered a selection of herbs and leaves, naming every plant and commenting on their properties and uses. I recalled and quoted Carys' comment *They teach us useful things here*, and complimented him on his knowledge.

'The human brain,' he answered, 'has a colossal capacity for information. Outside, it's quite often useless information, but in Nossex we like to remember more of the helpful stuff.'

Laden with bags, some of which were now dangling from my rucksack, we made our way back across the fields at a different angle, towards the early afternoon sun. It made walking warmish work, though the autumn air didn't have the heat of high summer; the light rain late the previous evening had freshened things up.

Re-entering woodland, the path began to climb again through mature beech-woods, and then through birch and pine. I was impressed by the size of a couple of wood ant nests, and noticed a few of those large ants crossing the path. On one tall pine, I saw a tree-creeper probing the deep fissures in the bark; and high in another I thought I saw a spotted woodpecker.

As the path steepened, and mercifully the Abbot slackened his pace a little, I took the chance to ask what he thought of Carys' betrothal.

'What was unusual about it,' answered the Abbot, 'was that he took her by surprise. Not easy to knock Carys out of her stride – a very confident young woman – and I noticed she was only disconcerted for a few seconds, even so.'

'Yes,' I said, 'she seemed to accept the situation very quickly. I asked her about it; I thought maybe she suddenly realised she loved him, but no, she said she didn't love him – yet.'

'Marriage, in Nossex,' said the Abbot, 'is not usually a response to romantic love, though that love may well exist by the time the marriage takes place.'

'So marriages here are arranged?'

'Not at all. We found long ago that too many failures – or shall we say less successful marriages – resulted from the older generation's over-estimation of their own wisdom. No, the youngsters make their own choices, but not, or not usually, based on falling in love.'

'That would seem very strange Outside,' I said, watching two Speckled Wood butterflies spiralling upwards towards the high canopy.

'No doubt. But the whole glorification of romantic love – the idea that it is irresistible, and that if fulfilled it leads to perfect happiness – never really caught on in Nossex. You studied English, you said.'

'Yes,' I admitted.

'So you've read CS Lewis' *Allegory of Love.*'

'Certainly.'

'You must know, then, that that whole Romantic Love paradigm only arose in Western Europe in the eleventh century, more specifically in France. It never really touched Nossex, because there was so little Norman or Angevin influence.'

'What about Alain FisBos?'

'He was Breton, and took a lot of trouble to keep the Normans out of Nossex.'

'So what motivates Nossexfolk to get married?' I persisted.

'Well, to put it bluntly,' said the Abbot, 'biological urges. Outside, people are often motivated by loneliness, but there's very little loneliness in Nossex. No, if people here feel they must marry, it's because they don't feel called to celibacy.'

'Does there have to be a call?' I wondered.

'*All* Christians,' said the Abbot firmly, 'in Nossex or Outside, are called to one of two states. If you're not called to matrimony, you're called to celibacy. If you're not called to celibacy, you're called to matrimony. And therefore, if you're certain of a call to matrimony, you need to organise yourself a spouse.'

'And on what basis do people choose, if not on love?'

'Whether you think you can serve God better together, as a team, than you can separately. Equally, the only justification for celibacy is if you can serve God better that way.'

'Though celibacy is the default situation,' I pointed out, 'because Christians have to remain celibate unless and until they are married.'

'Yes. In that situation, if someone is unwillingly celibate, it may be God's decision that they can serve Him better in that state, for the time being, even if they might not think so. That calls for great patience – have you heard the Tale of Esther Forester?'

'I have, yes, though why she had to wait so long, I'm not sure.'

'Well, in her case, there was great love, grounded in compassion, and she was prepared – even if it was very hard – to play the role of sister and friend until Andrew was ready to marry.'

The path was still fairly steep, and doubled back on itself a couple of times to

147

negotiate the steepest and shadiest part of the slope; hartstongue ferns and soft green moss grew in abundance. I wondered if the Abbot's own celibacy had been, or still was, unwilling, but decided I couldn't ask that directly.

'Do you enforce celibacy for the unmarried youngsters?' I asked instead.

'There's no force involved. We strongly *recommend* celibacy before marriage to Christian young people, but to the minority that are avowedly not Christian, we can only point out the issues and possible consequences of their choices. Actually the peer group has far more effect on people's behaviour than anything the older generation might say. Among the committed Christians there's a culture of caution in personal relationships, especially before the Years Out.'

'And do they usually get together with someone from a different community?' I asked. 'I've read that in the kibbutzes, the kids that are raised together look on each other more as siblings, and a kind of incest taboo operates.'

'It's not invariable,' the Abbot answered, 'but you do see that pattern. In any case, the majority of the children in any one community probably *are* related: first, second, third or fourth cousins. In most cases that wouldn't rule out marriage, but perhaps it contributes to looking a little further afield for a partner.

'On the other hand,' he went on, 'where there's a culture there may be a minority counter-culture. One young couple at the top end of the school are exceptions in almost every respect you can think of. They grew up together, and they're second cousins, but they're *an item*, as one calls it these days. They're not believers, and they are in a full sexual relationship. I know that not because I've been spying on them, but because a member of staff is ensuring a reliable supply of contraceptives. We don't approve, but with those two any strong expression of disapproval would only drive them to further rebellion, so we choose to be realistic, treat them as young adults, which they almost are, and agree to differ on the moral issue. At least they're devoted to each other, in their own counter-cultural style.'

'Would you agree with what Paul wrote to the Corinthians, that it's better to remain single?'

'As I said, some are called to one state, some to the other. If someone marries just because all their friends have married, so it seems the thing to do, then they're not really following a call. If someone pursues a single life because they think they will earn greater merit thereby, that's not a true calling either. The thing is to find out what is God's will for *you*. I don't recommend lifelong singleness to anyone explicitly, but I hope my being content to remain single might reassure someone who is uncertain whether they will be able to accept permanent singleness.

'I share my own story with anyone who might be helped by it,' he added. 'During my Years Out I met a wonderful Christian woman who would have made an excellent wife. She liked me too; we were very close friends. But I detested life Outside. So much aggression, selfishness, competition and hostility. I couldn't wait to finish my Years Out and come back. She was very involved in the church in her home town, and wanted to stay there. She didn't mind the noise, or the litter, or the

148

ugliness; she was happy to live in an environment of waste and excess, driven by money and advertising. Boasting, we call it in Nossex. She visited Nossex once, and said it was *nice and primitive*, which actually meant that she found it distressingly uncivilised, unsophisticated, and uncomfortable. I could see she wouldn't want to settle here, so I broke off the relationship to see if I could live without her. And I found I could, which told me that singleness was probably the right path for me.'

'And how did she feel?' I couldn't help asking.

'She was sad,' the Abbot conceded. 'But she soon found someone else, and she's still there, a key member of that same church. We're still in touch. We pray for each other's work.'

To my relief, the path became less steep as we came out of the woods onto the long curving ridge that we had already crossed much earlier. Here there was a scattering of cattle grazing on the rough moorland vegetation. Another skylark sang somewhere high overhead, lost in a blue sky streaked with wispy clouds.

Once we reached the far side of the ridge, Pinisk appeared below us, old honey-coloured stone buildings on the hillside, and beyond and below that, a good-sized lake or reservoir near the head of the valley. As we descended and came closer, a crowd of folk emerged from various doors, among them some black-clad figures who were presumably the friars, and a babble of voices arose. Clearly the Abbot had carefully timed his arrival for an afternoon break or perhaps the end of formal lessons.

A couple of young lads came towards us and offered to take the Abbot's gathered foodstuffs to the kitchens.

'I'm going there myself,' he said, 'but you can help carry.' He detached the bags that were hanging from various corners of my rucksack, and then extricated some containers from inside, reducing the weight on my shoulders considerably.

Martin was approaching, together with a tall, thin, and fit-looking woman that he introduced as his wife Lydia. They took on the task of showing me round the school and ancillary buildings, starting with a spartan dormitory where I was able to dump the rucksack before enjoying an unencumbered stroll up and down staircases and across steep grassy quadrangles. The buildings were ranged on a fairly steep hillside, so that two sides of each quad had roofs that stepped downwards, while the upper horizontal side had a view over the top of the lower, down to the lake and the Isk valley.

Outside the school quadrangles were farm buildings, a dairy, a tannery, and other sources of a rich variety of powerful aromas, some pleasant, and others less so. By the time I'd had the full tour, I was seriously hungry, and glad to hear a gong sound for the evening meal. As at Pinrose, part of the mealtime was free for conversation, but part of the time was silent, while an improving text was read. The Abbot took the reading himself.

'Charity never bargains,' said Anima, 'nor does she challenge her opponents or assert her rights. She is as proud of a penny as a gold sovereign, and as pleased with a grey home spun coat, as with a tunic of Tartary silk or finest scarlet. Charity rejoices with those who rejoice, returns good for evil,

149

and trusts and loves all whom our Lord created. She never curses and she bears no malice, and takes no delight in slander or making fun of others. For she trusts whatever men say and accepts it cheerfully, bearing patiently all manner of injuries. Nor does she covet any earthly goods, but seeks only the bliss of the kingdom of Heaven.'
    'But has she no sort of income?' I asked. 'No money, or wealthy patrons?'
    'She never gives a thought to money or income, for she is never without a friend to provide for her in need. Thy-will-be-done always helps her out, and the only supper she eats is a bowl of Trust-in-the-Lord.'

I thought of Tabby of the Grey Friars, sleeping in borrowed beds – as I was doing now, but then I was on holiday. I only found out afterwards, when the time came to write up and I looked up *Piers Ploughman*, that the Abbot had altered the pronouns, making Charity a woman.

The main course was a Nossex version of cottage pie, which had enough beef mince to be identifiable at least, though it was considerably bulked out with some very tasty mushrooms. The helpings were appropriately generous for growing children. It occurred to me that decades eating here would help explain the Abbot's considerable bulk. The blackberry and apple crumble that followed was equally filling, less sugary but more strongly spiced than would be usual Outside, and after a good bowlful I felt I'd fully made up for missing lunch.

In the course of conversation, I gathered that I had arrived on the right day for the Blackfriars Inquisition. Having heard how it had been founded by Andrew Breeze 350 years ago, I looked forward to the event with keen anticipation. Perhaps because of such high expectations, it turned out a little disappointing, seeming a touch uninspired, a little mechanical, rather routine. Nevertheless, there were a good number of adults present, which suggested that folk generally thought the Inquisition worth attending. Maybe their presence inhibited the school pupils.

The session began with a critique by two older pupils of a classic text, *The Presentation of Self in Everyday Life*, a book from the 1950s that I knew well, and progressed to a discussion on self-image, self-confidence, modesty, honesty, and related topics. The discussion was efficiently run by a senior girl, and largely confined to an inner circle of a couple of dozen pupils, with a larger crowd of pupils and adults sitting round the outside, listening and occasionally contributing briefly.

It appeared to be a topic that didn't really engage the Nossex youngsters, perhaps because they all knew each other so well that they couldn't quite imagine someone successfully projecting a misleading self-image. Those with more experience of Outside society seemed more aware of the issues. I was struck by their use of the words 'Boaster' and 'boasting', which they applied to any form of self-promotion: Twitter, selfies, CVs and personal statements. One boy expressed shock that the word 'loser' could be a term of abuse Outside.

150

At this, the Abbot explained that in schools Outside, competition was encouraged, to motivate children to strive to improve themselves. He quoted from William Law, who he said was a 'voice in the wilderness' arguing against this approach:

We complain of the effects of pride; we wonder to see grown men acted and governed by ambition, envy, scorn, and a desire of glory; not considering that they were all the time of their youth, called upon to all their action and industry upon the same principles. You teach a child to scorn to be out-done, to thirst for distinction and applause; and is it any wonder that he continues to act all his life in the same manner? Now if a youth is ever to be so far a Christian as to govern his heart by the doctrines of humility, I would fain know at what time he is to begin it; or if he is ever to begin it at all, why we train him up in tempers quite contrary to it?

'We do things differently here in Nossex,' he said. 'Winners and losers are not categories we divide people into. But you'll need to recognise that those concepts permeate Outside life.'

I realised that the topic of this Inquisition had been chosen partly to prepare teenagers for their Years Out; the Abbot had obviously had that quotation ready for the right moment to pop it in. Perhaps there were other Inquisitions that were less engineered.

Afterwards, a number of us wandered out into one of the quadrangles. The air was mild, and the night soft and dimly lit by a low crescent moon and one or two windows showing a gentle yellow light. Carys was on her own; she had been at the Inquisition with Howell, but he had disappeared for the moment, so I went and sat by her, and said: 'This would be a brilliant setting for one of the Tales of Nossex.'

'I'll tell you one,' she said, 'since I haven't yet. What have you heard? The Tale of Esther Forester, I know. I was there.'

'One I would like to hear,' I said, 'is Persis' story. I've heard the Tale of Quintus of Cyrene, but that finished when Persis arrived, and I don't know why she was late.'

'All right,' said Carys. 'It's a grim tale in parts, but inspiring in the end.'

As she was about to begin, Howell appeared, and Martin and Lydia also approached; but rather than interrupting or delaying the storytelling, they gathered round and sat on the grass in a little circle, waiting expectantly, even though they had presumably heard the Tale many times before.

Twenty: The Tale of Persis

How long will my enemy triumph over me? Look on me and answer,
O Lord my God. Give light to my eyes, or I will sleep in death. Ps 13:2

Persis daughter of Marcus Claudius was born in Rome of a prosperous family with military connections. Two of her uncles were army officers, and her father had a lucrative business in what would today be called logistics, or supply chain management: the army relied on businesses like his for all kinds of supplies other than weaponry.

She was slight and delicate, with great dark eyes, and while she was still in her late teens her father arranged a marriage to a handsome young officer. Although the marriage was arranged, there was love between them, and she was very unhappy when within two years he died of dysentery on campaign. Her parents did not know how to console her; there was no child, and at first she refused to consider remarriage. As a way of giving her some occupation to stop her brooding, her father allowed her to help in the business, and was surprised at the talent she had for organisation.

The work helped to take her mind off things, but she felt the need to talk to someone outside the family, and a sympathetic friend provided a good listening ear, as well as an introduction to a new and strange religion centred on a crucified man who had risen from the dead. Persis was intrigued, then fascinated, then convinced; and her faith healed her wounds and filled the emptiness. She found satisfaction in her work, and comfort in the fellowship of believers.

Not very long afterwards, her father died suddenly. Persis knew the people he had dealt with and was mistress of the accounts, and nobody else in the family wanted to take the business on. Because contracts had to be honoured, she carried on, and found that in fact the business prospered, for her father's and uncles' names opened doors and gained trust, and her winning smile, as well as the sympathy from those who had known her husband and her father, gained her new contracts on competitive terms. Already, she found, her accepted status had changed from young ornamental wife to rich widow and respected and competent businesswoman.

In time she made business connections among the Christian fellowship in Rome, and sometimes travelled together with friends and fellow-believers on business trips. One summer in the late 50s she travelled from Rome to Lugdunum in Gaul, together with Phoebe of Cenchreae, an older Christian who was a good friend. Along with their goods for sale, their invoices, and their letters of introduction, they took a copy of the apostle Paul's letter to the Roman church, as a gift to the church in Lugdunum; and during the voyage to Massalia, Persis made another copy for her own future use, just as Phoebe had done on the voyage to Rome, not long before.

When they arrived in Lugdunum they made contact with the believers there, finding a small but very warm fellowship, who had just received exciting news from a former member now in Britannia, where he reported that an entire tribe, albeit rather a small tribe, had become believers. He was asking for help in teaching these new

believers, and none of the Lugdunum congregation felt called to make the journey into the unknown.

That night Persis dreamed that she was on the way to Britannia. It was a frightening dream, for it seemed that she was locked in a small cell, and had been, she sensed, for many days; and she felt nauseous. All the same, within the dream she somehow knew that she would be released, and that she would yet arrive at her destination, which it seemed would be a place of peace and healing.

She told her dream to Phoebe in the morning, and her friend thought it must be a word from the Lord. To test it, on the next Lord's day they fasted and prayed with the believers, and it seemed to all that Persis should make the journey. Many prayers were said for her safe passage through the dangers that the dream appeared to predict; and Phoebe promised to return promptly to Rome and see that Persis' absence was covered and her business in good hands.

All went well on Persis' journey until she arrived at Portus Itius, and had to wait for a fair wind for the crossing. The weather was pleasant enough, and the white cliffs of her destination were tantalisingly visible, so that she became impatient, and eventually agreed to make the short passage with the first man prepared to depart, a stubbly little merchant, a dealer in fish and seafood, who looked rather like a dried fish himself. She did not quite trust him, but the voyage would be mercifully short, she thought.

She had forgotten, or perhaps had never fully realised, how far her family connections, and her general air of being somebody of substance, likely to have powerful friends, had kept her safe on her travels so far. At sea, beyond the borders of Roman Gaul, this counted for little.

Her trading goods, and her personal valuables, were probably stolen very soon; she did not see when, for she was fully occupied struggling with the fish merchant. Small though he was, he was still stronger than her, and soon had his pleasure of her, leaving her bruised, nauseated, furious, and a prisoner.

It did not end with the short voyage, either, for she was bound, gagged, and stuffed in a large basket, to be carried on shore along with basketloads of crabs and lobsters, and many tons of fish, and then released only into a locked store cupboard along with empty baskets that stank of rotting fish. It was the cell of her dream, more or less, though the smell, and the nausea, were far worse than she had imagined.

Her captor returned regularly, to leave food and water only after he had had what he wanted. She hardly touched the food, she felt so sick, though she was wise enough to drink at least a minimum to avoid dehydration. Everything about the fish merchant revolted her: his brutality, his air of self-admiration at having contrived so self-pleasuring a situation, his rotten teeth, his breath, fishier even than the baskets all around, and the prickliness of his greying stubble, somehow always the same length. The little things seemed to enrage her even more than the main violation, though she knew that would trouble her far longer. Faint and indistinct, beyond the anger and the nausea, the conviction that she would eventually be freed enabled her to struggle above total despair, and to pray.

How long her captivity lasted she had no notion at the time, though she worked out later that it had been around three months. One day her jailer seemed longer than usual in arriving; then there were voices outside, speaking Latin rather than that barbarous Celtic; then the door was burst open, splinters flying, and a Roman officer stood there, horror on his face.

He was still more horrified when he learned who she was. He had known her late husband, slightly, and knew her uncle well, and vowed vengeance on the fish merchant. He wanted Persis to be ready to give evidence against him, as soon as he should be caught, but she was eager to be on her way. She thought her impatience was entirely due to her errand from the Lord, so much delayed already, Nemet's fellowship waiting for her. Later she realised that it had been equally due to a desire to put as much distance as possible between her and that horrible fishy cell; for years afterwards she could not bear the smell of salt fish.

The officer gave her an escort as far as Londinium. At that point she collapsed and could travel no further. The danger was past, but her nausea grew worse, and she lay as if at death's door for many long weeks, realising in the end that she was expecting the fish merchant's child, which explained the extreme sickness, his final inescapable imposition on her.

It was winter before she could rise and get about. The sickness passed quite suddenly, and she recovered a good appetite. The weather was mild, and she became eager to travel; but although she felt healthy, her strength had been undermined, and she could not travel far without great weariness. Finally she staggered into Nova Castra, and asked for Quintus of Cyrene, to find that he was on the eve of departure; and then her pains began before she could explain why she was so delayed.

From this point things became much better. The midwife was wonderfully skilled, and like a mother to her; the labour, though excruciating, was at least brief, as if the child was in a hurry; and the baby was a joy. Persis found herself breathing in the scent of him, again and again, in disbelief at how sweet he smelled, and she realised that she had irrationally, ludicrously, expected him to smell of fish. Instead he smelt of warm bread, or milk, or something equally sweet and harmless; and he was not in the least stubbly. Her fears that the child would remind her of the unwanted father drifted away, and the memory of her jailer began to be more distant.

Cara the midwife, and all of the Nemetians that she met, cherished and supported her and the baby. Although a firstborn, he was named Quintus after the departed soldier. In between caring for him, Persis took up her task of working through the scriptures with the fellowship, and answering their many questions. She had the use of a Greek version of the Jewish scriptures, which Quintus of Cyrene had left to the Nemetian church, and her own copy of Paul's letter to the Romans, somehow kept safe through her captivity, though much crumpled.

In the times when young Quintus slept (and he slept long and peacefully), she made a fair copy of that letter, and as the months and then the years went by, work was begun on translating the scriptures into Nemsh: first, the letter to the Romans, then two short narrative books, Ruth and Jonah, then selected Psalms, Habakkuk, Malachi, and Hosea, because they were quoted in Romans. But Genesis, Exodus, and Isaiah were also heavily quoted in Romans, and eventually it was time to begin work on these larger tasks.

155

Before she set out for Britannia, Persis had vaguely thought of staying a year. But she had arrived late, and the first summer was far too soon to leave. By the second summer she was already feeling very much at home, missing only a few aspects of her former life, and sure that there was a large unfinished task for her in Nemet. Little Quintus was happy, getting into all sorts of mischief now that he was walking, and speaking only Nemsh. She shrank from the idea of taking him away from this safe haven and into the dangerous world outside. She was less aware of her deeply buried fear of once more venturing on a journey involving seaports and ships. The news had in fact reached her that the fish merchant had been hanged; the Roman officer had found enough crooked dealing in his accounts to justify execution, without having to charge him with the abduction and rape of the daughter of a Roman citizen. But she hardly rejoiced, and her confidence in travel throughout the Empire had gone.

So she remained, and in time married Glin, a skilled coppersmith and church leader in Caermorgan. She was still only twenty-eight, and this second marriage made her feel young again. Quintus was growing tall and sturdy, not in the least like his father; in fact he was the image of his grandfather, her late father, and although this sometimes brought a tear to her eye, it was still a great comfort. He became known as Quintus of Caermorgan, to distinguish him from Quintus of Cyrene, who was still revered, and of whom tales were often told.

Persis had five more children, four girls and a boy, which might have kept her fully occupied, if the life in Caermorgan, as in all Nemet, had not been so communal. Although this rested to some extent on the oral tradition of the early church, via Quintus of Cyrene and Persis, it was little different from how the Nemetians had lived previously. Each church, which in every settlement was the great majority of the population, had all property in common, and saw all work as a collective responsibility. It was understood, in fact often stated explicitly, that Persis had to be given time to work on supervising Scripture translation; and in any case, childcare from the age of three was seen as a communal task.

Occasionally Christian soldiers and officials, who knew Greek and were ready to help in translation, were posted to Nova Castra; and one great day, when young Quintus was almost grown up, an officer arrived with a copy of Luke-Acts, and thereafter the Nemetians were able to study a written Gospel. Persis put Isaiah aside, to concentrate at once on translating this new jewel for the Nemetians.

Everything that had been translated was swiftly copied, so that each church, and many families, had a steadily expanding Nemsh Bible. Literacy had been valued in Nemet before the Romans came; and the Nemetians never thought that anyone, boy or girl, might have no need to learn their letters. Persis was constantly encouraged in her task, especially by the church leaders, and she was still working on it the day before she died at the age of 92.

Thereafter translation progress was fitful, as the remaining books of the New Testament arrived in somewhat random order. In fact the Nemsh Bible was not complete until the days of Gaius the Elder, builder of Pinrose.

Twenty-one: Overnight in Pinisk; walk to Chittock *(9 miles)*

'A harrowing story,' I commented, 'but at least it had a happy ending. Why did she have to go through something so horrible, I wonder?'

'Maybe the Enemy was extra keen to stop her ever getting to Nossex,' said Carys, adding: 'but God is much stronger.'

'And then the delay and the trauma kept her here, when otherwise she would probably have gone back to Rome.'

'Yes,' Carys agreed. 'And the Nossexfolk realised she was sent by God, and gave her the title of Bishop, as successor to Quintus of Cyrene. So Nossex got round to women bishops nearly two thousand years before the Church of England.'

'Have there been many other female Bishops of Noaster?'

'Some; I don't know how many. It's not that important.'

'It is Outside,' I said. 'But the position of women seems different in Nossex. I really do get an impression of equality.'

'Maybe,' she said, 'I don't know; nobody's measuring it. We're not desperately *trying* to be equal; we *know* we are; it's only common sense. *There is neither male nor female, for you are all one in Christ Jesus.*[1]'

'So you would base the equality on Christian doctrine,' I suggested, 'but the Church elsewhere was male-dominated for centuries.'

'Because it grew inside male-dominated societies,' put in Lydia, 'and was tainted by them. Nemet wasn't like that, even before it became Christian. Steve, have you ever read anything by a sociologist called Hofstede?'

'Indeed I have,' I said, 'very relevant to my former occupation, working cross-culturally all the time. Nossex would score very low on Masculinity – no interest in quantity of things, only quality of life; and very little if any role differentiation. In that respect it reminds me of Sweden, only more so.'

'You know your stuff, then,' Lydia observed, not particularly impressed. 'Well, the pre-Christian Nemet was like that, rather more matriarchal than patriarchal, but actually not interested in a person's gender as a qualification for leadership, only age and wisdom. Nemet was run by the Heads of the Families – and in fact vestiges of that system persist informally today – and the Head was either the oldest member of the extended family, or the most suitable person out of the surviving oldest generation. It could be a man, but more often it was a woman. So the place of women in Nemet was never an issue, and nobody's succeeded in making it an issue since. Young men who wanted to be domineering found it easier to act like that Outside, so they tended to stay Out.'

'So Nossex systematically *exports* any male chauvinist piggery,' I said. 'A neat idea, but wouldn't it leave you with a surplus of females?'

'We also export girls who like shopping,' Carys pointed out, at which Lydia laughed and agreed. 'The numbers probably balance out.'

[1] Gal 3:28

157

'Going back to the story,' I said, 'I'm not suggesting you made it up, but how much of the detail is original, and how much has been added over the centuries?'

'Every story-teller has their own style,' said Lydia before Carys could answer. 'Carys made the story her own, but there was nothing in that narrative that would conflict with the story as I've heard it on other occasions.'

'After nearly two thousand years, how sure can we be that things happened as the Tale reports?'

'There are two early documents – admittedly not from Persis' lifetime, but not long afterwards – one in Latin, one in Nemsh, and then Esther Breeze wrote a definitive English version, based on the oral tradition but referring to the documents for confirmation. Any *Tale of Persis* you hear today won't be far from the Esther Breeze version, even if the storyteller learned the Tale orally.'

'I first heard it from Sister Christina,' said Carys.

'She would know Esther's version,' said Lydia.

Ben wandered over and asked a little awkwardly if I was interested in the Querimonia, explaining that it was a subversive counterpart to the Inquisition. I was intrigued, but none of the others showed any enthusiasm, so I followed Ben back inside, and through corridors and the main library to a smallish annexe, a room lined with books from floor to ceiling, and containing an eclectic selection of armchairs.

It was difficult to be sure when the Querimonia began. There was clearly no agenda or set structure, and it was hard to know whether anyone was taking the role of Chair, even once everyone was there. Though possibly not everyone who might have been there was there. It was a much smaller gathering than the Inquisition, but also had something of the same fishbowl setting, in that all the interaction was between a small group of half a dozen in the centre, while perhaps twice as many sat round the outside and did not participate apart from non-verbal reactions.

The leaders, it became clear, were three principal malcontents: Ben, who I already knew, and a remarkable couple who sat close together, often touching one another. They were displaying several fairly obvious signs of rebellion, rather more in-your-face than Ben's long hair. The boy Malachi was the first male I'd seen in Nossex with pierced ears; one of the ears had two steel rings in it. Despite a heavy black beard, the baby-smooth skin around his eyes gave away his youth. Like many Nossexmen, he was shortish, thickset and strong, but unlike most others, there was just a hint of aggressiveness in his demeanour. Both his meaty forearms were fully tattooed in the style currently fashionable Outside; again, they were the first tattoos I'd seen in Nossex.

The girl Lucy could have walked straight out of a St Trinian's film, all in black with a short dress and black stockings that combined to show frequent glimpses of upper thigh; altogether a very un-Nossex-like get-up. At least she hadn't disfigured an attractive face with any piercings. The face reminded me of someone, though at my age almost every face does that. Her eyes seemed sleepy, with a smile at the corners, and luxuriant wavy brown hair spread over her shoulders, much longer and

158

looser than most Nossexwomen kept their hair. She left most of the talking to Malachi, and smiled at his clever remarks.

The topic of conversation, or rather of complaint, moved here and there at random, showing a tendency to slide into flippancy whenever an issue became serious. I found it fascinating and frustrating at the same time, and thought I detected the same reaction from one or two of the silent outer ring of observers.

'Outside,' said Malachi at one point, 'they say men are from Mars, and women from Venus. I get that; I'm from Mars, and Lucy's definitely from Venus.' They caught each other's eye significantly. 'But most of the Nossexfolk are from Saturn or somewhere colder. Ben's from Mercury, I guess.'

I smiled at that, so Malachi challenged me: 'Where are you from, Steve?'

'Earth, I hope,' I said. 'I grant you, plenty of men Outside are from Mars. It causes a whole heap of problems. And maybe some women Outside are from Venus, though I think most are from Earth. But the Nossexfolk are definitely from Earth: they have their feet on the ground.'

'Yes, everything here is so wonderfully sensible,' Malachi complained. '*It's only common sense*,' he mimicked in a mocking sing-song, and I had to admit to myself that the phrase was rather frequently used.

'If you want somewhere where things often *aren't* sensible,' I suggested, 'try almost anywhere Outside. All the same, Nossex has some odd quirks: cross-gender wrestling seems a fairly wacky idea.'

'Huh! Even a daft idea like Nossex wrestling, they manage to organise sensibly. All so carefully controlled and monitored. Picture it: Day One, first lesson. Boys and girls lined up. Big diagram on the wall, stylised male & female figures, front and back view, red-shaded areas that cannot be touched on pain of disqualification. *Note the word pain, lads*, says the gym mistress. *You touch what you shouldn't, you're disqualified, you lose the bout. Your opponent's won, so she's got nothing to lose if she retaliates, and believe me, she can cause a lot of pain in a very short time.*'

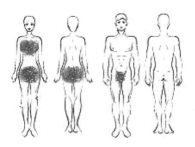

'All the boys went pale,' said Lucy with a smirk, 'and behaved themselves impeccably in the first bout. No disqualifications. Second bout, I was lined up against Mal, and he'd been winding me up in class, so I decided to get my retaliation in first. *Sorry, miss*, I said as he writhed on the floor, *I thought I heard the whistle.*'

159

'I was walking bow-legged for a week,' said Malachi. 'I owed her one, but I bided my time, and paid her back in private, with no referees watching.'

Lucy stretched like a cat, eyes half closed, showing yet more upper thigh. 'That wasn't the least bit painful.'

'It wasn't meant to be.' They smiled at each other.

'Does anyone know the history of Nossex wrestling?' I asked. 'Or how or why it became mixed?'

'For men, it goes back to Roman times,' said Ben. 'The idea of mixed wrestling came in from Outside about a hundred years ago: some modern educational theory or other. But for the Nossex establishment, it's like dancing: they think if they allow randy kids to get to grips with each other's bodies in strictly controlled situations, then they're less likely to end up warped and touch-averse, but at the same time everything's within limits. Doesn't work with the likes of Mal and Lucy, of course, but they would have been shagging each other silly anyway, they're past praying for.'

'Nobody's past praying for,' I couldn't help saying.

'Do you actually believe that?' Malachi sneered.

'In principle, yes,' I answered. 'I knew a man once, one of the quietest, nicest men you could hope to meet. God turned his life around when he was in jail for murder. He'd gone out with a gang one night, when he was about your age, and carried out a revenge killing. I don't know who was praying for him, but I know who heard the prayer. Why would I think anyone's past praying for?'

'Of course, nobody wants murder,' Malachi conceded, going off at another tangent rather than engaging with the issue of redemption, 'but there isn't even any *unrest* in Nossex – at least, all the unrest there is, is here in this room.'

One of the younger girls, who had been completely silent so far, suddenly spoke up. 'If you're so fed up with Nossex, why don't you leave? You and Lucy, you could have started your Years Out two years ago; Ben could have started last year. Why are you still here?'

Lucy sat up, roused out of her languorous pose, eyes now fully open. 'Because we're not as totally selfish as people think we are,' she said. 'Once we're Outside, we're probably not coming back. You know that, we know that, our families know that. My Dad doesn't want me to go just yet.'

With a shock, I suddenly realised why Lucy's features had seemed familiar. She must be Martin's daughter. Once I saw the likeness, it was unmistakable.

'Even if you do settle Outside,' I said, 'you are allowed to come back and visit, aren't you?'

'It's not as simple as that,' said Ben. 'I mean, yes, of course you can visit any time, but settling Outside makes you *seem* a long way away. Nossex puts you under pressure to buy into the whole philosophy, the whole ethic. If someone stays Out, it means they're rejecting the Nossex dream, and all Nossexfolk as well: it puts a massive psychological distance between you.'

'Are you not rejecting the dream already?' I asked.

'Ben doesn't reject it, said Malachi. 'He wants to *improve* it: more democracy, less religion, more innovation. Lucy and me, we're older and wiser, we know we'll never change Nossex so that we fit in; we just need to have a good moan now and again to let off steam.'

Which is why the Abbot is happy for the Querimonia to exist, I thought. 'And if you were Outside,' I said aloud, 'would you be having a good moan about the situation there – and would Ben be trying to improve Outside society?'

'Of course,' said Ben. 'Isn't that everyone's responsibility, here or Outside?'

That was true, I thought, realising that Ben was just an over-enthusiastic idealist who would probably be a pillar of the Nossex establishment in forty years' time. On the other hand, Lucy was probably being realistic in assuming she and Mal wouldn't stay in Nossex. It would leave Martin and Lydia with very mixed feelings, and no doubt they were happy to postpone the parting.

After a few more tangents, the gathering dissolved without any very satisfying conclusion or clear finish. It was late enough for me to be glad to tumble into bed and sleep soundly; my extra walk with the Abbot had left me physically a little weary, and the day had included a lot of new impressions and new ideas.

Wednesday 1ˢᵗ October 2014

I woke to the subdued sounds of a few folk getting up quietly, trying not to disturb others who were still sleeping. It reminded me that there had been mention of a pre-breakfast prayer meeting, and I stirred myself and followed, hoping that it was a meeting I could gatecrash.

Although there were no staff present, and the meeting was student-led, it seemed that visiting adults were welcome. Titus was there, and Carys, but not Howell. Perhaps he was incapable of early rising. The girl in charge was brisk and well-organised, and prayers were kept remarkably short. It reminded me of a Christian youth group I'd been involved in decades ago, which had a 'one-sentence prayer' policy, to encourage the nervous to participate and the confident not to dominate. They must have a similar idea here, I thought, even if nobody has mentioned it.

Most sat with heads bowed, but Titus knelt by a chair, as at Icclescombe, one lad lay flat on his stomach on the floor, and a couple were standing. Nobody was watching anybody else, but the slick turn-taking showed that they were aware of each other. In a quarter of an hour that passed in a blink the meeting was over and everyone piled into breakfast, which seemed designed to provide plenty of fuel for growing youngsters. I particularly enjoyed some rather spicy sausages.

As I ate, I looked back on the three meetings, the Inquisition, the Querimonia, and the early prayer meeting, and decided that the third had been the most impressive. The Inquisition had been competently run, but a bit bland, even on the edge of boring; the Querimonia, while messy and rambling, had had atmosphere and unpredictability; and the prayer meeting had shown what the students were capable of. It had been efficient, focused, and lively, and the fact that a good number of teenagers had got

161

there before breakfast said quite a lot.

After breakfast the clearing and washing up was all taken care of by well-drilled teams, so I went to collect the rucksack and made ready to leave on what might, I guessed, be a longer walk than some others I'd had in Nossex.

Titus was ready to set off too. 'Mr Steve!' he said. 'You are going back to Icclescombe?'

'Yes, but not today,' I answered. 'I'm going to Chittock first. But our paths lie together until we're in West Nossex, so I'd be happy to walk with you that far. We can follow those two.'

Carys and Howell were a little way ahead, walking close together, obviously delighting in each other's company, and without needing to mention it, Titus and I automatically remained a discreet distance behind them The path southwards from Pinisk climbed gently upwards around the head of the Isk valley, giving fine views of the lake below. A few hairy cattle were scattered on the slopes, and as we came up to the crown of the ridge, we encountered a few of Caermorgan's sheep, too busy grazing to notice us going by. If Carys and Howell had turned and looked back, they would have seen us, and perhaps waited, but they were engrossed in conversation.

'He is a lucky boy,' commented Titus. 'Even if perhaps she will wear the trousers, she will dominate him.'

'Maybe,' I said, 'but not in a bad way. He'll probably enjoy being dominated by Carys. I think you're right: he's done very well.'

'I have prayed for a wife,' said Titus. 'But in Nossex I am not sure how it goes, for a man to find a wife. The boy there, I think he surprised his girl. It was a big risk.'

'Yes,' I agreed, 'and Carys told me that wasn't the usual Nossex way, so I wouldn't try it if I were you.'

'Also, I am still not certain if I want to stay in Nossex or not. It is marvellous, it is a place of peace, they have been very good to me, but is this where God wants that I live?'

Before answering, I asked myself whether *I* would want to live in Nossex, and found no clear answer.

'He brought you here,' I said. 'Not many find Nossex. And you have brought something to the community here.'

'I have? Truly?'

'John told me you revitalised the prayer meetings in Icclescombe.'

'Only God's Spirit can do that. But if He has been gracious to use me, then I am content. Thank you for telling me that.'

Ahead of us, there was laughter from the happy couple; Carys punched Howell a couple of blows on the upper arm, light love-taps that rocked him sideways. He shoved her back, but made little impression. They bumped into each other again, the kind of childlike behaviour that lovers enjoy. I remembered Carys' words: *Who said I loved him?* and thought *Oh yes you do*. I also recalled what the Abbot had said the day before: *love may well exist by the time the marriage takes place.*

162

Could things have changed between Carys and Howell in just two days? They had spent a lot of that time together. I then remembered something I'd heard decades earlier, from a happy clergyman who had unexpectedly married in late middle age: *love calls forth love in return, just as God's love elicits our love in response.*

As we walked, Titus talked a little about people he'd become friends with in Icclescombe. Technically, perhaps, this was gossip, but since every story or detail Titus narrated showed the people he was referring to in a good light, it wasn't gossip as most folk would understand the term.

'In Africa, before I depart,' he said, 'I have seen from time to time, how bad men can be. In Nossex, I see how good men and women can be, with God's help. But the bad things that I have seen are still in my head. It is necessary that I talk to somebody.'

'You need trauma healing,' I said. 'A friend of mine at church has worked with such programmes in Africa. You need someone to listen to you. I can listen, but I guess you'll need much more time than we have today. I'm sure someone in Nossex can help.'

'I don't want to put a burden on friends in Icclescombe.'

'There will be someone from another community who can listen,' I said with all the confidence I could muster.

'Sometimes I feel afraid for Nossex,' he went on. 'It is so beautiful, so peaceful, and so easily evil could damage it.'

'I think it's robust,' I said. 'It's kept going thousands of years; it's not afraid to change and improve. And it's under God's protection.'

'It is still important to pray for that protection to continue.'

'Of course. And they do pray.'

We turned right, leaving the crown of the ridge, and following a winding path down the slope under oaks and birches, with the shady, tumbling Caermorgan Brook on our left, and the path from Caermorgan beyond it, which descended parallel to our path, before crossing the brook to join our route out of East Nossex. As before, the din of the dual carriageway was a sudden unwelcome shock when our path came out from the sheltering trees and then ducked under the road. We were glad to leave the traffic roar behind and regain the peace of the West Nossex woodland.

Carys and Howell paused on the second of the bridges over the Tivvy. I guessed this might be their parting of the ways, and touched Titus' arm to suggest we stop and wait a few minutes, rather than disturb them too soon.

'Let me pray for you, Titus,' I said, and briefly I committed his needs for counselling and for a wife, and his decision whether to remain in Nossex, into God's safekeeping. He responded by praying for the rest of my time in Nossex, and for the book I was hoping to write.

It was heartwarming. I might well have hesitated to pray so freely with a young Englishman, unless I knew him a bit better than I knew Titus. But there was an openness about the tall African that made it easy, and possibly the atmosphere of Nossex was affecting me.

163

Carys gave Howell a brisk hug and a kiss, and set off with sudden decisiveness. Howell lingered on the bridge for a moment, watching her depart.

'Go with God, Mr Steve,' said Titus. 'Walk with the boy; he should not be alone. I will run after the girl.' He grinned, eyes shining, as he realised the double meaning of what he had said.

'Go with God, Titus,' I said.

Titus loped a few yards in his easy, rangy African stride, and Carys turned and greeted him; they were soon hidden from view round a bend in the path to Icclescombe. It took me a little longer to catch up with Howell, walking at my best brisk tempo.

'Hi,' he said, 'are you going to Chittock?'

I said I was, as part of my aim to see all the Nossex communities before leaving.

'Yes, you shouldn't miss out Chittock. You can stay in Portervert Castle, and learn the history of all the earls and countesses.'

'Sounds fascinating,' I said. We went on some way in silence, along a woodland track that rose steadily under big oaks. The forest floor was green with many ferns and thick hair moss. I recognised the leaves of woodruff and wood spurge, and there were scattered spots of colour: pink campion and herb Robert, yellow herb Bennet. There were some fine big mushrooms, too, but Howell made no move to collect them. I wondered how soon Carys would transmit her automatic gatherer instinct to him. A jay screeched in the middle distance, and wood pigeons cooed, but the sounds only emphasised the surrounding peacefulness.

'So what made you choose Carys?' I asked, eventually deciding to break the silence between us. We were walking along a shady path, quiet, but for the song of a robin, posing truculently on a low branch and watching us go by.

'I'm just daft about her,' answered Howell, 'I have been for years, but I didn't see her all that often, and when we were teenagers I was too shy to say anything. Then our Years Out have been spent a long way apart, and I never quite found the right way... And if I spoke, and she said no, that would have been it, finished, but if I waited, there was still hope. Daft, I know. In the end I spoke to the Bishop; actually, I was seeing him about something else, but he sensed there was something troubling me, and got me to open up. And he said *Just tell her.*'

'In the way that you did? Was that his idea?'

'No, at first I think he meant normally, but I made some sort of joke, and the idea sort of grew between us. He has a great sense of mischief, and once the idea was there, I think he wanted to see what would happen.'

'You weren't worried about the effect on Carys?'

'Well, I wanted to shock her, I suppose. But I know she's tough enough to take a shock. I wrestled with her, once.'

'I know,' I said. 'She told me.'

'Then she probably told you she won two-nil in a best of three.'

'She did.'

'She wouldn't have won so easily,' said Howell firmly, 'if I hadn't been so distracted by the feel of her arms around me. I fell in love before I hit the floor.'

I laughed. 'The Abbot was telling me yesterday,' I said, 'that young people in Nossex have never bought into the idea of Romantic Love.'

'What does he know,' retorted Howell, 'celibate all his life.'

'Celibate people can still fall in love,' I said. 'I was celibate until I married in my mid-thirties, but my wife was the third person I fell in love with. But that's not what the Abbot meant. He meant that here, you're not *guided* by that in your choice of a partner – and you seem to be an exception.'

'I love Carys, and always will,' he said. 'But I guess the Abbot's right up to a point: I wouldn't want to marry her unless I thought she'd make a good wife, a real partner in Christ. Don't you think she would?'

'*Above Rubies*,'[1] I quoted. 'I think you've made a brilliant choice, and you're very lucky – or blessed, rather – that she said yes. The question is, are you up to it?'

His smile disappeared. 'In my own strength, no. But with God, all things are possible.'

'Of course,' I said. 'Hold on to that, in the painful times.'

Howell seemed deep in thought, so deep that although we walked fairly close by a group of workers who were pollarding trees and sawing the poles into manageable lengths, he made no move to get involved in the work. I felt slightly guilty, as the sounds of busy work faded behind us, and the path wound on through denser woodland. A little way ahead of us, a young roebuck bounded across the path.

'After my grandfather died,' began Howell, 'Gran said – you met my grandmother, didn't you?' I nodded. 'She said: *don't get the idea that fifty years of happy marriage was pain-free or difficulty-free. You only stay together that long if you can accept the pain and overcome the difficulties together.*'

'My grandfather was a very special man,' he went on. 'I was named after him: Howell Thatcher. He was responsible for all the electricity in Nossex, as well as the fact that we're just about in touch with the twentieth century, and even the twenty-first, in one or two respects.'

'Is he another of the Twelve Tales of Nossex?' I asked, half joking.

'Well, he could be – it's a good enough story. The Twelve Tales aren't fixed in stone; they could be different for different people, though some Tales are classic and shouldn't be left out. Which ones have you heard so far?'

'Quintus of Cyrene, and Persis,' I answered, remembering them in historical order rather than the order I'd heard them, 'Gaius the Youngest, Cennis, Alain FisBos – actually three Tales about him and his family – Judah ben David, Bishop Andrew Breeze, and Esther Breeze. So ten Tales so far – and I'm here three more days, so I'll have time to hear twelve, from twelve different people, as they say is the tradition.'

'But nothing so far later than the seventeenth century. In that case,' said Howell, 'you should hear something newer, and my grandfather's story could fill the gap.'

[1] Prov 31:10

165

Twenty-two: The Tale of the faithfulness of Sparky Thatcher

Guard yourself in your spirit,
and do not break faith with the wife of your youth. Mal 2:15

'Howell Thatcher, my father's father,' said Howell, 'was born in 1923, so he started his Years Out in 1938, just before the Second World War. Through family connections he managed to get into quite a good school, and he concentrated his energy on subjects that would help him in engineering: particularly maths and physics. Being a Nossex boy, he was already very handy practically with woodwork and metalwork and all kinds of bodging and improvising, but he made sure he learned more if he could, getting involved in clubs that specialised in such things. At this point he picked up the nickname "Sparky", from his enjoyment of playing with electricity.

'People could already see there was another war coming, and this had even caused some debate in Nossex. We'd kept well out of the First World War, and thought it a horrific cause of unnecessary suffering, but the situation in the late thirties seemed different. Because of our Jewish communities here, we were especially sensitive to what the Nazis were doing; in fact, a small number of refugees found their way here, so we knew at first hand what was going on.

'This explains why young Howell joined the school cadet force. Nossexfolk don't like uniforms and militarism and all the swagger that goes with it, and still more we hate weapons. But Howell swallowed his dislike and eased his way into roles dealing with telephones, electricity supply, logistics generally, and when he left school, he joined up and somehow made sure that he ended up in the Royal Engineers. He wanted a way of playing his part in defeating the Nazis without actually fighting; and in fact, although he was fully occupied throughout the war, he never saw combat.

'It took until 1946 to get himself demobilised, and then when he came back to Nossex, at first he couldn't settle. He'd travelled a lot in the war, North Africa and the Middle East and a lot of places between there and here; he'd seen many different situations and cultures, and Nossex felt very quiet in comparison. Partly he enjoyed that peacefulness, but another part of him was restless, so he went off and lived in a kibbutz in Israel for a year.

'It gave him a lot to think about. He wasn't very impressed, he said, by how the women seemed to end up doing largely childcare, cleaning, and catering, because he knew from Nossex life that that could be avoided. But what he found interesting was that it showed that a community that had all things in common could exist, separately but openly, *within* a capitalist individualist society. There was quite a lot of debate in Nossex at that time about possibly opening up, becoming visible, joining on to the rest of the country. The founding of the Welfare State made people wonder whether Outside might be moving in the direction of the kind of society we would be happy with. For the time being, however, caution prevailed, and Nossex decided to wait and see how things played out.

'Howell was more in favour of remaining secret and separate, but still he was curious about the outside world, and off he went again as a volunteer with "Christian Reconstruction in Europe", which was a forerunner of Christian Aid and VSO. It took him to some unusual places, and he learned a lot about what people really need, what they can do without, and what might come in useful. I wish I'd asked him more about where he went and what he saw,' admitted Howell, 'but he died six years ago, and it's too late now.

'Anyway, when he was thirty-two, he decided to settle down, and married my grandmother, and right away he began wondering how to bring electric power into Nossex. There was quite a lot of prejudice to overcome, because Nossex was still in a very anti-technology mindset. At the time of the industrial revolution, Nossex rejected steam power and heavy machinery and factories, because of the dirt, the noise, and the horrible working conditions; and we went on using hand-looms for weaving and water power for milling flour. In the twentieth century, we rejected the internal combustion engine because of the noise, again, and because it uses oil, which we can't produce ourselves. So you must have noticed: there's not a car, tractor, motor-bike or chainsaw from one end of Nossex to the other.'

'I have noticed,' I said, 'it's wonderful.'

'But Howell thought: electricity is quiet and clean in itself, it's just a question of how you generate it. He'd seen a lot of noisy and dirty ways of generating electricity, but also some hydro projects that got him thinking. He talked my grandmother round first, then spoke to a few others who had some technical knowledge, though nobody else had his breadth of practical experience.

'There were several watermills that were rather under-used, only grinding flour part of the time. Howell started with the Pinrose mill, and found a way to generate electricity from the waterwheel; then he refurbished an old windmill to grind flour. Wind power was too unpredictable to give a steady source of electricity, but flour could be ground whenever the weather was favourable.

'Waterwheels were acceptable to Nossexfolk, because they were familiar, and electric light in a couple of rooms, for studying in winter evenings, was welcome. There was resistance to most kinds of labour-saving gadgets; we Nossexfolk really like our work, and we don't see why we should have to give it up to a noisy machine. But fridges folk could see the sense of, in the summer, and we soon realised that freezers helped us make more frugal use of food resources, so before long all the communities wanted their hydro scheme.

'Howell got really busy, and from here on he was like Mr Electricity, and his Sparky nickname was resurrected. He mobilised all the folk he could find with any aptitude for the work, but it was clear that the youngsters needed further training, especially to keep up with advances in the technology. He persuaded the Nossex Purse to invest in supporting several people through electrical engineering degrees, and others through electrician apprenticeships.

'So as the sixties and the seventies went by, Sparky found himself working more and more with young people, which he loved; he said it kept him fresh. But it had its dangers as well. I only heard this part of his story after he died; my grandmother told me. In the early seventies a girl called Abigail turned up, fresh from her Years Out, with a degree in electrical engineering, and specialising in grids, switchgear, and energy storage, all the things that Sparky needed more expertise on. He only knew her slightly; she was from Pinginna, on the far side of Nossex from Iddicombe, and he hadn't seen her since she was a little girl. Now she was full-grown, and as soon as Sparky set eyes on her, that was him, head over heels, hopeless case. Trouble was, they locked eyes, and she seemed to have fallen for him, too, even though he was thirty years older. He was quite a handsome chap, my grandfather.

'*Abigail had short brown hair in a cute spiky style*, said my grandmother, *a cheeky grin that put dimples in her cheeks, and forget-me-not eyes. And there was me, just turned fifty, tired and saggy and going grey.*

'So what did Sparky do? He prayed, of course, in our family that goes without saying. But he also reorganised the Power Supply Task Force so that Abbi was reporting to someone else, not him, and he took himself off switchgear work, though he was really interested in that at the time, and from then on he made sure, as far as possible, that they were working in different places.

'It took two years, according to my grandmother, before he was fully over it. Of course he hadn't kept the struggle secret from her, she knew, and they prayed together. They prayed for Abbi as well, and were pleased when she eventually got married. And so that was that, seemingly.

'In the eighties and nineties, Sparky got into computing; he understood the hardware, and he made some progress in programming, and he pressed for young people to be trained in this area too. It led to him being involved in teaching at the Blackfriars School, which he enjoyed no end – and then Abbi turned up there, teaching maths and physics. One day, in a momentarily empty corridor, their eyes locked again, and they knew. Hopeless. He was over sixty by now, and she was in her thirties, but that didn't make any difference to how they felt.

'So Sparky left the school; retired, in effect. Of course hardly anyone stops *working* in Nossex, but he withdrew from the whole electrical and computing research sector, and stuck to the everyday jobs that everybody does, in the kitchen, in the fields, in the woods, whatever. He stayed with my grandmother, and they celebrated their golden wedding three years before he died.

'There were plenty of younger folk to take up the work on power supply and technical education; Abbi became a leading figure in both areas. But none of it would have happened without Sparky's pioneering determination in the fifties and sixties.'

Twenty-three: Overnight in Chittock; walk to Icclescombe *(3 miles)*

'I like it,' I said. 'Is that a story about love, or about faithfulness?'

'Both,' answered Howell. 'Love *is* faithfulness.'

'There's a minister at our church,' I said, 'who shocks young couples on marriage preparation courses by asking them: what will you do when you fall in love with someone else? *When*, not *if*. The marriage candidates don't know what to say, but it's something that it's wise to prepare yourself for.'

'Yes,' said Howell. 'I guess if it's happened to me once, it could happen again.'

'Probably will. Love at first glance doesn't happen to everyone, but it does happen, and it would appear to run in your family. So be ready to hold fast.'

'Did it ever happen to you?' he asked.

'No,' I said, 'it always crept up on me gradually, so that I was off my guard. I'd start off thinking I just fancied someone, and only realise it was more serious when it was too late.'

A blackbird sang from an oak above our heads, and somewhere in the distance the cackle of a green woodpecker sounded under the trees.

'My grandmother added in a few more details,' said Howell. 'She said *When your grandfather said I Love You, even though it might not have been a truthful description of his feelings, I knew it was a trustworthy expression of commitment.* She also told me he said once, *Do you know, I literally never touched the girl. Never even shook hands.* She said, *You don't need to convince me.* He said, *I'm not, I'm just kind of amazed.*'

'He sounds a pretty amazing bloke,' I said.

'He was,' said Howell. 'I heard all sorts of things after he died, but he was very modest, and wouldn't have dreamed of boasting about the things he'd achieved or the different ways he'd helped people.'

'*I love you* is commitment, not description,' I said, half to myself. 'I'll remember that: it's a performative.'

'What's one of those?' asked Howell.

'When you do something by saying something: *I name this ship Victory*; or *I now pronounce you man and wife.*'

As we climbed the slope, the trees thinned out, and the path ran out onto a grassy hillside, with the brown stone houses of the village of Chittock a little way above us.

'What did Carys' parents – or your parents – think when they heard the announcement?'

'Carys' mother died some time ago,' said Howell. 'But we don't ask parents' permission in Nossex. Our two fathers celebrated on Sunday evening with a couple of tankards of cider each. They've been friends a long time.'

We were close to the edge of the village now. A slightly larger building stood to one side, in shape something like a tithe barn, and I wondered if it was the communal hall/school/church that most Nossex communities seemed to have.

'What time do they have lunch here?' I wondered. 'I'm starving.' It was well on in the day, and the walk from Pinisk Blackfriars had been the longest of my rambles in Nossex so far.

'We've probably missed it,' said Howell. My heart sank and my stomach rumbled. 'Not to worry,' he went on, with a smile at my long face, 'if we go to the kitchen they'll find something for us.'

Just then the Countess appeared from a wide archway in the barnlike house. 'Welcome to Portervert Castle,' she said. 'Come inside. I thought you'd be along soon, and I've kept some food for you.'

She led us into a sizeable hall with high stone walls, not as large a space as the communal halls in the different Nossex communities, but larger than any individual dwelling I'd seen so far. There was a long table down the centre of the room, and a strong-looking squareish chap of about my age, completely bald but with a close-cropped grey beard around a square jaw, was laying four places around one end of the table.

Countess Mary introduced me to her husband Owen, and we all sat down to a good helping of a spinach, potato and sunflower seeds concoction, which was almost cold, but tasted none the worse for that, being well spiced with a kind of herby pepperiness that I couldn't identify, but half thought I could link to a vaguely familiar woodland smell. I guessed it must be one of the many edible wild plants whose edibility has been forgotten Outside, except by writers like Richard Mabey.

'So you didn't stay with Carys any longer?' said Mary to Howell.

'No, I want to hitch from the lay-by beyond the North Hedge, as early as possible in the morning. She's spending one more night with her family, then going over the hill and taking the train from the station beyond Cennis' Chair.'

'Cennis was sitting in the Chair when I came into Nossex,' I said, 'but I didn't know it was named for her.'

'It wasn't,' said Owen, 'it was named for the first Cennis, the founder of the Abbey.'

'You've heard the Tale?' asked Mary; and as I nodded, she went on: 'the tradition is that she sat there for a night and a day, after Howel the Infirmarer died. It's been a place of prayer ever since.'

'I thought perhaps it was a guard post,' I said.

'It has that function, too, and prayer is part of keeping Nossex safe, but you don't sit there for three hours saying *Lord, please keep evil-doers out of Nossex* ten thousand times. There are too many other things to pray for, and the association with the Tale of Cennis means that it's natural to spend plenty of time in prayer for the bereaved.'

'And there are always bereaved people,' said Owen. 'One thing that's exactly the same in Nossex or Outside – the death rate is 100%.'

We had cleared up every scrap of the spinach and potato, and Owen brought out half a good-sized apple pie, cut it into four portions, and served us. It was very good, and I noticed that cinnamon was one of the items that Nossex was prepared to import.

'Hezza buttonholed me after the Gathering,' said Mary to Owen.

'Trouble?'

'He wanted to know why we'd explicitly invoked Nossex Oppression Law on behalf of John Smith, but not on behalf of gypsies and travellers.'

'Always the stickler for fairness,' said Owen. 'What did you tell him?'

'That John was a new case, with protection being offered for the first time, whereas protection was extended specifically to gypsies 353 years ago, and it shouldn't need to be repeated unless there's actually been a complaint.'

'You'd done your preparation well.' Her husband was impressed.

'Abbot Peter briefed me. We thought someone might ask, and we wanted to check it had actually been formally announced, and not just assumed.'

'What is Nossex Oppression Law?' I asked.

Mary was about to answer, but Owen, with the tiniest hint of a smile in the corner of one eye, forestalled her. 'You've studied it quite recently, Howell,' he said. 'How would you summarise it?'

Howell looked far from delighted at this challenge. 'The definitive text,' he began, 'was written by Andrew and Esther Breeze, and it runs to five thousand words. They were trying to be really concise.'

I chuckled.

'No, really. It's very tightly packed. But the principle at the heart of it is that no person or group should put pressure on another person or group. This covers all sorts of things: harassment, ostracism, humiliation, political parties, lobbying, bullying, emotional blackmail, nagging... in fact it's hardly possible for people to avoid breaking Oppression Law. And of course you come up against Andrew's Paradox: that you can't accuse someone of breaking Oppression Law without breaking it yourself in the process.'

'Well done, Howell.' Owen looked genuinely pleased. Turning to me, he added: 'Of course it has to be applied with the maximum amount of common sense. For example, the young children's threat of a Helping Strike to back up their request for mobile phones – that technically breached Oppression Law. But there would have been no advantage in refusing their request on those grounds. We had a quiet word afterwards with the children who organised it.'

'It very seldom comes to the point of a formal legal action,' said Mary. 'I doubt if that's ever happened in Howell's lifetime, for example.'

'Not that I remember,' said Howell. 'The real point is that all sorts of nasty behaviour that would be perfectly legal Outside, and very difficult to stop, in fact you see it all the time there – here in Nossex, you just say *Oppression* quietly, and people back off. It's great for getting a nagging parent off your back.'

'I wish you luck, trying that on Carys,' said Owen drily. 'Wives are more of a challenge.' He cocked an eye at Mary, but she didn't rise to the bait.

'The Law didn't originate with Andrew and Esther,' she said to me. 'They simply codified a general principle that had been applied in Nossex Common Law for centuries, but without clear boundaries or definitions.'

'How does Nossex Law operate in general?' I asked.

'You've seen it. You were at the Gathering. The Council is judge, usually represented by me or Matthew, but in theory it could be any member of Council. And the people of Nossex are jury. Simple. Technically, it's inquisitorial rather than adversarial.'

Owen was already serving coffee before I'd finished my pie. I took a sip and found it delicate, like Iddicombe's, but this time I recognised the flavour: cardamom, like Arab coffee. Another spice that could hardly be home-grown. It might even have been real coffee, though very weak. Then I remembered that the Sprat Collective had Chittock connections. Perhaps they regularly brought in a few exotic treats.

My eye had been caught by a huge map of Nossex in a carved wooden frame, hanging against the high stone wall of the hall. As soon as I'd finished eating, I took my coffee and went over to scan every part of it, tracing where I had walked. It appeared to be of roughly 1:25000 scale, and like the Ordnance Survey, every hedge, building, pool and bridge was marked. Deborah's Stones were there, and Cennis' Chair; the lock at the end of the Wall Dyke, and even the lay-by that Howell intended to hitch from, on the busy road that sliced between East and West Nossex.

The style, however, was very different from the OS: much more imaginative and pictorial, with tiny figures walking along the tracks, and sheep or cattle grazing in the fields. There was considerable detail, too, in the Outside areas around the edges of the map; the footbridge I'd crossed on the way to the Yew Tree Stair was marked, and even the railway station I'd walked from was just visible at the edge.

'Can I make a copy of this?' I asked.

'For the book?' was Owen's cautious reaction.

'I was going to ask you about maps,' said Mary. 'Obviously it will help your readers follow the route as they read, but how will you safeguard security?'

'An intelligent reader,' said Owen, 'can look at which way the river runs, and a few other details like that, and be much nearer a good guess at which part of England Nossex lies in.'

All three of them, the Countess, Owen, and Howell, fixed their eyes on me expectantly.

'The book will purport to be pseudo-factual fiction,' I said. 'Well, some of it can *be* fiction. I'll need a fairly accurate map, but then I can turn it through 90° or 180° before going over the text to make sure details such as where the sun rises agree with the orientation I've given the map. Equally I could record this conversation and leave the map alone, so that readers think the map's been altered when in fact it hasn't.'

'Better to turn it anyway,' said Owen.

'More than that,' I went on. 'Several of the tales mention towns and cities Outside: Lincoln, Leicester, Stamford. It would not be difficult, and it would not affect the underlying truthfulness of the book, to substitute other places far enough away to create muddle in the minds of any who try to locate Nossex.'

'That sounds safe enough,' said Mary, 'but you will check the whole book?'

'Don't worry,' I said, 'by the time any of my books arrives at the printers, I've read every last word dozens of times. I won't let any dead giveaways through. One thing that puzzles me, though,' I added, 'is how you managed to get hold of one of my books.'

'No mystery,' she answered. 'I was visiting an old friend from my Years Out, she had a big round number birthday bash. She lives in Oxford now, and in her spare time she's a volunteer fundraiser for Helen & Douglas House, the children's hospice. She sold me *Upper Thames & Wiltshire Ramble*, and I was happy to spend some of my Outside money in a good cause. After I'd read it, I put it in the Noaster library, and that's why you saw one or two others had read it.'

We drained the coffee and Mary gathered the used dishes on a tray. Owen asked me if I'd ever used a scythe, and when I said I hadn't, he told me to bring a whistle. It seemed a strange alternative, but I stuck a D whistle in my trouser pocket and assumed all would become clear in due course.

We walked up through the village together. The stone cottages were quite closely packed, closer than Icclescombe or Caermorgan or Iddicombe, and the narrow alleyways between were paved, so that the heart of Chittock was surrounded by stone. It might have been a little bleak, if the stone had not been of such a rich variety of warm shades, from yellowish honey to a coffee or cinnamon brown, to an almost orange russet in places.

Mary turned aside to leave her tray in the village kitchen, while the three of us went on further, to a shed which was obviously a tool store. Owen greeted the woman there in Nemsh, and the nasalisation seemed even more pronounced here than in Caermorgan. Could two villages a few miles apart have developed distinct accents? It occurred to me that Caermorgan had been hosting the Hughes clan for centuries, and their pure Welsh might have softened the Caermorgan Nemsh, in which case the really thick accent I was hearing now would be the more authentic dialect.

The woman had handed scythes to Owen and Howell, and made to offer me one, but Owen said to me: 'if you've never done it before, you'd need more than the odd hour to get the hang of it, and you might well put your back out. Not worth the risk.' He then dropped back into Nemsh, and was fairly obviously discussing me with the storewoman. There was no way of telling what the adenoidal jabber referred to, but I imagined that the woman was saying that she knew who I was, she'd been at the Gathering, and Owen seemed to be relaying a summary of our recent conversation about the map of Nossex.

'Sorry to exclude you,' said Owen as we came away, 'but the language needs to be used.'

'Absolutely,' I said. 'No need to apologise. My mother-in-law's a native speaker of Gaelic, in the Hebrides, and when I'm there I sometimes feel guilty that I'm part of the reason the language struggles to survive.'

173

We went on, out of the village, to a broad meadow of very long grass and wildflowers, which was already being mown by several folk with scythes. I recognised some members of the Sprat Collective, working away steadily, and on a low bank at the edge of the meadow sat the concertina player, entertaining the workforce with her music.

'Bith birinn?' Howell greeted the workers. It seemed to be a rhetorical question, for one looked up and gave a wave, but nobody spoke, and he didn't wait for an answer, but found a place to work and began swinging his scythe with practised ease.

'You might like to join Jo?' suggested Owen, nodding towards the concertina player, whose name I realised I'd never asked when we swapped tunes in Noaster. I was grateful for his pragmatic thoughtfulness in suggesting bringing a whistle, and went over to sit beside her and join in some moderately paced Morris tunes that suited the steady rhythm of the swinging scythes.

After a while she asked me to play over *Ursula*, the slide I'd played in Noaster, so that she could learn it. We took it through half a dozen times, and it seemed natural to follow it with a couple of well-known Irish slides, and then I added *Fourpence Ha'penny Farthing*, which she seemed to half know, and was able to busk along to.

'What was that?' she asked afterwards.

I told her its name, and said I'd only ever seen it written in 6/8, but she agreed that it felt very similar to the slides.

Fourpence Ha'penny Farthing

Mary was approaching, carrying a scythe, together with a tall lad that I half recognised, then suddenly realised it was Ben, looking rather different with his hair cut short, and wearing Outside-style jeans and T-shirt. There was an intense expression on his face that I couldn't interpret at all. He hesitated, then came over to sit by me, while Mary went to join in the work.

'I want to speak to Howell,' he said, 'but I won't interrupt his work.'

I wasn't at all sure what to say, so prayed for a way to find out what he was so wound up about.

'You were at the Querimonia,' he said suddenly.

'Yes,' I said, and waited.

'You remember the challenge? *If you're so fed up, why are you still here?* I couldn't sleep for hours, thinking about that. And then in the darkest part of the night, I felt Someone. Or Something. The believers would say it was God. I'm not sure. I just felt imperfect, unsatisfactory, substandard. Like a tune with a bum note. Or a clay pot with a crack in it. Or a carving where you've just taken off what you didn't mean to. I would have rejected me, thrown me out and started again. But somehow I didn't feel rejected. I can't describe it.'

'You're describing it very well,' I said, noticing that Jo was listening, yet trying not to make it too obvious she was listening.

Howell happened to glance our way, and Ben waved. Howell came across and offered his scythe. 'Want a go, cousin?' he said.

'I want to come with you in the morning!' said Ben. 'I've decided to start my Years Out after all.'

Howell looked very dubious and reluctant. 'There's not a lot of call for clog-cutters where I'm going,' he said.

'It's not the only thing I can do!' said Ben impatiently.

'Oh!' cried Jo, looking up. 'You can cut clogs?'

'He cuts as good a clog as anyone in Iddicombe,' said Howell.

'We sell clogs,' explained Jo, 'but I'm not very good at the cutting and shaping, I prefer the decorative work. Why don't you join us? We've room for one more, and you could help with the locks and the boat maintenance.'

'Really?' The intensity in Ben's face relaxed into a smile. 'Maybe God really does answer prayer!'

'No maybes,' said Howell. 'You'll see.'

'I'm not a believer yet,' retorted Ben. 'I want more evidence.'

Shortly afterwards there was a drinks break, and Jo explained the idea to Jack and Rachel Sprat, who endorsed it enthusiastically. I thought Howell looked mightily relieved.

As the afternoon wore on, some younger folk came out to the meadow, and took over the scythes a few of the older workers were using. Owen and the Sprats and one or two others went back to the village, taking me along with them, and Owen showed me the dairy, which smelled powerfully of goat's cheese. From there we went to the kitchen, where I found myself useful employment in chopping, peeling, and occasionally stirring things.

For the evening meal the Countess and Earl Consort ate in the main hall with everybody else, the Sprat Collective included. I took the chance to ask about a Nemsh phrase, *birinn dai*, that had been exchanged when some of the mowers left the meadow.

'It doesn't really translate into English,' said Owen. 'Here in Nossex, the English farewell might be *work with God*, but *birinn dai* means *work well*, and could also mean *good job*, as a comment. *Birinn* is an allotted or chosen task, almost like a vocation, but specific to the day, rather than referring to a career. It means doing exactly what God wants you to do, right now. In some contexts it can mean a privilege, and that's how Nossexfolk have always felt about work.'

'Yes, I've seen that,' I said.

'One of the pithiest comments I ever heard on Outside,' said Mary, 'was from a lad who came back from his Years Out and just said *dim birinn*. He didn't mean there

175

was no work at all, but no work, or not enough work, that you could take a real pleasure in. Too much work Outside is no fun at all.'

'On the other hand,' added Owen, 'while we're comparing Nemsh and English, there's no Nemsh word for *drudgery*.'

The meal was very filling, and people seemed happy to turn in early afterwards. Howell said he wanted to be up at first light, Ben was yawning repeatedly, and that set me off, although I had less reason to be tired. All the same, I slept like a log in Portervert Castle, after we had shared a short time of prayer. Ben joined us, which surprised Howell, but said no prayers aloud.

Thursday 2ⁿᵈ October 2014

We were up before the dawn, and had a hasty and very early breakfast with Howell, proving that he could get up early if he had to, before he set off to return to 'the Land of Litter, Noise, and Exploitation,' as he put it. 'It's quite fun if you're in the right mood,' he said, his intonation suggesting he often wasn't.

'If you want to visit us in Manchester,' I said, shaking hands, 'you're very welcome. Plenty of litter and noise, but we won't exploit you. And the church is good.'

'I might take you up on that,' he said, as he hefted a small rucksack and went out.

'That's him on his way,' said Ben. 'But you can tell he doesn't really want to go. He'll never really escape from Nossex. He's grown up here, so he's conditioned, like most Nossexfolk. I'll find it hard in some ways too, even though I'm not satisfied with the way Nossex operates.'

'So you think Nossex is a psychological prison for those born and raised here,' I suggested.

'No,' said Owen, 'even for children, Nossex isn't a prison. I'll give you a for instance. Bronwen Forester, thirteen years old. She has an uncle and aunt in Derby, used to visit them fairly often. She came back to Nossex from one visit, then three days later, she turned round and went back to Derby. She had a return train ticket; the return half was meant to be for her next visit a few months later.'

'When her parents realised she was missing,' put in Mary, 'they were pretty worried for a couple of hours, because she was – is – the kind of scatterbrained accident-prone kid who could easily do herself an injury in the woods somewhere. But do her justice, she sent emails to various people, and one of them was picked up fairly soon, and she Skyped her parents that evening.'

'And you know why she felt she just had to go back Outside?' demanded Owen, a rhetorical question; of course I had no idea. 'She couldn't bear,' he went on, 'she just couldn't live with the idea of not knowing what would happen in the next episode of *Eastenders*.'

'Silly, really,' said Mary, 'because she could have organised access to a computer and checked it out on iPlayer, here in Nossex.'

'But that's not really the point,' said Owen, unconsciously contradicting himself.

176

'It's the whole experience: watching the programme on the sofa, with the takeaway from MacDonald's and all your friends, the whole lifestyle.'

'Shopping,' said Mary, 'concerts, cinemas, chocolate, boyfriends.'

'Would she not have had boyfriends here in Nossex?' I asked.

'Well, probably not. Boys in Nossex tend to hold off a bit longer. There's no rule or law, no official prohibition, but most boys – and girls – tend to avoid close relationships before their Years Out begin, which is usually at sixteen. It's only common sense. On the other hand, although it wasn't – as far as we know – for a specific boy that she went back to Derby, a lively thirteen-year-old girl there could expect to enjoy some gratifying attention from boys, at least, and could live in hope of a boyfriend much sooner than in Nossex.'

'Three more years,' sighed Owen, 'and she would have been encouraged to head Outside anyway. And you could be pretty sure she would have been one of those who stay out. So if she really preferred life Outside in every way, she might as well be there already. At least she was safe with family.'

'But I don't suppose it occurred to her,' added Mary, 'that she represented a significant extra expense for her uncle and aunt. We do our best to get the message across to our youngsters, but when food, clothing, and shelter come free in Nossex, it's hard for the ones who aren't great thinkers to understand that such things have to be paid for Outside.'

'It could be argued,' I said cautiously, 'that she wasn't just freeloading on her uncle and aunt, but on the whole system Outside: presumably she got free education, but her parents weren't paying taxes here in Nossex.'

Owen frowned, and I wondered if I'd gone too far. 'Freeloading,' he said. 'It's been an issue since the NHS and the welfare state began. Way back in time, if the king raised taxes, it was nearly always for war, and Nossexfolk had no qualms about not paying for soldiers to go and kill foreigners. But now, quite a lot of the money – not all, mind you – is spent on things we would approve of. So we do need to ask ourselves if we're sometimes freeloading.'

'And are you?'

'Individually, one or two might be. But take Nossexfolk overall, we don't think so, though the sums are hard to work out. Almost all our young people do three Years Out, some several more, and they pay their taxes during that time, but 99% of them draw no benefits from the system. If they can't get paid work, they'll do the kind of volunteering that offers board and lodging; if they can't even get that, they'll come back to Nossex. Nobody draws unemployment benefit, the most they might take from the welfare state is treatment at A & E if they break a leg or whatever while they're Outside. That's pretty rare, so we think Nossex as a whole is in credit with the system.'

'Pensions?' I asked tentatively.

'Who needs a pension in Nossex?' demanded Owen. 'Old people are fed and housed; they're looked after if they're sick. Nobody really *retires*; they work as much as they want to, which might gradually decline with age, and they might slow down a

177

bit, but nobody's counting or measuring. A lot of folk here are still busy well into their eighties. Mind you, even Outside, if people enjoy their job they tend to keep going rather than retiring. Or they put as much time and energy into their hobby as they ever used to put into their job. Retirement's only really necessary for people doing a job they dislike.'

'So why are you sitting here nattering?' asked his wife.

In an apparently Pavlovian reaction, Owen got up without showing any other response. 'Let's go,' he said to me.

'Do some people have a career Outside and then retire to Nossex?' I asked as I lifted my rucksack.

'It's not common,' said Mary, rising to her feet as well. 'If people have spent their working lives Outside, then usually they've got children, and probably grand-children, that they want to be in close touch with, so they stay Out. But if there's no family or other complications, then occasionally a couple, or more often a single person, might sell their house, give the money to the Council of Nossex, and have their pension paid into the Nossex Purse for the rest of their lives.'

'That's not freeloading,' said Owen as we headed out of the great door of Portervert Castle. 'The individual's only getting back from the state Outside what they put in; and Nossex may be doing quite well in the end, but most likely the Purse made a biggish investment in that person's education or training, forty years earlier.'

We headed down through woodland towards the North Brook. The path was steep, and in places had been made into steps, carefully maintained and in good order, unlike so many stepped footpaths Outside. The first signs of yellow were appearing in the leaves of some trees, the only real indication that the year had advanced to October, for the weather continued mild.

'Does it make much difference to you, that Mary's a Countess?' I asked. 'Does it give you a title?'

'I'm called Earl Consort, officially,' he said, 'but that's not really a title, it's more of a leg-pull. Earl bloody Consort!' he muttered, with a blend of scorn and amusement. 'Owen Smith a Countess's husband! I knew she'd make a good Countess, mind, and I'm glad she didn't try to wriggle out of it.'

'Has it changed your life much?' I asked.

'A bit,' he said, 'not much. We get to live in the Castle, which means we can do more hospitality, and that's nice. I lose Mary one evening a month, and a few other odd bits of time; but then because of that we make a bit more of an effort to do things together, so it probably evens out. It's not like being nobility Outside would be, more like one of us being on the committee of a local charity.'

We came to the bottom of the slope, and crossed the North Brook on a clapper bridge of a design I recognised from Dartmoor, though this was on a much smaller scale. I looked up the deserted valley, where the grass and wildflowers were growing long, perhaps ready to be mown by the Chittock scythes. The distant guttural croak of a raven sounded far up the valley, where a couple of black specks floated in the sky.

'Talking of what we put in, and what we get back from Outside,' said Owen, 'I'll tell you the story of someone who put in a lot of work, total commitment – that is, he put his life and health on the line – and brought back only trauma and something else we didn't expect and certainly didn't want.'

'Is this one of the Twelve Tales of Nossex?' I asked.

'It could be. It's very new, so it's not traditional, but it's a better story – I think so, anyway – than some of the old ones.'

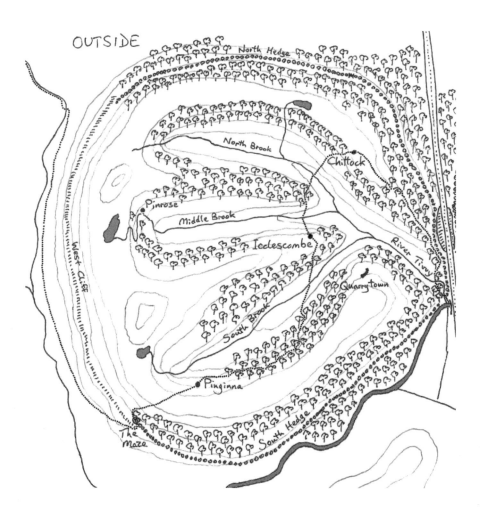

Return route through West Nossex

Twenty-four: The Tale of Happy Day and the Stolen Scimitar

I will search for the lost and bring back the strays.
I will bind up the injured and strengthen the weak. Ezek 34:16

James Day, like a few other teenage boys, found Nossex a bit lacking in excitement. He was a lively lad, often up to mischief, and looked forward to his Years Out. However, an abysmally-paid job stacking shelves in a supermarket in Scunthorpe didn't provide quite the thrills he had been looking for, nor the cash to go and find them. The elderly couple he was staying with tried to interest him in church activities, but James wasn't interested in spiritual things at that stage, and there were virtually no young people in the church. For lack of any attractive alternative, he fell for the temptation to enlist in the army.

At first it proved more fun than stacking shelves; he enjoyed the camaraderie and the banter, and it was early on in his army days that he gained the nickname 'Happy'. He was built like a typical Nossexman, stocky and broad-shouldered, and was already pretty fit when he joined up, so they introduced him to rugby union and gave him a crash course in the dark arts of the front row. He had been adept at wrestling, back in Nossex, so he took up judo as well, and soon progressed through increasingly colourful belts. Pumping iron in the gym, he became even stockier, and yet mightier in the shoulders. He represented the battalion at rugby, and that day he almost split his shirt with pride.

Life was good for Happy Day, until one fine day a scrum collapsed – as they do – and he ended up with what seemed to be a pinched nerve, somewhere in his shoulder or lower neck. The way Happy was built, it was hard to tell his neck from his shoulder anyway. It was enough to stop his sport, but not enough to stop the army training. He battled on, often in quite a lot of pain. He took to drinking a fair amount to dull the pain, and gambling to substitute for the excitement of competitive sport.

Through unlucky timing, or bad planning on his part, he found himself in rather a lot of debt when the time came either to leave the army, or sign on for several more years. He knew that if he went back to Nossex, he would effectively be welching on the debt; so he felt he had to sign on.

At that point he was posted to Afghanistan, and things got better in some ways, and worse in others. At least he drank a lot less, and gambled hardly at all. There was quite enough excitement to be going on with, though it came in short bursts with days and weeks of boredom in between. But the bad experiences began to pile up. Three times his patrol lost a man to an IED; each time Happy was apparently uninjured; but he was close enough to feel the blast, and to be first on the spot to pick up the pieces.

Outwardly, he seemed unmoved, and he won praise for coolness under fire. But it was too easy for others to look at his rock-like stature, and assume that he was equally strong emotionally. And although scientific research was beginning to establish that *any* exposure to blast affects the brain, as far as the army were concerned, if you were still walking and talking, you were OK.

180

Deep inside, Happy was not OK. He had come across civilian casualties, women and children, that might well have resulted from air strikes his unit had called for, and that preyed on his mind. Because of the persistent pain in his neck/shoulder, he slept little; and in some ways he was glad of this, for the dreams he had when he did sleep were not good.

Somehow, he got through the tour; back in the UK, he reported to the MO with both the physical and mental ailments. After a lot of delays and bureaucracy, it was finally established that he had had a broken neck, which had healed, but not very helpfully, so the cheerful conclusion was that he would probably have 'low-level' pain for the rest of his life. As for the bad dreams, and the depression that he was slumped in most of the time now, he was diagnosed as 'borderline' with regard to PTSD – in other words, they couldn't make up their minds whether he was suffering from it or not.

Happy decided he was suffering from too much army, and from making bad decisions earlier, so when they offered him a medical discharge, he took it, and declined most of the offers of help with resettlement, apart from the cash, which he took. But then he found himself at a loss. He had enough to live on, even after he had paid off the last of his debt, so that there was no immediate need to work.

Yet he wanted to work, though he didn't know what at; and he wanted to go home to Nossex. And still he hesitated to do that, for his moods were volatile now, and he had been close to violence a few times. Fortunately he looked so formidable that men usually backed off, even if he tried to pick a fight; but that couldn't last. His thoughts circled endlessly; he felt unworthy of Nossex, or at least that he would hardly fit in there now. Sleep was still a rare commodity, and his dreams were still evil.

One day he was walking down a suburban cul-de-sac, when he saw a Scimitar armoured car, outside on a driveway with the engine running, but no driver in sight. Something snapped inside Happy Day, and he hopped in and drove off smartish.

Bizarrely enough, nobody noticed for a while. The Scimitar was owned by an enthusiast, who had bought it in an army surplus auction and added it to the collection of large miltaria that overflowed his garden. It was road legal, and he used to drive it here and there for fun, so the neighbours thought nothing of it when they heard it drive off. He'd left the engine running to charge the battery and warm up, for it was a cold December day, and he was in the loo when Happy drove off, so he noticed nothing for a little while.

By the time the alarm was raised (and it took the enthusiast some time to persuade the police that he was serious and sober), Happy was quite a few miles away. The Scimitar can do up to fifty miles an hour on an open road with a good surface, and he was choosing little-used B roads that in those parts were long and straight. By now it was dark, around five o'clock in the early evening of a sharp, clear night. He drove fast but sensibly, for he was stone cold sober and very focused on one objective – to get to Nossex as soon as possible.

181

In fact, that wasn't all that far, forty, fifty miles perhaps, and within an hour and a half he was heading down the series of farm tracks that leads to the only vehicle access to Nossex. It's designed for horse-drawn carts and wagons to come and go on an occasional discreet basis, and on the way in you eventually come to a padlocked metal five-bar gate a few hundred yards outside the North Hedge.

Happy didn't have a key, but nothing was going to stop him reaching Nossex, now that he was so close, so he drove through and over the gate, flattening it in the process, and carried on to the North Hedge, where there's another, narrower wooden gate with stone gateposts. The Scimitar was too wide for that, but he kept going, thoughtfully demolishing only one of the gateposts rather than both, and carried on up the slope on the far side of the hill from Chittock.

Now that he was in Nossex, he drove more slowly, which was just as well, for he was able to stop when the Guardian on duty stood ahead, in the middle of the track, and held up a hand. Demolishing a couple of gates is one thing; demolishing your own father quite another, and worth avoiding. Happy tumbled out of the Scimitar and into his father's arms.

'Sorry, Dad,' he said.

'Good to see you, James,' said John Day. 'You can tell me about it afterwards, but just now you need to hold yourself together a little longer, because you're going to have to drive that thing back out of Nossex tonight. At least the night is still young. We can do a lot before sunrise.'

They walked over the hill to Chittock, where happily it was evening meal time, so almost everyone was in the hall. John kept his son discreetly outside, and sent a messenger inside for the Fire Quenchers. They came out at a run, a dozen capable folk, and there was a short consultation. Everyone saw the situation as an immediate emergency: the defences of Nossex had after all not been breached to this extent for over a millennium.

Two or three went back into the Chittock hall, to recruit more helpers, and keen young runners were sent to Icclescombe and Quarrytown. Meanwhile most of the Quenchers went back with the Days, father and son, to the Scimitar, which looked very out of place in Nossex woodland.

Nobody said much; they took it from John Day's demeanour that now was not the time for talking, and they didn't even seem very surprised. As was commented afterwards, 'we didn't really expect someone to drive a tank into Nossex, but if anyone was going to do that, it would have to be James Day.'

With familiar faces around him, and totally surrounded by prayer, though he wasn't aware of it at the time, Happy felt strong enough to keep going. He backed carefully down the track, found a place to turn, and proceeded at walking pace back through the gap in the North Hedge, where a gate had stood two hours earlier. Two Quenchers stayed there and made a start on clearing the debris and rebuilding the gatepost.

The rest followed the Scimitar on down to the flattened five-bar gate. Here they first had to locate the padlock. Providentially, the full moon was rising, large and orange, over beyond the Wall Dyke, and it cast a strong light. John Day found the padlock, used his key to detach it from the twisted gate, and they were then able to tease the gate away from the drunkenly leaning gateposts, and leave two more Quenchers to reinstate those posts.

They then took the Scimitar and the ruined gate a half-mile further on, where an identical, but undamaged gate led off the track into a field. Checking first that the field contained no livestock, they took the good gate off its hinges and sent it back down the track to replace the flattened one. The idea was to put the damaged gate where the good one had been, and park the Scimitar in the field, so that it would at least be found three-quarters of a mile outside Nossex, rather than right on the borders.

All this time they were praying like mad that the farmer wouldn't notice the commotion. He was a Friend of Nossex, actually, but they were really twitchy about the defences being breached, and they felt very apprehensive about whether he would still be a Friend of Nossex if he knew they'd dumped a Scimitar armoured car in one of his fields.

In the midst of their prayers, before the Scimitar had turned into the field, the farmer strolled up.

'Hi, guys,' he said, 'would you be wanting to fly-tip that tank?'

There was an embarrassed pause.

'Because if you were,' he went on, 'by God's amazing providence I happen to have a hired flat-bed trailer in the yard, which has to be back at the hire base by nine tomorrow morning. I was going to make an early start anyway, but if you grant me three wishes, I'll make an even earlier one, and I know a deserted lay-by twenty miles away in the middle of nowhere, which would be a much better resting-place for that lump of metal. Wait right there and I'll back down with the trailer.'

In a few minutes he was back, and Happy turned the Scimitar again, and reversed it carefully onto the trailer. The farmer went inside to look at the controls, and Happy showed him how to start up.

The farmer gave Happy a long look.

'Afghan?' he asked.

Happy nodded.

The farmer squeezed his shoulder – or at least, the small part of the shoulder he could get his hand round.

'My boy's out there now,' he said, 'pray for him.'

'I will,' said Happy, and smiled for the first time in weeks.

They climbed out, and the farmer stood face to face with John Day.

'Three wishes,' he said.

'You can have thirty-three,' said John fervently, '*and* a new gate.'

'I'll sort the gate,' said the farmer. 'First wish: team of four, two days' hedging next week. Second wish: next autumn, team of four with scythes, sort out our wildflower meadows in the traditional way, and leave one scythe behind when they go. Last wish: a free meal in Chittock tomorrow night for myself and my better half, and we want to hear the story in full and at our leisure.'

'Cheap at the price,' said John, shaking hands. 'See you tomorrow night, and if you think of any more wishes, you're still in credit.'

The trailer drove off one way, and Happy walked the other, back to Nossex, between his father and his uncle, their arms round his shoulders: three burly men who could have taken on any front row anywhere. As they went they passed a horde of hard-working sweepers, carefully obliterating tracks all the way back to the North Hedge.

'I was praying the farmer wouldn't hear anything,' said John Day.

'So was I,' said his brother.

'There are times when No is better than Yes,' said John.

Twenty-five: Overnight in Icclescombe; walk to Pinginna *(4 miles)*

'Was Happy one of those I saw baptised last Sunday?' I asked.

'He was,' said Owen. 'It took a couple of years for him to work through a lot of anger, and fear, and horror. I had to listen to some of it; I was one of the counselling team, and pretty shocking it was. Some things he couldn't tell anyone for a long time, and when you heard them, you could understand why not.'

'Titus could do with that kind of help,' I said.

'That's one reason I'm on my way to Icclescombe now. He hasn't asked, but we reckoned there would be a need. We were only giving him time to settle in and feel at home here. Perhaps we could have been a bit prompter. Did he open up to you?'

'Only to say he needed to talk to someone, preferably not from Icclescombe.'

'We can respect that. Don't worry, he'll get all the time he needs. I'm glad he feels ready.'

'The Abbot told me he thought the early Nemetians had some sort of post-traumatic stress,' I said, 'and it all came from a battle they won.'

'I need to update him,' said Owen. 'We've been digging in the Old Nemsh archive, and just the other day, I found a poem. Some of the vocabulary's guesswork, but my attempt at an English translation goes like this:

Brittle their swords that broke on our shields
Keen our blades, slicing through bone
Drunken their warriors, not feeling the wounds
Sober our fighters, with faces of flint
Feeble their arms and weary their wrists, their mouths open and panting
Sturdy our shoulders and strong our hands from the forge and the axe
Three of ours died, with us no more
Three of theirs survived, captive in honour and shame
Their women wept, their little children wailed
They could not be comforted

A hand with no arm, a head with no body
Guts spilling into the red ditch
Ravens pecking at sightless eyes

What have we done?

'It's even starker in the Nemsh,' he commented. 'Hits you like a whip. Even before then, they didn't like fighting, but they would defend their land, and their smithwork was so much better than their neighbours' that they won easily if it came to a fight. This last battle, though, was the most one-sided of all, they just carved the enemy to pieces, effectively wiped out the menfolk of the other tribe.'

185

They took in the widows and orphans out of remorse, rather than triumphantly seizing them as slaves, but they felt dreadful about it, and closed the borders to avoid any repetition. They couldn't bear to use swords again, or even look at them, and the rather distinctive Nossex scythe owes its shape to its swordblade origins.'

'Not ploughshares?' I said.

'No, a sword doesn't actually make a very good ploughshare. But the Nossex scythe, they say, could take the hairs off a Fox Moth caterpillar without its noticing.'

'When and where did this happen?'

'Good question,' said Owen. 'From genealogies, the date might be around 275BC, allowing 25 years per generation. As to where, we don't know for sure, but did you notice on the Nossex map that one corner has no settlement?'

'The north-west,' I said, remembering the empty space.

'There's something unpleasant about Raven Hill. Nobody feels comfortable being there for very long. The sheep aren't bothered, and the grass grows, but we couldn't live there.'

'I don't care how many soldiers fall,' I quoted,

'I am the grass, I'll cover them all.'

Owen did not answer. Further into the woods, we came across an area being coppiced, and as usual briefly joined in the forestry work – at least, in my case, the tasks that were not too specialised. Owen showed his versatility by working the bodger's pole lathe for a quarter of an hour and turning a few chair legs, though he left it to the bodger to apply the final touches to his own satisfaction. I tried my hand at some bark-stripping, though I was mainly proving my incompetence, and soon went back to simple sawing tasks, until Owen judged it was time to move on.

'Birinn dai,' I said proudly in my beginner's Nemsh, as we headed off.

'Cirth dai,' was the response this time, so that I had to ask Owen again for a translation.

'Good walking,' he said.

We came out of the woodland and saw how our path ran down to a neat little stone bridge over the Middle Brook, then up the far slope to the clustered cottages of Icclescombe. I glanced sideways at Owen's strong square-jawed profile, and recognised that despite his self-deprecating manner, he was a key member of the Nossex community.

'Talking of those who were baptised on Sunday,' I said, 'I saw Hezekiah Hughes and John Smith, the following morning, talking and, I think, praying together.'

'Yes,' said Owen. 'That's a high risk, but I would hope a high reward situation. They both have a need to deal with the old man, the unregenerate parts. Sanctification takes time. But it could benefit Hezekiah to have a weaker character to encourage and build up, and the friendship of Hezekiah could build up John's confidence. A lot of his problems stem from lack of confidence. I could tell you a story or two, but that would be gossip.'

'Does Nossex try to avoid gossip? That must be difficult where everybody knows everybody else.'

'It certainly is difficult, it's a sin we often have to confess. We like to look after each other, we want to make sure everybody's supported, but the hard thing is to care for people without compromising their autonomy, and to take an interest in their welfare without encroaching too far into their lives. People are more independent these days – of course, not as much so as Outside, but we're slowly moving a little in that direction. In the old days nobody tried to be independent. There's no Nemsh word for *privacy*, for example. If I was speaking Nemsh I'd probably refer to it as *privisi*, which makes it rather obvious that it's a foreign concept. But all the same, it's better not to force assistance on people if they resist being helped.'

As we came towards the dinky one-arched bridge over the brook, a heron rose from the shallows, flapping awkwardly at first to gain height, then regaining its dignity with slow measured wingbeats on a typical curved trajectory downstream. I felt impelled to pause on the bridge for a moment and take in the views upstream and down, hoping that Owen wasn't in a hurry. But he seemed happy to stand for a moment.

'I used to fish here as a boy,' he said. 'It's still one of my favourite places.'

We watched a water wagtail, bobbing on a damp stone near the bank. A couple of mallard drakes drifted aimlessly in the current, and a white butterfly flew jerkily around yellow and purple flowers at the water's edge. The silence surrounding the bubbling of the stream was momentarily broken by the squawk of a moorhen. At the head of the Middlebrook valley I could see the Pinrose buldings, in their idyllic setting, high up but in the lee of the encircling hillside, sheltered from the prevailing winds. It was easy to see why Gaius the Elder had chosen to build his villa and his community there. Somehow it made the whole valley seem homely.

'I envy you digging in the archives,' I said. 'I meant to have a good look in the Blackfriars Library, but what with the Inquisition and the Querimonia, there wasn't the time.'

'That's not the only archive,' said Owen. 'We have a Nemsh archive in Chittock, then there's a substantial store in the Noaster Library, and most of the oldest and most valuable originals are in a cave behind Quarrytown – temperature and humidity controlled. The Quenchers insist that there should be at least two copies of every original, so that if there is a fire or a flood, they don't have the burden of having failed to prevent irreparable loss. But if you're leaving Nossex via Pinginna, then you have missed your chance of a good dig in the old documents.'

'I wanted to see Esther Breeze's notebooks,' I said.

'Of course – you're a musician. You'll have to come back and do a One-in-Twelve as an archivist. They're always looking for folk to help with copying and digitising.'

'Seriously?'

'Why not?' he answered. 'It's only Outside busyness that would stop you.'

We moved on, up the gentle slope towards Icclescombe. I wondered if I would meet all the same people: Megs, Titus, John and Ruth. If Megs' English conversation class was on, I could perhaps sit in and be a little more involved this time.

As we approached the village, from a slightly different angle from my first visit the previous week, I noticed the smell of roses and lavender, and remembered that I'd been told that one of Icclescombe's cottage industries was perfumes and essences, mostly for export Outside. Most Nossexfolk preferred to leave the nice smells where they were, someone had said, but they had enough to spare for those Outside who liked to carry smells round with them.

Titus was there, digging over a patch of ground. As he saw us approaching, he stuck his spade in the earth and drew himself up to his full lean height, flexing his back, before coming over to greet us.

'Mr Steve,' he said. 'You bring us an Earl. A great honour for us.'

'Earl *Consort*,' said Owen. 'My wife's the one with the responsibility.'

Titus laughed delightedly. 'Nossex is upside down,' he said. 'The men are humble, and the women are strong.'

'Not like that where you come from?' suggested Owen.

A shadow passed over Titus's face. 'Some of our women need to be very strong,' he answered. 'But the men with guns and grenades, they are not humble.'

'You could tell me about that,' said Owen. 'After lunch?'

Titus looked at me. 'Your prayers are answered very fast, Mr Steve.'

'It's not who prays that makes things happen,' I said, 'but who you pray to. And Owen was coming anyway.'

'God hears our prayers before we say them,' answered Titus. 'It's an answer all the same.'

Owen walked across to where Titus had been digging, and picked up another spade lying nearby. I left them working away in silent togetherness. Digging is not one of my top skills, and in any case I couldn't see a third spade. I went on to the kitchen, which as I'd foreseen had plenty for a spare pair of hands to do. John and Ruth were there, peeling and chopping, and I joined in to shorten the task. We talked a little of the book that was already growing rather amorphously in my mind, and I told them of some of the experiences I'd had since leaving Icclescombe the week before.

Ruth made the point that the weather had been particularly kind. 'You could easily leave a reader with the impression that Nossex weather is always perfect,' she said. 'Of course, we have just the same weather as the nearest bits of Outside.'

'And it's an outdoor life a lot of the time for most of us,' said John. 'You have to be able to cope with a bit of wind and rain sometimes.'

'And snow,' said Ruth. 'Though we get a lot less than we used to.'

John had moved on to cooking enormous pancakes, thick oatcakes rather like those called Staffordshire or Derbyshire oatcakes Outside, depending where you happen to be. Here they had to be Nossex oatcakes, and today the recipe included a generous admixture of sweet peppers. The pans were almost a yard across, and as each one was done they were set aside to cool. One of my tasks was to take them out to the dining hall, where each one took pride of place on a table for a dozen folk. A slim woman of my age, or close to it, was putting bread, cheese and fruit out, and as our tasks were finished, and folk began to come in for the meal, it seemed natural to sit together. I was keen to see what the oatcakes would taste like.

'Hi, I'm Abbi,' she said, with a smile that put creases in her cheeks and laughter lines around a pair of startlingly blue eyes. It was a handsome face, suntanned and framed by close-cropped grey hair.

'I'm Steve,' I answered, and as I explained that I was just a visitor, and recounted a little of what I'd seen of Nossex, echoes of phrases that Howell had reported ran through my mind: *hair in a short spiky style… a cheeky grin that put dimples in her cheeks… forget-me-not eyes…*

More like speedwell, or even alkanet, I thought pedantically, but of course forget-me-not made a much better metaphor. Could this be Sparky's requited but unchosen love? From what Howell had said about his grandfather, he must have been of my father's generation, which would make Abbi about my age. If this was her, it was not difficult to see what had bowled Sparky over.

'What do you do?' I asked.

'Electrical maintenance and computer support,' she answered, which more or less clinched it. 'Hardware, software, and I help train the wetware, which is the most challenging part.'

She asked me my plans for the rest of my stay, and on hearing that I was soon leaving, via Pinginna the next day, she offered to walk there with me, providing we left reasonably promptly after breakfast. I was happy to agree, silently marvelling once more at how Nossex always seemed to come up with a companion for the next leg of my journey.

Megs was nowhere to be seen, and Titus told me she was teaching in Quarry-town, and so there wasn't an English conversation class on a Thursday. I certainly couldn't be any help with Abbi's tasks for the afternoon, installing and customising software on Icclescombe's communal computers, so I went outside and found myself employment picking plums in one of the orchards, then carrying baskets into the kitchen.

After begging a little vinegar for a wasp sting, I stayed to help in the lengthy de-stoning operations, until there was a break for some herbal tea.

Feeling I'd had enough of de-stoning by then, I decided to catch up a little with writing notes for the book, and went over to where my rucksack was propped in a corner of the hall. Before I'd scribbled more than a line or two, however, a tune floated back into my head that had been there before, when I'd had no chance to write it down. Now that I had paper and pencil in my hand, it was too good an opportunity to miss.

I tried snatches of the new tune on the whistle, writing it down in abc notation bar by bar:

d2 d2 A2 | GE2 FGA | FG/A/Bc/d/ed/c/ | Bee^GAA/G/ |
F2 A2 f2 | ed2 Adc | BG2 cBA/G/ | FD2 EFG |
AfecdA | Bd2 c/B/AF | GeFdEc/e/ | dc/B/AF/E/D

I looked up as I made the last alteration, and there was Megs.

'Are you composing, or remembering?' she asked, with one of her bewitching smiles.

'I hope I'm composing,' I said, 'but how to be sure? Can I play it for you?' I explained its purpose of rounding off a set of tunes, and played *Orleans Baffled*, then *Madge's Maggot*[1], and finally the new tune.

'Yes, that's nice,' she said when I'd finished. 'It does the job.'

'OK,' I said, 'I'll call it *Megs' Approval*.

'A tune with my name on!' She smiled again. 'You'll never be able to forget me now.'

Now what did she mean by that, I wondered, before realising that it was just a joke. Meanwhile she was looking at my scribbled abc notation, and asking if I could write it out in staff, which I did:

She was ready to try it out on one of the recorders from the bag on her shoulder, when Titus came by with an invitation for me to join him at the prayer meeting. He looked at Megs, and was about to speak. She shook her head: a tiny movement, without her usual smile, but Titus accepted it, and we went off together, leaving her playing the new tune.

The prayer meeting was as intense and noisy as before, and the focus just as international. There was much thanksgiving for the newly baptised, and prayer for their future. I thought particularly of the men and the boy whose stories I had heard.

[1] see *Upper Thames & Wiltshire Ramble*

190

The evening meal once more featured large tasty pies, and I wondered if Icclescombe Pie was a staple. This time it wasn't rabbit and mushroom, but duck, carrot and hazelnut. By now I knew enough about Nossex cuisine not to expect large amounts of duck, but I was a little surprised by some banter on the far side of my table.

'Warning: May Contain Duck,' said one.

'If you're very lucky,' added his neighbour.

'Mock Duck,' was another comment, leading to a series of facetious suggestions: Virtual Duck, Notional Duck, and Theoretical Duck.

'Chef dreamed of Duck last night.'

'A duck flew past the window as he was rolling the pastry.'

It seemed almost cruel, especially as the pie was particularly tasty and really did taste of duck. I had the impression with every mouthful that the next mouthful might be at least partly duck. Finally I realised that the man in the midst of the banter, almost choking with laughter, was actually the creative chef, who finally admitted having made nine large pies from one small mallard.

Once the washing up was finished, the evening seemed short. Folk were chatting, reading, writing, knitting or practising different kinds of embroidery or craft. The hall was full of shadows, with little bright pools where people were sitting who needed light for what they were doing. I took the chance to catch up on some notes, completing what I'd intended to write before I was sidetracked by the hornpipe.

Reaching a stopping point, I wandered outside, to find the landscape bathed in moonlight; it actually seemed brighter outside than it had in the hall. A half moon shone in the star-strewn sky over the hill above Pinrose, and a little way off stood Megs, all alone, her blonde hair like molten silver in the moonlight. Perhaps she was wondering if her distant lover was gazing at the same moon.

Titus came out of the doorway behind me, and looked across at his English teacher. He said nothing, and I could not guess at his thoughts. Was he concerned for her salvation? He must have known she was not a believer. Was he simply feeling compassion for her loneliness, able to empathise because of his own lack of someone to love? Or did he in fact love her, without hope for at least two reasons?

I suppressed an impulse to go over and talk to Megs, and strolled a few yards in a different direction. One or two others were emerging into the moonlit evening. I noticed that a stocky dark-haired girl began chatting to Titus; it was Carys' friend, that she had spent time with when I first came to Icclescombe. They made an incongruous couple, for he had to bend his lanky frame in order not to tower over her. But it was good to see a happy grin brighten his face, and to hear his characteristic chuckle. I wondered if this might be the beginning of another answer to prayer. At least it was cheering him up just now.

Going back in, I met Ardil, the newly baptised Kurd, who I knew from Megs' conversation class. He invited me to join him in the room he shared with Titus; there was another bed there, he said. I was glad to accept, as I'd been wondering if it would be in order for me to invite myself to John and Ruth's again.

As we turned in, Titus came to join us, and we shared a brief time of prayer, mostly giving thanks. Titus particularly mentioned 'answered prayers', and I noted the plural. As he blew the candle out, he said: 'He is a good man, the Earl Consort. Both humble *and* strong. I think I make no more jokes about Nossexmen.'

'Behind every good Nossexwoman,' I said, 'there is a good Nossexman in support. Don't stop making jokes, they're a Nossex currency.'

I suddenly thought of Tabby, on her own – but of course, not on her own, she had the best man of all in support. The perfect man.

Friday 3ʳᵈ October 2014

I had wondered how exotic breakfast might be, with an African and a Kurd. They say that everyone's tastes are most conservative at breakfast, and we crave familiar childhood food. To my surprise, Ardil prepared authentic Scottish oatmeal porridge, with salt, which he said he had learned from a Scottish doctor in Kurdistan.

It prompted me to tell the story of Ishbel and myself in Turkey nearly thirty years before, trying to find oats to make up some muesli for ourselves, looking the word up in the dictionary, and being referred to a narrow side-alley where the dealer seemed very surprised that we wanted just one kilo. Only when we got the oats home and found how coarse and nubbly they were, did we realise we'd been sent to a supplier of horse fodder.

Ardil laughed and said his Scottish friend had had the identical experience in northern Iraq.

Outside, it was another fine morning, and I was soon on my way, walking down to Deborah's Stones with Abbi. As I had done the previous week, I paused at the spot where Quarrytown came into view. Having been there and seen it close up and from the inside, it seemed even more impressive.

Abbi was more prepared to linger than Megs had been. 'Superb engineering,' was her comment.

'Did you go to school there?' I asked.

'No chance, I'm not at all creative. Maths was my strong point in the village school, so I went to the Blackfriars, and got into physics and engineering.'

We went on down to the South Brook, and at various points I noted that the leaves were just beginning to turn. Views that Megs had shown me, that had been almost entirely green, were now showing attractive patterns of yellow and green. A couple of times we paused to gather hazelnuts, but Abbi seemed conscious of needing to get to Pinginna before too much of the morning had gone.

Down in the valley, a pair of lapwing flapped away upstream in their distinctive style, crying their querulous pee-wit into the middle distance. As we came to Deborah's Stones, Abbi asked me if I knew the rhyme.

'What rhyme?'

'The one the children chant as they cross the brook.' She quoted:

Tears of sorrow; tears of joy;
Lose a girl and gain a boy.
Lose a son and gain a daughter;
Death will come and grant no quarter.
Nine shall sleep before December;
Twelve the stones that help remember.

'The rhyme's a bit obscure if you don't know the story behind it,' she said. 'It's one of the Twelve Tales of Nossex; have you heard it?'

'No, I haven't; but I've already heard twelve Tales, from twelve different people, as they say is traditional.'

'No reason why you can't hear another one. We'll call it a Nossex dozen. In any case, you shouldn't cross Deborah's Stones without having heard the Tale.'

'I've already crossed them once,' I admitted. 'Megs brought me this way from Icclescombe to Quarrytown.'

'And she didn't tell you the Tale of the Stones? Shame on her.'

'She told me the Tale of Abbess Tilflæd and Earl Alain.'

'Did she now?' said Abbi, half to herself.

'It followed on from the Tale of Alain's arrival in Nossex, which I'd heard the evening before.'

'Of course. Well, let me tell you about Deborah and her Stones.'

We sat down beside the brook, almost opposite where I'd sat with Megs nine days earlier, but facing upstream so that the view was quite different, with the Stones in the foreground, and Abbi began.

Twenty-six: The Tale of Deborah's Stones

...he will swallow up death for ever. The Sovereign Lord will wipe away the tears from all faces. Is 25:8

Deborah Cohen was born in Pinginna, probably in the late 1320s, a few years after the horror of the Great Murrain. By the time of the Black Death, she was married with a young son, and another baby on the way. Judah ben David and Naomi his wife, who had been prominent in the defence against the Murrain and the evil weather of that time, were still alive, and at the first rumour of the Black Death's arrival in the south of England, they insisted that the borders of Nossex be sealed, with no exceptions. And so in 1349 that awful scourge passed Nossex by.

In Pinginna this good outcome was not credited particularly to Judah and Naomi. They had not been spoken of by the Jews of Pinginna, since their conversion and departure, and the Christians of Pinginna respected this silence. But everyone was glad to have escaped the plague, especially when they learned of the devastation it had caused Outside.

Time passed; Deborah had six more children, all of whom survived infancy, and she counted herself blessed, especially so because her husband Caleb was exceptionally loving, kind, and helpful. He loved to spend time with his children, and would even help with housework if he could do so without people noticing.

In 1361 there was talk of a fresh outbreak of plague, but it seemed much less virulent than the original terrible pandemic, and the Nossex borders might have been left open (at least, as open as they were normally), if Naomi had not insisted on closing them again. By now she was very old, and Judah was dead, but the intensity of her argument carried the Council with her. Nossex escaped once more.

When Deborah was some forty years old, Caleb her husband fell ill, of a sickness that had no precise location, simply leaving him increasingly weak and short of breath. At first he tried to keep going as if nothing was amiss, but one day he slipped on a stepping-stone and fell full length in the South Brook. There were men with him, and they fished him out and got him home quickly, but it was a cold day, and he caught a chill, from which he never really recovered.

At first Deborah assumed that her husband would eventually get well again, even though he showed little sign of improvement. Meanwhile her anxiety was focused in anger over the state of the crossing of the South Brook. There was a series of wobbly little stepping-stones, liable to be submerged in times of flood; and in one place a rather long stride between stones that challenged the timid, the frail, and the short-legged. She decided that one useful thing at least would come out of Caleb's fall: she would make sure that this long stride was shortened, with solid flat-topped stones either side.

With five strong young sons, she had no need to carry stones herself. But she specified the height and placement of the new 'stone' (it was really more like a small pillar), supervised the choice of component slabs, and watched over the construction process, making sure nothing was skimped. The largest slab at the bottom of the pillar

194

was firmly embedded in the streambed, and the top was carefully levelled off, rough side up. On the day it was finished, Caleb died, and through their tears the boys called it 'Father's Stone'.

Impressive as the stone was, it was not much help without another of similar design to stride to and from, and the 'boys' (the eldest two were really young men) carried on. It gave them something to do that helped them handle their grief, and they could work with less supervision now that they had a template to copy.

Deborah was less free to supervise them anyway, for her mother-in-law Miriam had fallen sick in her turn. It did not appear to be the same sickness as Caleb's, but was perhaps connected in that old Miriam had insisted on doing most of the caring for her son, and had exhausted herself in the process, before seeing him lose his hold on life. Now Deborah had to do the nursing, and her anger intensified. She had always got on well with her mother-in-law, unlike some, and she could not bear the thought of losing her as well.

She took to repeating prayers for the sick, until she lost patience and spoke to God directly in her own words, like Hannah of old, asking him to show whether he really was compassionate and merciful. A strange sense of peace stole into her heart, and then Miriam fell into a deep sleep and lay without moving for hour upon hour. Deborah wondered if she had been presumptuous, and was about to be punished, but deep down the peace was still there, and eventually her mother-in-law sat up and said 'Is there any food in the house?'

With tears of gratitude, Deborah hastened to prepare a meal. When the boys came back to report that the second stone was finished, they saw their grandmother dressed and tucking into chicken broth, and the stone became 'Grandma's Stone' forthwith. Rejoicing, the boys went on to begin a third stepping-stone, and from now on the aim was to complete the crossing with all stones at the same level and to the same standard.

They did not neglect their normal duties, or school work in the case of the younger boys, but with five of them the work progressed well. Their three sisters were not directly involved; one was not inclined to that kind of labour, and the other two were too young. The youngest, eight-year-old Esther, was desperate to help, but her brothers would not allow it. She was a lively, active child, and one day she was playing on a dilapidated wall when part of it collapsed, and she fell. She did not fall far, but somehow she was flipped over, and her neck was broken on landing. There was barely a mark on her body, but there was no breath in it.

The whole community wept for little Esther, Jews and Christians together. She had been everybody's favourite, full of gaiety and mischief. Her brothers took one of the stones from the offending wall, and incorporated it in 'Esther's Stone', the third to be completed.

Deborah was distraught, and furious as well: angry with God for the way he was treating her, and angry with the community for not dealing with wobbly stepping-stones and rickety walls before they caused unnecessary death. She said bitter things about lazy builders and men who left essential jobs to be done by somebody else.

Her sons took note, and later, when the dreadful events of that year were past, and Deborah's Stones were complete, they became a band of builders, or rather rebuilders, going all over Nossex seeking out cracks and bulges in walls, dry rot and wet rot and mould, sagging roofs and dangling guttering. This was the start of the Corps of Stone Surveyors, also known as the Plummeteers from their constant use of plumb-lines to check the verticality of walls. To this day the Surveyors ensure that Nossex has no ruins or dereliction.

Meanwhile, by an odd coincidence, little Esther's funeral was shared with a cousin of Deborah's, a widow whose death left her only son an orphan. Young Nehemiah was twelve, of an age with Joseph, the youngest of Deborah's boys, and they were fast friends. From now on Nehemiah attached himself to the gang of five working on the stones, and the fourth stone was called 'Nemi's Stone'. It did not escape Deborah that 'Nehemiah' means 'God's comfort', but even if she was ready to feed him, consider him part of the family, and praise her sons for allowing him to help in their task, it seemed little comfort to think that she still had eight children. She was angry, hurt, and confused.

The trees were in full leaf, hawthorn blossom and cow parsley splashes of white amid the burgeoning green, as the fifth stone was completed. Through her sorrow and grief, Deborah was focusing on the approaching wedding of Reuben, her eldest, when her second son Jacob came to speak to her.

'Mother,' he said, 'I have to tell you that I am a Christian. I believe Jesus of Nazareth is the Messiah.'

Deborah was appalled. 'My son,' she wept, 'how could you do this? Now, of all times. After your father's death. After your little sister's death. And your brother about to be married. It will be hard enough to rejoice – and now you load shame on the family. What were you thinking of? Who has deceived you? Who enticed you away? Was it some shameless Christian girl?'

'It was no girl, mother,' he answered. 'It was Jesus himself. I have been reading the Christian scriptures. If you don't want your sons to become Christians, don't forbid them to read the Christian scriptures.'

'I did forbid you to read them,' she cried indignantly, mishearing him.

'That was what made me pick them up; I thought there must be something very interesting there, and there was.' He smiled, but his smile was hateful to her.

'Out!' she shouted. 'Out of that door and don't come back! I won't have you in Caleb Stamford's house.'

He hesitated for a moment, but she reached for a clay pot of little value, and as he darted out, it shattered on the door behind him. He was not present at his brother's wedding the following week, and Deborah varied the customary formula slightly but significantly, saying with forced cheerfulness 'we have not lost *this* son, and we have gained a beautiful Jewish daughter.'

The sixth stone had been finished off the day before the wedding, and the four remaining brothers named it 'Rachel's Stone' for their new sister-in-law. The fifth

196

stone remained nameless, though they all thought of it as 'Jacob's Stone'.

The days were shortening into the autumn of that hectic year of 1368, when one of the community returned from a journey Outside, coughing as if from a chest infection. At first nobody thought too much of it, but the patient's health worsened rapidly, and soon he was coughing blood. Inside two days he was dead, and soon afterwards, three others that had been in contact with him sickened.

The rumour of yet another flare-up of the plague, now more or less endemic Outside, had not reached Pinginna. Old widow Naomi was no longer alive to remind people of the danger, and the response had been half-hearted: some entrances sealed, but not all. Everybody had left the task of informing Pinginna and sealing off the Maze entrance to somebody else, and nothing had happened. Later, Deborah made a formal complaint to the Senior Rabbi, who spoke to the Earl and Council, and the border guards were reorganised, expanded, and given extra responsibility under the new name of the Band of Guardians, which still functions efficiently today.

Meanwhile, immediate action had to be taken. The first essential was to isolate Pinginna from the rest of Nossex. The sons of Deborah undertook to act as sentries by the brook, as they continued work on what were already known as 'Deborah's Stones'. Deborah herself volunteered to act as nurse, more than half hoping that her own death would release her from the grief of this nightmare year. Still, she took what precautions she could, covering herself from head to foot, wearing gloves and a mask, less for her own protection than to encourage the other nurses to be cautious.

Caution also dictated separation between those who were sick, those who had been in contact, and those who, it was hoped, were still uninfected. Although in those days the transmission of bubonic plague was mysterious, in this pulmonic outbreak it was clear enough that coughing and sneezing and physical contact were transmitting the disease person to person. Until the end of the year Deborah had no more contact with her children than shouted greetings and instructions at a distance of thirty yards. The new bride Rachel found herself cooking for nine under her grandmother-in-law Miriam's direction, and learned rapidly.

Nursing could do little more for the plague victims than reduce their suffering. Hardly any recovered, and nine died. But by November there were no longer any new infections. They kept potential contacts isolated until Christmas, at which point all came together to share both thanksgiving and grief. Jews and Christians had suffered alike, for the first contacts had been nurses from both sections of the community.

Deborah's Stones were also finished by Christmas, twelve in number. For her family the first six each held their memories, sad or happy; for other bereaved families, who had assisted with the later stones, some of the last six were special. In later years they came to have other, more general names, and while children might skip across chanting the 'Tears of Sorrow' rhyme, older folk might use the stones as an aid to remembrance and prayer, pausing on each stone and meditating on the associations of its name: Bereavement; Healing; Sudden Death; Adoption; Betrayal; Marriage; Suffering; Patience; Determination; Faithfulness; Sacrifice; and Restoration.

Twenty-seven: Overnight in Pinginna; Departure from Nossex *(4 miles)*

'When I heard the story of Judah ben David,' I said, 'I didn't think about the effect on the community they left behind. It must have been a shock to lose a whole extended family like that.'

'Not a whole family,' Abbi corrected me. 'Esther left her siblings, her mother, her nephews and nieces and cousins behind, which was very hard. I should know. In terms of numbers, the Jews of Pinginna could take the loss. At that time, they were quite prolific, outnumbering the Pinginna Christians, because several families had arrived in the years leading up to the 1290 expulsion, and then many children were born in the next twenty years. But the sense of betrayal was still very strong, which accounts for Deborah's reaction to Jacob's announcement.'

'Is there still a reaction like that if a Jew becomes a Christian?' I asked.

'There's no way of saying what's typical, because I'm the only example in living memory of a Pinginna Jew who has converted and stayed in Nossex. There may have been conversions Outside, of people who have stayed Out and haven't kept in touch, but we wouldn't know about them. You see, the Pinginna Christians have bound themselves not to proselytise, so it's only possible for someone with a background like mine to hear the Gospel Outside, or at least elsewhere in Nossex. And although they're not bound in the same way, elsewhere in Nossex they're very cautious.'

'Where did you hear the Gospel, then?' I prompted.

There was a long pause, while Abbi seemed far away in memory. I watched the brook swirling through the narrow channels between the Stones. A little way upstream, a duck quacked, long and stridently.

'In Edinburgh,' she said finally. 'I was very fortunate – or blessed – to get a grant from the Nossex Purse on the strength of my maths and physics, and I went to Heriot Watt, which had only recently gained full University status. Scotland was quite a culture shock for me, and so was the student counter-culture of the late sixties. I was tempted, shocked, attracted and repelled, nervous and inquisitive all at the same time. I'd been curious to find out more about Christianity for a long time, but my curiosity hadn't been encouraged in Pinginna. Now I was a long way away, which was both liberating and frightening.

'By the grace of God, I found myself sharing a room with Catriona, a girl from the Hebrides, who had come from a very strict Presbyterian background. She was a committed believer, but she had questions about some of the stricter practices of her own denomination, and like me, she wanted to explore new ideas, but was repelled by the atheism and sexual permissiveness that surrounded us. We encouraged, support-ed, and I guess protected each other.

'I managed to avoid the relatively small Jewish community in Edinburgh, but Catriona wasn't as completely off the leash as me, because there were churches of her own denomination in Edinburgh that she was expected to attend. She compromised by attending one of them on Sunday mornings, taking me along, and then in the evenings we did the rounds of other Edinburgh churches.

'After a while we ended up at Charlotte Baptist Chapel. At the same time we were going to Heriot Watt CU meetings. I was impressed that they used the whole of Scripture, and that the Christian writings, what they called the New Testament, referred back again and again to things that were already familiar to me. I'd shared with Catriona that I was Jewish, but otherwise I kept quiet about that, and just asked questions, observed the Christian students, and read the four Gospels again and again.

'I suppose I already believed by the end of my first year, but I put off making a full public commitment till near the end of my second year. I was baptised at Charlotte Chapel, and then had to come home to Nossex and tell my family.'

'What happened?'

'It was like being swept up in a whirlwind. I didn't know which way was up. The family reacted more with grief than anger, but the grief was so extreme that it put me under incredible emotional pressure. Pinginna Jews don't give a fig for Nossex Oppression Law. The Rabbi spoke pleadingly to me. I could have coped more easily if he'd been angry. All my childhood friends came to see me, one by one, and cried. I'm sure it was orchestrated, at least to some extent, and at first I almost lost my grip on reality, and was tempted to doubt the authenticity of my own experience. But in the end they overdid it, and it awoke a stubbornness in me.

'I had to move out, and become part of one of the other communities, so that I could worship with Christians without spoiling things for the Pinginna community. And the relationship with my parents has never been the same, though at least we managed to avoid a total rift.'

'That's something,' I said.

'It was an answer to prayer. It cost them a lot, to overcome their feelings of betrayal, and forgive me up to a point – enough to keep in touch, anyway. I took a while to settle down and get married – I kept being attracted to the wrong men – but when I did, my parents wanted to meet Gareth, my husband, and persuade him to allow our children to be brought up in the Jewish faith. He never absolutely agreed to that, but in the end it was a non-issue, because we didn't have children of our own, and so we fostered teenagers, who mostly already had their own ideas about what they believed.'

'You don't do that any more?' I asked, as we set off again, and began to cross the stepping stones. Abbi lingered on the first stone.

'Gareth died six years ago,' she said quietly. 'And he was ill for a couple of years before that, so when our last foster-child went on her Years Out, we said to the Council that we were no longer available.' She continued across the stones, and conversation had to pause until we reached the far bank.

'It must have been very hard for you,' I said, conscious that anything I said would be inadequate.

'Of course, but oddly enough I was more upset by something else. That same year another special person died, an older man, a former colleague that I admired very much. In fact, I'd had a bit of a crush on him once, but when I heard he'd died, I'd

199

not seen him to speak to for years. No chance to say goodbye.'

'Unfinished business,' I suggested.

'Unstarted business,' she said, 'and much better so, but it hit me quite hard. With my husband, I could see it coming, and when he finally died, in some ways it was a relief: no more suffering for him, and less strain for me. I did a lot of my grieving in advance.'

The path slanted upwards through woodland that was a mixture of pine and birch. Small birds were cheeping incessantly in the canopy, keeping out of sight, though by the sound they were goldcrests.

'It's really difficult to see someone suffer,' I ventured after a pause.

'To be fair,' she said, 'Tabby and her team did a good job of pain control. We may not have the full range of modern drugs available in Nossex, but we're not ignorant either. There's a great bank of knowledge of herbal remedies and how to use them safely, and Tabby worked Outside for quite a few years as a Macmillan nurse, so she knows about tailoring the drugs to the individual. They worked out what suited Gareth. He wasn't in a lot of pain, but being ill frustrated him. He liked to be helpful, and in his last days he couldn't.'

We came out of the trees, and ahead and slightly higher on the hillside were two long terraces of dwellings, one above the other. As we approached there was a powerful smell of cheese, borne towards us on a westerly breeze. Abbi took a deep breath.

'Welcome to Pinginna,' she said.

We walked along the lower terrace until we came to a handsome stone building that I guessed was the usual communal hall. Abbi explained that because Yom Kippur would begin an hour before sunset, at about half-past five, the *kaparot* meal, that Jews and Christians traditionally ate together in Pinginna, would be an early afternoon meal in place of lunch. This meant that she had until the meal to get her upgrades installed, and so she was keen to get started. Spotting a youngish man she knew, who didn't appear too busy, she introduced me to him, and asked him if he had time to show me round the village.

Sam said he would be happy to do that, and at once had to field my first question about the *kaparot* meal.

'It's an old custom,' he said, 'probably from eastern Europe, which symbolises atonement, God's removal of our sins, and the substitution of an innocent victim. It was traditionally carried out the day before Yom Kippur, and originally a live chicken was waved over your head, before it was killed and given to the poor. Nowadays there are issues of animal welfare, so here in Nossex we don't do any bird-waving. And there isn't anyone poorer than us, so we eat the chicken ourselves.

'In Pinginna the tradition has developed of sharing the meal with both communities. Once Yom Kippur begins, the Jews will withdraw and celebrate by themselves, but in the run-up they like to share with the Christians as far as possible. Both communities believe that everyone is sinful, and that only God can remove sins. The

200

only disagreement is about how He does so. And the Jews certainly don't believe that the death of a chicken *achieves* atonement. It's only a symbol.'

Sam led the way into the main hall, a long building at the centre of the village, and pointed out that there was a kitchen at either end of the hall. In this way all the food could be stored and prepared separately, but the two communities could eat under one roof and establish a degree of togetherness. In the case of today's meal, he said, the chef would be Jewish, and the chicken would be prepared in the Jewish kitchen, while the Christian kitchen would prepare vegetables to the chef's specifications.

'We'll come back here and lend a hand,' he said, 'but I said I would give you a tour,' and he headed back out into the sunshine. One long street ran along the hillside above and behind the hall, while another ran parallel below, passing in front of the hall. We walked up to and then along Higher Street, which was flanked on our left, the upper side, by a long terrace of two or sometimes three storeys. This, Sam told me, was where the Jews lived. The ground floor was mostly byres and stables for a variety of livestock, with some workshops here and there, and there were external stone staircases to the upper floors, which appeared to be dwellings. On our right was a fine view over the roofs of the terrace houses along Lower Street, and across the valley to the wooded hillside opposite.

As we strolled along, Sam filled me in on Pinginna history: how silver had been discovered in Roman times, and the villagers were afraid of the intense interest the Romans would surely take in Pinginna if the discovery became generally known. A pair of Jewish traders had promised to keep the secret, and undertaken to smuggle the ore out via Noaster and London. It was in their interest to keep the secret, and even if the traders kept a good proportion of the profit, the Pinginna folk considered that a price well worth paying to remain undisturbed. Even back then, they were more interested in peace than profit.

Soon there were a few Jews among the small band of miners, and a few others settled in Pinginna as well, until there were sufficient men for a synagogue to be formed. They traded in wool, and flax, and woven linen, partly as a cover for the transport of the silver. And so when the silver was finally worked out, towards the end of the Roman period, there were enough alternative commodities for a small trading community to survive. Some left when the borders were closed at the Breaking of the Bridge, but enough remained to continue as a distinctive group. They became tailors to all of Nemet, and also specialised in gardening, in particular cultivating plants for fruit and spices, often plants that were not frost-hardy, and that required extra care. I realised that some of the more exotic spices I'd noticed might not have been imported after all.

At the western end of the village, Sam showed me the synagogue, which was simply the end of the long terrace, taking the shape of a hall two storeys high. Across the road was an entrance to the attic of the end house of the terrace below. Sam took me inside, where we descended a staircase into a well-stocked, indeed well-packed library, with bookcases lining stairs and landings like a second-hand bookshop Outside. By this time, however, I had been in Nossex long enough not to imagine that these books might be for sale. I assumed, without even bothering to ask Sam, that they would be common property, available to all and treasured by all.

The great emphasis on study and learning, among the Pinginna Jews as well as the Nossexfolk, and Nemetians before them, must go back to the earliest times, said Sam, for the Jews had maintained a knowledge of Hebrew, to the extent that Cennis had consulted them when translating, or supervising the translation of the Scriptures into Saxon in the seventh century.

I could have lingered in the library for hours, but Sam seemed keen to move on, and led the way through tall canyons of bookshelves, down more stairs and out onto Lower Street. Terraced houses lined the right hand side, as we strolled back to the hall, while on the left was a fine view across and down the South Brook valley. We paused in one house to leave my rucksack where Sam said I could get a bed for the night.

Back in the hall, I offered my services in the kitchen as usual, but found myself redundant for once; they had enough workers, they said, so Sam and I sat with our backs to the high stone wall of the main hall and listened to the music.

Three musicians were practising in a corner, a clarinettist, an accordionist, and a fiddler, trying over klezmer tunes. I was delighted by one slow melody in particular, and later made a note of its name.

Ki Hinei Ka'Chomer

The woman chopping vegetables sang a verse in a powerful contralto, and I asked for a translation, which Sam provided: *As clay in the hand of the potter, who stretches and squeezes it as he chooses, are we in Your hand, O God of loving-kindness; look at the covenant, not at our sin.*

'The melody is from 19th century Ukraine,' he added, 'but the words are many centuries older, developed from a verse in Isaiah.'

'Is there a strong eastern European connection here?' I asked.

'Pinginna Jews come from a lot of different traditions,' said the fiddler. 'Some families have been here centuries, but different people have arrived at various times, especially in the last hundred and fifty years, and so Pinginna practice has ended up as a compromise. People who couldn't adjust a bit just had to leave. We didn't throw anybody out for not conforming, but people left when they couldn't accept that their neighbour might have different ideas. Those who stayed were those who could agree to differ, or those who liked arguing. Most of us like arguing.'

'No we don't,' said the clarinet player.

'Yes we do. You're arguing now.'

'I'm not arguing, I'm simply making sure that an alternative viewpoint is not overlooked.'

'That's called arguing. That's what the word *arguing* means.'

The accordion player squeezed a fat chord and hurtled into a tune at furious tempo, which I half recognised as a well-known *freylech*. The two others stared at each other as if ready to pursue the argument, but meanwhile their fingers, and the clarinettist's mouth, picked up the melody almost as if the instruments were controlling their hands. Sam, too, had automatically started playing air guitar, the twisting of the fingers on his left hand proving that he was a genuine guitarist, not a wannabe. I wished I'd had my whistle to hand, though I'd hardly have been able to keep up.

When the time came for the chicken meal, it turned out to be a real feast by Nossex standards, with proper helpings of meat rather than occasional hints. I found myself sitting with the musicians, and we talked klezmer tunes, comparing the beauty of the Sephardi melodies and the Hasidic dance tunes.

Abbi came and sat on the other side of Sam, and apologised for having been rather curt earlier, offloading me onto him because she had so much to get done. Now her tasks were completed, and she asked after Sam's news. He talked about his mother-in-law's cancer remission; it was amazing what Outside medicine could do now, he said, with more targeted chemo and follow-up monitoring. Then he seemed to realise he'd been a bit crass, talking of survival rates to a widow.

'No need to apologise,' said Abbi calmly. 'Gareth knew what the trade-off was when he decided to stick with Nossex care and treatment. He died earlier than he might have done, but he had less unpleasant treatment, and less hassle with appointments and consultations. Health care comes to you in Nossex. And on average people live longer in Nossex anyway, because of the healthy diet, healthy lifestyle, and generally very healthy population.'

'Have some hereditary susceptibilities to illness been eliminated, then?' I asked. 'Either by natural selection, or by people who expected to need treatment leaving? Does Nossex export unhealthiness, the way it exports dissent?'

'Nobody's thrown out, or even politely asked to leave,' answered Abbi, just a little sharply. 'I'm sure you know that by now. But a young couple who knew they had a measurable chance of their child suffering from an inherited condition that would need modern medical support might well freely decide to make sure the child was born Outside. The effect of a number of decisions like that, over time, would be to export some types of health problem. But it's still fair for the Nossex lifestyle to claim most of the credit for our healthy population.'

When the meal was over, the Jewish community remained in the hall, while the Gentiles left, a number of the Christians adjourning to a largish house for a prayer meeting. There most of the prayer was for individuals. From the names, and the fact

203

that the person praying generally assumed that everyone there would know the person being prayed for, it was clear that they were praying for their Jewish neighbours, one by one and family by family.

After the prayer meeting Sam suggested reading in the library, and we headed that way, along with a few others that had had the same idea. I took some time to choose a book, fascinated by the ancient-looking volumes in Hebrew script, which I couldn't have begun to read. In the end I settled for *Pinginna Horticulturalists: Forty Gifted Gardeners*, which was a collection of brief biographies, ranging all the way back to Roman times, with lengthy digressions into the care of tropical and subtropical plants and trees. It was fascinating, but I was tired, and Sam spotted me nodding off and suggested we turn in.

Saturday 4ᵗʰ October 2014

Having gone to bed early, we both woke early, and headed off for an early breakfast in the hall: poached eggs and fried potato with a rather bland lightly roasted coffee substitute that was not the best I'd tried in Nossex.

We foraged for materials for a packed lunch for me – Sam said he would be home for lunch – and found a crusty rye loaf, hard sheep's cheese, a tomato, an apple, and walnuts and almonds, all of which promised to take a little of the Nossex experience beyond the border. It was soon packed, and we made our way back to our temporary abode, Sam also having been there only a couple of days.

'So are you a Nossexman,' I asked, 'or do you really belong Outside?'

'Am I a Nossexman? It's a question I sometimes ask myself' he said. 'My life has been like a mirror image of a young Nossexman's CV. I took Years In while my cousins took Years Out.'

'You have family connections, then,' I said, feeling very quick on the uptake.

'Well spotted. My grandparents on my mother's side were born here, in the Jewish community, but they stayed Out after their Years Out, got married, and drifted right away from religious observance. All the same, they kept a sense of Jewish identity, and were glad when their daughter, my mother, married a nice Jewish boy. He was also minimally observant, and that probably suited them well. But the family kept in touch with their Pinginna relatives, and there were visits in both directions. So I came here from time to time as a boy, and I loved it – perhaps especially the music, but also the sense of peace.'

'It's amazingly peaceful, isn't it?' I said.

'Perfect for a week or two, to get away from pressure and rush, and most of all, from fear. I came in for a fair amount of bullying at school. Anti-semitism is alive and thriving Outside, and a couple of the worst bullies lived quite near me, so even out of school time I couldn't forget about them. But once I set foot in Nossex they seemed a thousand miles away. Yet I never really thought about settling here, until everything went haywire in my first year at Uni.'

204

As Sam was telling his story, we had been descending an increasingly steep grassy hill, the path made safer by the natural steps caused by the passage of many feet over time. Below us, and to our left, a thick tangled hedge stretched away into dense woodland. Below and to the right, it looked as though the cliff I'd scaled on my way into Nossex curved round to meet the hedge, so that we would either have to climb down the cliff, or veer slightly left and find a way through the hedge.

The path steered us in the latter direction, plunging at first into thick shoulder-high bracken, then after three hairpin changes of direction, so that twice we were actually climbing briefly uphill again, it entered a vast mass of blazing yellow gorse that rose well above our heads. Here the twists and turns became more numerous, and there were often choices of path to be made. I followed Sam, who never hesitated for a moment, though he often chose what appeared to be the less well trodden alternative. It became clear that we were in a maze, and only the slope and the sun enabled me to keep any sense of direction. A very handsome yellowhammer, as bright as the gorse flowers, distracted me so that I completely lost track of the sequence of turns we had made before we finally emerged from the furze maze and squeezed through a narrow opening in a hawthorn hedge.

'I presume we're now Outside,' I said.

'We are indeed.'

'Can you tell me what changed your view of Nossex?'

'Sure.' We set off down a sloping meadow of lush long grass, with hardly a wildflower to be seen, except here and there round the edges. A buzzard mewed as it soared above trees in the middle distance. Gradually the path swung round to the north, until it was parallel to the cliff, and looked likely to lead us back to where I'd first ventured into Nossex.

'I studied Law,' Sam began. 'First big mistake. Just because I got good A level results, and my parents and the people advising me, and advising them, thought that the whole idea of life was to get into whatever profession would make you the most money. Nobody asked me whether I was interested in Law, though to be fair, I didn't know myself how boring I would find it, until I actually started. And I didn't realise either that I had no burning desire to make a stack of money, till I found it impossible to push myself to do any studying.'

'Did you think of changing courses?'

'There wasn't really anything else I was desperate to do,' said Sam. 'I enjoyed my music most, but I'd never studied the theory, so I wouldn't have got onto a music course. I was only nineteen, and very immature. I just ran away from the problem – skipped lectures and tutorials, missed deadlines for assignments, retreated into alcohol, soft drugs, and music. Then a girlfriend dumped me in favour of another member of a band I was in, so I left the band, and everything kind of caved in. I went home, and my youngest sister made the one sensible suggestion out of all the advice that was suffocating me. She said *Go and stay in Nossex for as long as it takes to calm down.*'

'How long did it take?'

205

'To calm down and get a sense of perspective? Maybe a few weeks. I was helped a lot by Abbi, actually, and her late husband. They kind of specialised in sorting out crazy mixed-up kids, mostly a bit younger than me. But even when I was more sorted and stable, I still felt I wanted to stay right out of the rat race. I had no wish at all to go back to university, or to start a career, or to make a lot of money. The Nossex life seemed infinitely preferable, so I stayed, for months and then for years.'

'But you didn't actually settle permanently,' I said. 'You referred to this period as *Years In*, so you must have gone back Outside.'

'After a while,' said Sam, 'I realised that my crisis at Uni had only been a surface problem, and there was a much bigger problem underneath. I started to see that the peacefulness of Nossex, its sensible approach to life, its healing qualities for someone suffering from anxiety, all these things didn't exist in a vacuum, but were based on what nearly all Nossexfolk believe, Jews or Christians: that ultimately God is in control, and we have to be in a right relationship with Him. And I wasn't. I'd ignored Him completely.

'So I spoke to the Chief Rabbi, and he talked to me on the assumption that I was a Jew, which of course technically I was and still am. Both my parents are Jewish, and their minimal observance did at least include having me circumcised. So for the Rabbi there was no hindrance to welcoming me back into the fold and filling in the gaps in my understanding of the faith. Yet as he talked, over the course of several meetings, I had a sense of incompleteness, something missing.

'I said as much to him, and he said I should check out Christian teaching, just to get a balanced perspective. Now the Pinginna Christians are under a strict obligation not to preach the Gospel to Pinginna Jews. I found out later, by the way, that they'd been praying for me for years. The agreement doesn't stop them from doing that, and a girl who'd had a soft spot for me since primary school insisted on praying for me regularly. She's my wife now, she still prays for me.

'Anyway, back to the story, the Rabbi told me to go and talk to the Bishop, which I thought was very brave and fair of him. Perhaps he was hoping and praying that I'd see no advantage in Christian teaching over Judaism. Unfortunately, from his perspective, it didn't turn out like that. Matthew was brilliant at linking everything from Genesis to Revelation. *Behold the Lamb of God, that takes away the sins of the world.* The scapegoat taking away the sins of the people. The Passover lamb dying instead of the firstborn. The ram in the thicket, slaughtered instead of Isaac.'

'He is the sacrifice,' I said.

'Exactly. Everything fell into place. So instead of being welcomed back into the Pinginna synagogue after my family had been missing for two generations, I was baptised in Noaster ten years ago. And after my baptism, Kate came and told me how long she'd been praying for me. I was really touched. And...' Sam laughed. 'I noticed she was really good-looking. Before long we were going out together. I knew her family, everyone knows everyone in Pinginna. So I took her Outside to meet my family; they're not far away.

'At the same time I had to tell them I was now a Christian. It didn't bother them at all, because they didn't believe at all. As far as they were concerned, it was as if I'd taken up Morris dancing, or joined Greenpeace. *Sure, if that's your thing now. Whatever.* Kate was totally shocked, she'd expected opposition.'

'Indifference is worse,' I said. We had come some distance northwards by now, and high on the hillside to our right I could see Cennis' Chair, with a small figure seated there, though it was too distant to identify, hardly more than a white spot on the rock. Close by on our left was a brook, and suddenly the familiar rudimentary bridge appeared. Sam led the way across, and we were back on the path I had walked almost two weeks before.

'We went to church on the Sunday,' Sam continued, 'which I'd never done in my home town before, and that was an interesting experience for both of us. For me, it seemed both like and unlike Christian fellowship in Nossex. The minister sounded on the right wavelength, but I wasn't sure about the congregation. Kate had had experience of strong churches during her Years Out, and she wasn't impressed with this one. It brought her back to a conviction that she'd felt during her Years Out, that the need for the Gospel was greater Outside, and even if she enjoyed life more in Nossex, that wasn't where she was called to settle. So when we started talking seriously about marriage, if I hadn't been prepared to come back Outside, that would have been a deal-breaker for Kate.

'There were actually some aspects of Outside life that I missed in Nossex. Amplified music – my electric guitar had gathered dust while I'd been in Nossex. Football. Beer. Marmite. And I felt strong enough now to cope with the things I didn't like. But I had to be sure I had my own call, and wasn't just hankering after trivial things, or agreeing to anything just to be with Kate. We prayed, and in the end we both had peace about it. We got married, and we settled in the town we're walking towards now. Kate's got a small gardening business; I help with that some of the time, and I'm in a ceilidh band and a klezmer band, both of which earn a little bit of money. We're part of a newish growing church, and we're close enough to Nossex to walk there when we're not too busy.'

'You mean this town just beyond the station? You really are close to Nossex.'

'Very near – and yet a whole world away,' said Sam. We emerged from the footpath onto the approach road to the back of the station, and found ourselves back in the land of yellow lines, concrete, and piles of litter. Sam said a brisk farewell, as he was already behind the time he'd promised to be back, and I was left to walk up onto the platform, and find out when the next train would deign to stop at the minor station that served this small town.

There was only half an hour to wait, to my relief; just time to scribble a few more notes and reflect on a fortnight in a different sort of society. I wondered if I would ever see Nossex again. At least I had a taste of it in my lunchbox.

207

Bibliography

Aaron, D (2007) *Living a Joyous Life* Trumpeter
Anon (1649) *Tyranipocrit Discovered*
Armstrong, K (2ed 1995) *Through the Narrow Gate* Flamingo
Armstrong, K (1983) *Beginning the World* Macmillan
Atkinson, P, Coffey, A, Delamont, S et al eds (2001) *Handbook of Ethnography* Sage
Backhouse, H ed (1985) *The Cloud of Unknowing* Hodder & Stoughton
Barnavi, E (1992) *A Historical Atlas of the Jewish People* Hutchinson
Bede (1990 tr Sherley-Price, L) *Ecclesiastical History of the English People* Penguin
Berneri, ML (1982) *Journey Through Utopia* Freedom Press
Borrow, G (1851) *Lavengro*
Briggs, A (1983) *A Social History of England* BCA
Brooke, C (1969) *The Twelfth Century Renaissance* Thames & Hudson
Bruce, FF (2ed 1982) *The Spreading Flame* Paternoster Press
Bruce, S ed (1999) *Three Early Modern Utopias* Oxford University Press
Burroughs, J (1648) *The Rare Jewel of Christian Contentment* Banner of Truth
Cannon, V (2011) *Gypsy Princess* Headline
Cavendish, M (1666) *The Blazing-World*
Chester, T & Timmis, S (2007) *Total Church* IVP
Claeys, G ed (2010) *The Cambridge Guide to Utopian Literature* CUP
Claeys, G & Sargent LT eds (1999) *The Utopia Reader* New York University Press
Clark, C & Greenfields, M (2006) *Here to Stay* University of Hertfordshire Press
Clark, D (2006) *The Rough Guide to Ethical Living* Rough Guides
Cohn-Sherbok, D (2000) *Messianic Judaism* Continuum
Comenius, JA (1638) *Didactica Magna*
Conkin, PK (1964) *Two Paths to Utopia* University of Nebraska Press
Csikszentmihalyi, M (1990) *Flow: the Psychology of Optimal Experience* Harper Perennial
Curtis, SJ & Boultwood, MEA (4ed 1965) *A Short History of Educational Ideas* UTP
Eliot, TS (1939) *The Idea of a Christian Society* Faber & Faber
Ellul, J (1978) 'Symbolic function, technology, and society' *J Social Biol Struct* 1/3
Ferguson, N (2009) *The Ascent of Money* Penguin
Ferns, C (1999) *Narrating Utopia* Liverpool University Press
Fokkema, D (2011) *Perfect Worlds* Amsterdam University Press
Gallet, P (1973) *Freedom to Starve* Penguin
Galtung, J (1969) 'Violence, peace, and peace research' *Journal of Peace Studies* 6/3
Galtung, J (1990) 'Cultural violence' *Journal of Peace Studies* 27/3
Gerson, M (1978) *Family, Women, and Socialization in the Kibbutz* Lexington
Gidley, M & Bowles, K eds (1990) *Locating the Shakers* University of Exeter Press
Goffman, E (1959) *The Presentation of Self in Everyday Life* Doubleday
Goldsmith, M (2014) *Storytelling* IVP
Griffiths, J (1984) 'Village Justice in the Netherlands' *Journal of Legal Pluralism* 23
Harris, JR (1995) 'Where is the Child's Environment?' *American Psychologist* 102/3
Harris, JR (1998) *The Nurture Assumption* Bloomsbury
Harris, JR (2000) 'The Outcome of Parenting: What do we Really Know?' *J Personality* 68/3
Henderson, G (1944) *The Farming Ladder* Faber & Faber
Henderson, G (1950) *Farmer's Progress* Faber & Faber

Herman, N (ca 1690) *The Practice of the Presence of God*
Hibbert, C (1987) *The English: A social history 1066-1945* Guild
Hill, C (1973) *Winstanley: The Law of Freedom and other writings* CUP
Hill, C (1975) *The World Turned Upside Down* Penguin
Hill, C (1977) *Milton and the English Revolution* Faber & Faber
Hilton, M & Marshall, G (1988) *The Gospels & Rabbinic Judaism* SCM
Hofstede, G (1980) *Culture's Consequences* Sage
Hostetler, JA (1974) *Hutterite Society* Johns Hopkins University Press
Jacobs, J (1892) 'Notes on the Jews of England under the Angevin kings' *Jewish QR* **4**/4
James, S (1993) *Exploring the World of the Celts* Thames & Hudson
John of the Cross (ca 1584) *Ascent of Mount Carmel*
Johnson, P (1987) *A History of the Jews* Weidenfeld & Nicolson
Julian of Norwich (1395) *Revelations of Divine Love*
Kerr, J (2007) 'Heavenly Hosts' *History Today* **57**/11
Kopciowski, E (1988 tr Clifford, P) *Praying with the Jewish Tradtion* Triangle
Lambert, R & Millham, S (1968) *The Hothouse Society* Weidenfeld & Nicolson
Langland, W (1959 tr Goodridge, JF) *Piers the Ploughman* Penguin
Law, W (1728) *A Serious Call to a Devout & Holy Life*
Lawrence, CH (2ed 1989) *Medieval Monasticism* Longman
Leland, CG (1873) *The English Gypsies* Trübner & Co
Lewis, C, Harding, P & Aston, M (2000) *Time Team's Timechester* Channel 4 Books
Lewis, CS (1936) *The Allegory of Love* Oxford University Press
Lieblich, A (1982) *Kibbutz Makom* André Deutsch
Lofland, J (1971) *Analyzing Social Settings* Wadsworth
Mabey, R (1972) *Food for Free* Collins
Maddicott, JR (1997) 'Plague in Seventh-century England' *Past and Present* **156**/1
Makin, B (1673) *An Essay To Revive the Antient Education of Gentlewomen*
McNamara, JA & Halborg JE (1992) *Sainted Women of the Dark Ages* Duke Univ Press

Merton, T (1961) *Seeds of Contemplation* Anthony Clarke

Milton, J (1644) *Areopagitica*

Morris, C (1968) *Include Me Out!* Epworth Press

Morris, W (1892) *News from Nowhere* Kelmscott Press

Mortimer, I (2008) *The Time Traveller's Guide to Medieval England* Bodley Head

Mortimer, S (2015) 'What was at stake in the Putney debates?' *History Today* **65**/1

Mundill, RR (1998) *England's Jewish Solution* Cambridge University Press

Neill, AS (1969) *Summerhill* Gollancz

Neill, SC (1952) *The Christian Society* Nisbet & Co

Newfield, TP (2009) 'A cattle panzootic in early 14th century Europe' *AgHR* **57**/2

Okely, J (1983) *The Traveller-Gypsies* Cambridge University Press

Packer, JI (1991) *Among God's Giants* Kingsway

Page, C (2010) *The Christian West and its Singers* Yale University Press

Paine, T (1791-2) *Rights of Man*

Pearlman, M (1938) *Collective Adventure* Heinemann

Peterken, GF (1996) *Natural Woodland* Cambridge University Press

Pinker, S (2002) *The Blank Slate* Penguin

Platt, C (1978) *Medieval England* BCA

Plattes, G (1641) *A Description of the Famous Kingdome of Macaria*

Pollard, E, Hooper, MD & Moore, NW (1974) *Hedges* Collins

Rackham, O (1986) *The History of the Countryside* JM Dent

Richardson, HG (1960) *The English Jewry under Angevin Kings* Methuen

Rivers, P (1978) *Living on a Little Land* Turnstone

Robson, M (2006) *The Franciscans in the Middle Ages* Boydell Press

Roffe, D (2007) 'Decoding Domesday' *History Today* **57**/6

Romain, JA (2ed 1988) *The Jews of England* Michael Goulston Educational Foundation

Roth, C (3ed 1964) *A History of the Jews in England* Oxford University Press

St John Climacus (1959 tr Moore, L) *The Ladder of Divine Ascent* Faber & Faber

Schama, S (2013) *The Story of the Jews* Bodley Head

Scullard, HH (1979) *Roman Britain* Thames & Hudson

Smith, D (2014) *The Book of Boaz* instantapostle

Spiro, ME (1954) 'Is the Family Universal?' *American Anthropologist* **56**/5

Spiro, ME (2ed 1970) *Kibbutz: Venture in Utopia* Schocken Books

Spiro, ME (3ed 1975) *Children of the Kibbutz* Harvard University Press

Stockins, J (2000) *On the Cobbles* Mainstream

Taylor, R (2011) 'A People on the Outside' *History Today* **61**/6

Thomsen, M (1971) *Meat is for Special Days* Souvenir Press

Tiger, L & Shepher, J (1977) *Women in the Kibbutz* Penguin

Torrance, DW & Taylor, G (2007) *Israel, God's Servant* Paternoster

Trivers, RL (1974) 'Parent-Offspring Conflict' *American Zoologist* **14**/1

Watson, T (1663) *All Things for Good* Banner of Truth

Williams-Ellis, C (2ed 1975) *England and the Octopus* Portmeirion

Willis, R (2009) 'Playful learning' *History Today* **59**/2

Winter, J (2000) *Depression: a rescue plan* DayOne

Wood, MF (1973) *In the Life of a Romany Gypsy* Routledge & Kegan Paul

Yoors, J (1967) *The Gypsies* Waveland Press

Yount, D (2008) *America's Spiritual Utopias* Praeger